SOUNDS ALL AROUND

A Guide to Onomatopoeias Around the World

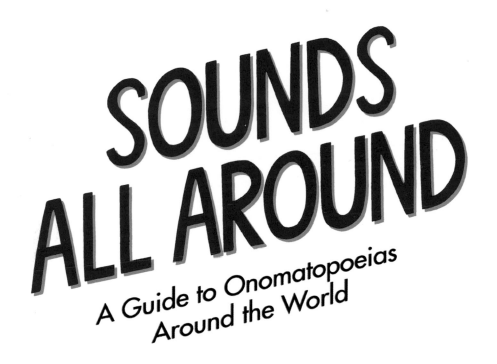

SOUNDS ALL AROUND

A Guide to Onomatopoeias Around the World

Dr. James Chapman

Andrews McMeel
PUBLISHING®

Let's Make Some Noise

Learning the sounds animals make is an essential part of language learning. Spending hours and hours pretending you're a chicken or a dog is not only great fun, it's educational, too. If you grew up speaking English, you probably already know your woofs and meows from your clucks and quacks—but how does the rest of the world describe sounds?

IN JAPANESE, CATS DON'T GO MEOW

NYAN!

IN GERMAN, PIGS DON'T GO OINK

GRUNZ!

IN HINDI, FROGS DON'T GO RIBBIT

TARR!

There's a whole world of words for all the sounds you know and love! (And even some words for sounds that don't show up in English.)

The words that imitate sounds are known as "onomatopoeia." These words are a wonderfully strange and interesting part of language. After all, we hear the same sounds, but we interpret and write them differently in different languages.

If you sing "Old McDonald Had a Farm" in French, your farmyard ducks go "coin coin" instead of "quack quack," and in Russian they go "krya krya." From the sound of a speeding car, to the sound a dog makes, to the sound of rain, there are almost as many words for these sounds as there are languages!

Early Beginnings

Many linguists (the people who study language) believed that onomatopoeic words partly explain how early humans began communicating and may hold the key to the origin of language itself! There are a few nicknames for these theories.

The Bow-Wow Theory
Language first came about from imitating animal noises like barking dogs and bird song.
The Pooh-Pooh Theory
Language evolved from imitating natural human sounds, like crying babies and laughter.
The Ding-Dong Theory
Language began by imitating sounds in nature, like thunder or the wind.

No one knows for certain how language first came about, but one thing is for sure: onomatopoeias are a fascinating part of how we understand the world and each other. Come and join us as we learn more about these sounds all around!

Bon Voyage

This book is going to take us on a journey around the world to learn about the different ways people describe sounds. We'll look at fireworks, heartbeats, clocks, lions, thunder, even the sound of brushing your teeth!

But who will take us on this noisy journey? We'll need an expert to guide us along the way . . .

PLEASED TO MEET YOU!

I HEARD YOU WANTED TO SOUND LIKE A FINNISH GHOST. DON'T WORRY, I KNOW A THING OR TWO ABOUT A THING OR TWO...

YOU CAN COUNT ON ME!

ANIMALS NOISES

Animal sounds are the perfect place to start this onomatopoeic journey. Of course it's common to learn the noises of cats and dogs growing up (every language has their own version of these), but some languages have animal sounds that are a little more obscure.

In Japan, foxes are a big part of their culture and some religions, so naturally they've been given their own special sound!

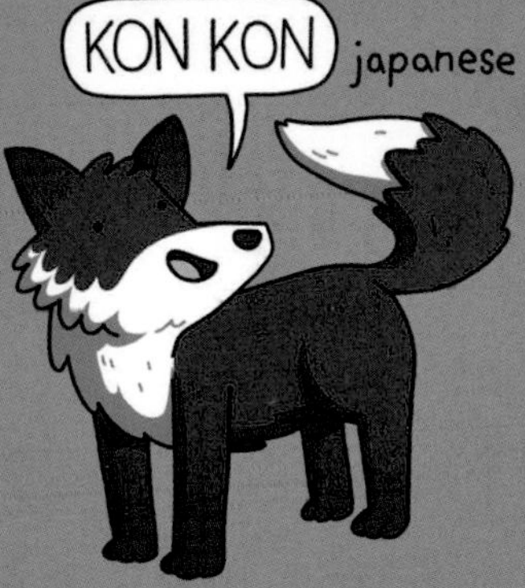
KON KON
japanese

Turtles get in on the action, too.

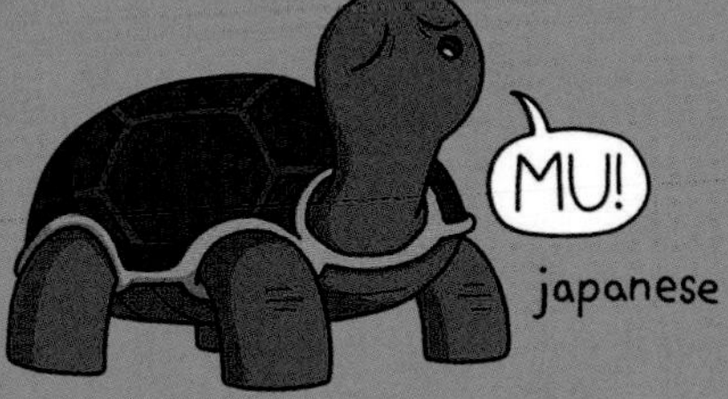
MU!
japanese

There's a sound for hamsters in Latvian, . . .

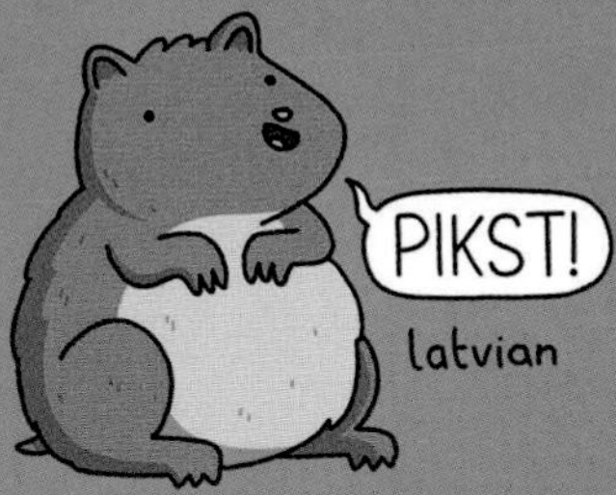
PIKST!
latvian

and even a word in Korean for the sound of rabbits hopping!

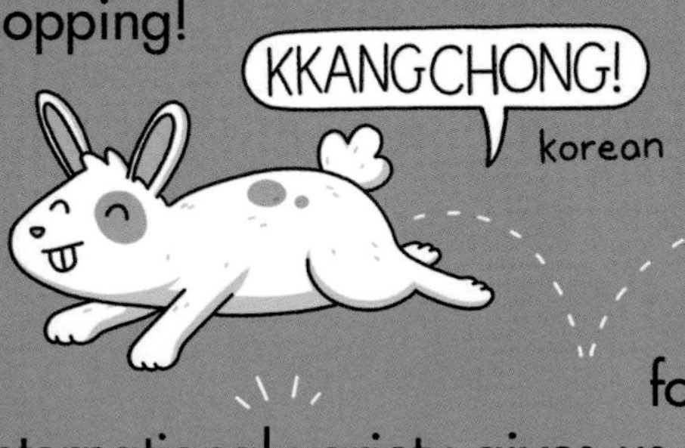
KKANGCHONG!
korean

The world is full of different words for sounds, and all that international variety gives us a load of alternatives you might never have seen before. Let's see how they compare to the ones you grew up with!

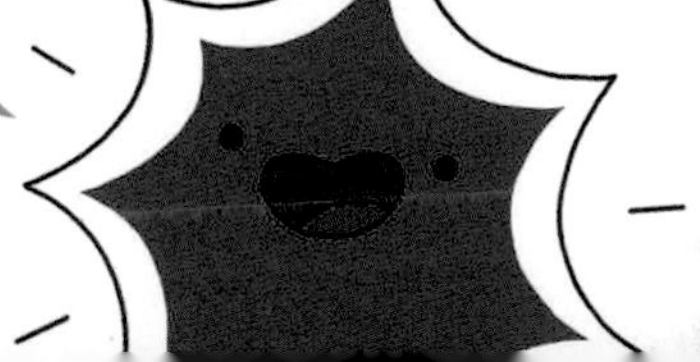

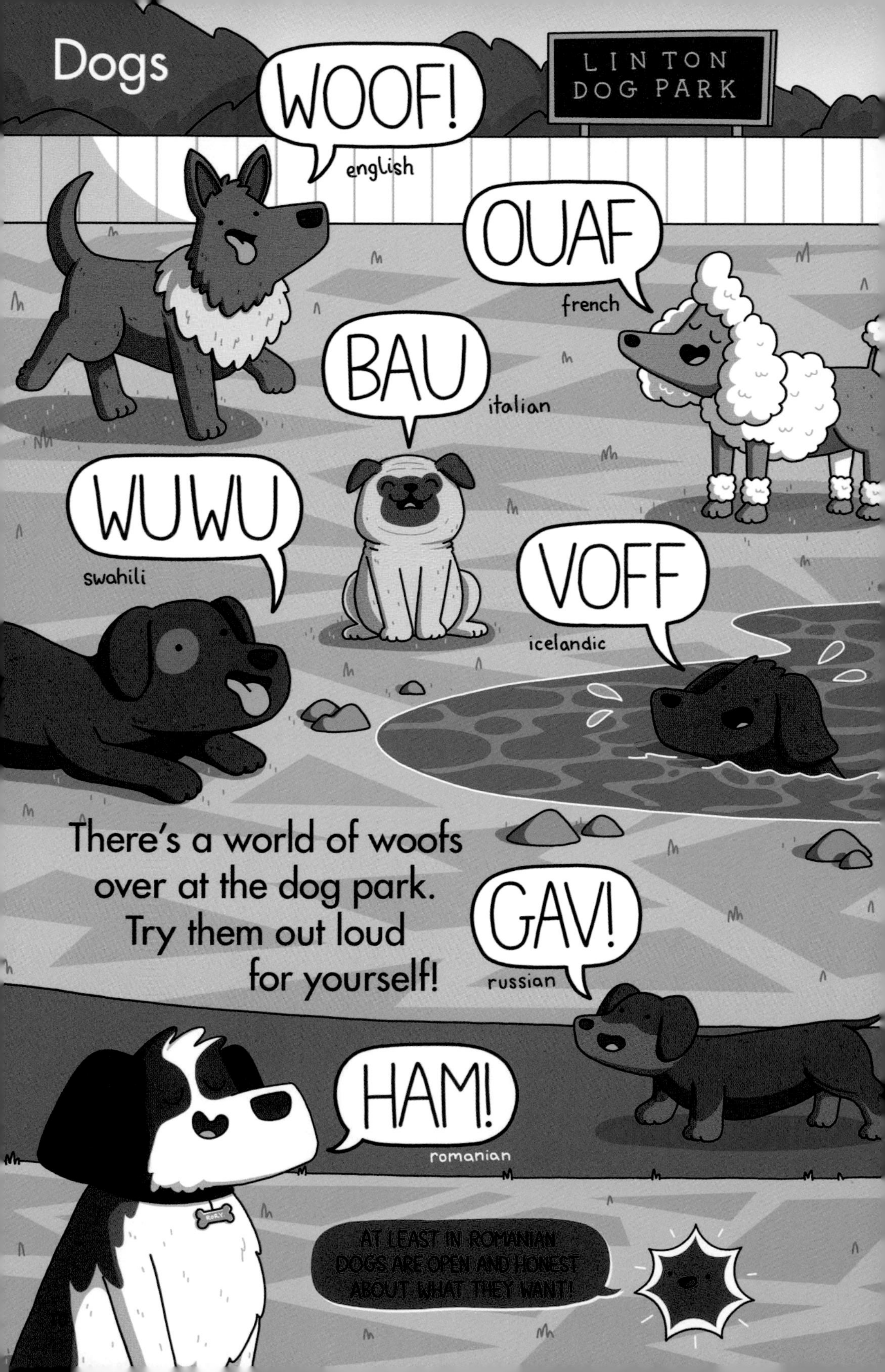
Dogs
LINTON DOG PARK
WOOF!
english
OUAF
french
BAU
italian
WUWU
swahili
VOFF
icelandic
There's a world of woofs over at the dog park. Try them out loud for yourself!
GAV!
russian
HAM!
romanian
RORY
AT LEAST IN ROMANIAN DOGS ARE OPEN AND HONEST ABOUT WHAT THEY WANT!

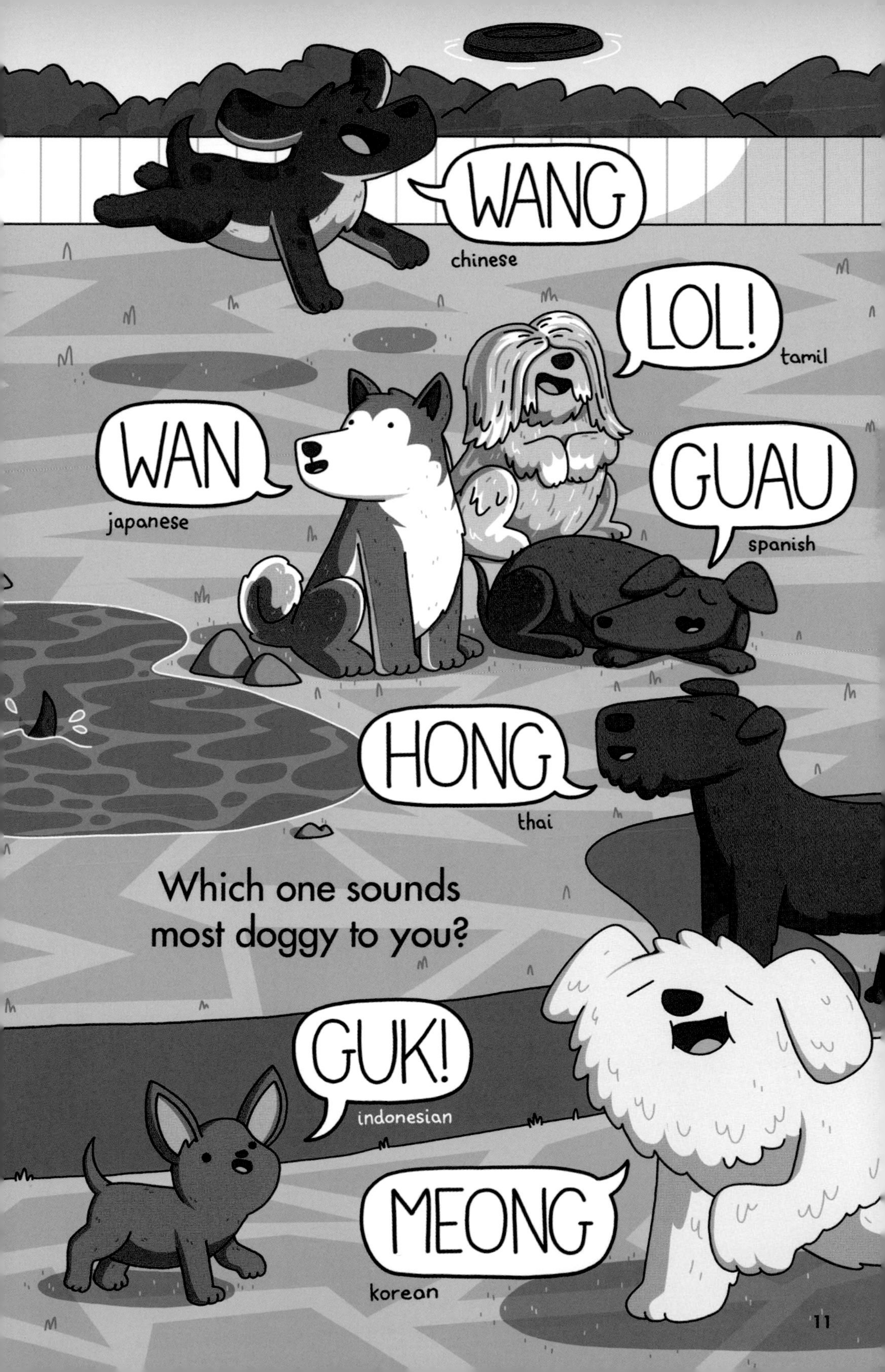
WANG
chinese
LOL!
tamil
WAN
japanese
GUAU
spanish
HONG
thai
Which one sounds most doggy to you?
GUK!
indonesian
MEONG
korean

Cats

Most languages agree on the sound cats make,

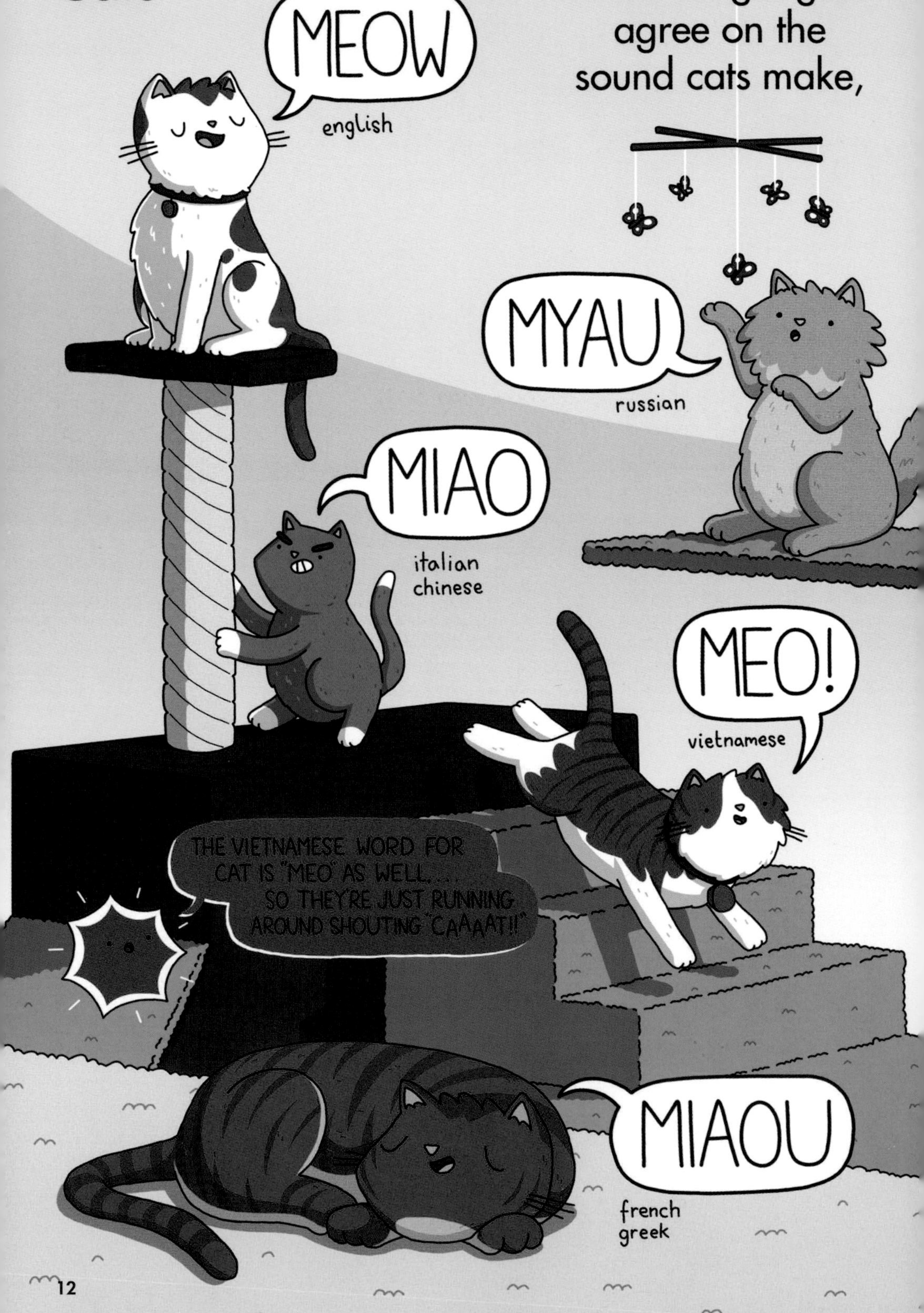
MEOW
english
MYAU
russian
MIAO
italian
chinese
MEO!
vietnamese
THE VIETNAMESE WORD FOR CAT IS "MEO" AS WELL... SO THEY'RE JUST RUNNING AROUND SHOUTING "CAAAAT!!"
MIAOU
french
greek

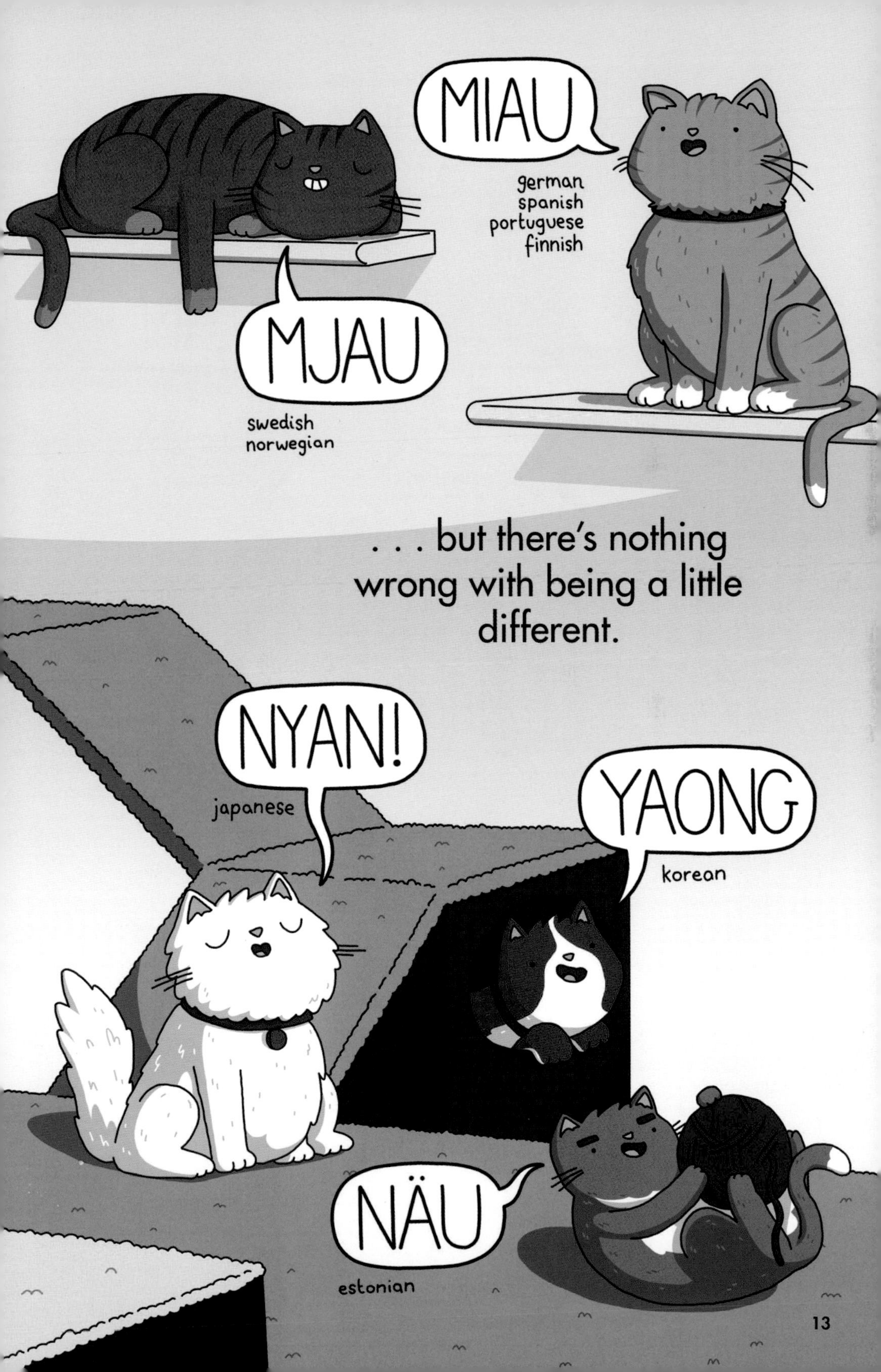
MIAU
german
spanish
portuguese
finnish
MJAU
swedish
norwegian
. . . but there's nothing wrong with being a little different.
NYAN!
japanese
YAONG
korean
NÄU
estonian

Mice

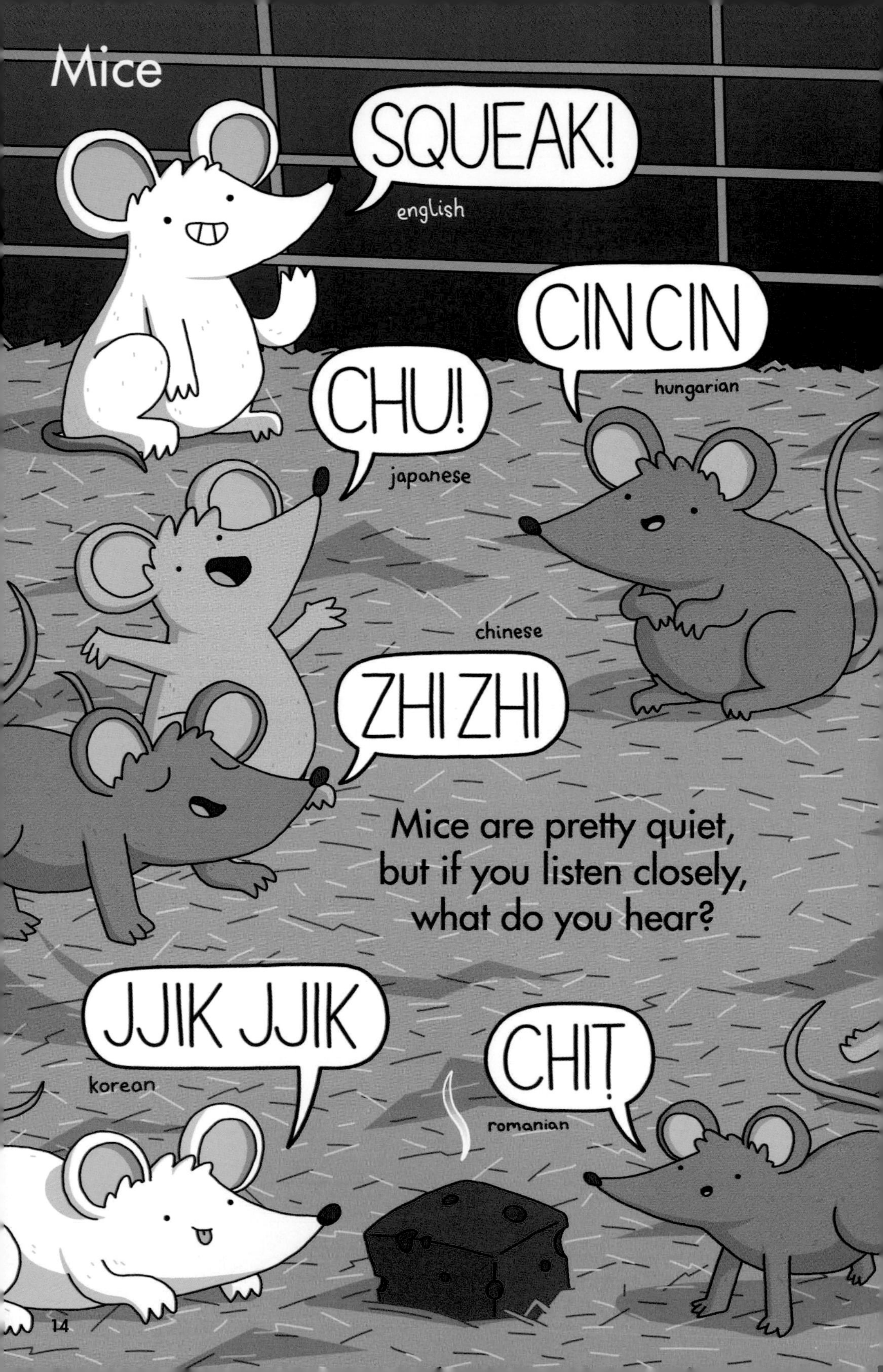
SQUEAK!
english
CIN CIN
hungarian
CHU!
japanese
chinese
ZHI ZHI
JJIK JJIK
korean
CHIT
romanian

Mice are pretty quiet, but if you listen closely, what do you hear?

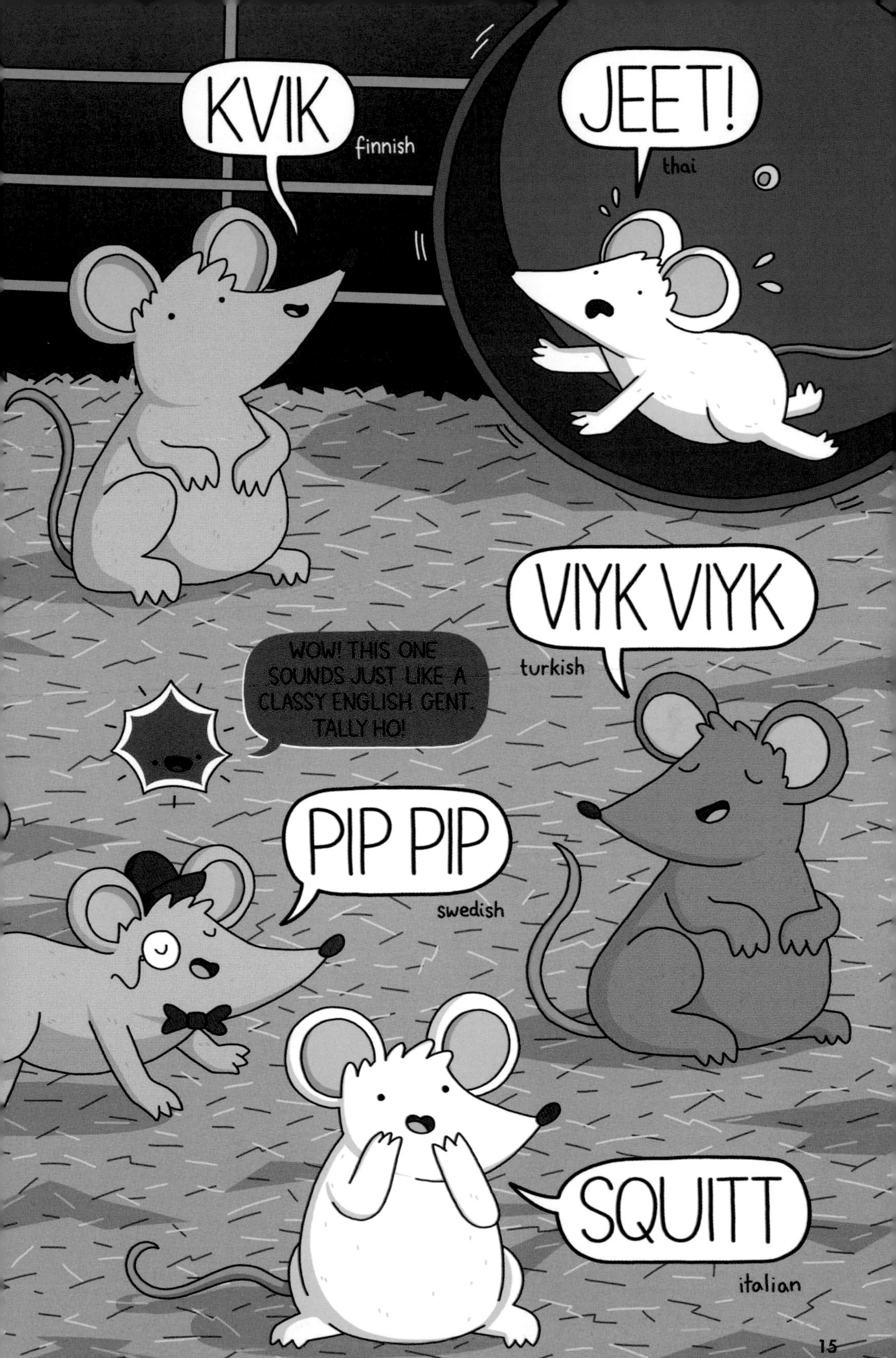
KVIK
finnish
JEET!
thai
VIYK VIYK
turkish
WOW! THIS ONE SOUNDS JUST LIKE A CLASSY ENGLISH GENT. TALLY HO!
PIP PIP
swedish
SQUITT
italian

Birds

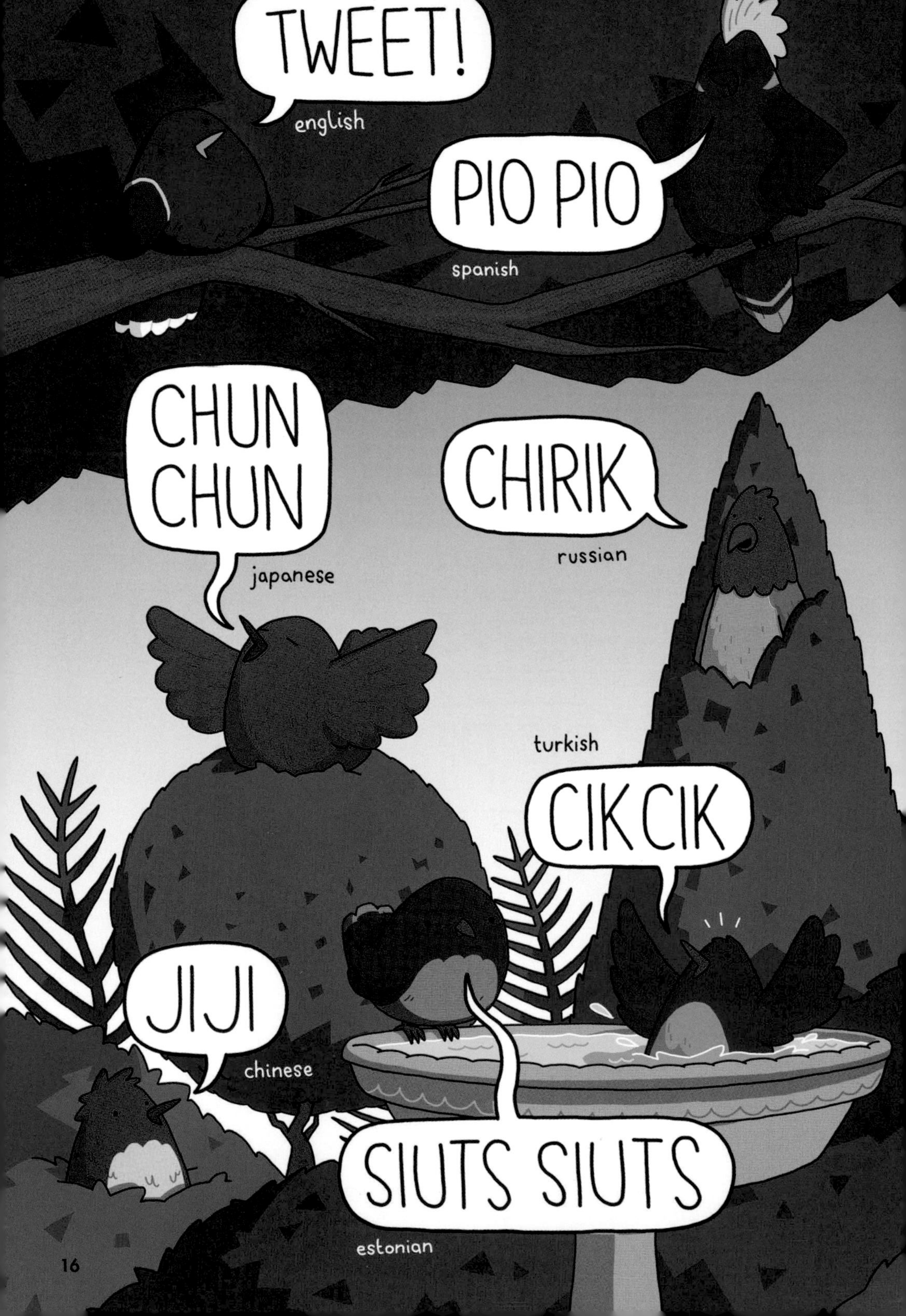
TWEET!
english
PIO PIO
spanish
CHUN CHUN
japanese
CHIRIK
russian
turkish
CIK CIK
JIJI
chinese
SIUTS SIUTS
estonian

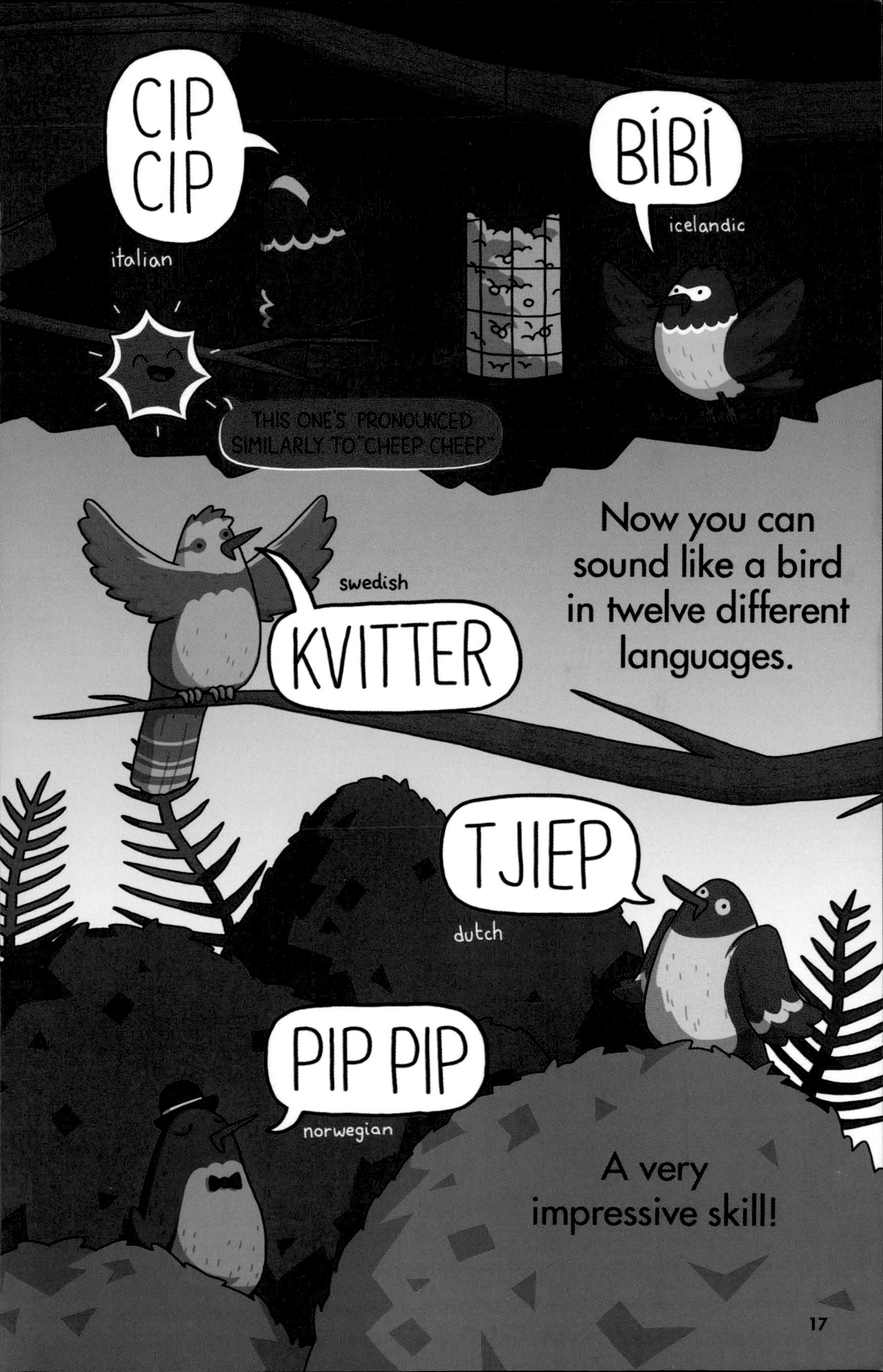
CIP CIP
italian
THIS ONE'S PRONOUNCED SIMILARLY TO "CHEEP CHEEP."
BÍBÍ
icelandic
swedish
KVITTER
Now you can sound like a bird in twelve different languages.
TJIEP
dutch
PIP PIP
norwegian
A very impressive skill!

Bees

These words might look a little different, but all of them are the bees' knees.

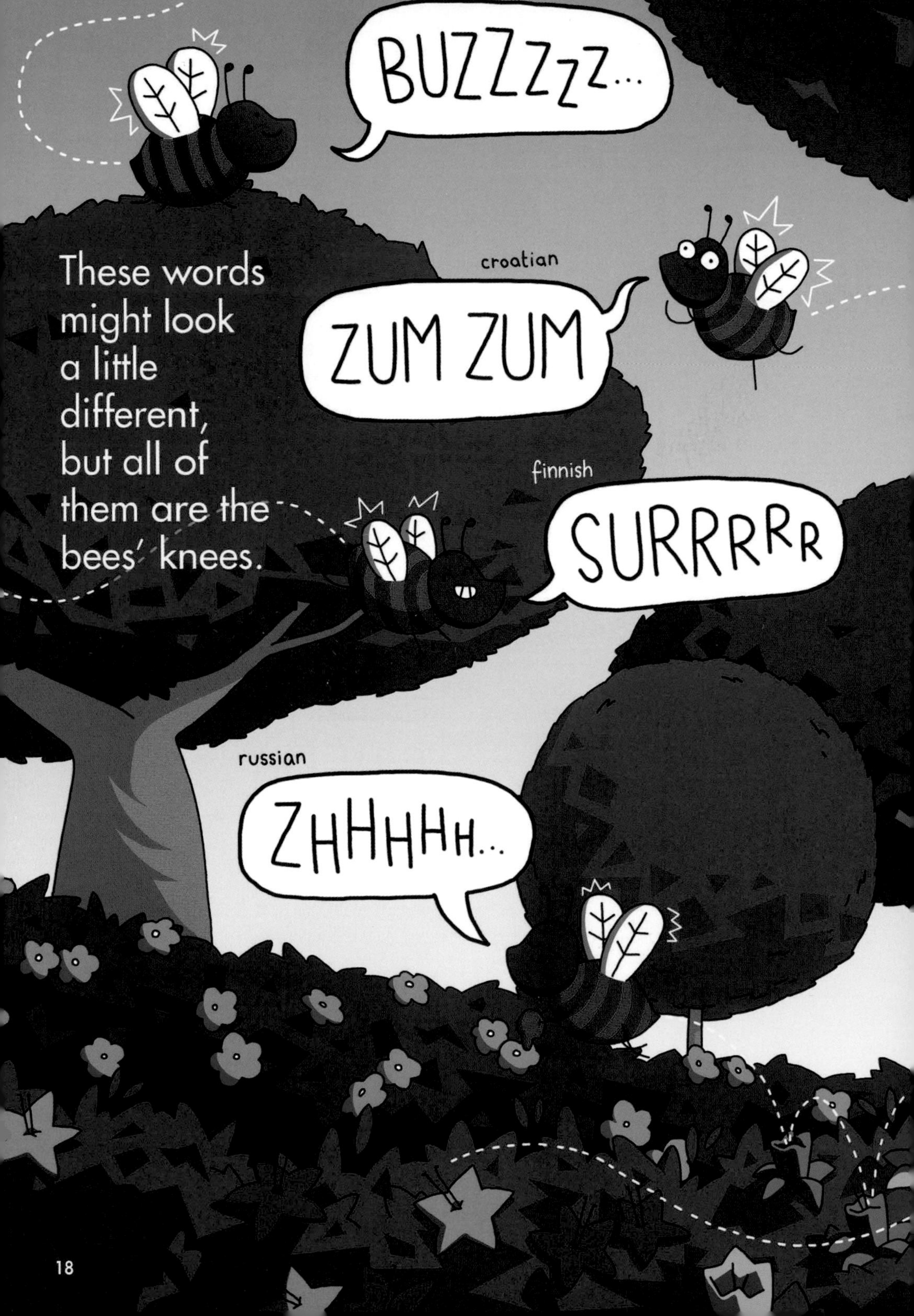
english
BUZZZzz...
croatian
ZUM ZUM
finnish
SURRRRR
russian
ZHHHHH...

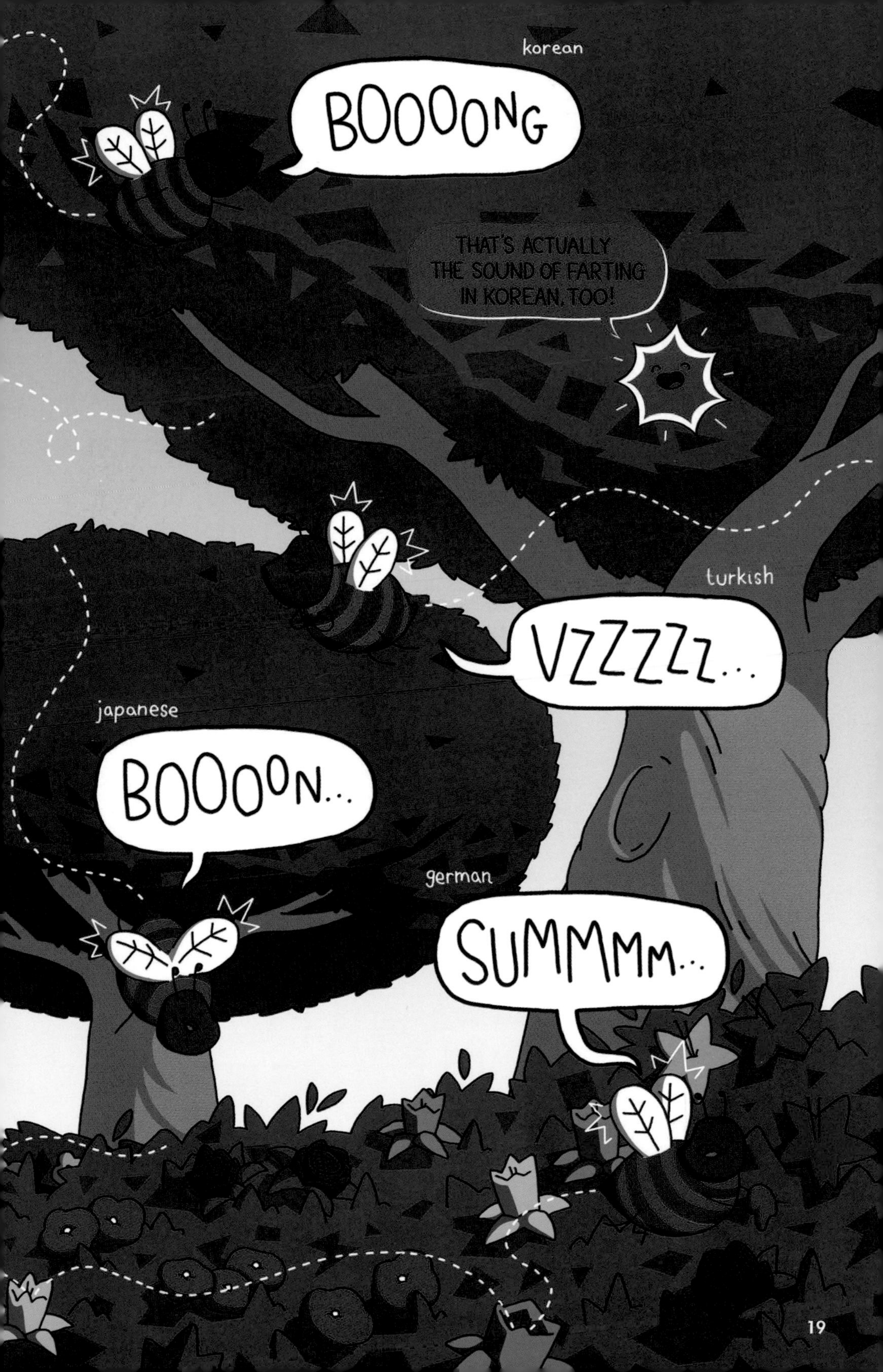
korean
BOOOONG
THAT'S ACTUALLY THE SOUND OF FARTING IN KOREAN, TOO!
turkish
VZZZZZ...
japanese
BOOOON...
german
SUMMMM...

Pigeons

Pigeons often live in the city, and with all the hustle and bustle, their sounds fit right in.

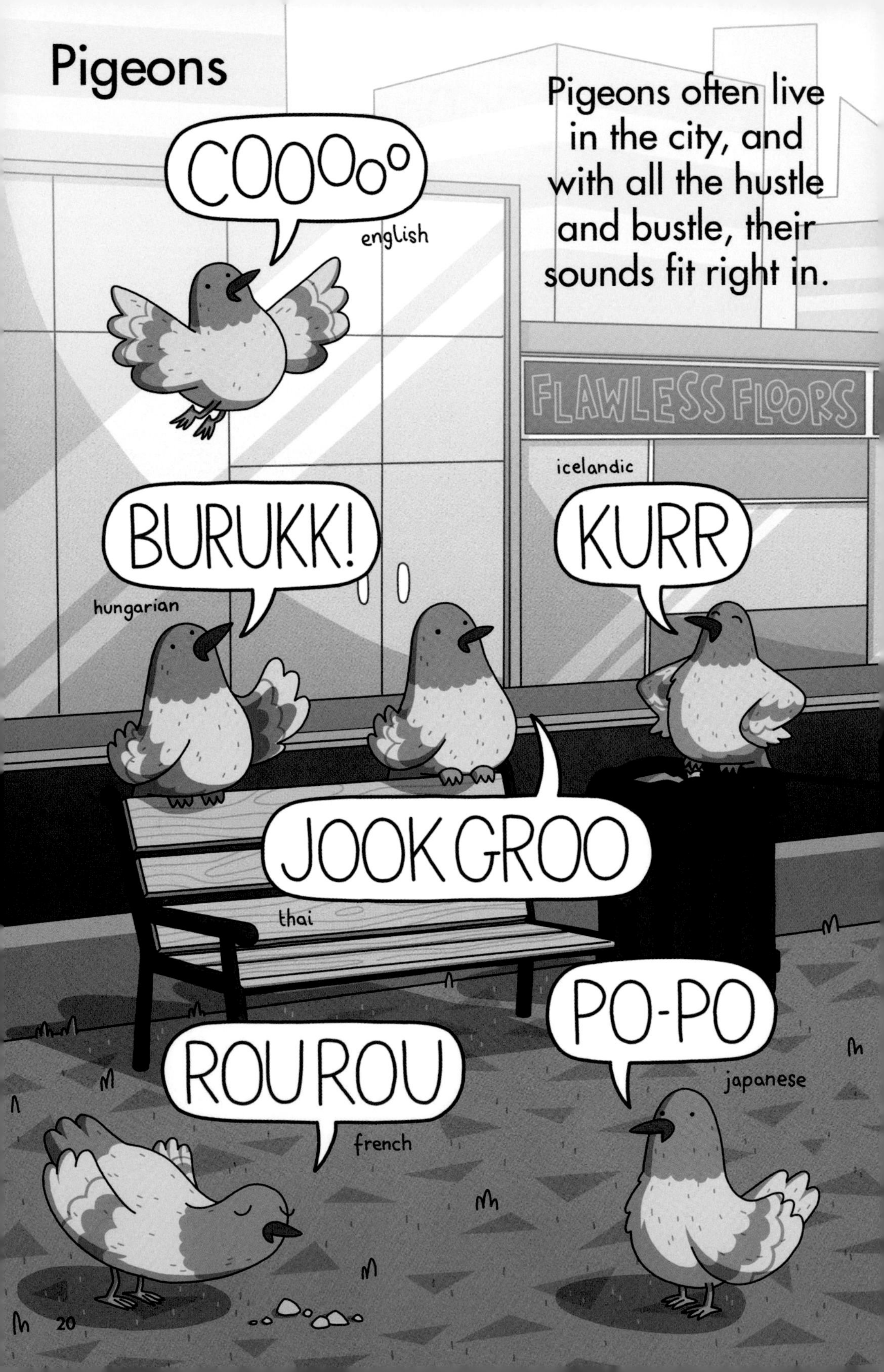
COOOoo
english
FLAWLESS FLOORS
icelandic
BURUKK!
KURR
hungarian
JOOK GROO
thai
PO-PO
ROU ROU
japanese
french

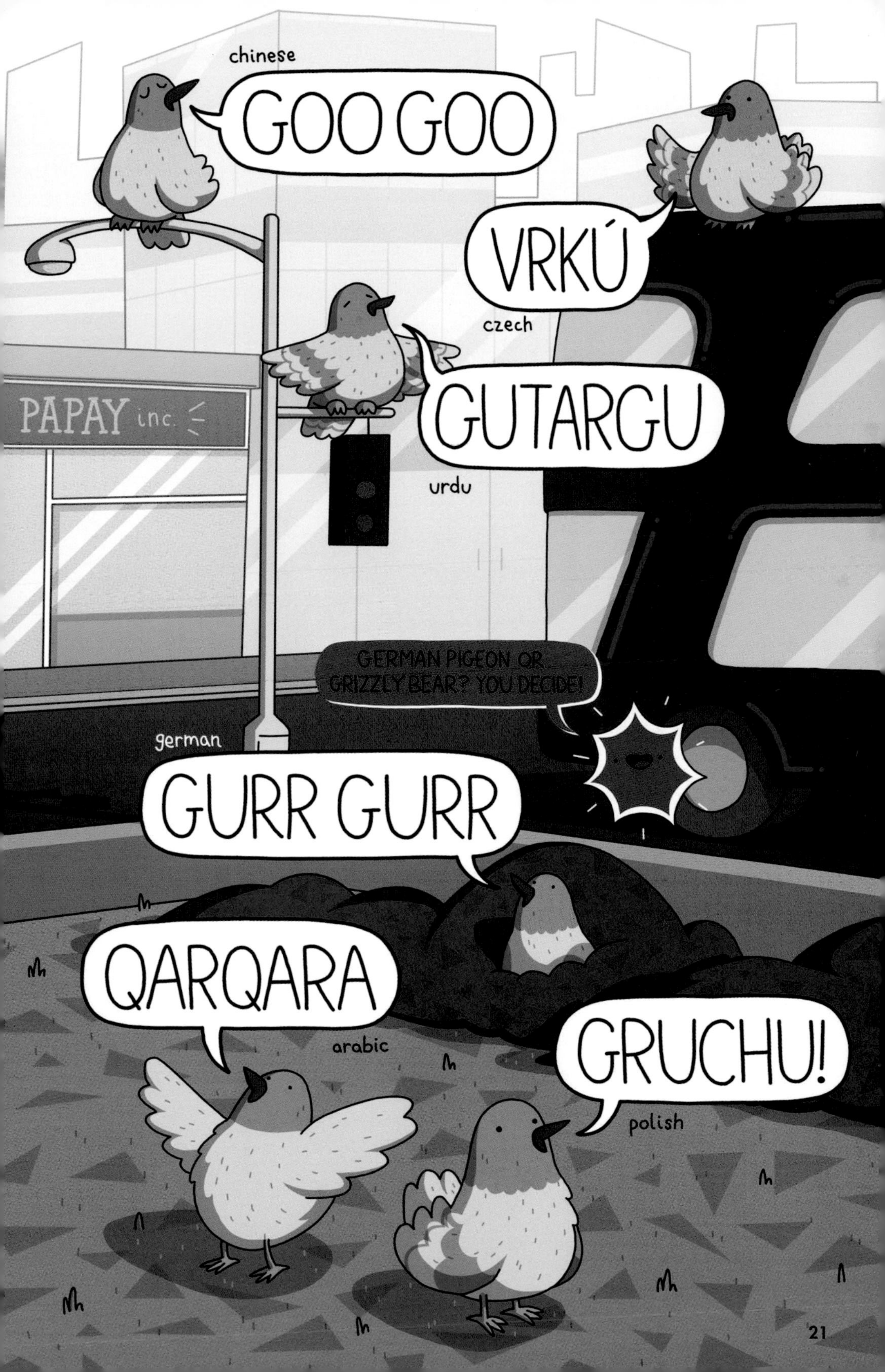
chinese
GOO GOO
VRKÚ
czech
GUTARGU
urdu
PAPAY inc.
GERMAN PIGEON OR GRIZZLY BEAR? YOU DECIDE!
german
GURR GURR
QARQARA
arabic
GRUCHU!
polish

Purring

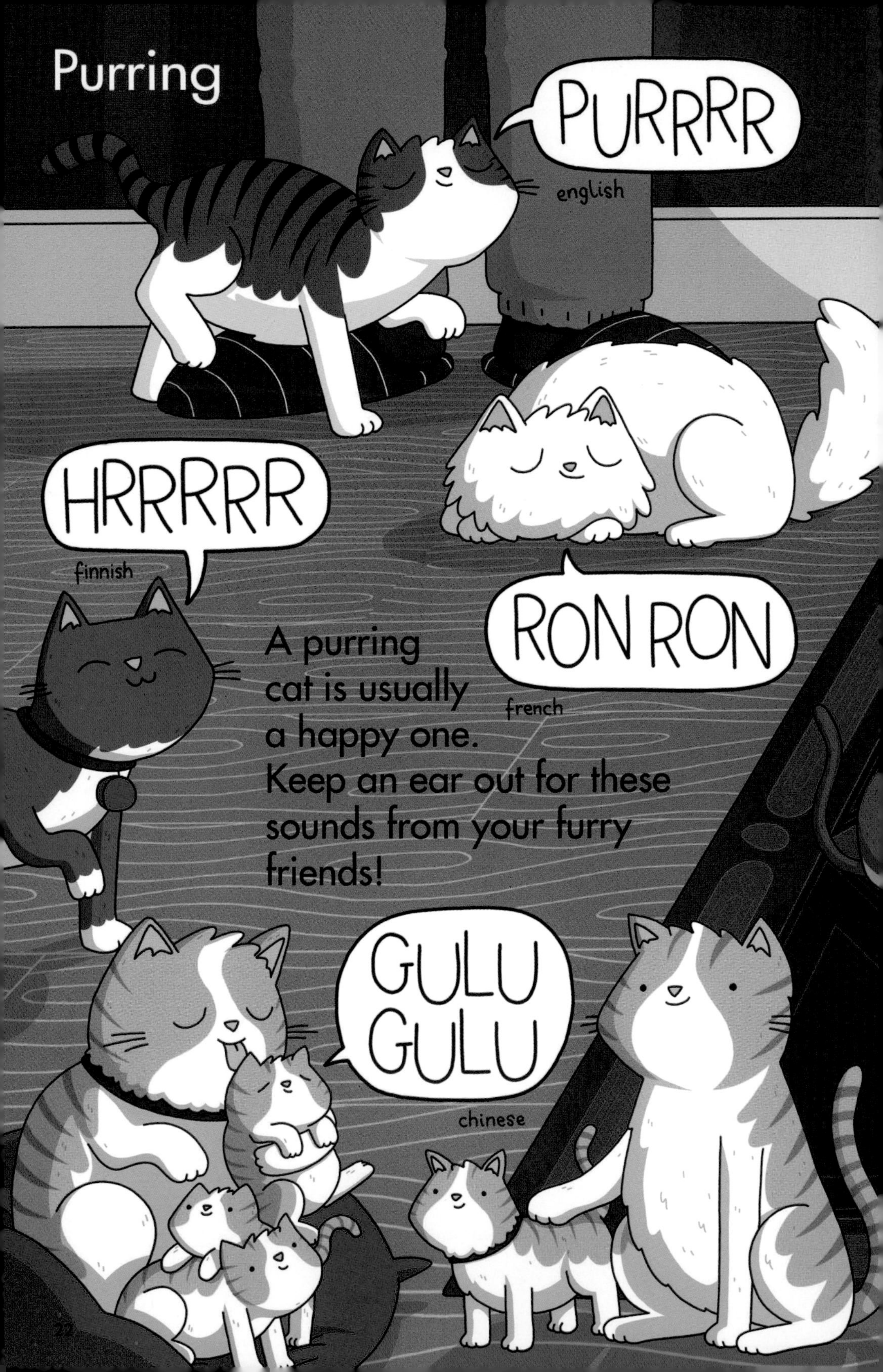
PURRRR
english
HRRRRR
finnish
RON RON
french
GULU GULU
chinese

A purring cat is usually a happy one. Keep an ear out for these sounds from your furry friends!

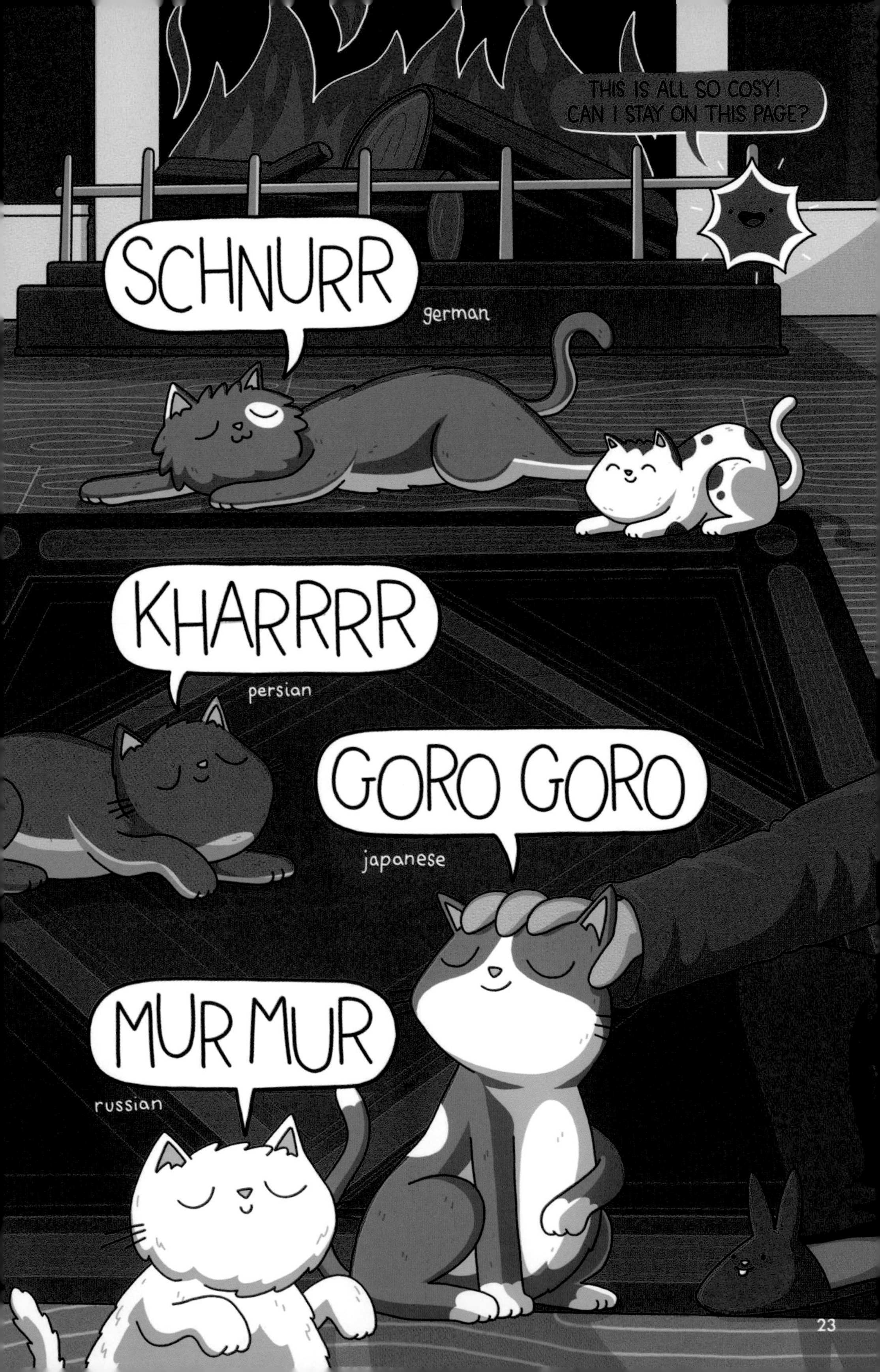

THIS IS ALL SO COSY! CAN I STAY ON THIS PAGE?
SCHNURR
german
KHARRRR
persian
GORO GORO
japanese
MUR MUR
russian

ON THE FARM

Old McDonald is world famous for his incredibly noisy farm animals, and rightly so. They're a fun group!

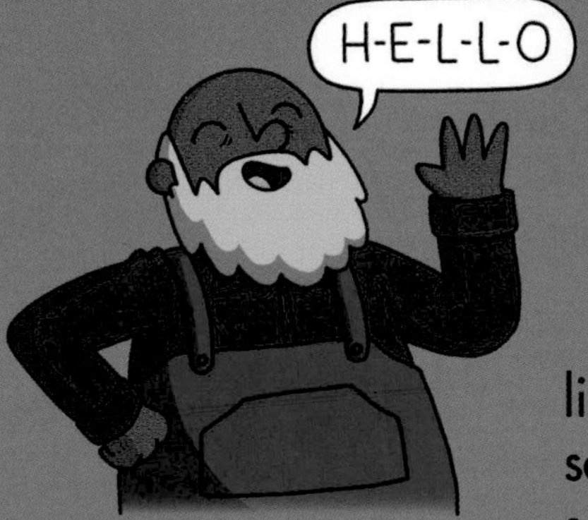
H-E-L-L-O

Quack quack, oink oink, moo moo—there's a great collection of sounds on the farm.

We already talked a little about how farmyard sounds are different as the song is translated around the world, but sometimes even Old McDonald himself becomes someone else!

In China, he's Old Mr Wang.
In Germany, the farm belongs to Uncle Jörg.
In Iran, he's just a Kind Old Man.
In Finland, Grandpa Piippola,
and in Italy, they sing about Uncle Tobias.

Now, off to the farm we go!

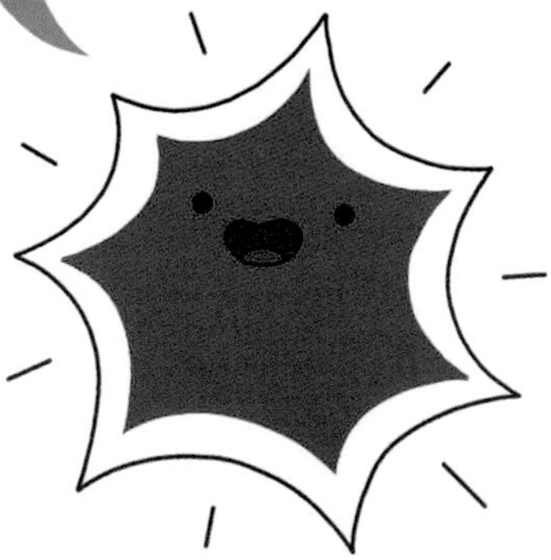

Pigs

Over on the farm, these mucky pigs make quite a ruckus.

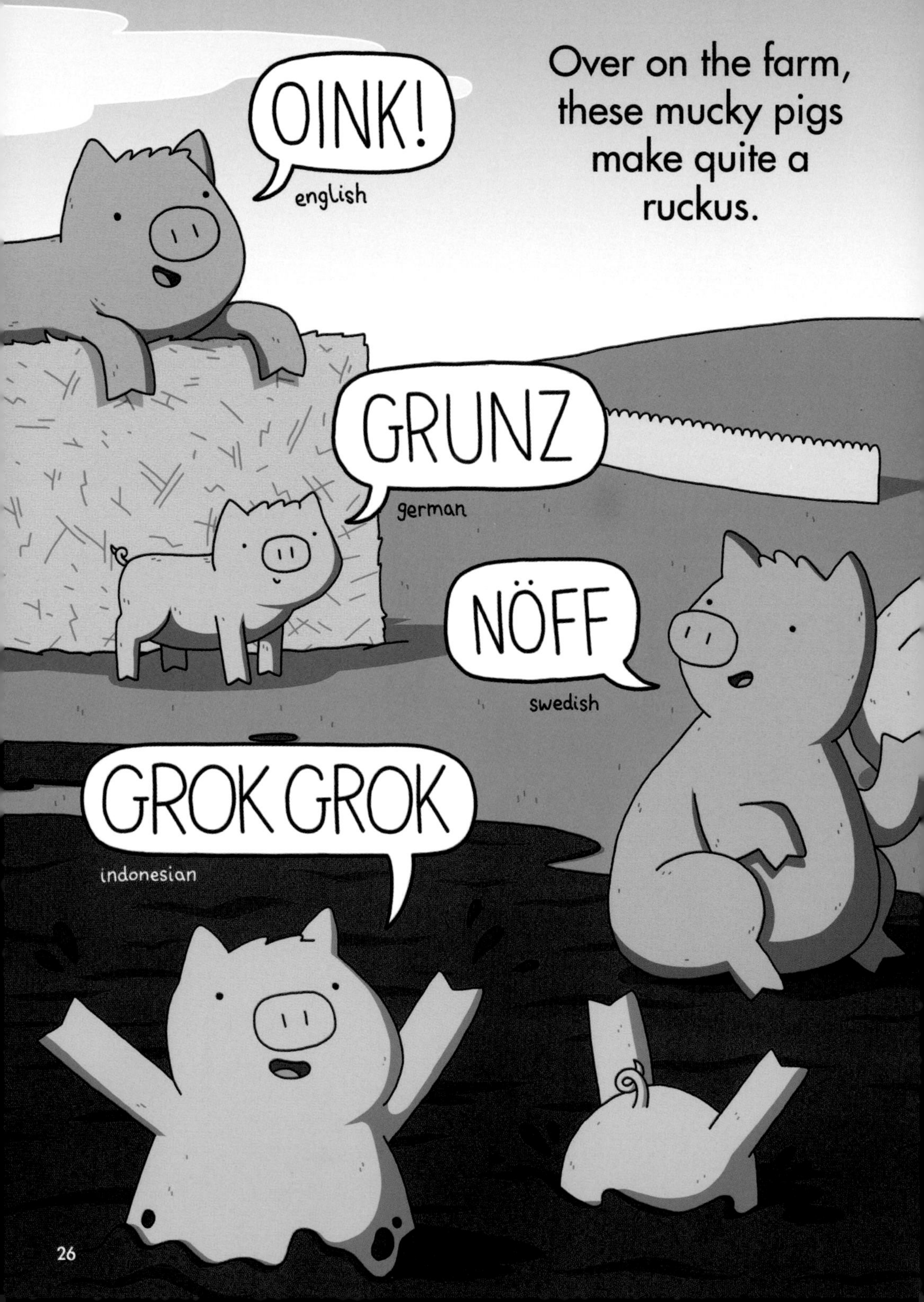
OINK!
english
GRUNZ
german
NÖFF
swedish
GROK GROK
indonesian

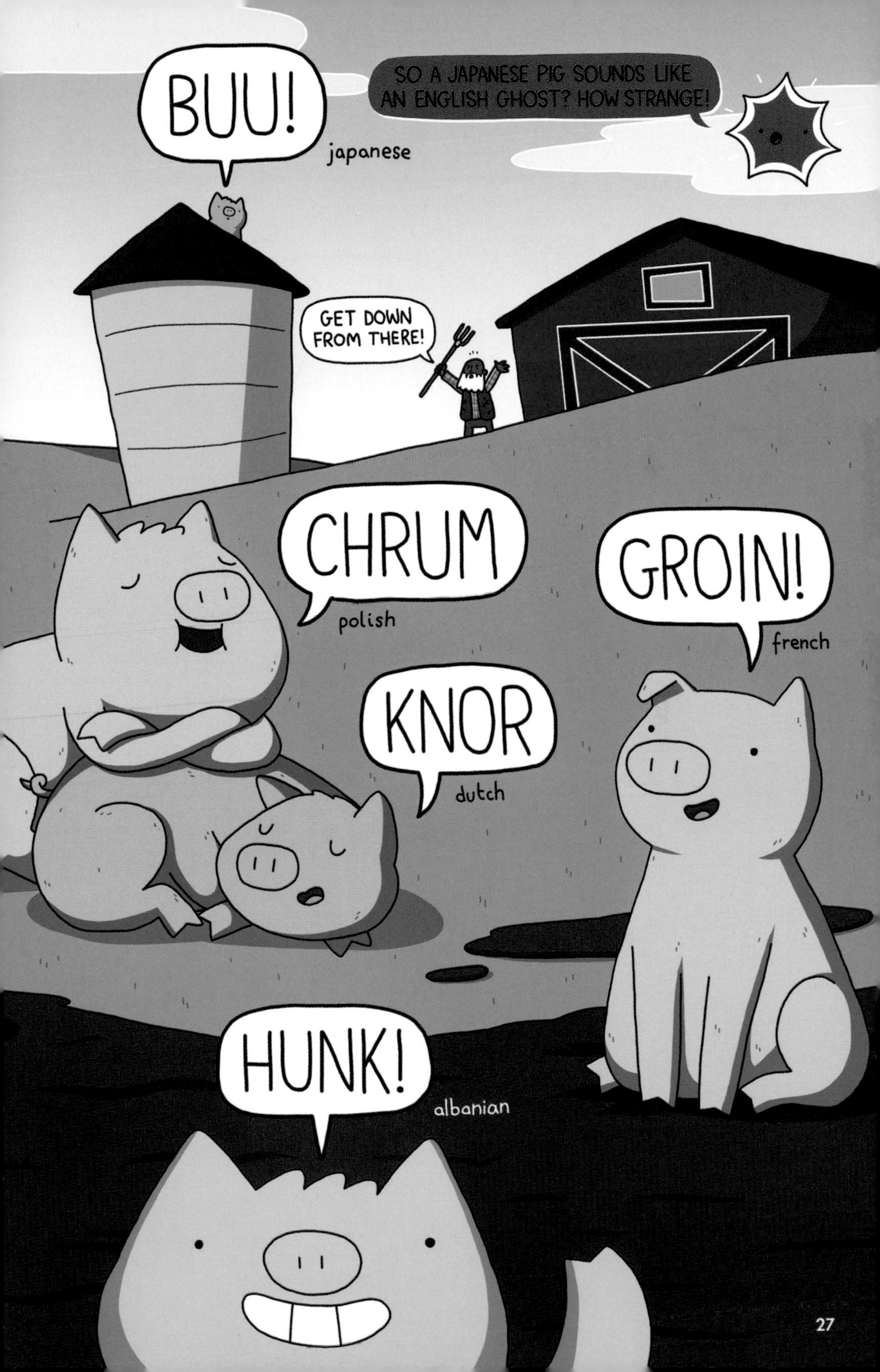

BUU!
japanese
SO A JAPANESE PIG SOUNDS LIKE AN ENGLISH GHOST? HOW STRANGE!
GET DOWN FROM THERE!
CHRUM
polish
GROIN!
french
KNOR
dutch
HUNK!
albanian

Cows

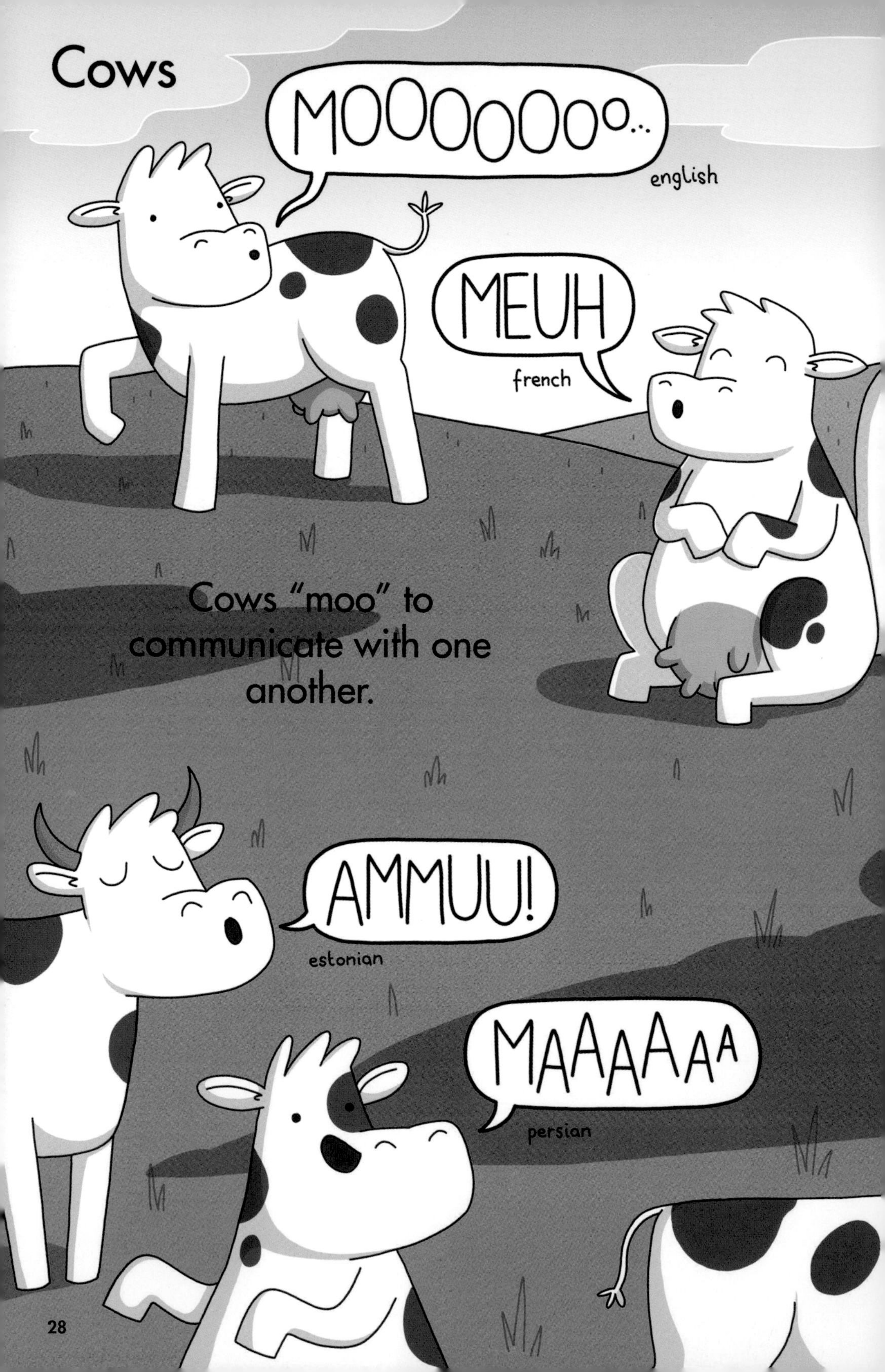
MOOOOOOo...
english
MEUH
french
AMMUU!
estonian
MAAAAAA
persian

Cows "moo" to communicate with one another.

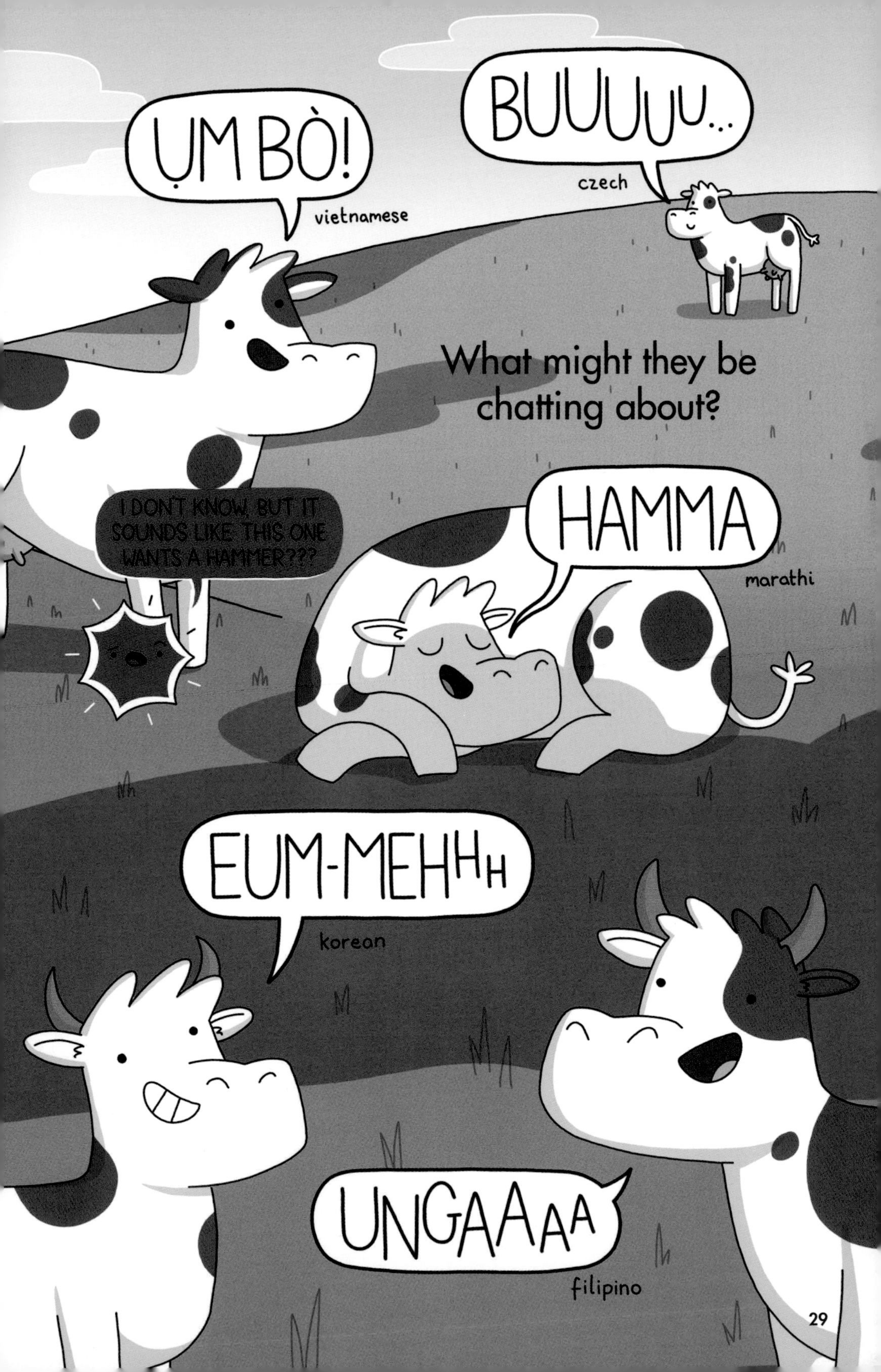
ỤM BÒ!
vietnamese
BUUUUU...
czech
What might they be chatting about?
[redacted]
HAMMA
marathi
EUM-MEHHH
korean
UNGAAAA
filipino

Sheep

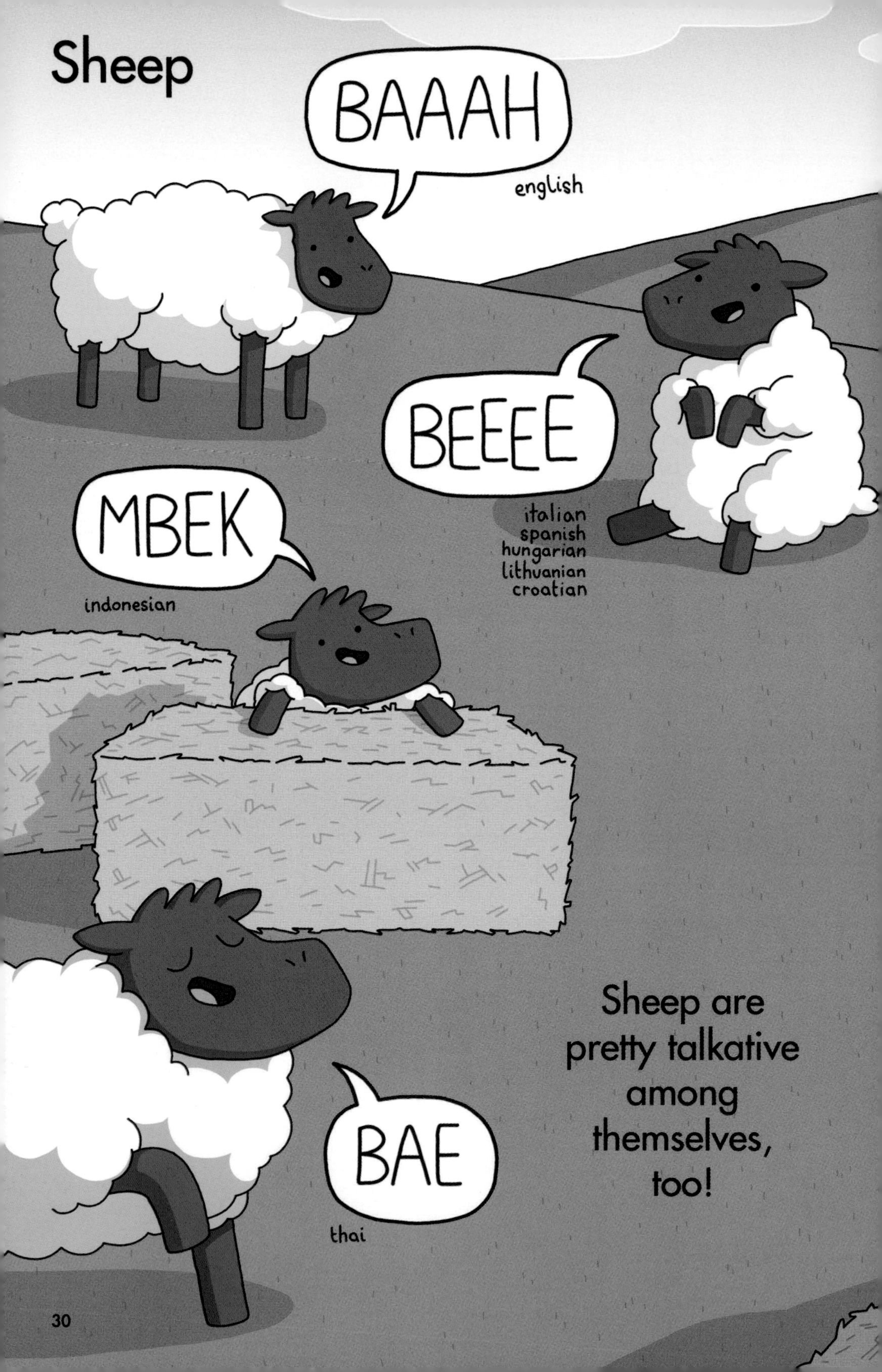
BAAAH
english
BEEEE
italian
spanish
hungarian
lithuanian
croatian
MBEK
indonesian
BAE
thai

Sheep are pretty talkative among themselves, too!

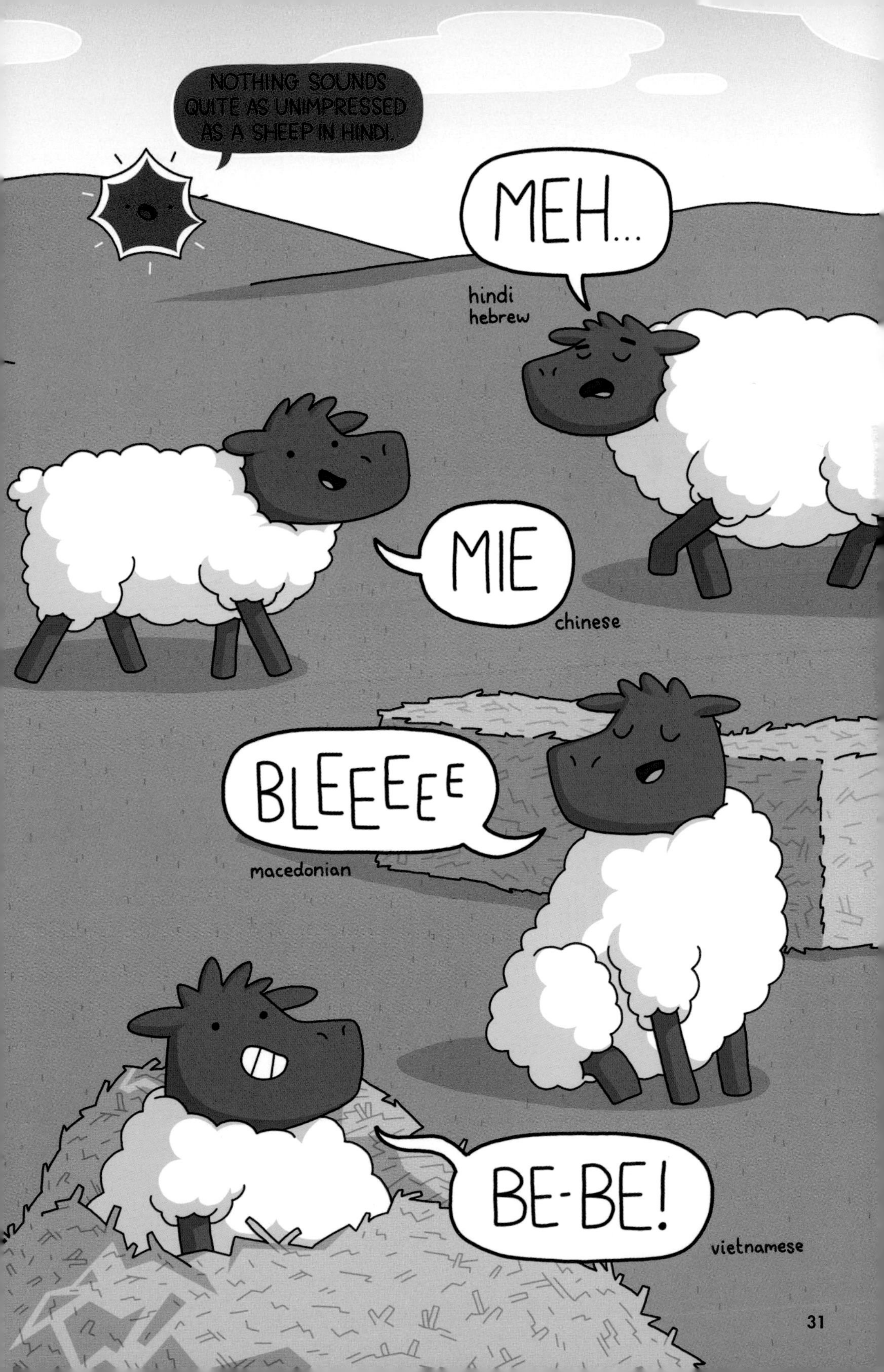
NOTHING SOUNDS QUITE AS UNIMPRESSED AS A SHEEP IN HINDI.
MEH...
hindi
hebrew
MIE
chinese
BLEEEEE
macedonian
BE-BE!
vietnamese

Roosters

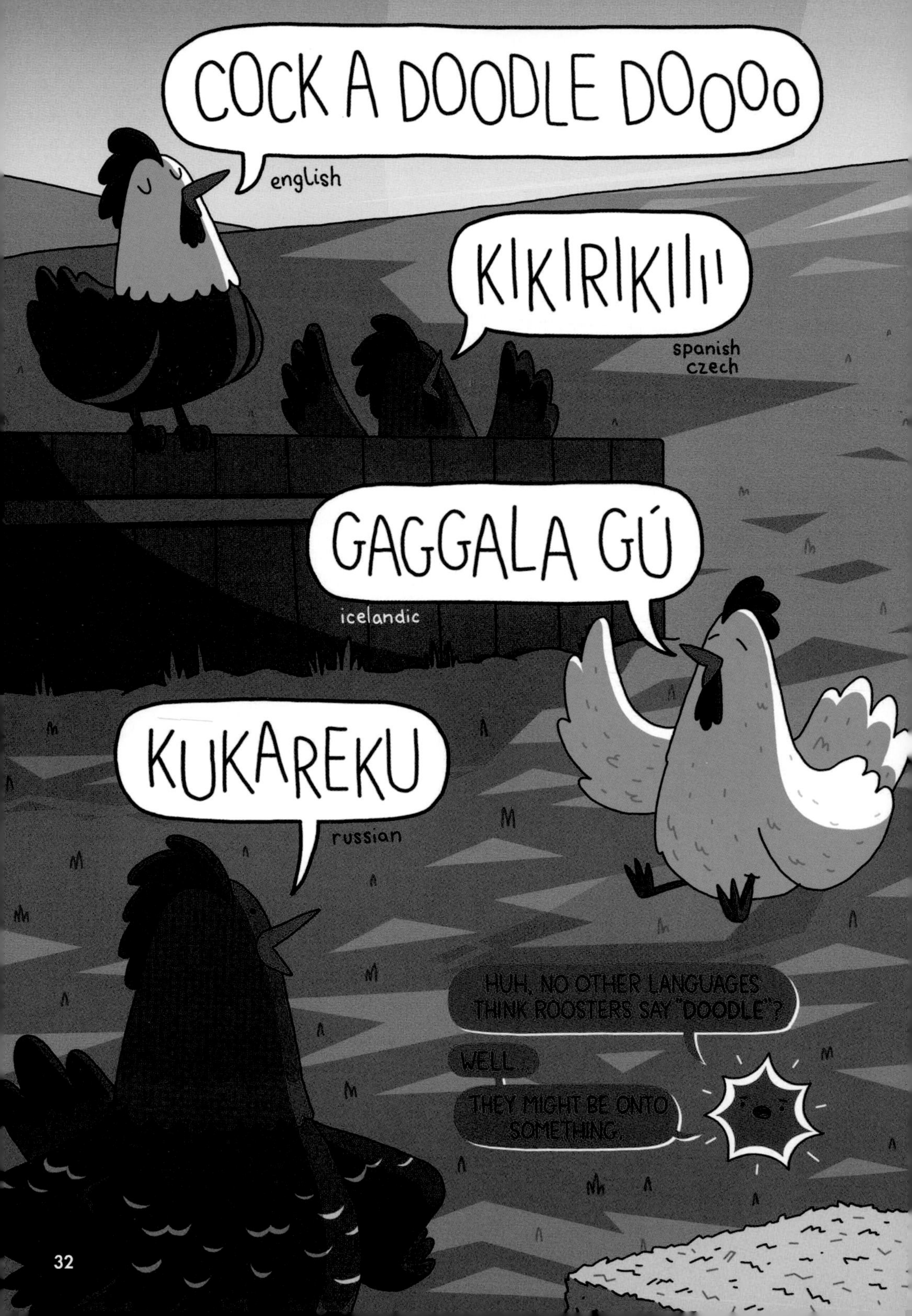
COCK A DOODLE DOOOOO
english
KIKIRIKIIII
spanish
czech
GAGGALA GÚ
icelandic
KUKAREKU
russian
HUH, NO OTHER LANGUAGES THINK ROOSTERS SAY "DOODLE"?
WELL...
THEY MIGHT BE ONTO SOMETHING.

Rise and shine!
It's a noisy start to the day
all over the world.
KOK E KOK KOOooo
japanese
CHICCHIRICHI
italian
COCORICOOoo
french
KUKELEKU!
dutch

Chickens

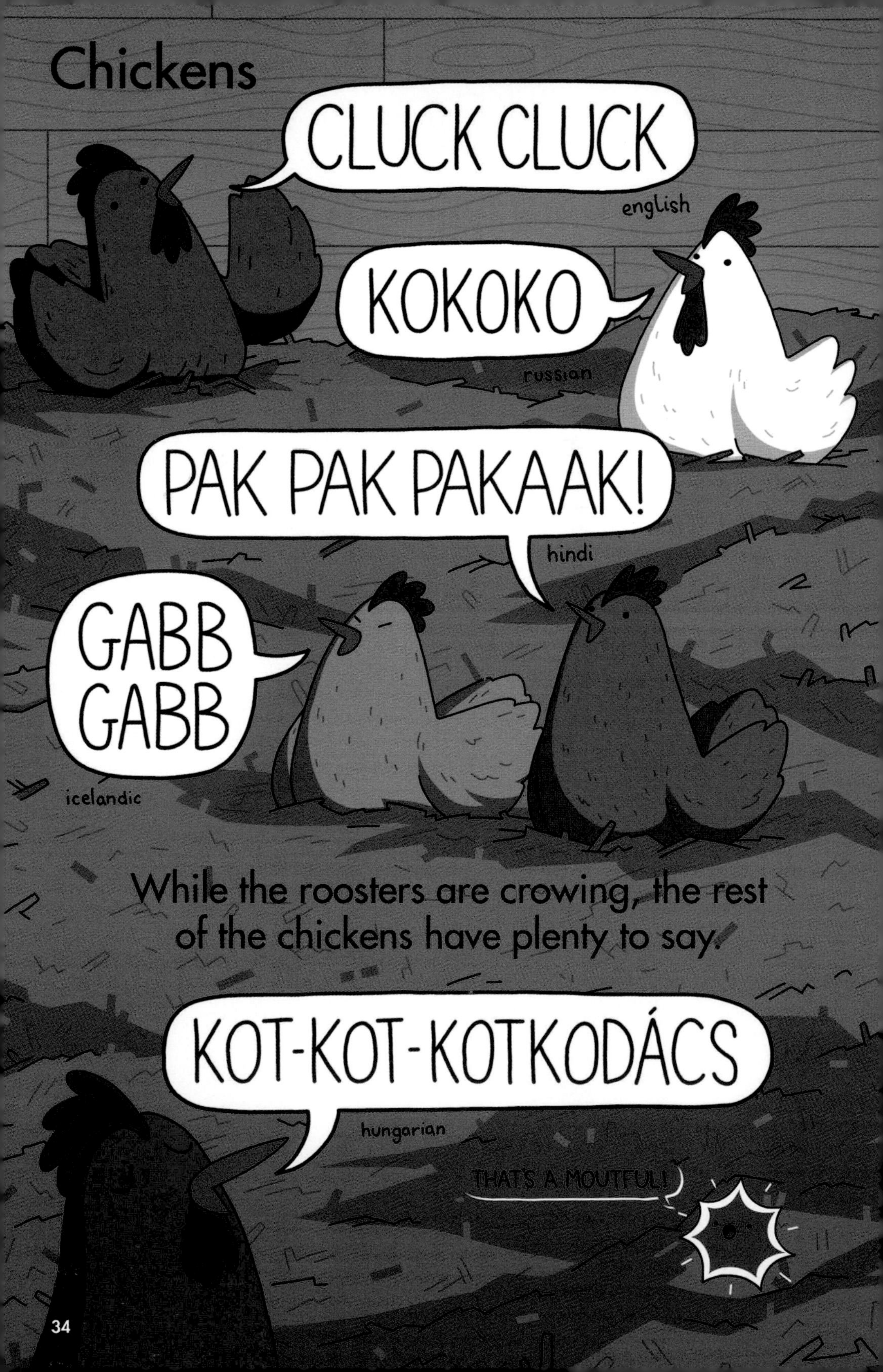
CLUCK CLUCK
english
KOKOKO
russian
PAK PAK PAKAAK!
hindi
GABB GABB
icelandic
KOT-KOT-KOTKODÁCS
hungarian
THAT'S A MOUTFUL!

While the roosters are crowing, the rest of the chickens have plenty to say.

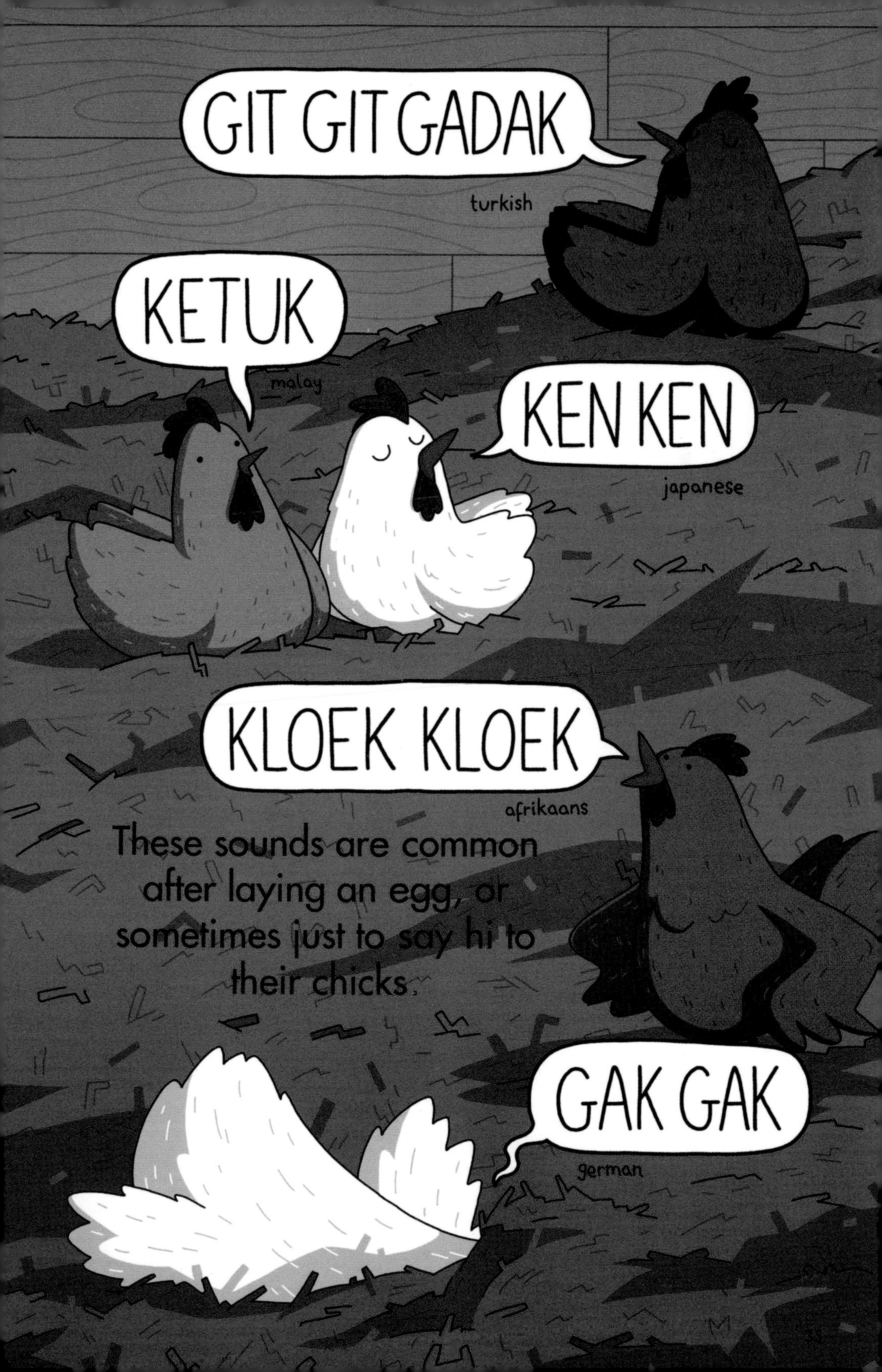
GIT GIT GADAK
turkish
KETUK
malay
KEN KEN
japanese
KLOEK KLOEK
afrikaans
GAK GAK
german

These sounds are common after laying an egg, or sometimes just to say hi to their chicks.

Chicks

Cute baby chickens have their sounds, too.

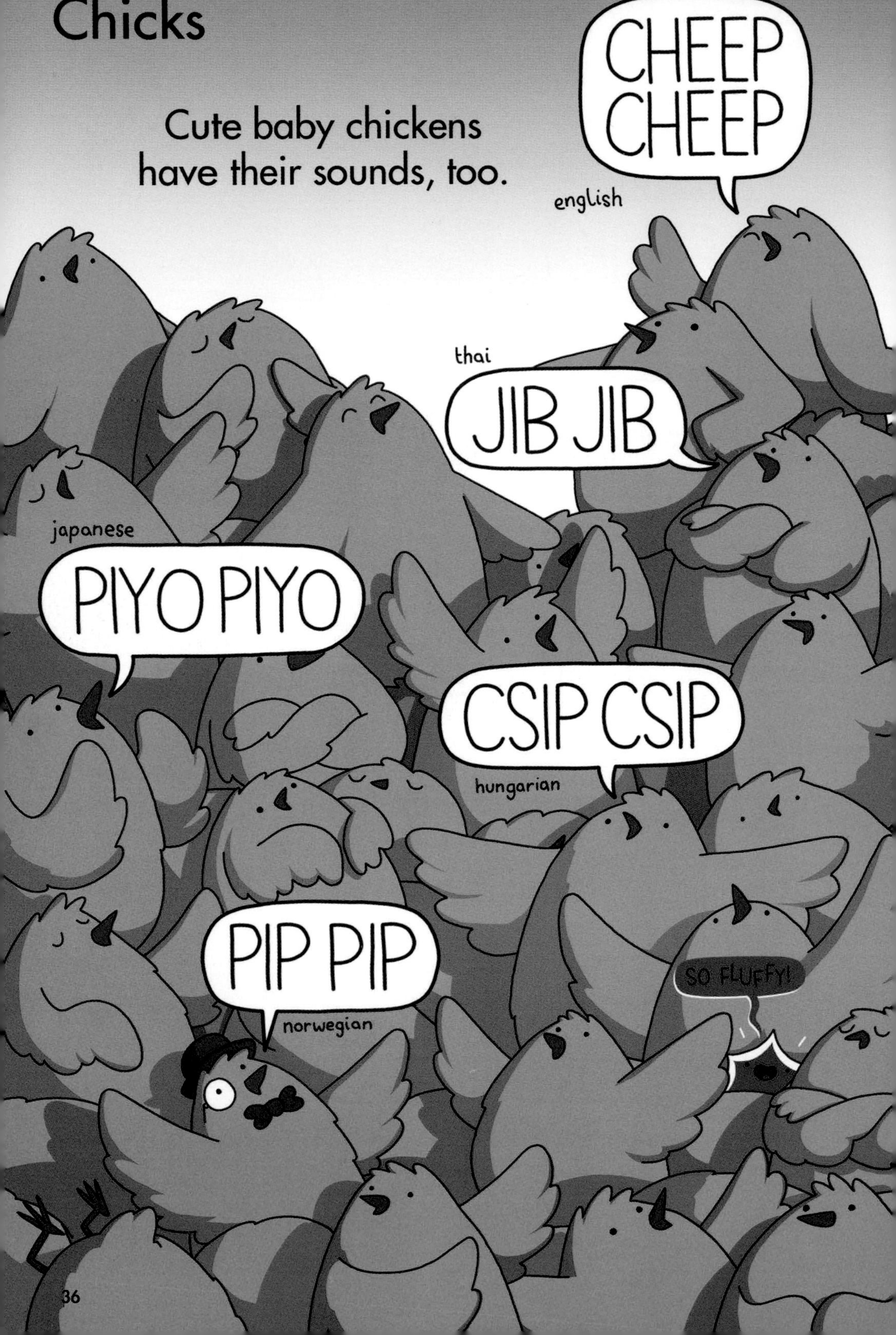
CHEEP CHEEP
english
thai
JIB JIB
japanese
PIYO PIYO
CSIP CSIP
hungarian
PIP PIP
norwegian
SO FLUFFY!

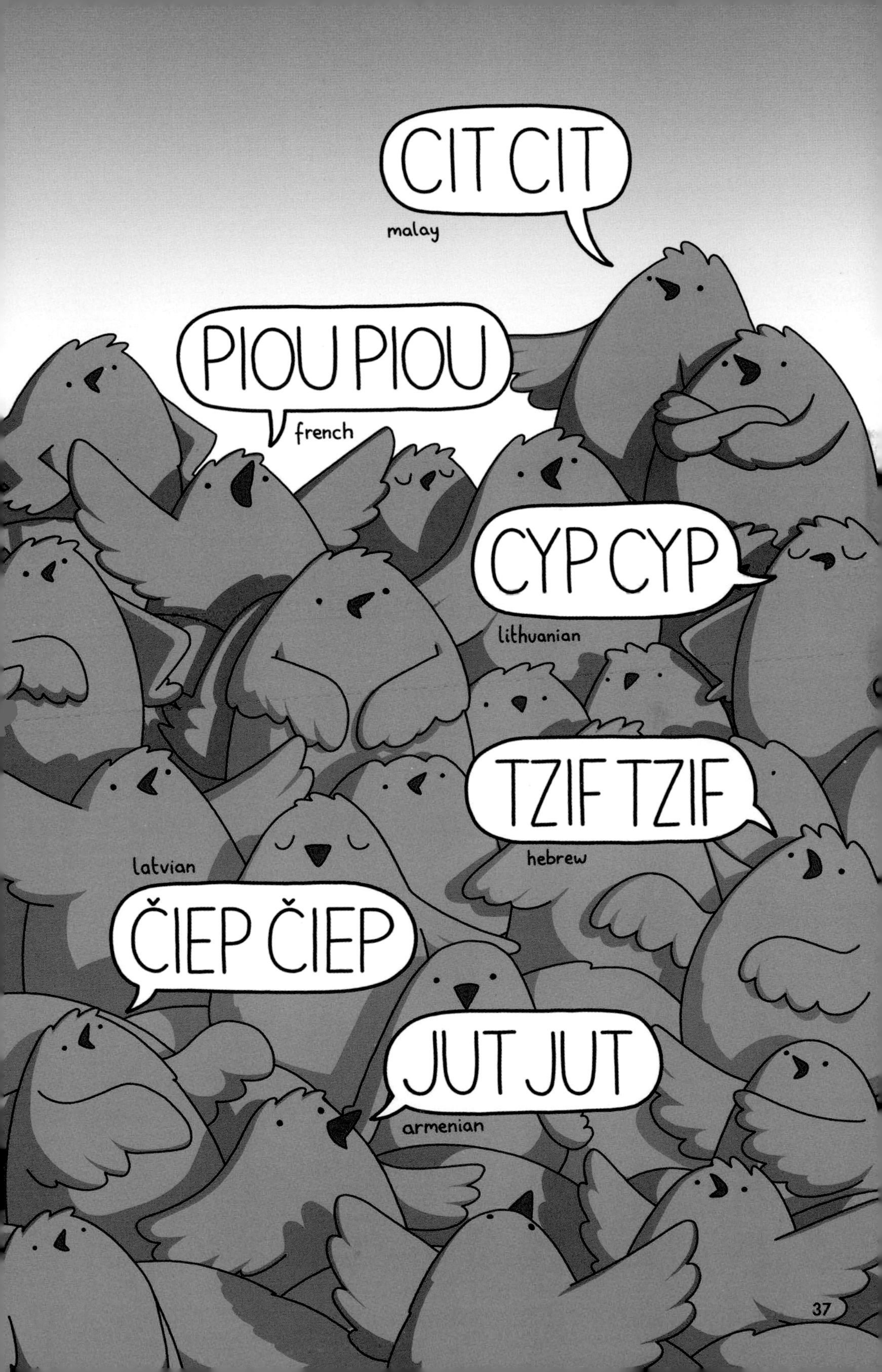
CIT CIT
malay
PIOU PIOU
french
CYP CYP
lithuanian
TZIF TZIF
hebrew
latvian
ČIEP ČIEP
JUT JUT
armenian

Horses

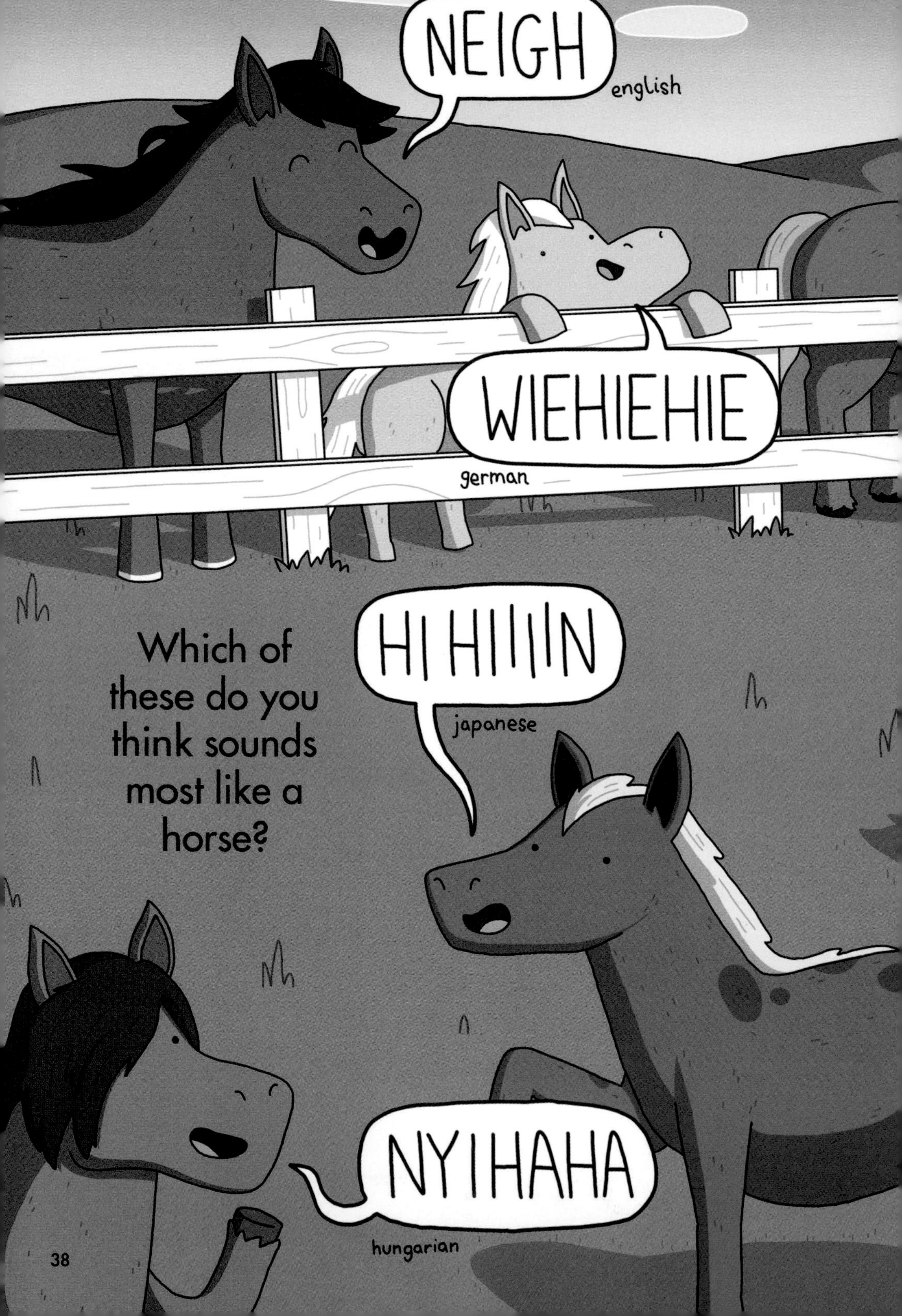
NEIGH
english
WIEHIEHIE
german
HI HIIIIN
japanese
NYIHAHA
hungarian

Which of these do you think sounds most like a horse?

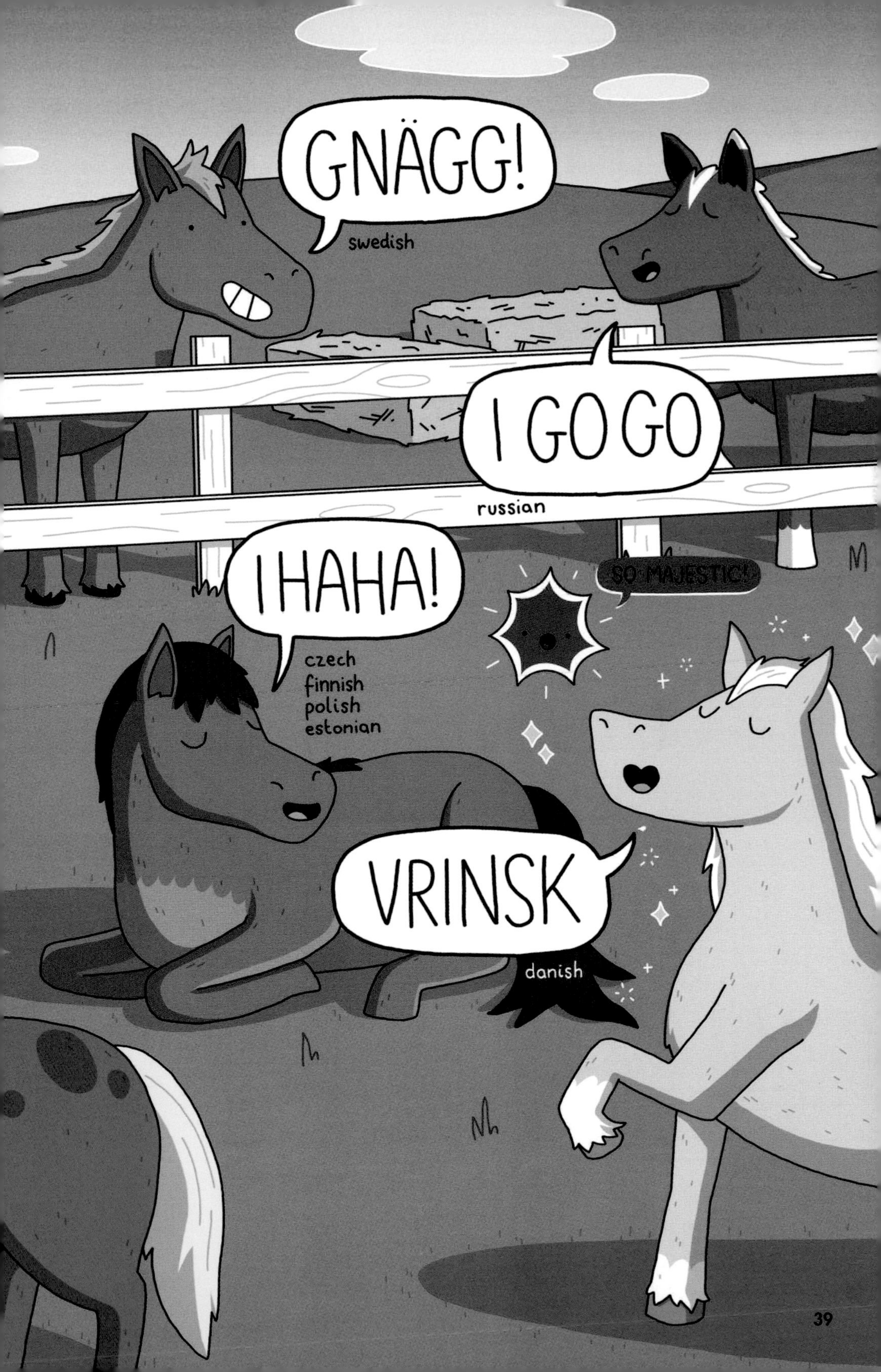

GNÄGG!
swedish
I GO GO
russian
IHAHA!
czech
finnish
polish
estonian
SO MAJESTIC!
VRINSK
danish

Hooves

Horses on the move make such lovely sounds. Giddy up!

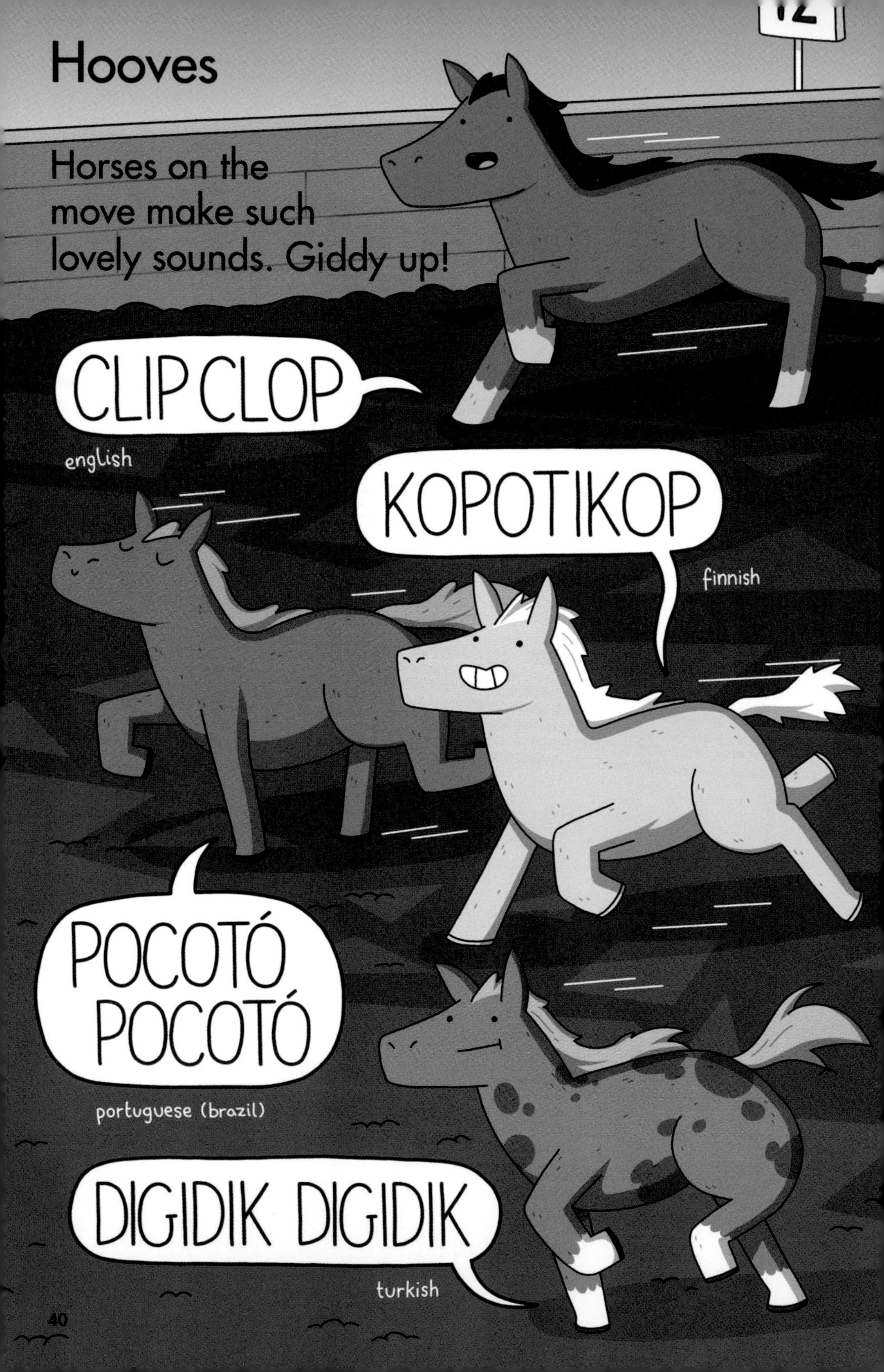
CLIP CLOP
english
KOPOTIKOP
finnish
POCOTÓ POCOTÓ
portuguese (brazil)
DIGIDIK DIGIDIK
turkish

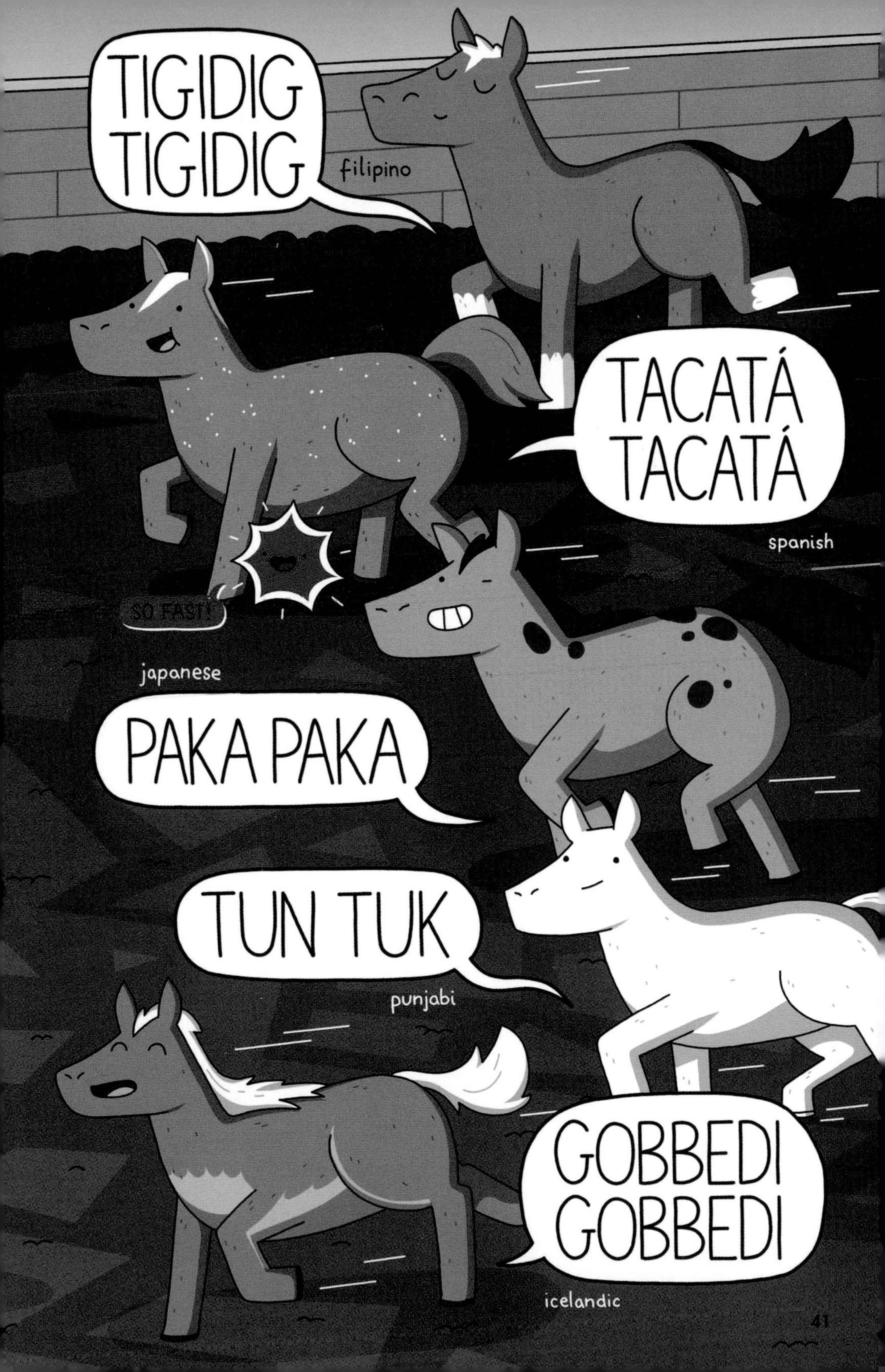
TIGIDIG TIGIDIG
filipino
TACATÁ TACATÁ
spanish
SO FAST!
japanese
PAKA PAKA
TUN TUK
punjabi
GOBBEDI GOBBEDI
icelandic

Ducks

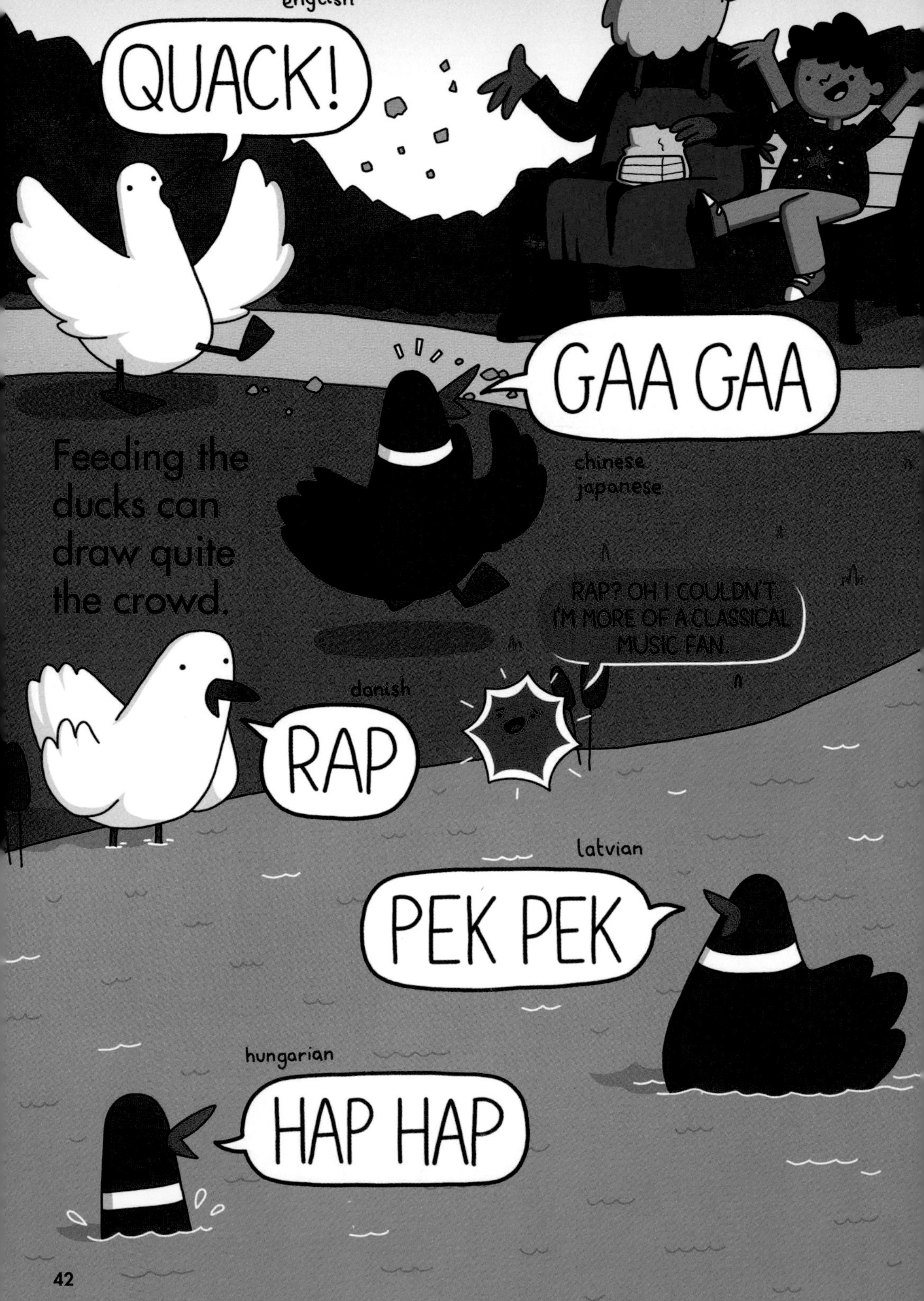
english
QUACK!
GAA GAA
chinese
japanese
RAP? OH I COULDN'T. I'M MORE OF A CLASSICAL MUSIC FAN.
danish
RAP
latvian
PEK PEK
hungarian
HAP HAP

Feeding the ducks can draw quite the crowd.

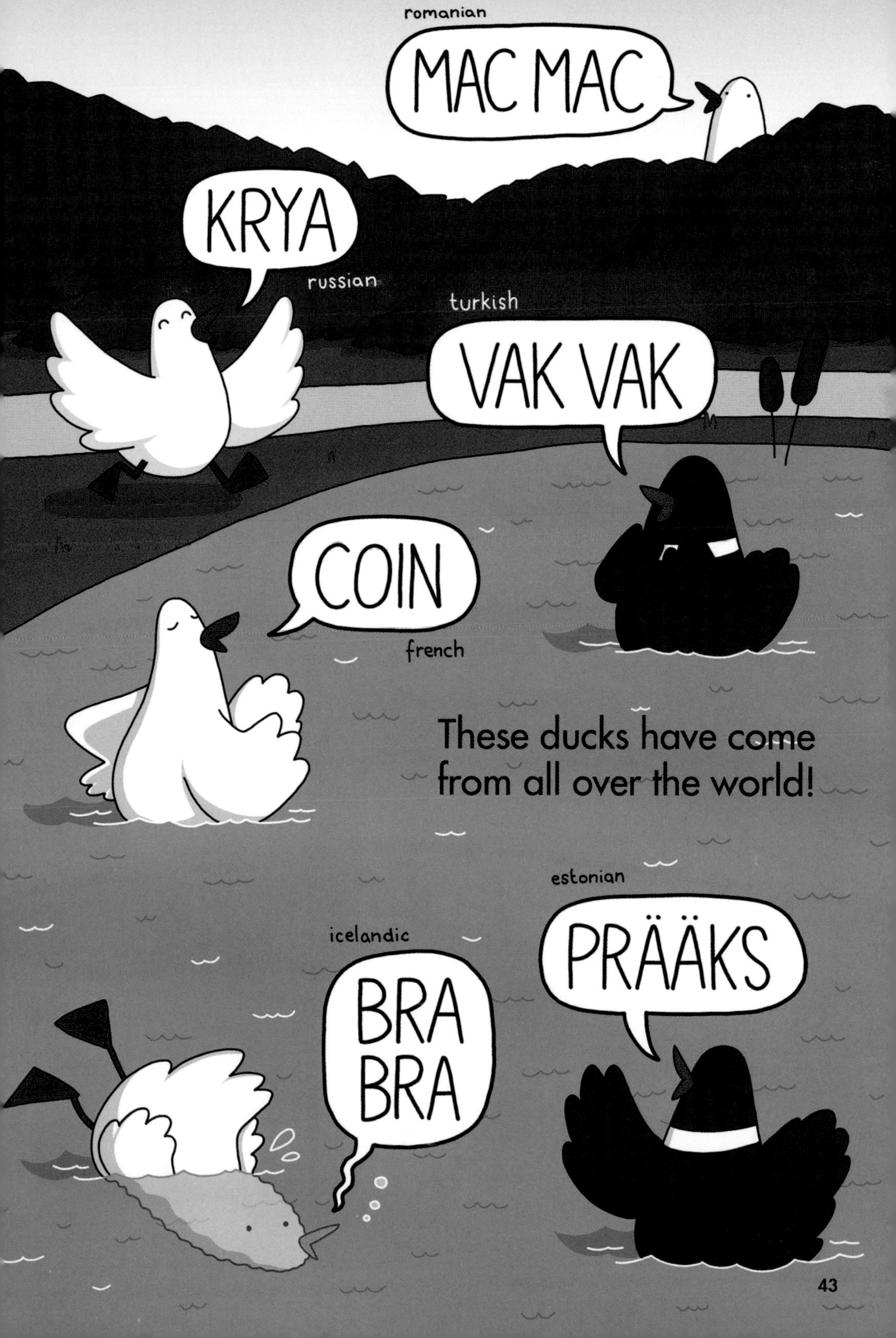
romanian
MAC MAC
KRYA
russian
turkish
VAK VAK
COIN
french
These ducks have come from all over the world!
estonian
PRÄÄKS
icelandic
BRA BRA

Turkeys

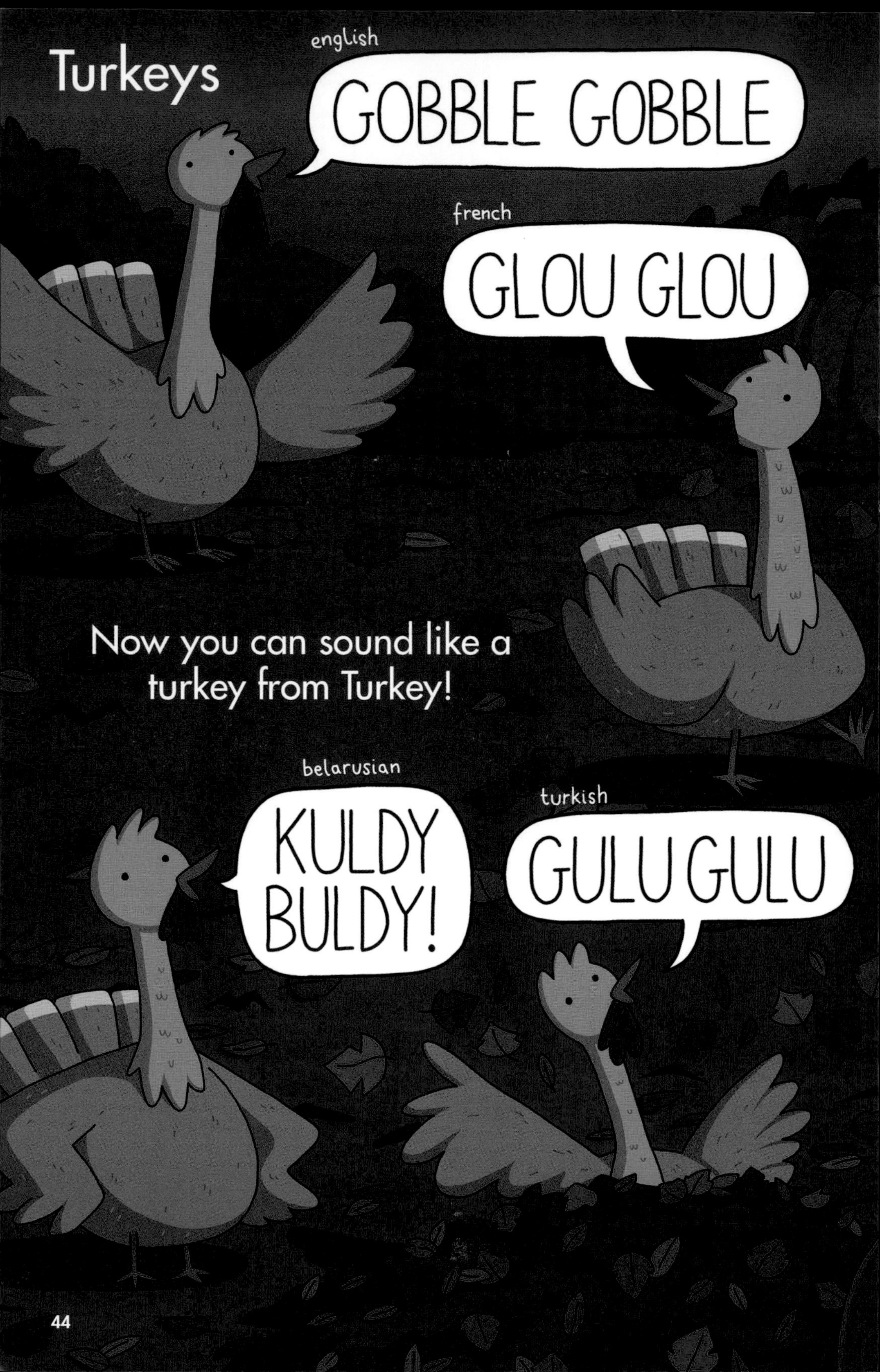
english
GOBBLE GOBBLE
french
GLOU GLOU
belarusian
KULDY BULDY!
turkish
GULU GULU

Now you can sound like a turkey from Turkey!

spanish (parts of mexico)
GORO GORO
HEY I'VE SEEN YOU BEFORE! AREN'T YOU A CAT SOUND?
persian
BOOGHALAMOON!
(also the persian word for turkey!)
ŠULDU BULDU!
lithuanian
czech
HUDRY HUDRY

IN THE ZOO

All kinds of animals can be found at the zoo, so we've got a whole new world of sounds to explore. It turns out a fair few creatures actually get their names from onomatopoeia for the sounds they make. Not just the cuckoo, no no no.

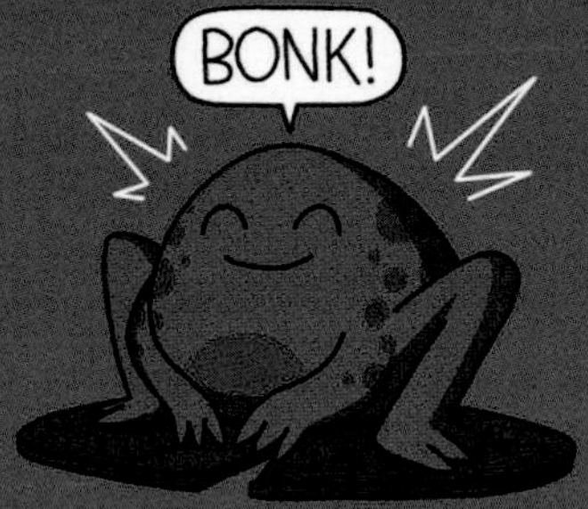
BONK!

There's a type of frog in Australia called a *Pobblebonk* (or the Western Banjo Frog), named after the banjo-esque **BONK** sound it's known to make.

The *Dik-dik,* a small antelope from southern Africa, gets its name from the whistles the female of the species makes.

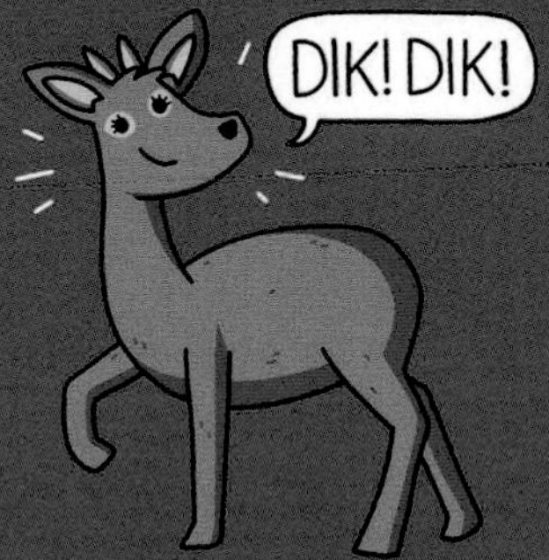
DIK! DIK!

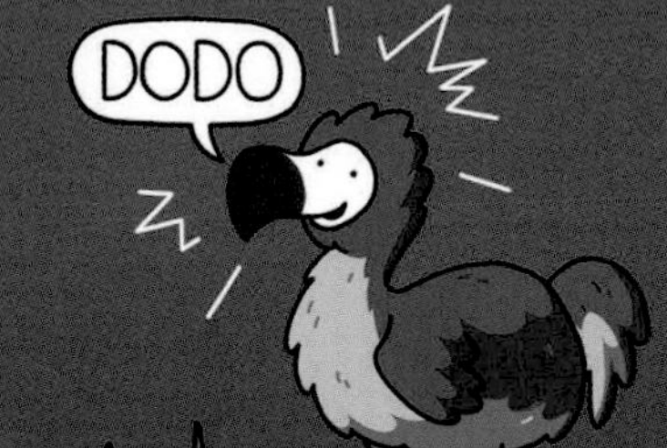
DODO

And some people say that the *Dodo* was named for the sound it made (while it was still around).

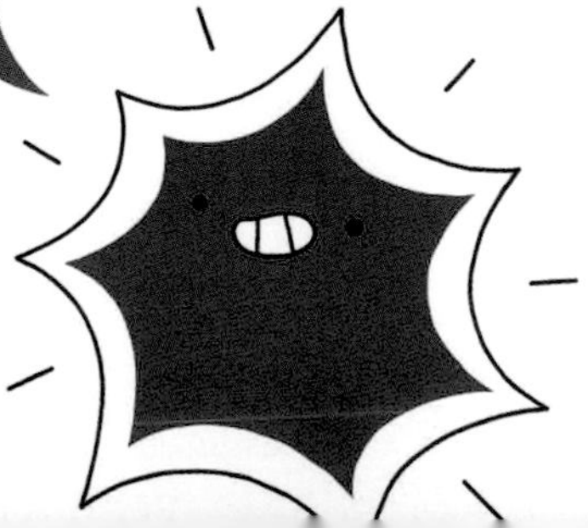

Lions

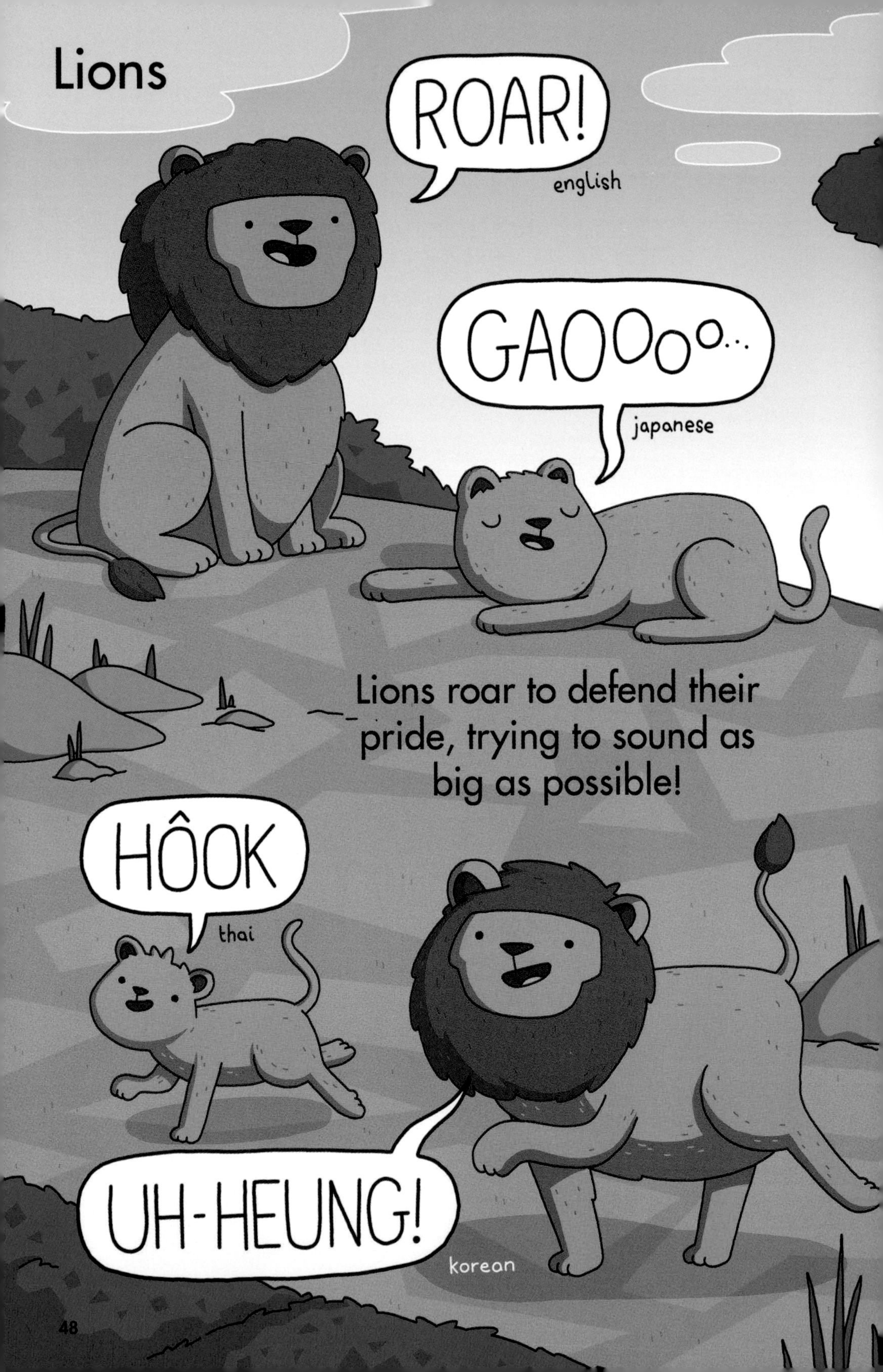
ROAR!
english
GAOOOO...
japanese
HÔOK
thai
UH-HEUNG!
korean

Lions roar to defend their pride, trying to sound as big as possible!

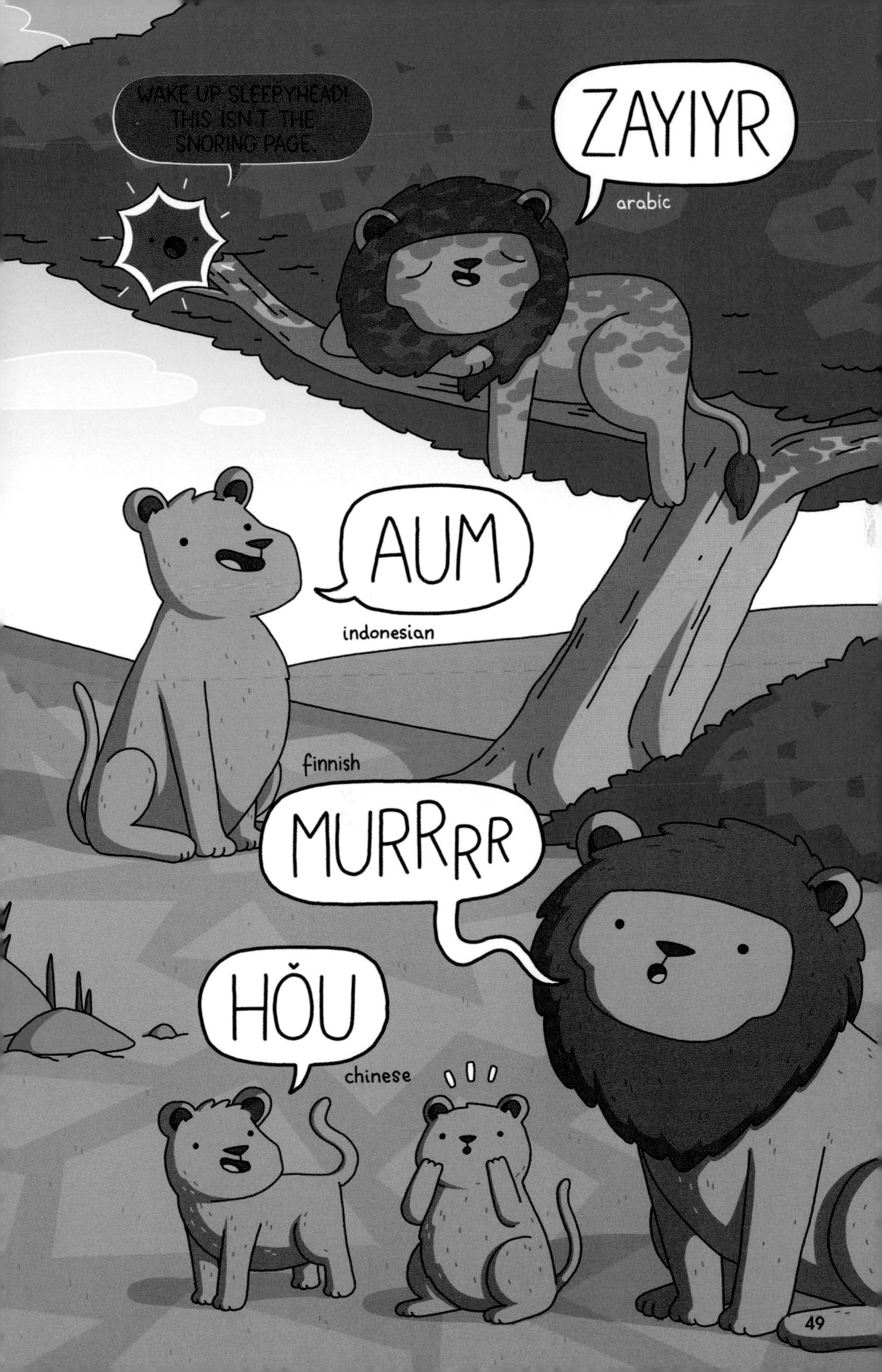
WAKE UP SLEEPYHEAD! THIS ISN'T THE SNORING PAGE.
ZAYIYR
arabic
AUM
indonesian
finnish
MURRrR
HǑU
chinese

Elephants

There's not really a word for the elephant's sound in English.

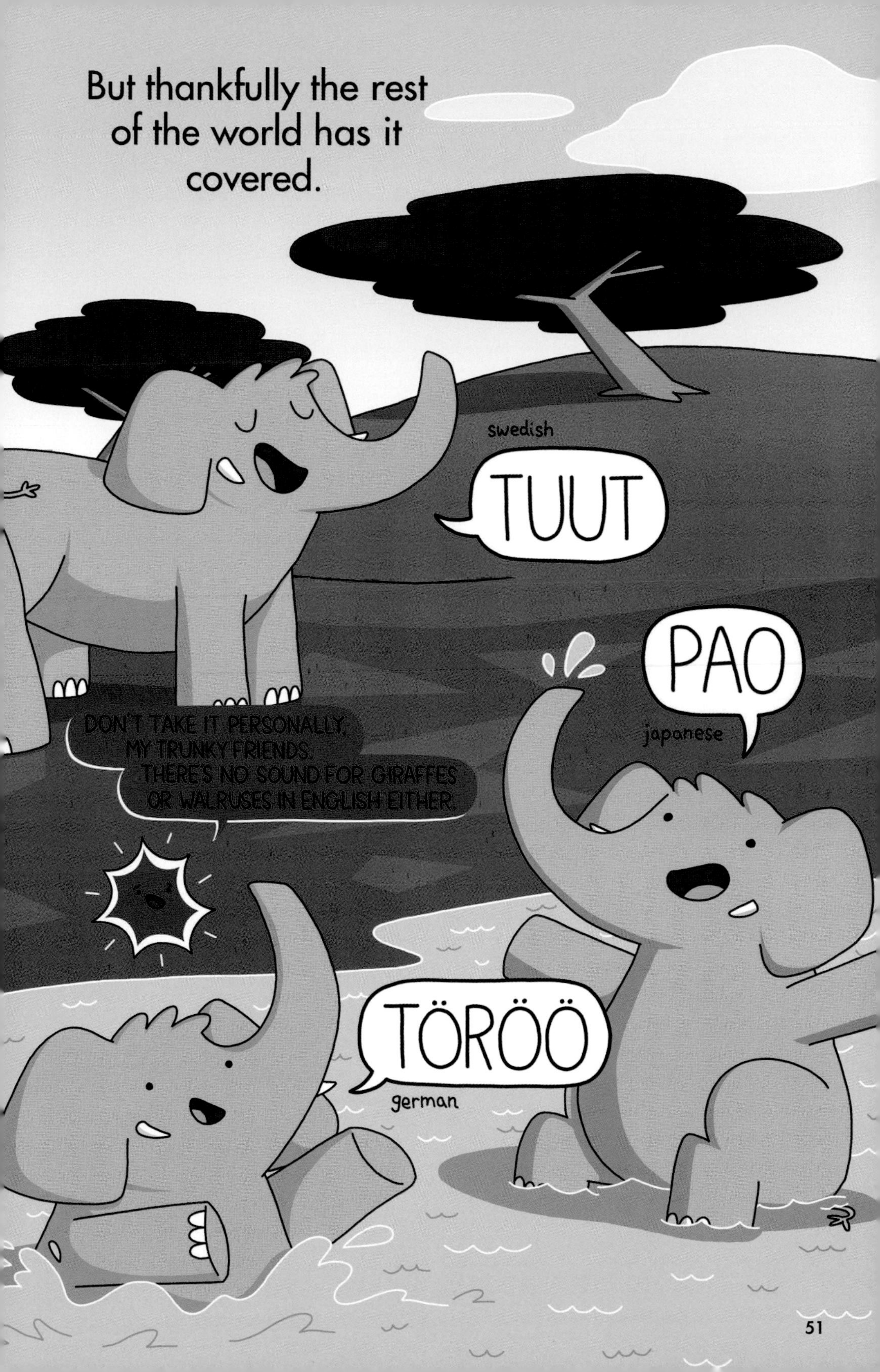
But thankfully the rest of the world has it covered.
swedish
TUUT
PAO
japanese
DON'T TAKE IT PERSONALLY, MY TRUNKY FRIENDS. THERE'S NO SOUND FOR GIRAFFES OR WALRUSES IN ENGLISH EITHER.
TÖRÖÖ
german

Snakes

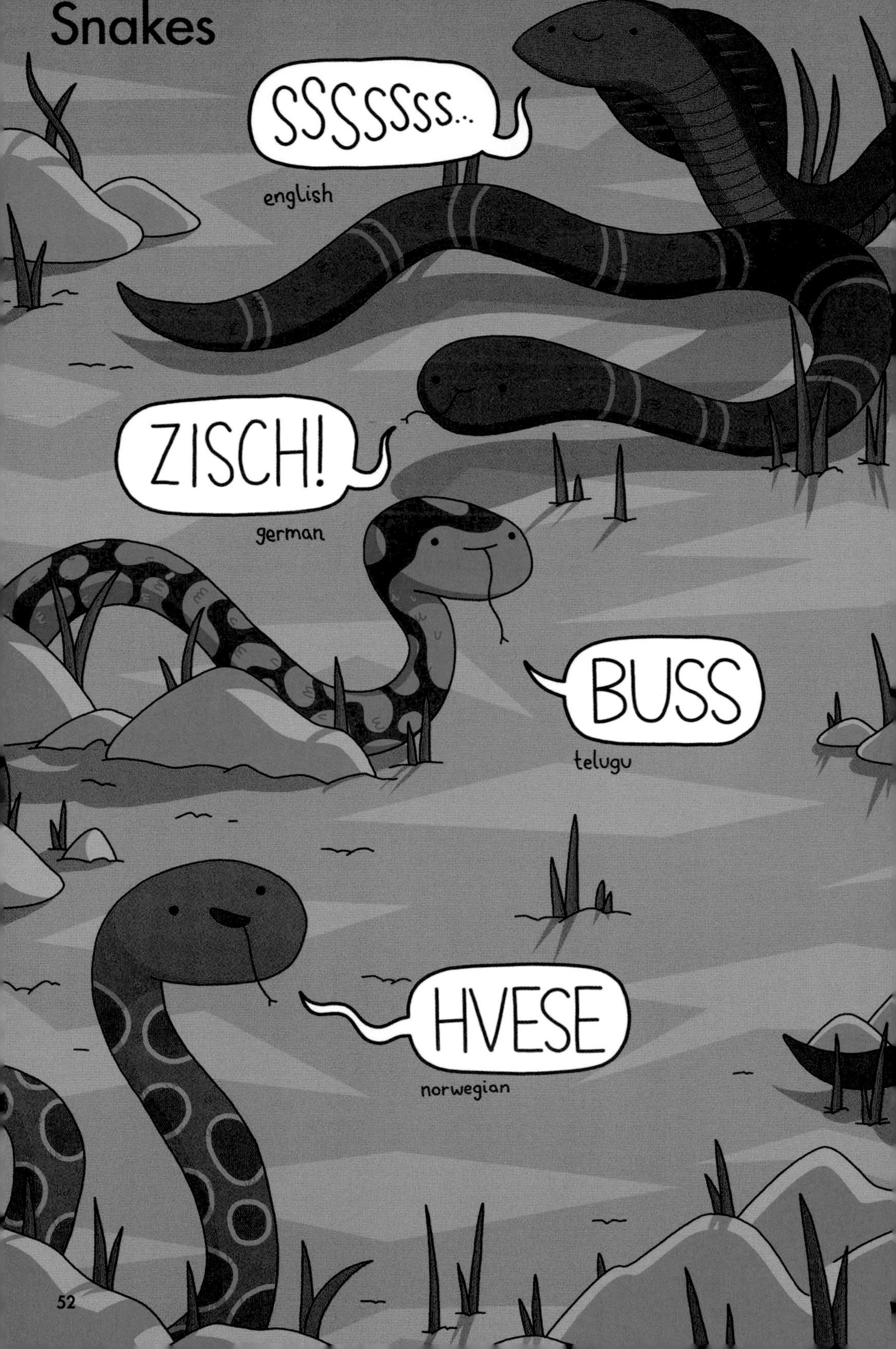
SSSSSSS...
english
ZISCH!
german
BUSS
telugu
HVESE
norwegian

Snakes don't hiss to chat, they do it to scare off their predators.

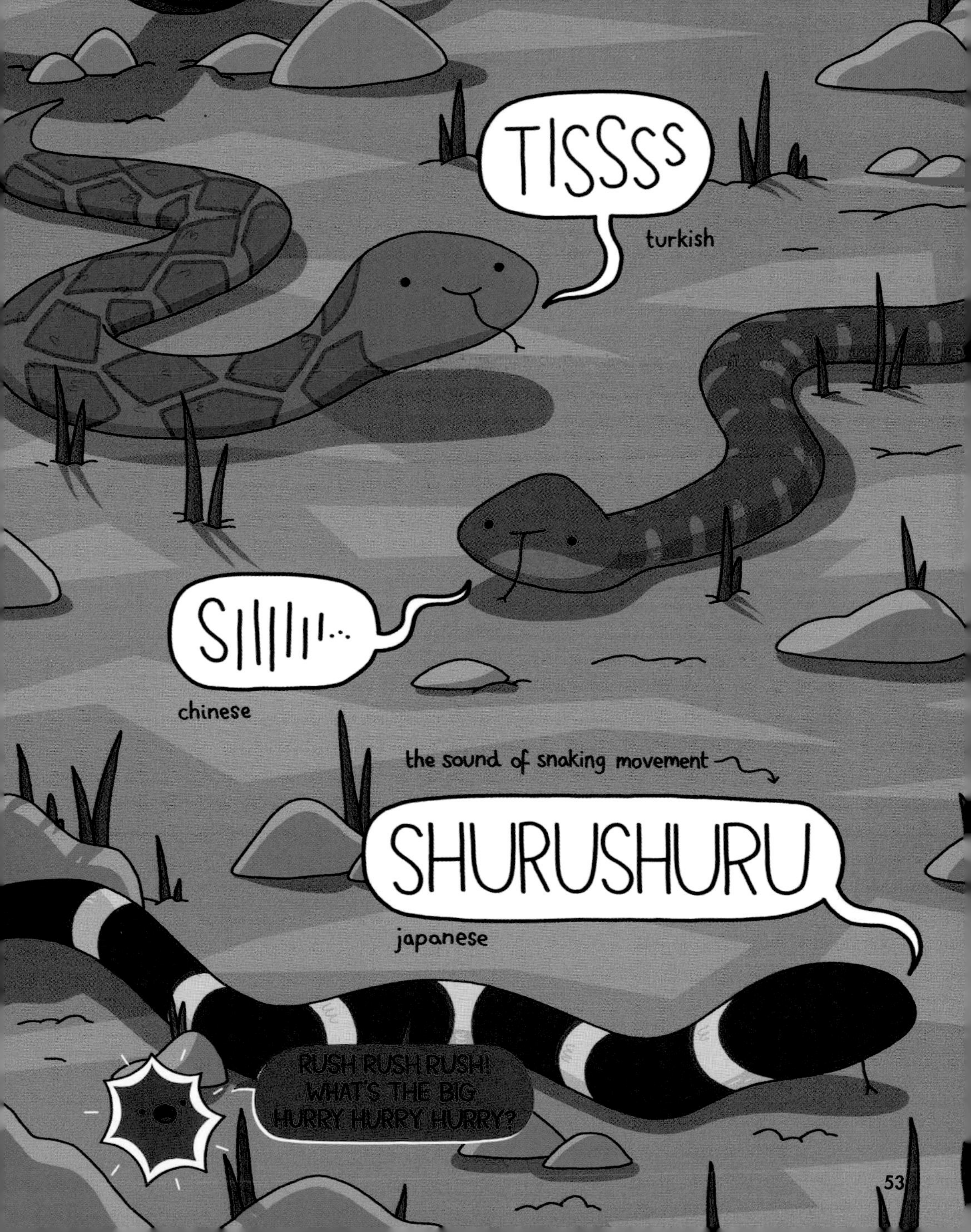
TISSSS
turkish
SIIIII...
chinese
the sound of snaking movement
SHURUSHURU
japanese
RUSH RUSH RUSH!
WHAT'S THE BIG
HURRY HURRY HURRY?

Frogs

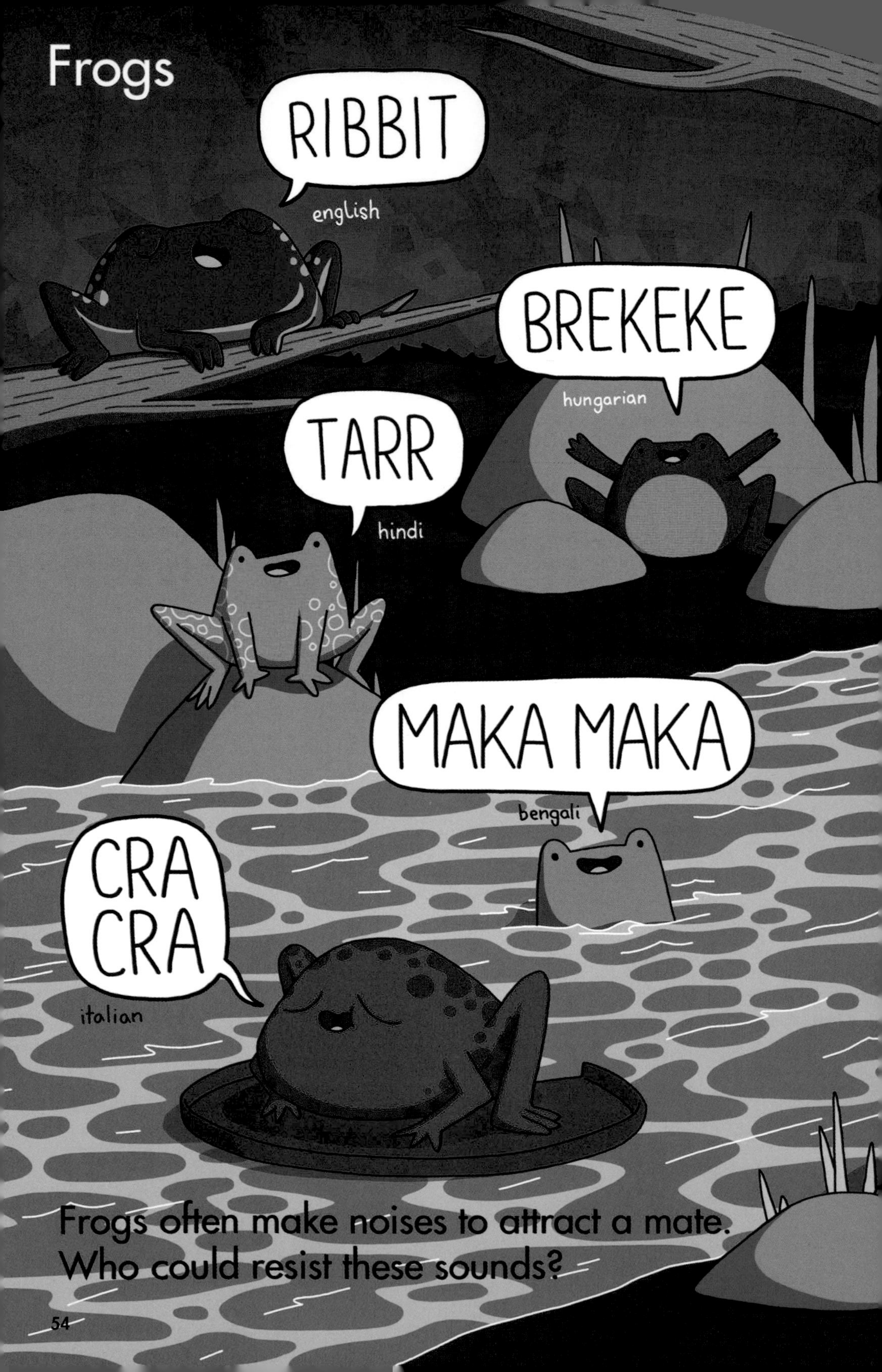
RIBBIT
english
BREKEKE
hungarian
TARR
hindi
MAKA MAKA
bengali
CRA CRA
italian

Frogs often make noises to attract a mate. Who could resist these sounds?

OPOP
thai
VRAK
turkish
KUM KUM
polish
GUA GUA
chinese
KROOKS
estonian
KEROKERO
japanese
WHAT A BEAUTIFUL SOUND!

Owls

There's some debate about the sound owls make, even in English.

But when owls come out at night, they make big noises to mark their territory.

Monkeys

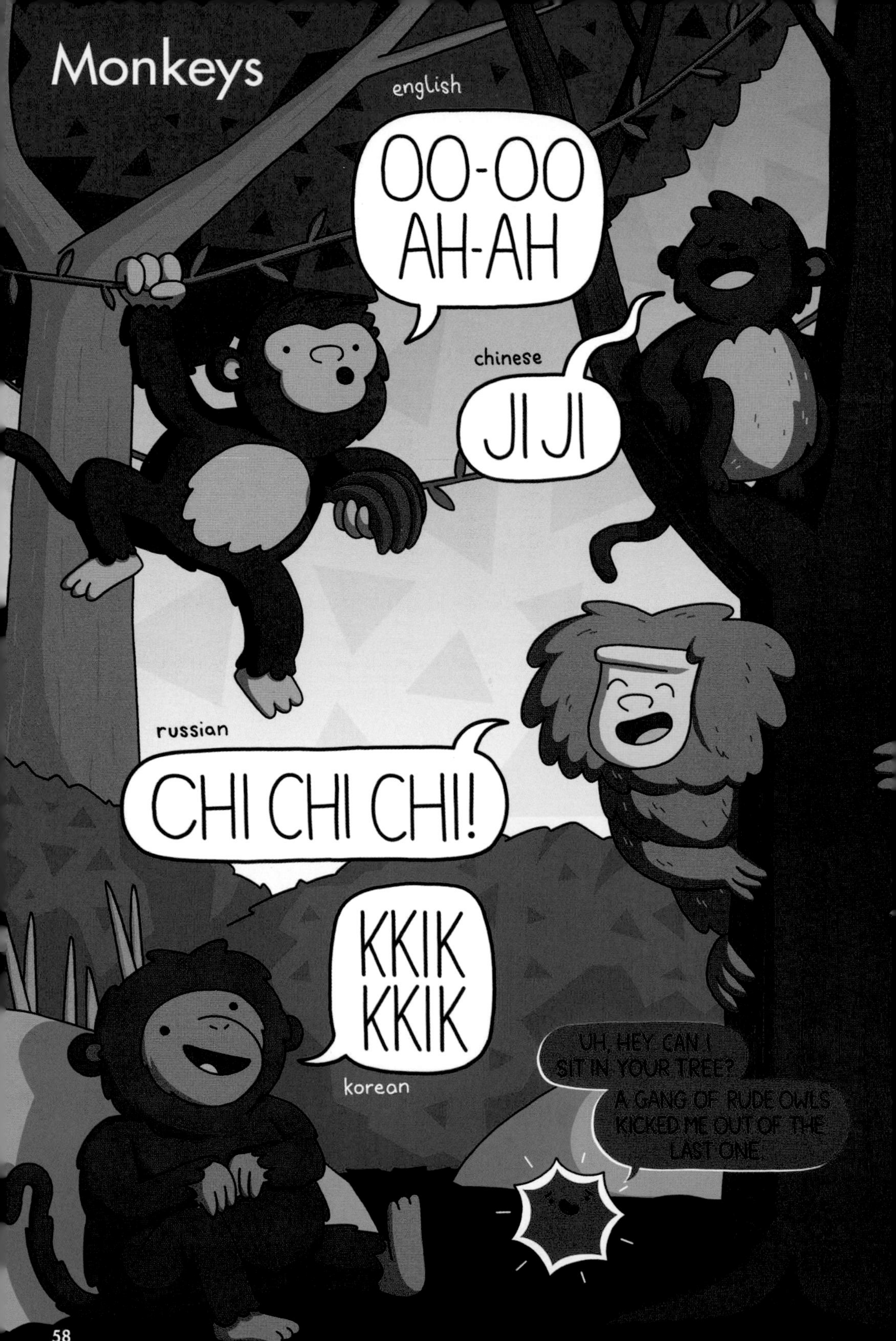
english
OO-OO AH-AH
chinese
JI JI
russian
CHI CHI CHI!
KKIK KKIK
korean
UH, HEY. CAN I SIT IN YOUR TREE?
A GANG OF RUDE OWLS KICKED ME OUT OF THE LAST ONE.

Mischievous monkeys make marvellous music.

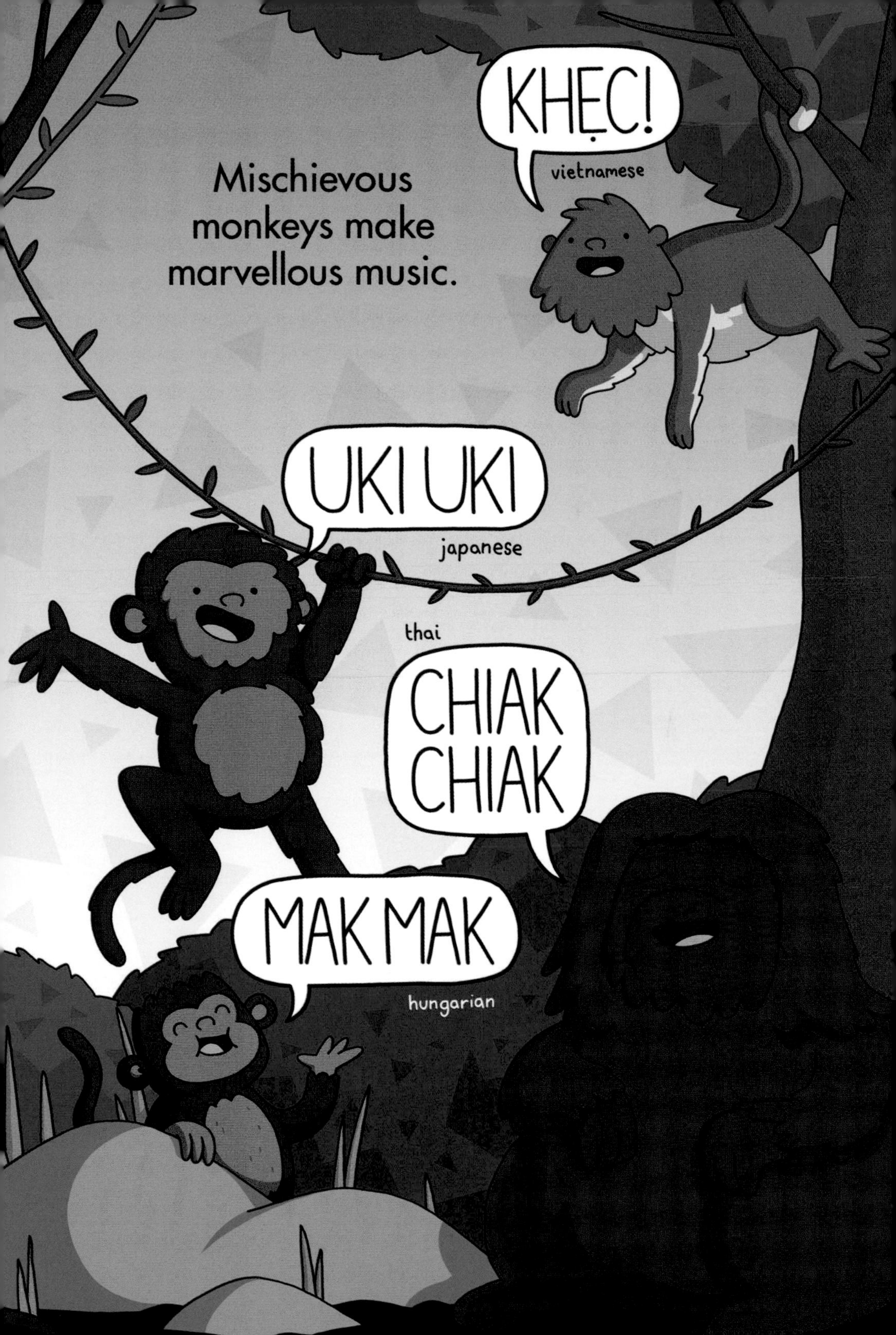

Bears

GRRRRR...
english
PAO
chinese
MÕMM
estonian
GAAAAH
arabic
BRUMM
czech
GẦM GỪ
vietnamese

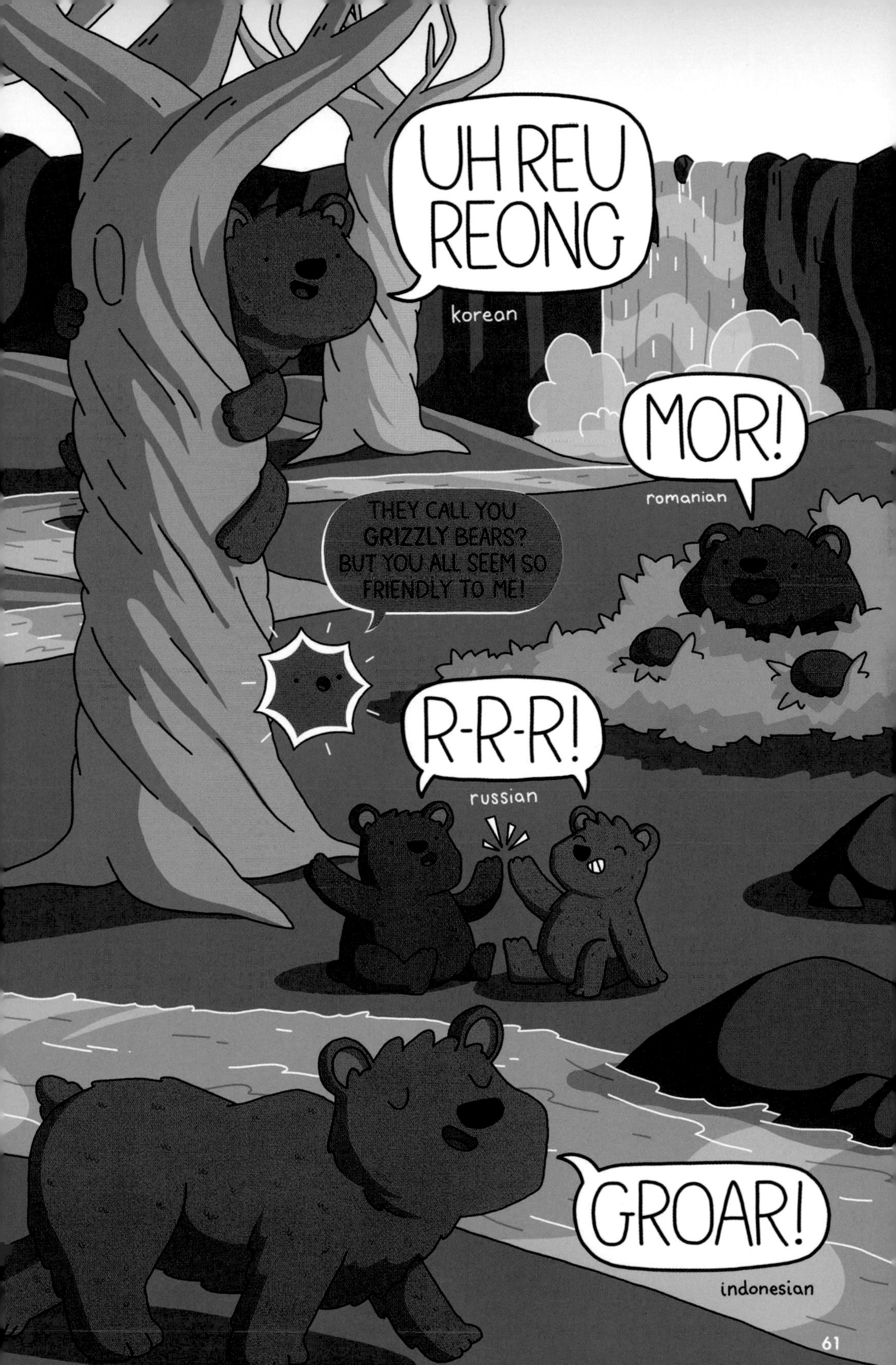

UH REU REONG
korean
MOR!
romanian
THEY CALL YOU GRIZZLY BEARS? BUT YOU ALL SEEM SO FRIENDLY TO ME!
R-R-R!
russian
GROAR!
indonesian

Wolves

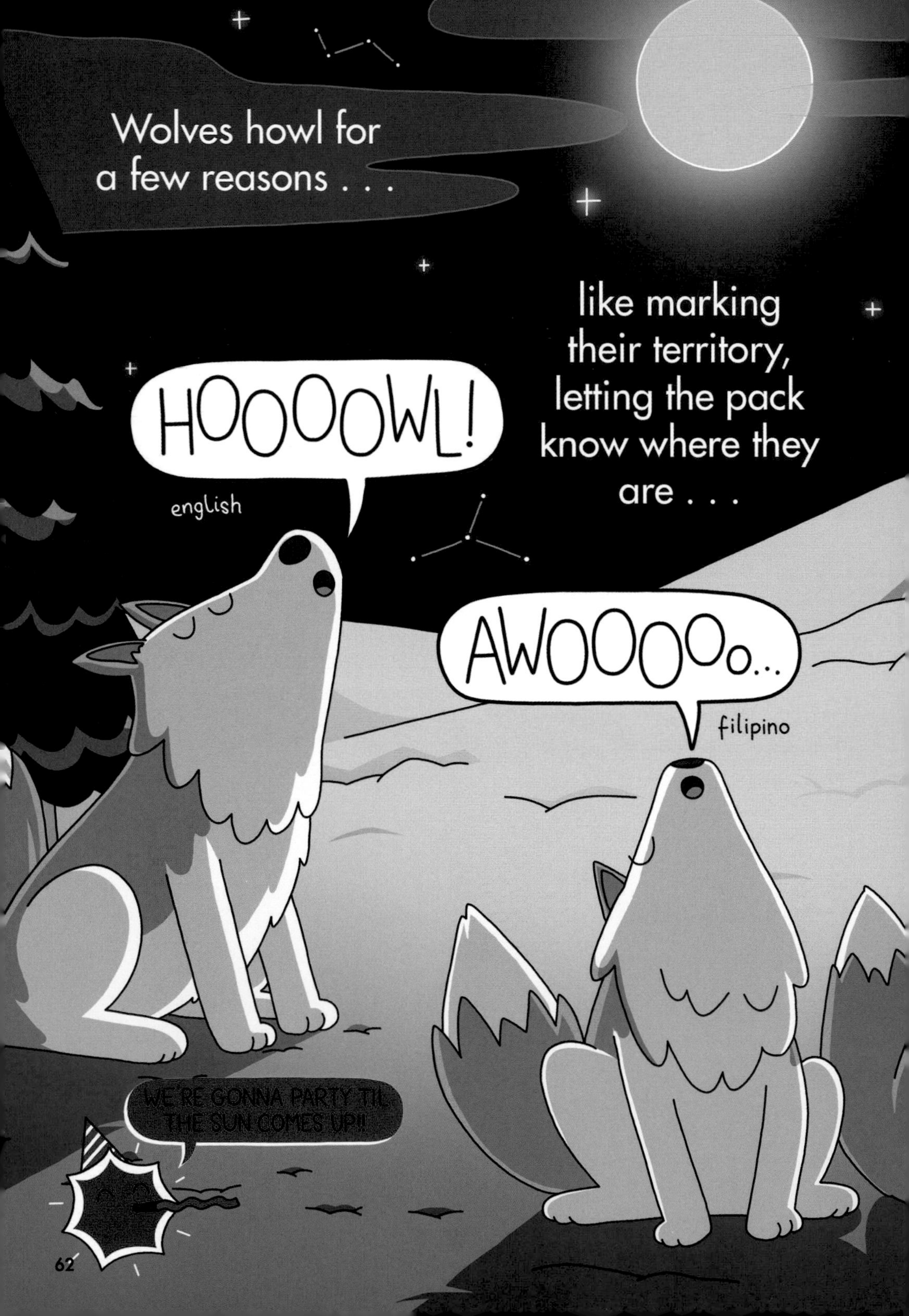
Wolves howl for a few reasons . . .
like marking their territory, letting the pack know where they are . . .
HOOOOWL!
english
AWOOOOo...
filipino
WE'RE GONNA PARTY TIL THE SUN COMES UP!!

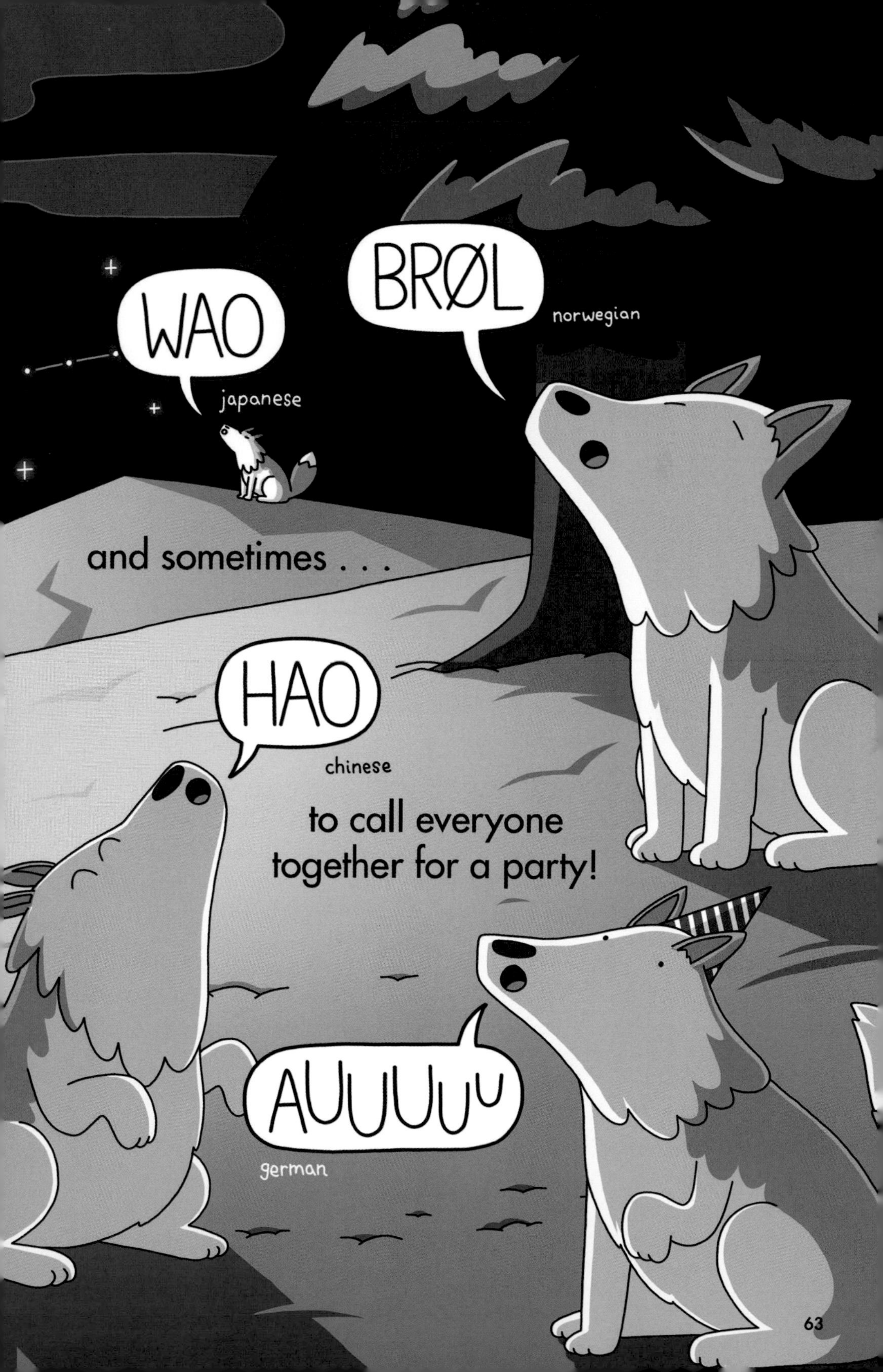
WAO
japanese
BRØL
norwegian
HAO
chinese
AUUUUU
german

and sometimes . . .

to call everyone together for a party!

LOUD NOISES

When something exciting is happening, loud noises are usually close behind, and all this onomatopoeia is great for the exhilarating world of comics.

The

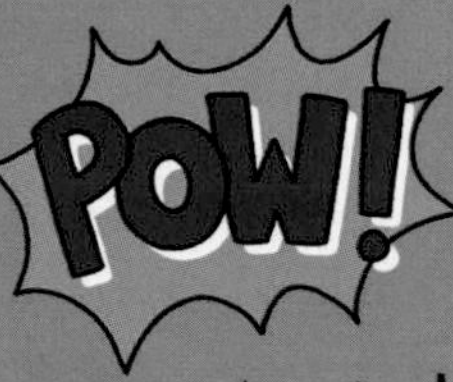
POW!

of a punch.

A window breaks,

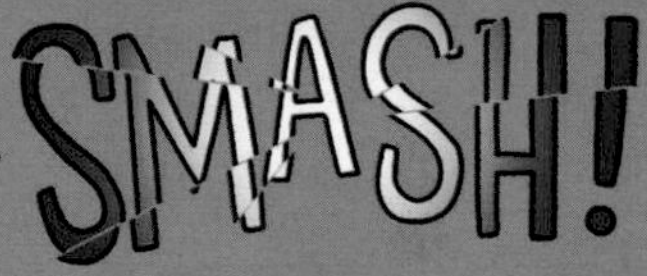
SMASH!

And

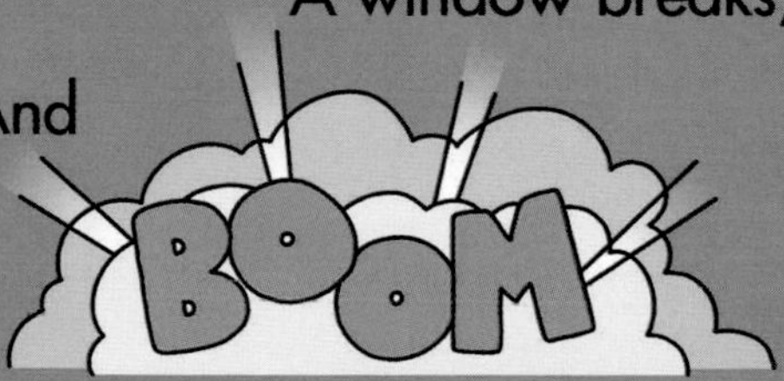
BOOM

goes the dynamite!

Big moments need big sounds, and in comics those noises appear right in the panel. You might've noticed some changes from English sounds if you've read comics originally published in different languages, like *Tintin* or *Asterix the Gaul* (whose French punches go **paf!**), not to mention the extensive sound effects in the world of Japanese manga comics.

Next time you hear a loud noise, think how you'd draw it in a comic panel. How would you write it down?

Now let's get a move on. There are some fireworks I want to see!

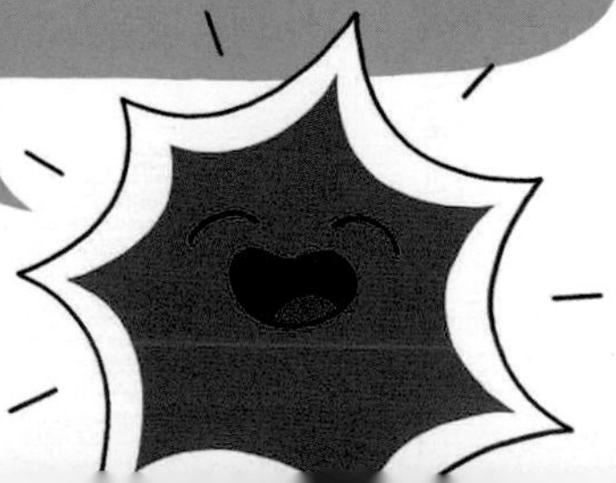

Fireworks

english
BOOM!
portuguese
CA-BUM
japanese
DOKAN
indonesian
DUAR!
PATAKA
hindi
finnish
JYSÄYS!
OOOOOH AAAAAH
THEY'RE SO PRETTY

It's time to celebrate loud and proud!

And what better way to do that than with beautiful fireworks.

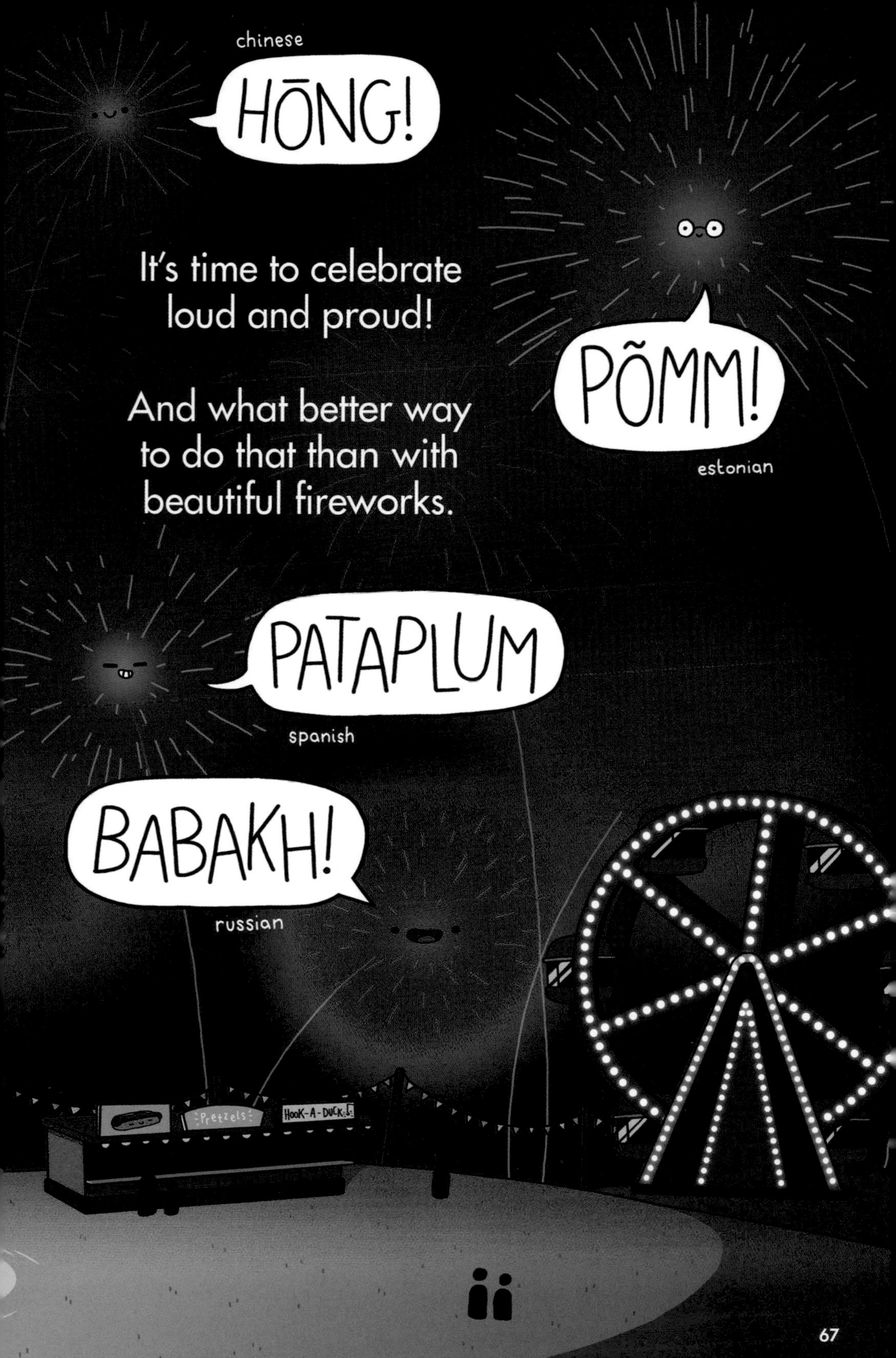
chinese
HŌNG!
PÕMM!
estonian
PATAPLUM
spanish
BABAKH!
russian
Pretzels
HOOK-A-DUCK

Smashing

There's nothing much noisier than a bull in a china shop.

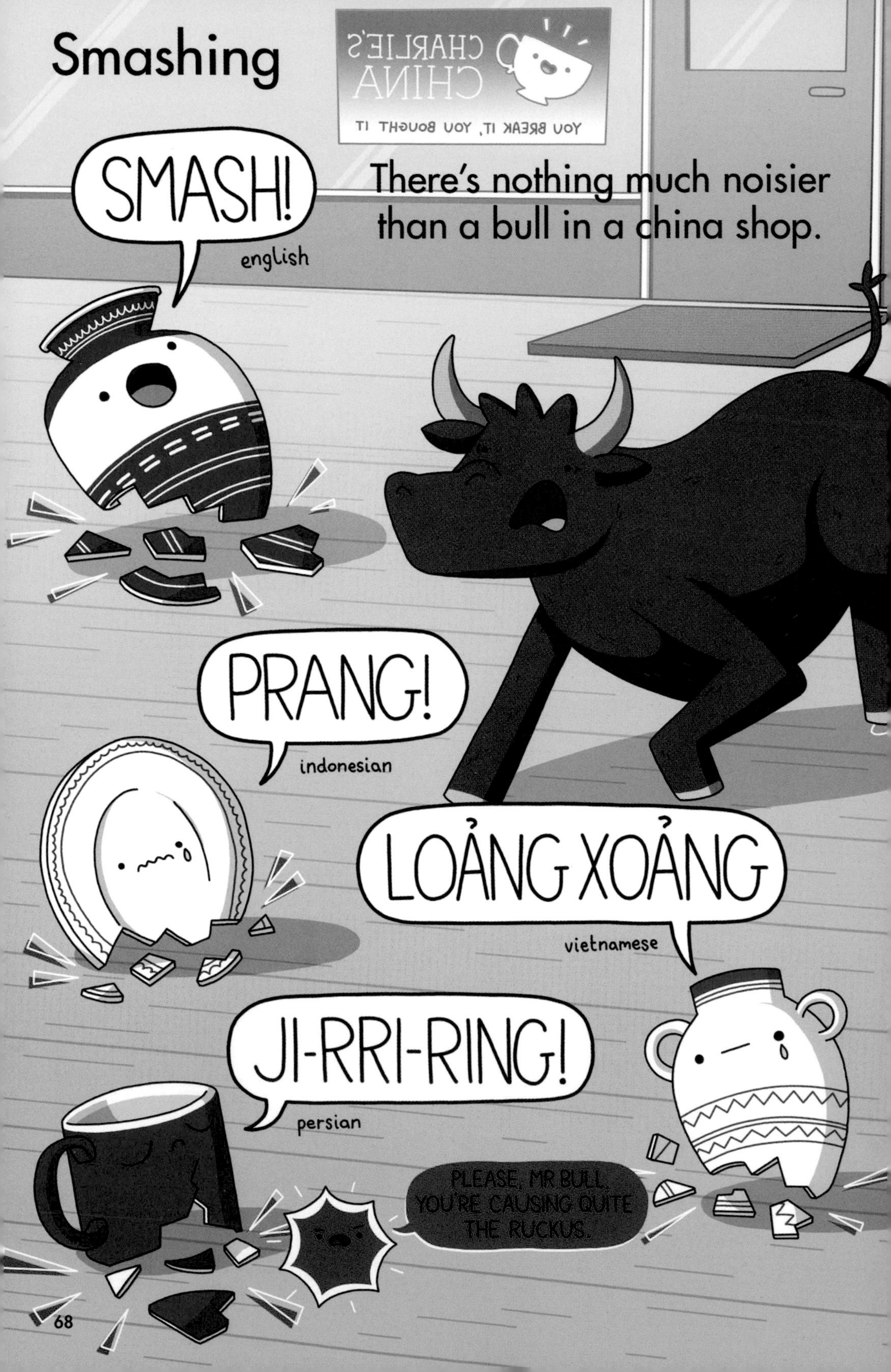

CHARLIE'S CHINA
YOU BREAK IT, YOU BOUGHT IT
SMASH!
english
PRANG!
indonesian
LOẢNG XOẢNG
vietnamese
JI-RRI-RING!
persian
PLEASE, MR BULL, YOU'RE CAUSING QUITE THE RUCKUS.

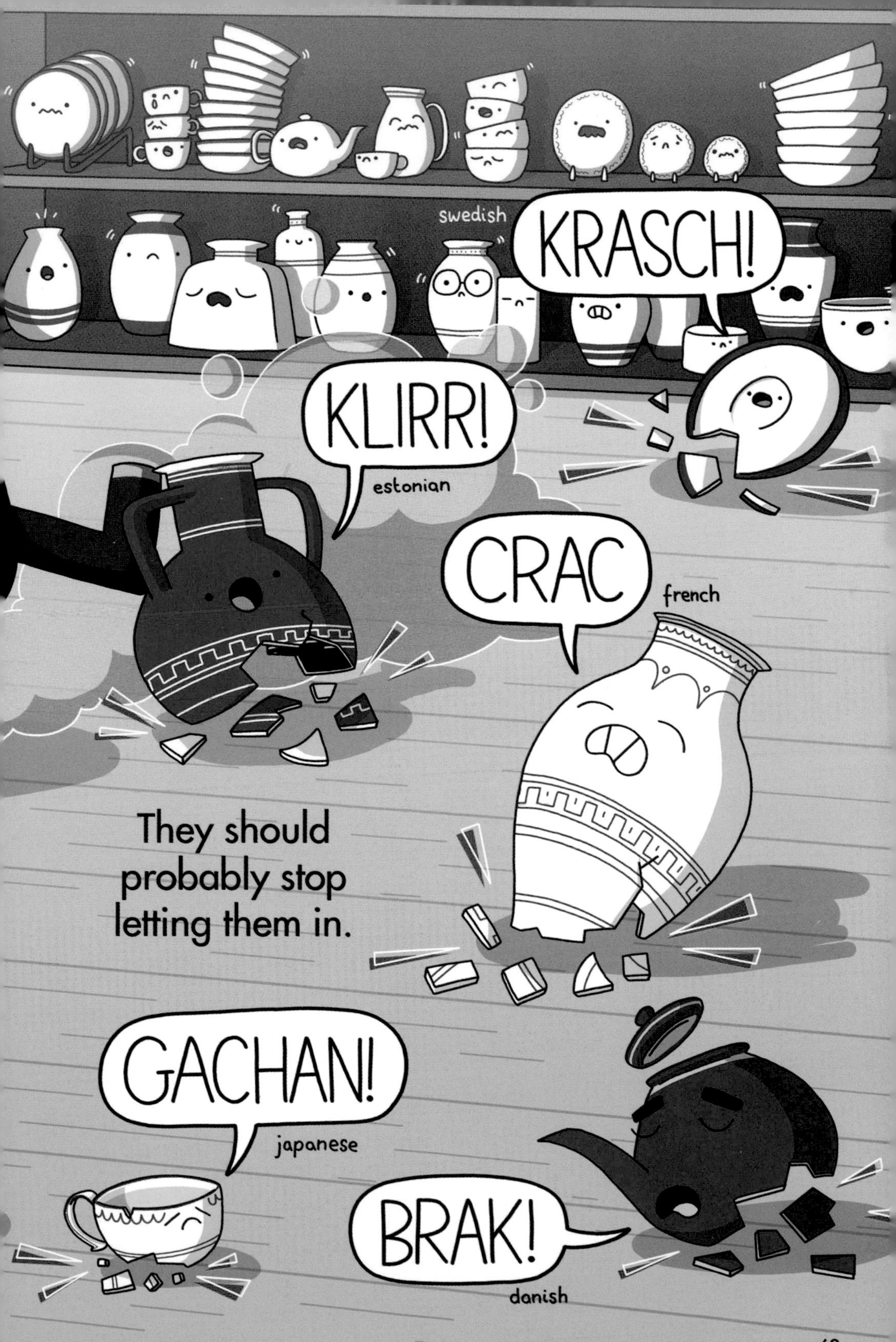
swedish
KRASCH!
KLIRR!
estonian
CRAC
french
They should probably stop letting them in.
GACHAN!
japanese
BRAK!
danish

Gunfire

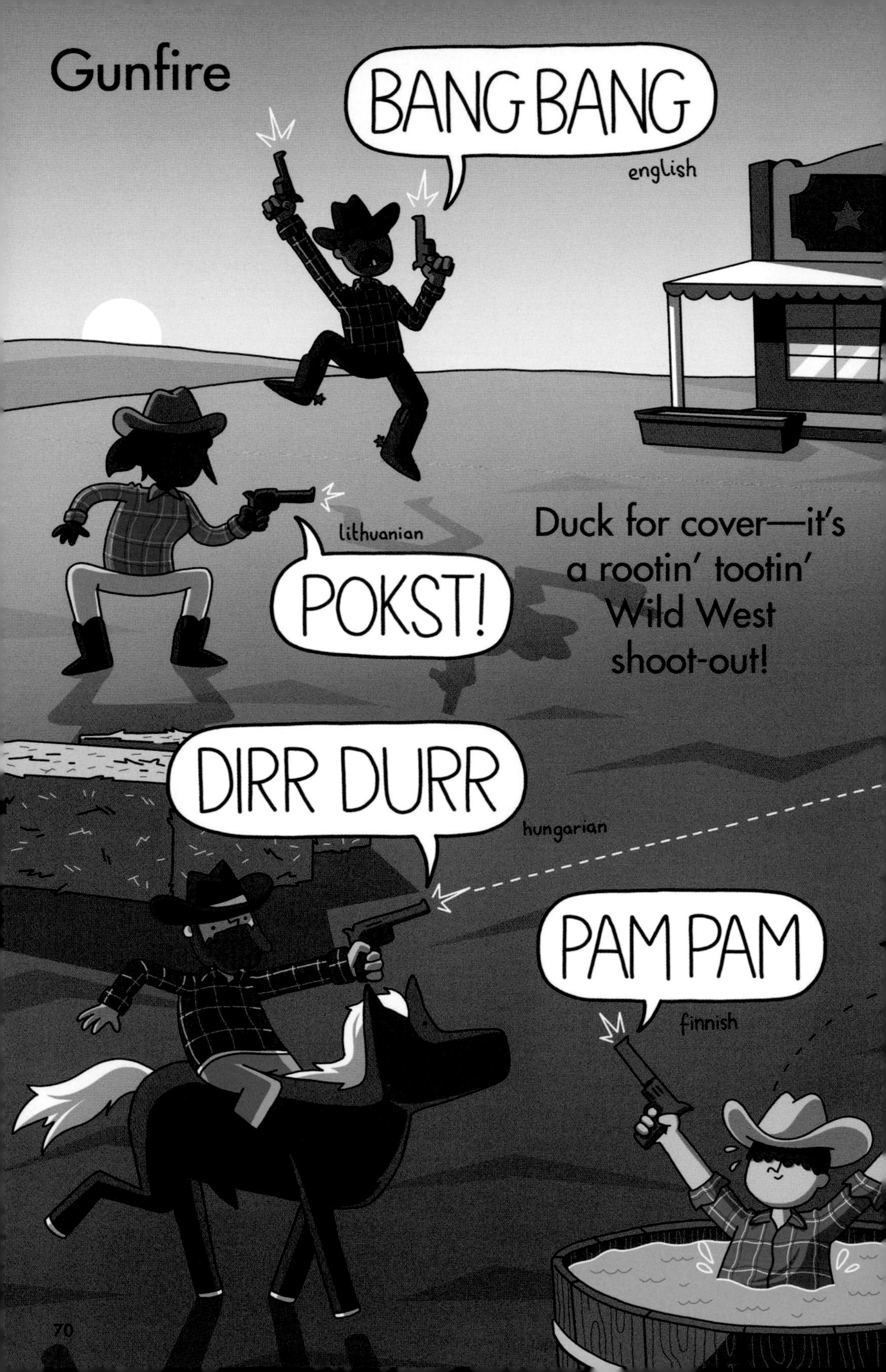
BANG BANG
english
POKST!
lithuanian
DIRR DURR
hungarian
PAM PAM
finnish

Duck for cover—it's a rootin' tootin' Wild West shoot-out!

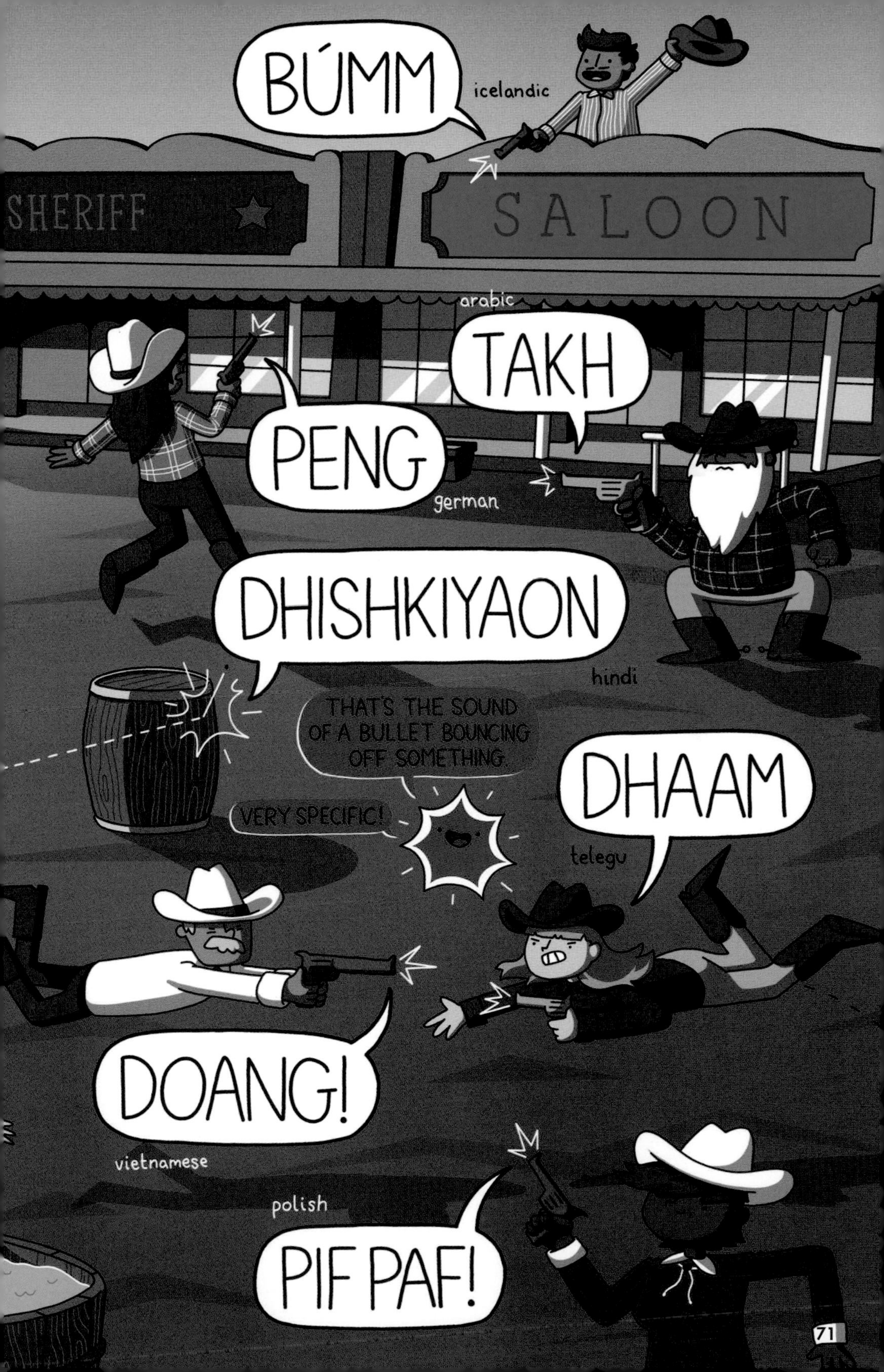
BÚMM
icelandic
SHERIFF
SALOON
arabic
TAKH
PENG
german
DHISHKIYAON
hindi
THAT'S THE SOUND OF A BULLET BOUNCING OFF SOMETHING.
VERY SPECIFIC!
DHAAM
telegu
DOANG!
vietnamese
polish
PIF PAF!

Sword Fights

The clangs of a medieval battle!

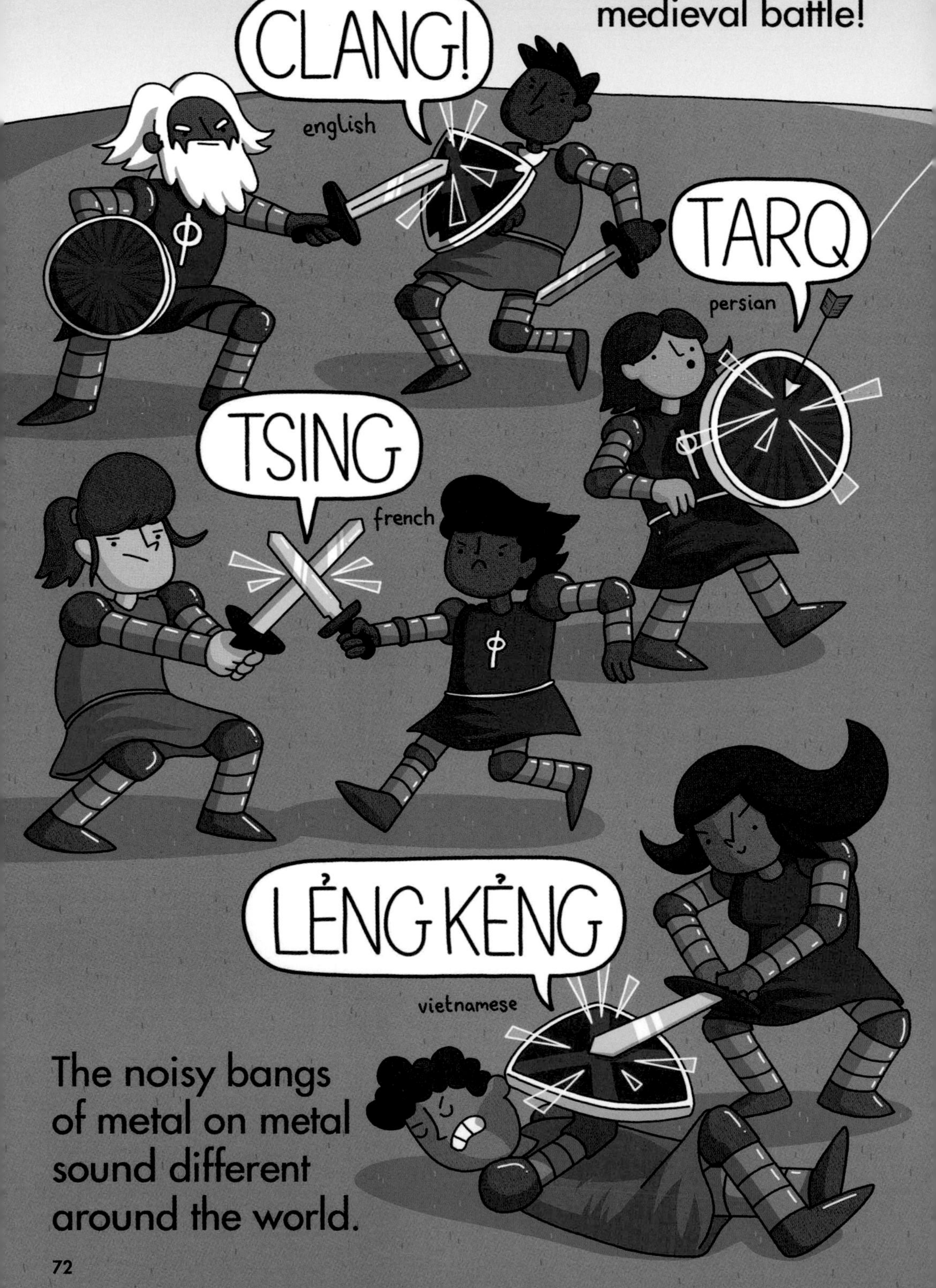
CLANG!
english
TARQ
persian
TSING
french
LẺNG KẺNG
vietnamese

The noisy bangs of metal on metal sound different around the world.

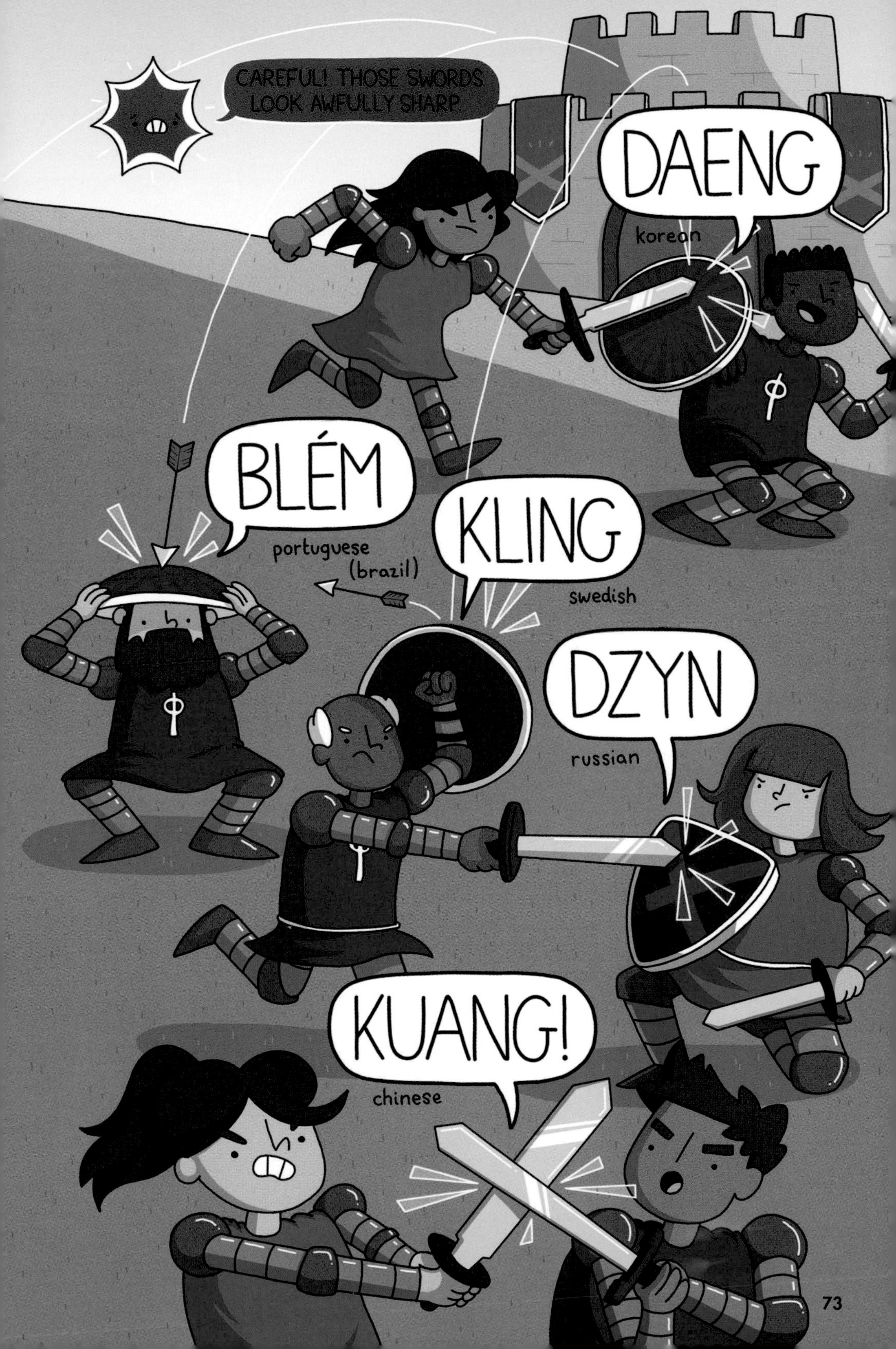
CAREFUL! THOSE SWORDS LOOK AWFULLY SHARP.
DAENG
korean
BLÉM
portuguese (brazil)
KLING
swedish
DZYN
russian
KUANG!
chinese

Splatting

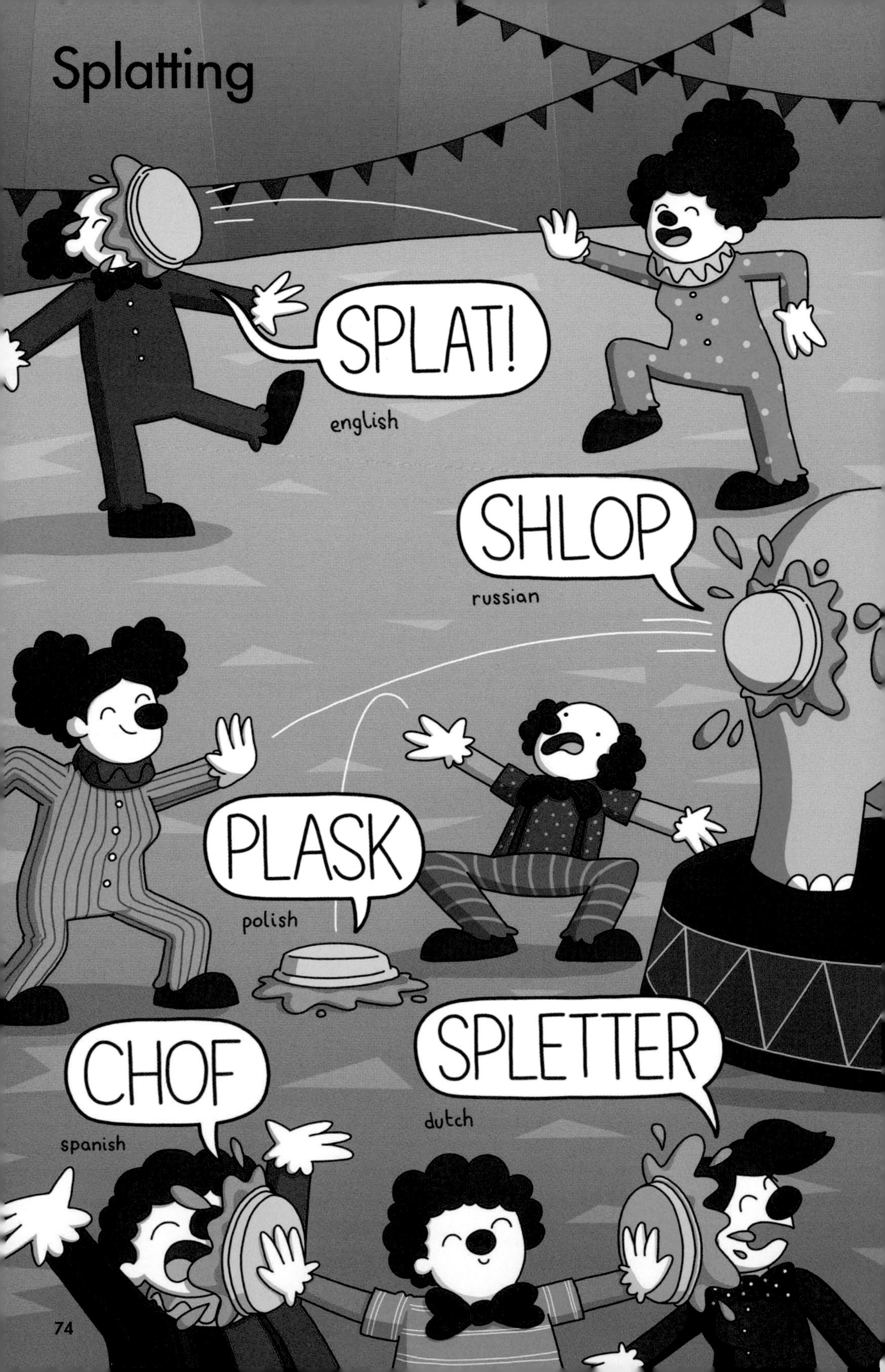
SPLAT!
english
SHLOP
russian
PLASK
polish
CHOF
spanish
SPLETTER
dutch

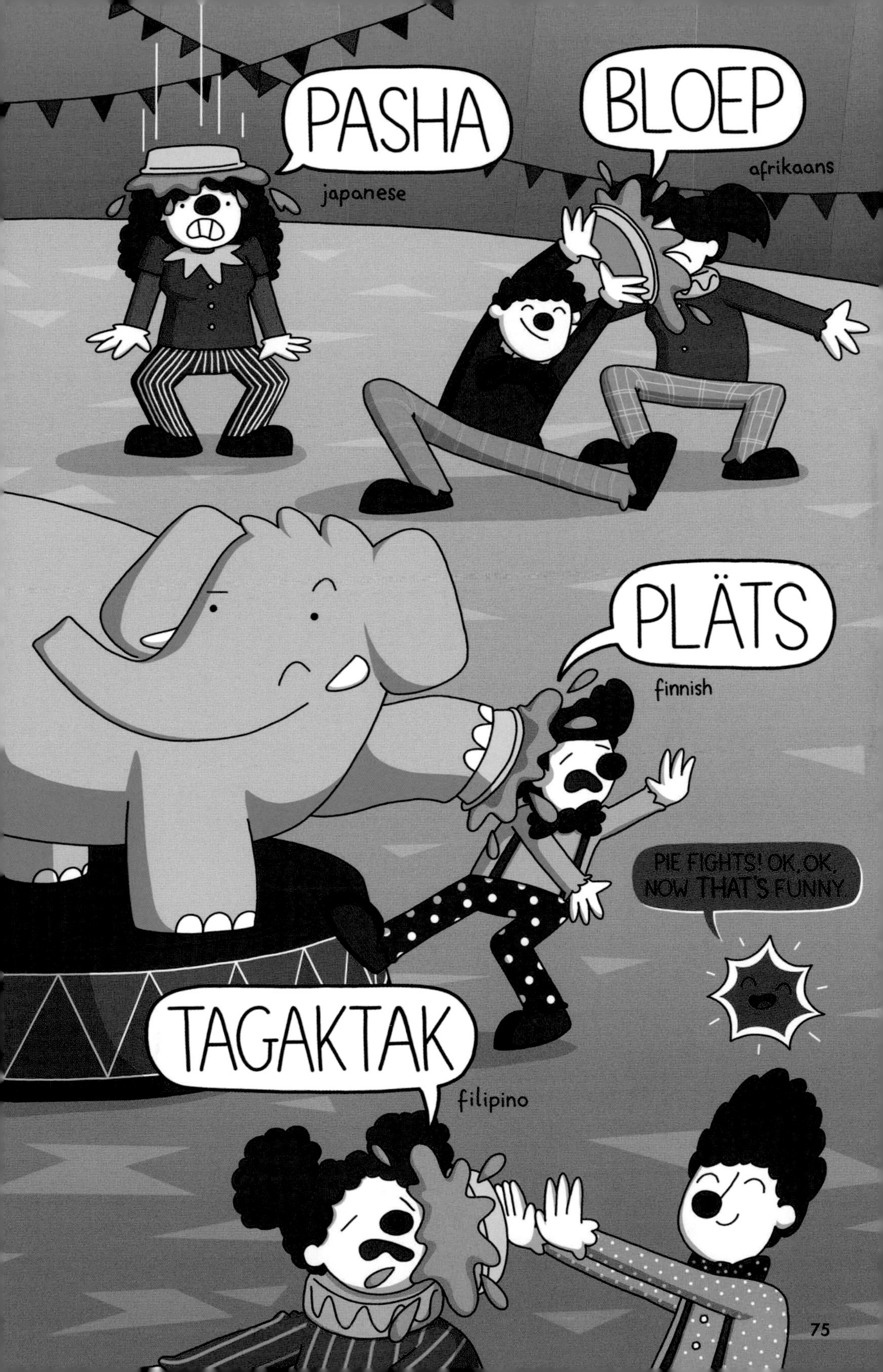
PASHA
japanese
BLOEP
afrikaans
PLÄTS
finnish
PIE FIGHTS! OK, OK, NOW THAT'S FUNNY.
TAGAKTAK
filipino

Popping

When balloons and bubbles get too big, you're moments away from this sound!

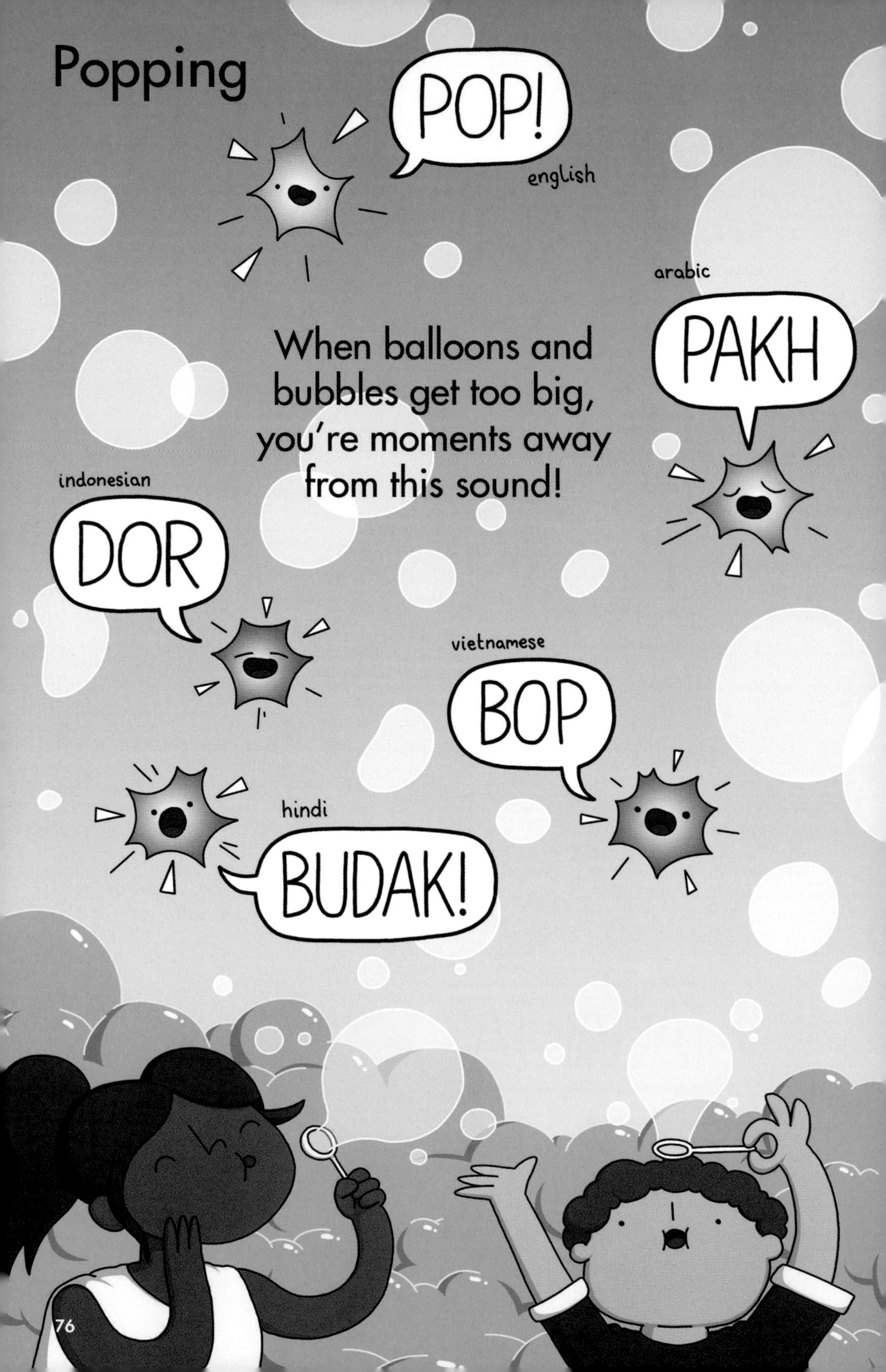
POP!
english
PAKH
arabic
DOR
indonesian
BOP
vietnamese
BUDAK!
hindi

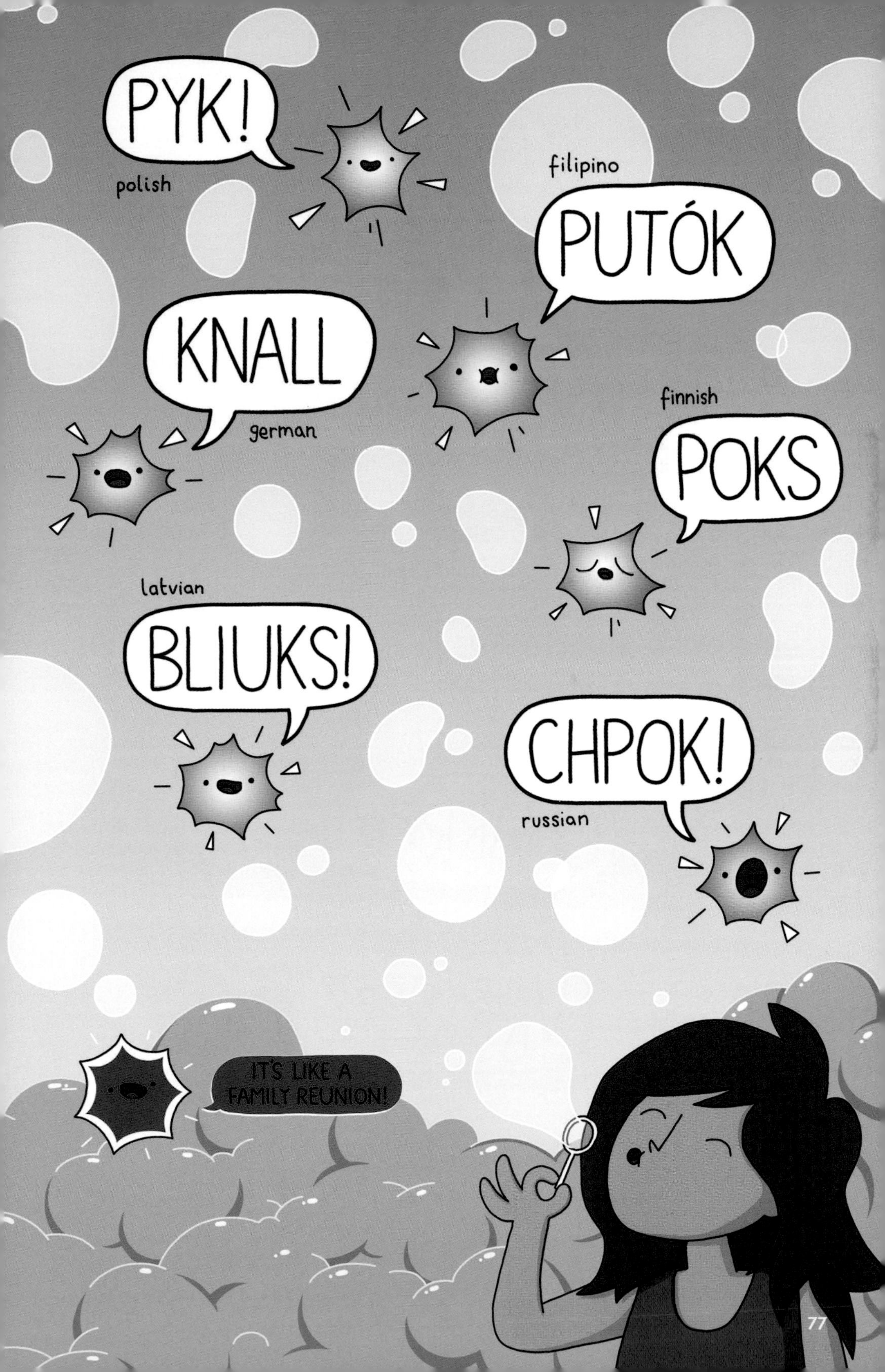
PYK!
polish
filipino
PUTÓK
KNALL
german
finnish
POKS
latvian
BLIUKS!
CHPOK!
russian
IT'S LIKE A FAMILY REUNION!

Creaking

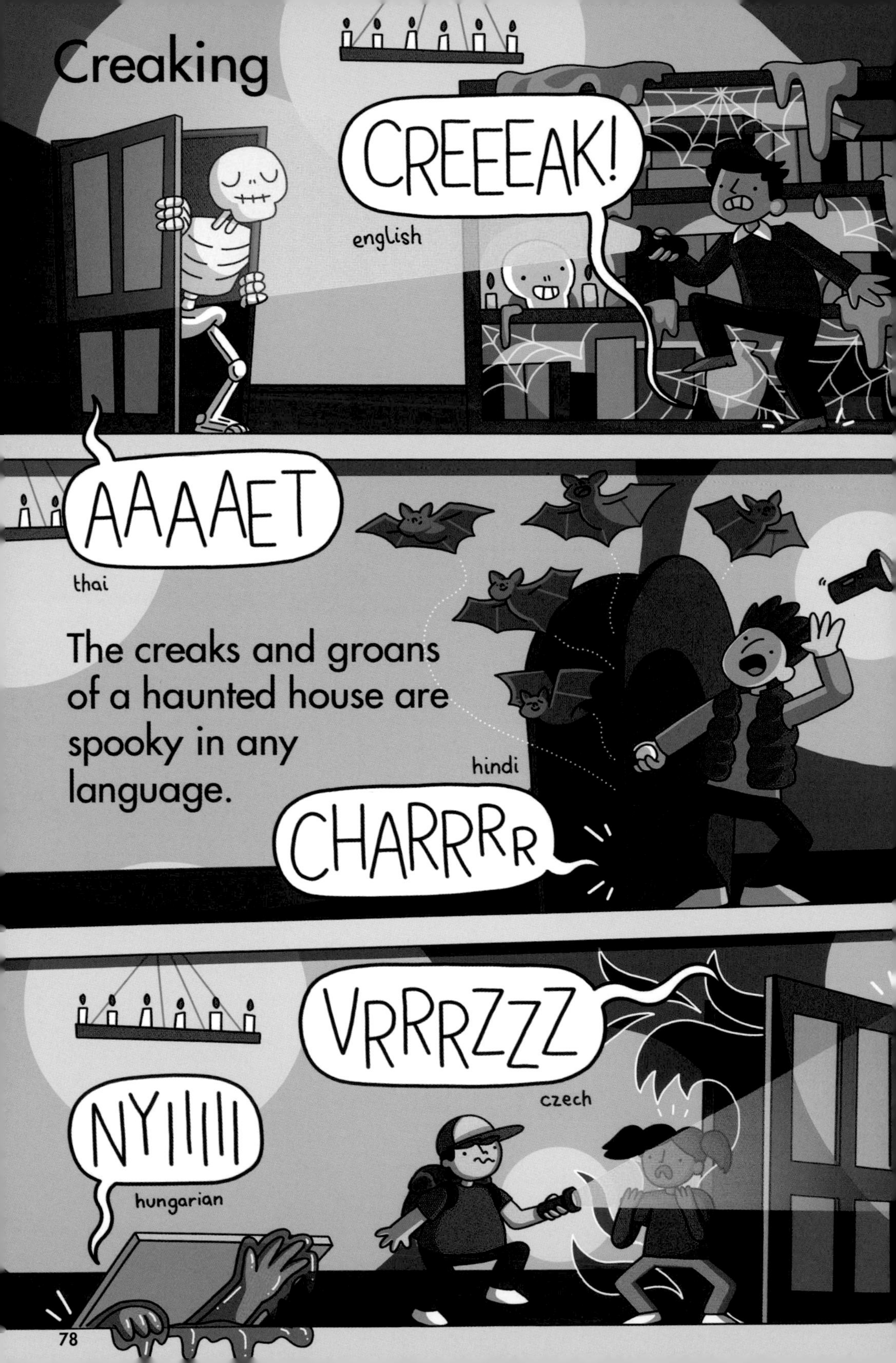
CREEEAK!
english
AAAAET
thai
hindi
CHARRRR
VRRRZZZ
czech
NYIIIII
hungarian

The creaks and groans of a haunted house are spooky in any language.

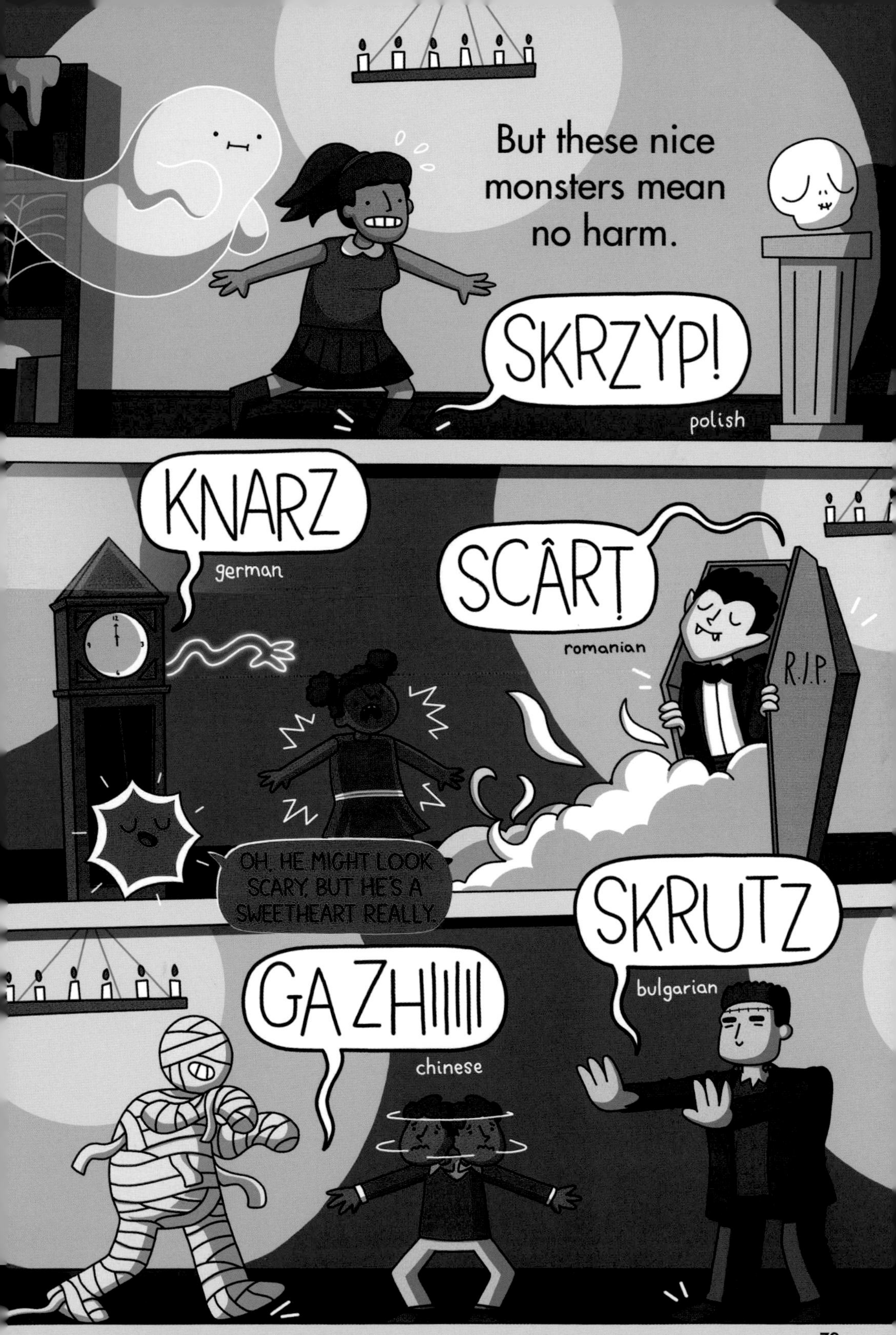
But these nice monsters mean no harm.
SKRZYP!
polish
KNARZ
german
SCÂRȚ
romanian
R.I.P.
OH, HE MIGHT LOOK SCARY, BUT HE'S A SWEETHEART REALLY.
GAZHIIIIII
chinese
SKRUTZ
bulgarian

Speed

english
ZOOM!
korean
SSHING!
swedish
SVISCH
norwegian
VOOSJ
icelandic
HVISS
VZHEEH
russian

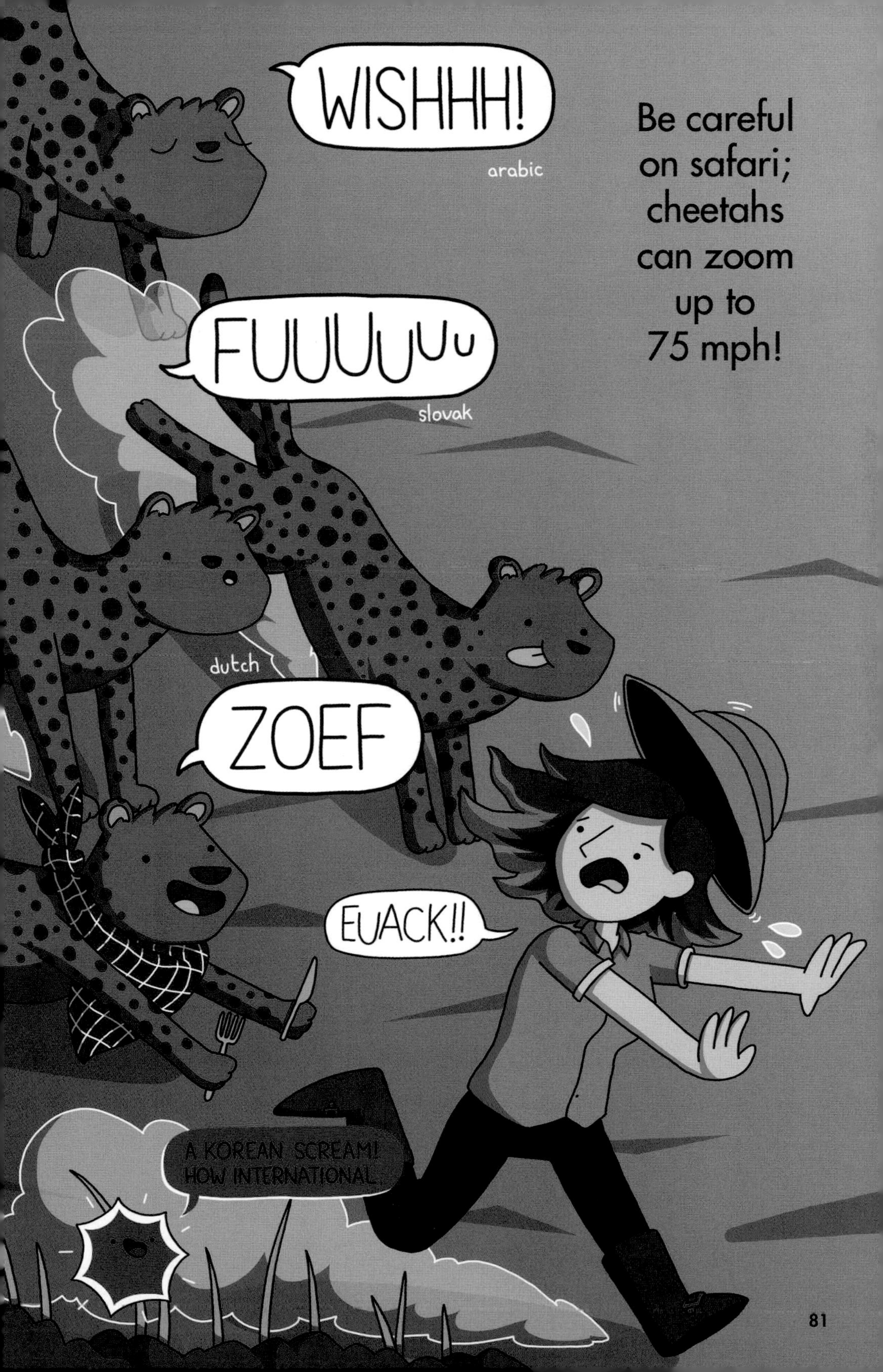
WISHHH!
arabic
Be careful on safari; cheetahs can zoom up to 75 mph!
FUUUUuu
slovak
dutch
ZOEF
EUACK!!
A KOREAN SCREAM! HOW INTERNATIONAL.

Knocking

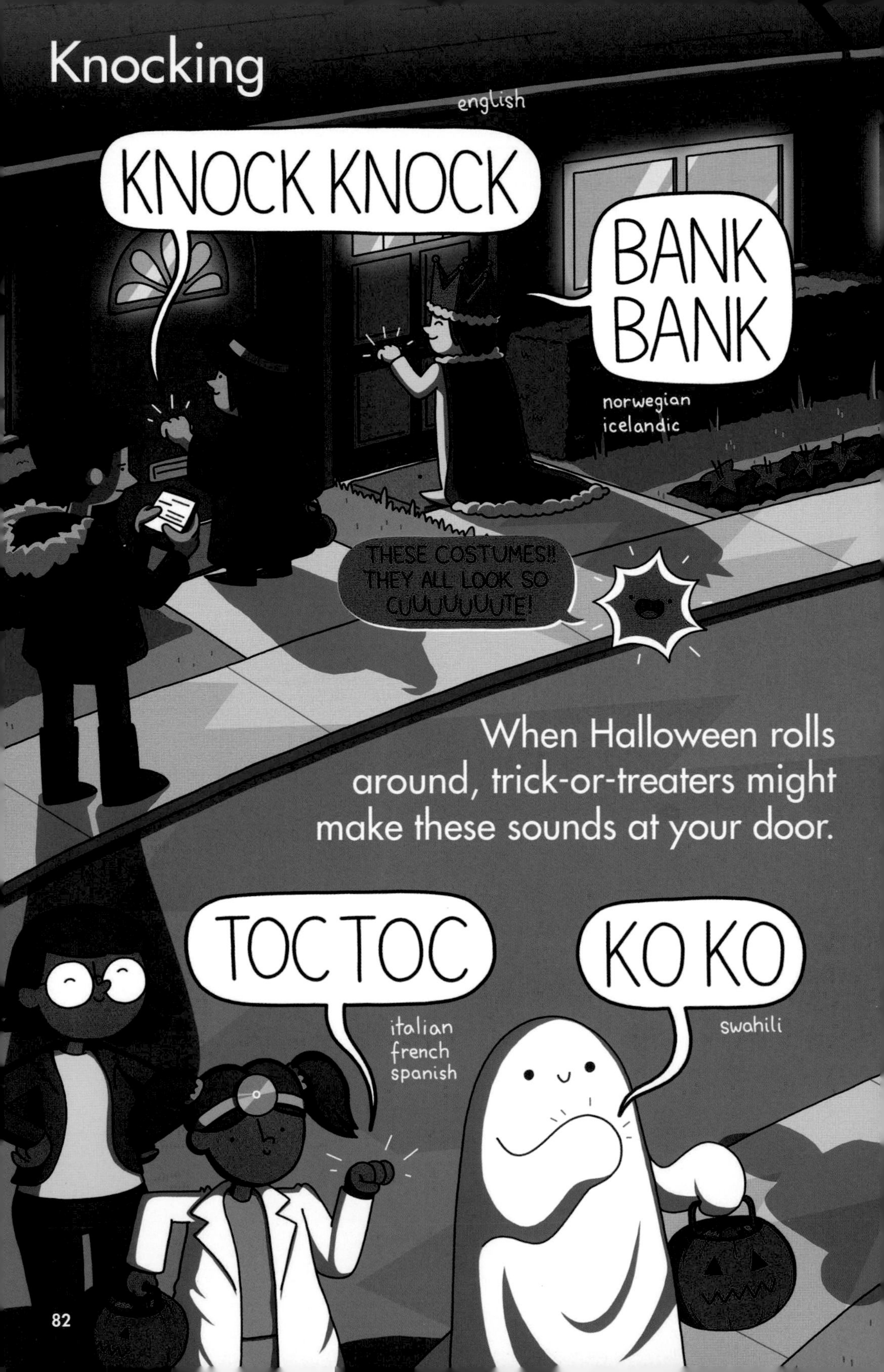
english
KNOCK KNOCK
BANK BANK
norwegian
icelandic
THESE COSTUMES!! THEY ALL LOOK SO CUUUUUUUTE!
TOC TOC
italian
french
spanish
KO KO
swahili

When Halloween rolls around, trick-or-treaters might make these sounds at your door.

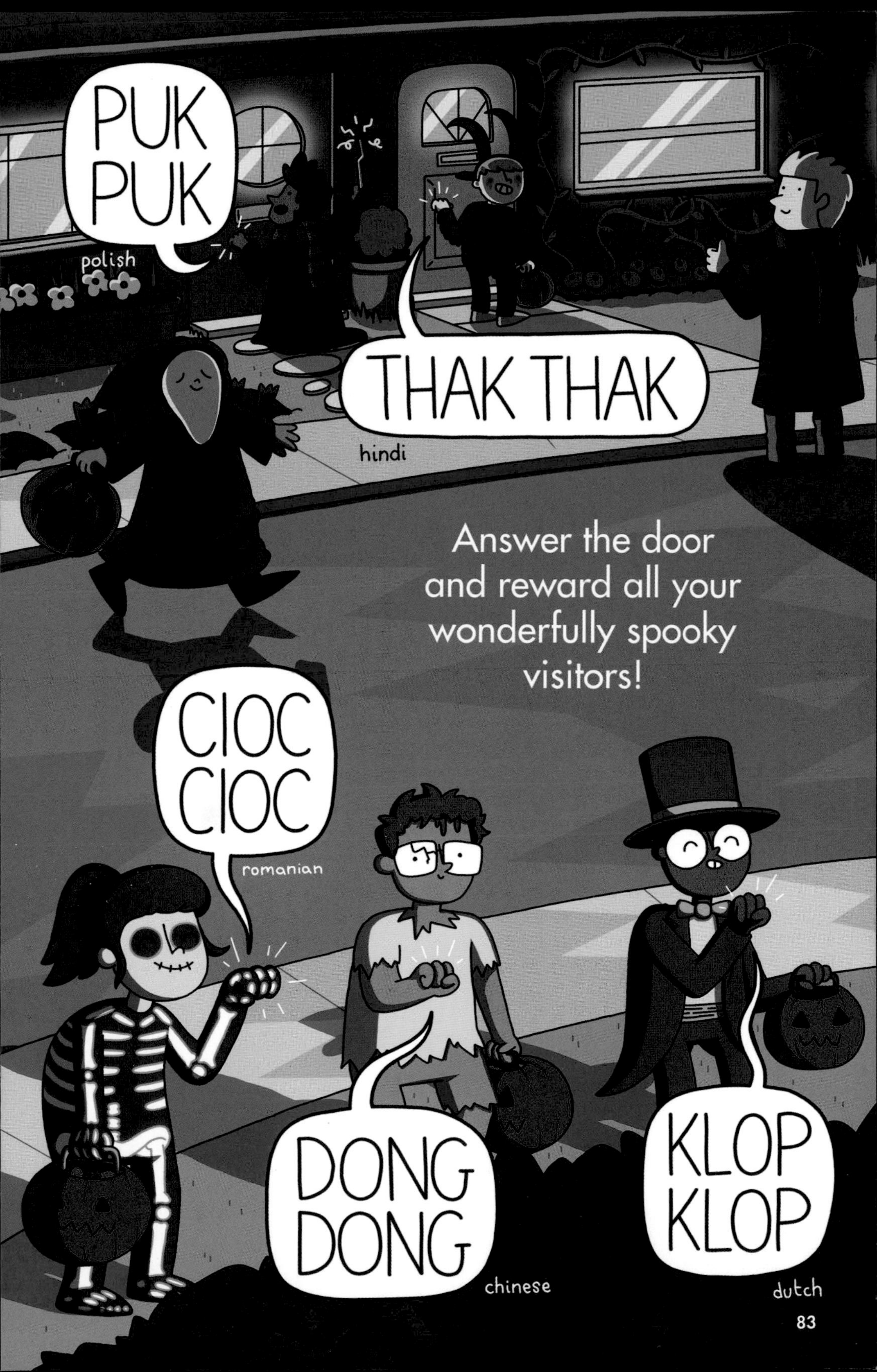
PUK PUK
polish
THAK THAK
hindi
Answer the door and reward all your wonderfully spooky visitors!
CIOC CIOC
romanian
DONG DONG
chinese
KLOP KLOP
dutch

Bells

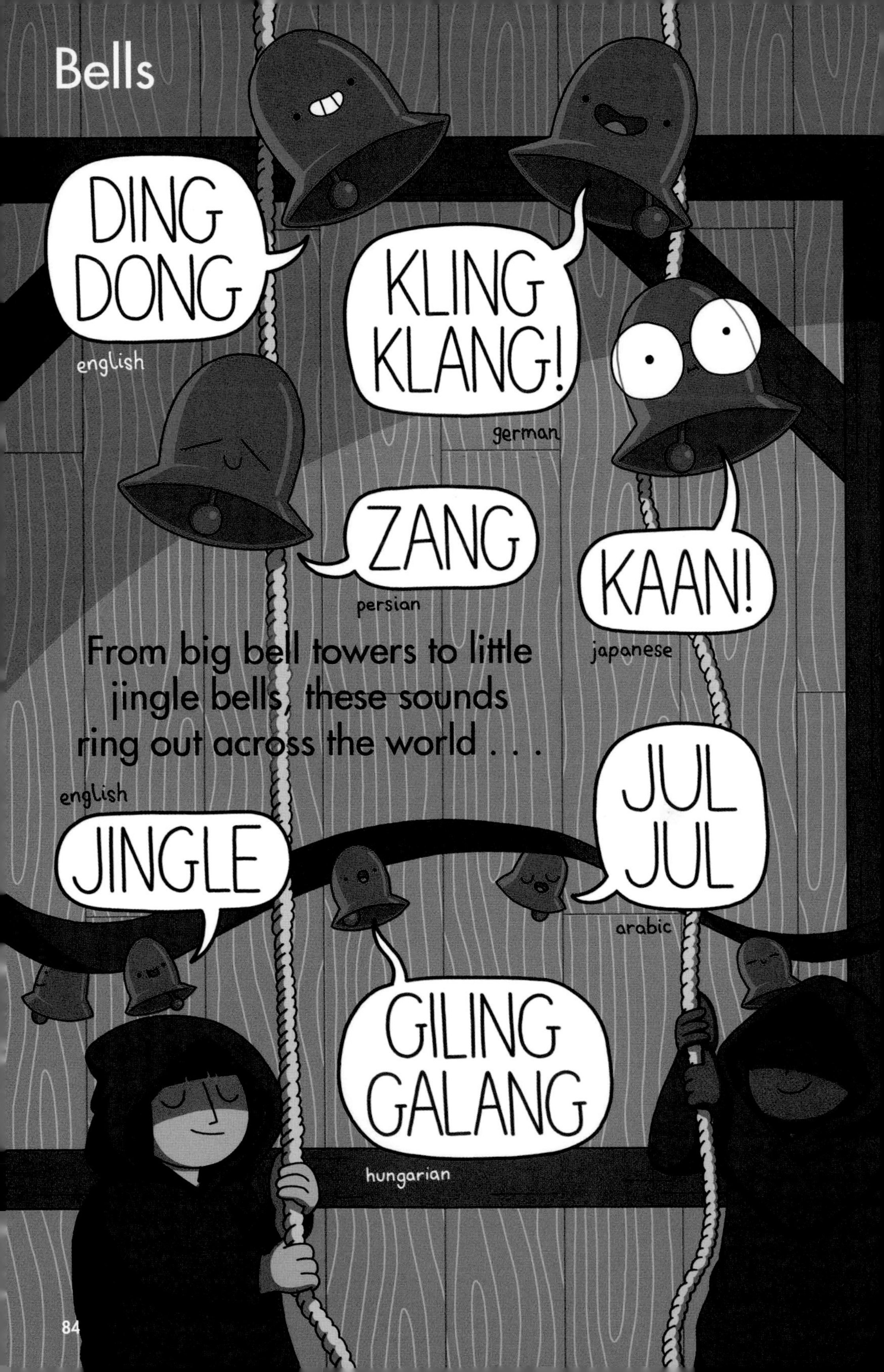
DING DONG
english
KLING KLANG!
german
ZANG
persian
KAAN!
japanese
From big bell towers to little jingle bells, these sounds ring out across the world . . .
english
JINGLE
JUL JUL
arabic
GILING GALANG
hungarian

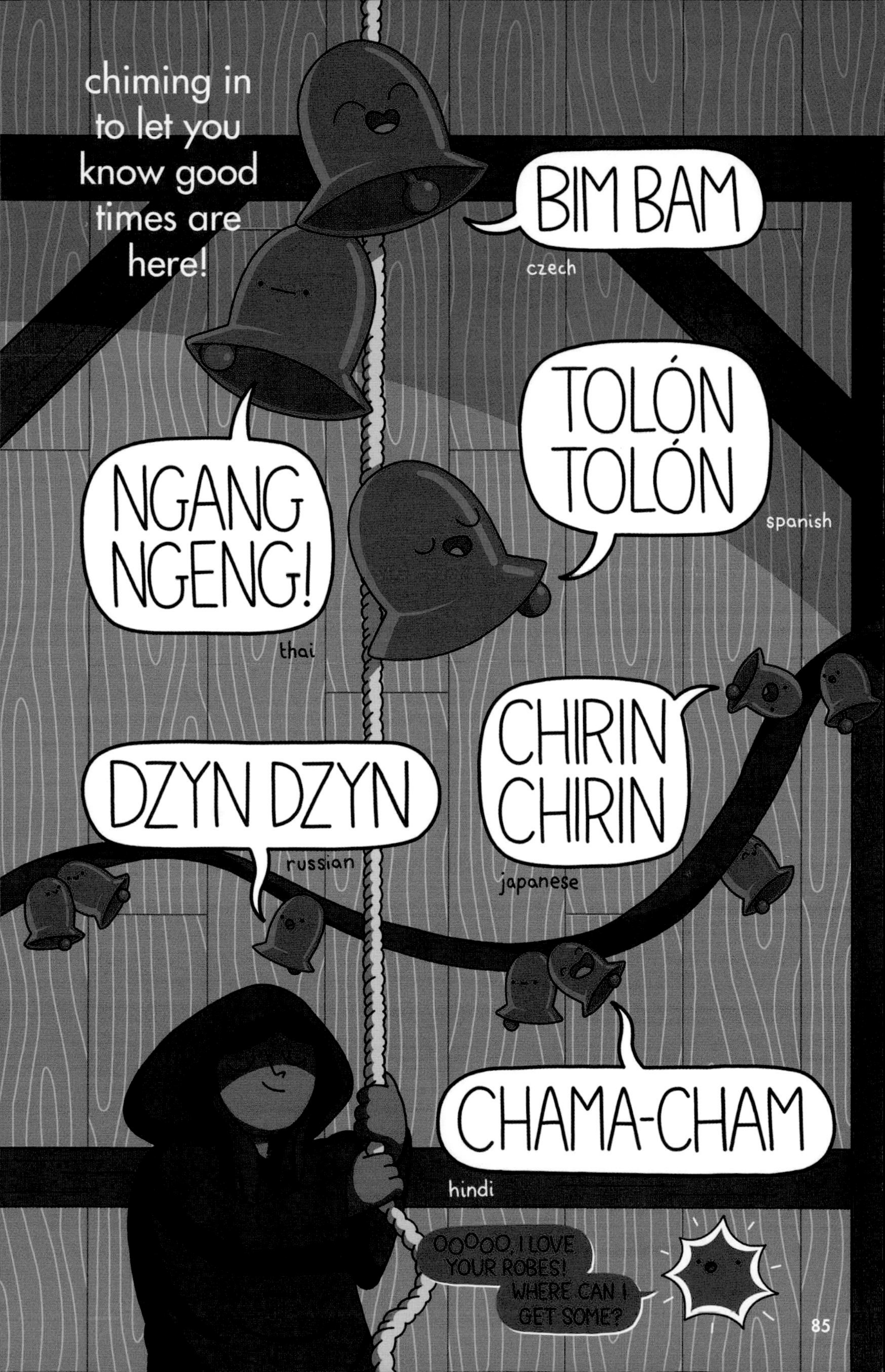
chiming in to let you know good times are here!
BIM BAM
czech
NGANG NGENG!
thai
TOLÓN TOLÓN
spanish
DZYN DZYN
russian
CHIRIN CHIRIN
japanese
CHAMA-CHAM
hindi
OOOOO, I LOVE YOUR ROBES! WHERE CAN I GET SOME?

NATURAL NOISES

Even if you ignore people and animals, the world would still make quite a bit of noise, from the crash of lightning and the splash of a waterfall to the rush of wind and the crackle of a roaring fire.

In the Ding-Dong Theory of the origin of language, it was thought that maybe cave people developed language around the sounds the natural world made. The clouds are booms. The rivers are splashes. It makes sense that sounds might be a good start when you haven't quite mastered what words are yet.

But then how do you name things that don't make a sound? Those poor prehistoric hedgehogs, living their lives namelessly!

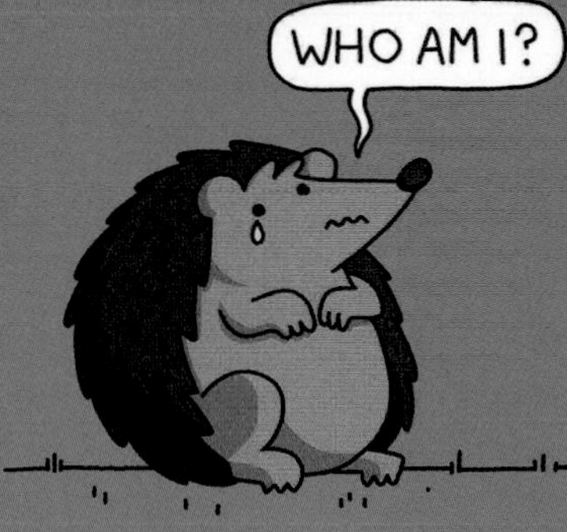
WHO AM I?

It's a good thing language has come a long way since then—now we've got names for *evvvverything*. There's even a word in German for weight gained from too much comfort food in times of stress, kummerspeck, which translates into English as . . . *"sorrow bacon."* Spectacular specificity!

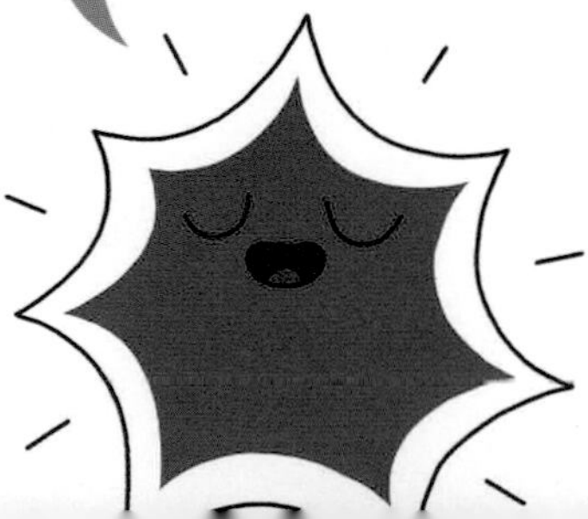

Rain

On drizzly days, it's tempting to stay inside.

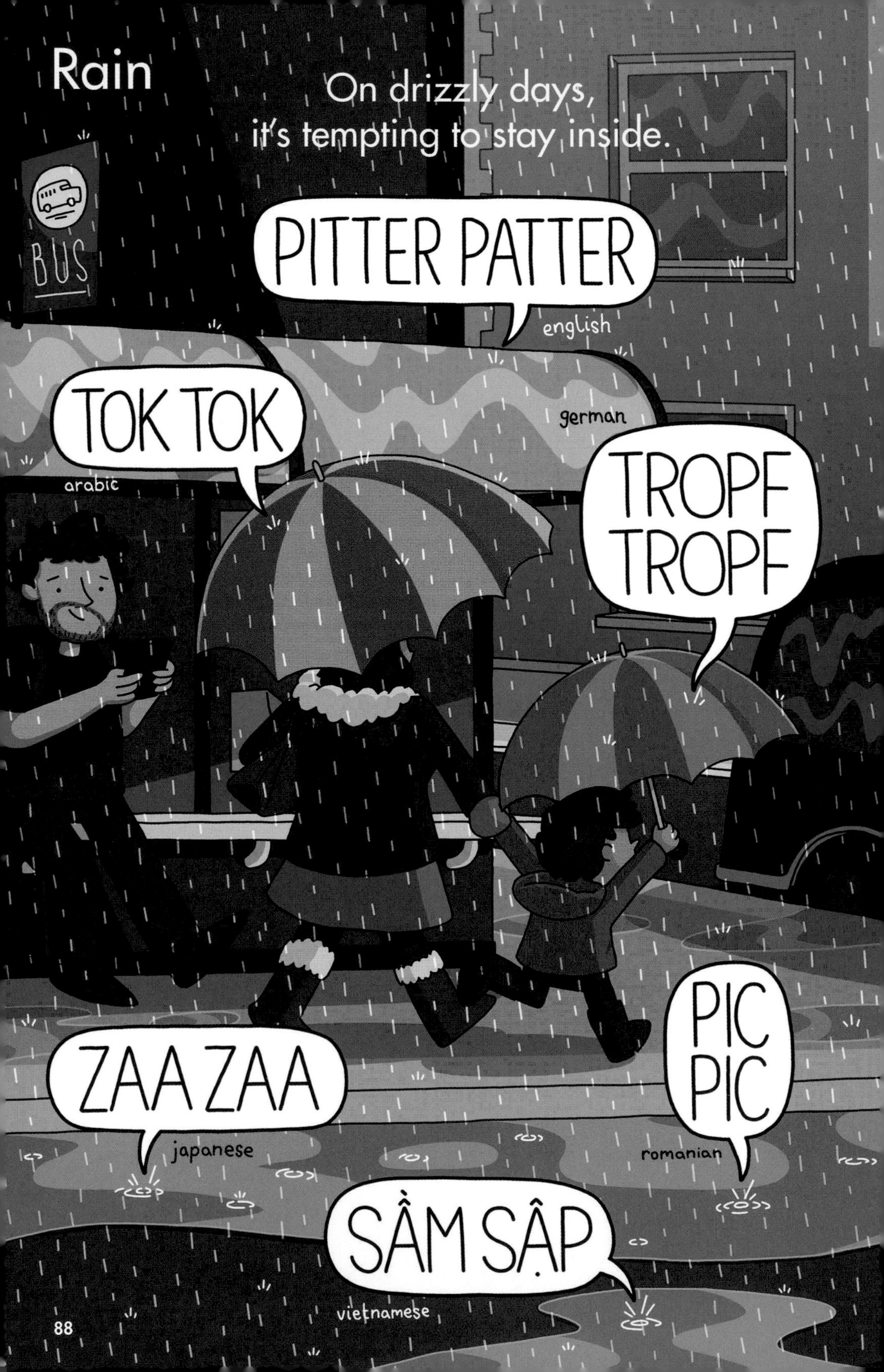
BUS
PITTER PATTER
english
TOK TOK
arabic
german
TROPF TROPF
ZAA ZAA
japanese
PIC PIC
romanian
SẦM SẬP
vietnamese

But a whole world of sound is out there waiting for you.
TEEF TAF
hebrew
estonian
TILK TILK
FEELS LIKE I'M IN AN EMOTIONAL MUSIC VIDEO.
PLIC PLOC
french
korean
JU-RUK JU-RUK
CSIPP CSEPP
hungarian
CHITA-PATA
telugu

Thunder

The distant rumble of thunder on a stormy night might sound a little scary.

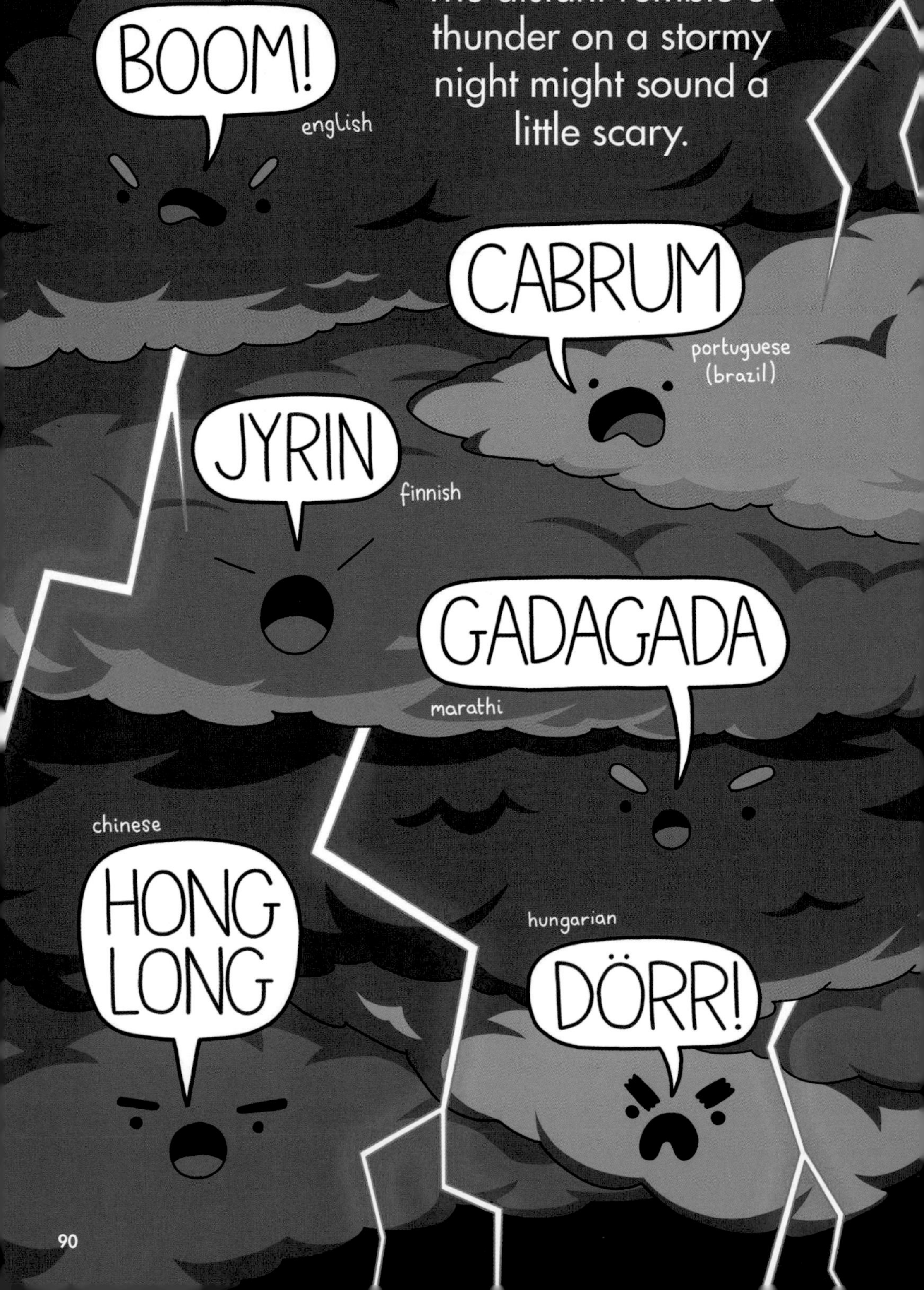
BOOM!
english
CABRUM
portuguese (brazil)
JYRIN
finnish
GADAGADA
marathi
chinese
HONG LONG
hungarian
DÖRR!

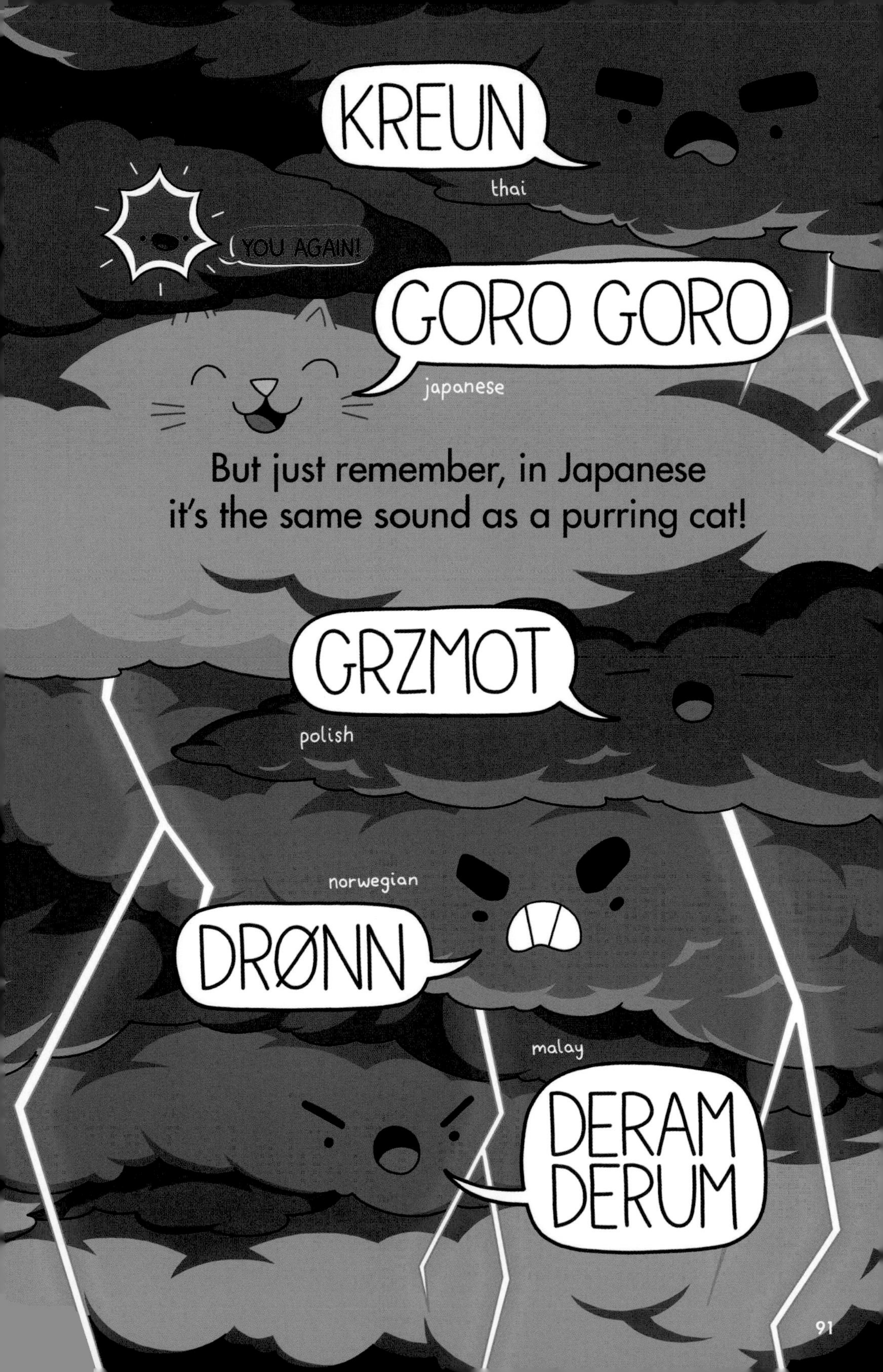
KREUN
thai
YOU AGAIN!
GORO GORO
japanese
But just remember, in Japanese it's the same sound as a purring cat!
GRZMOT
polish
norwegian
DRØNN
malay
DERAM DERUM

Wind

Blustery days are great for kites.

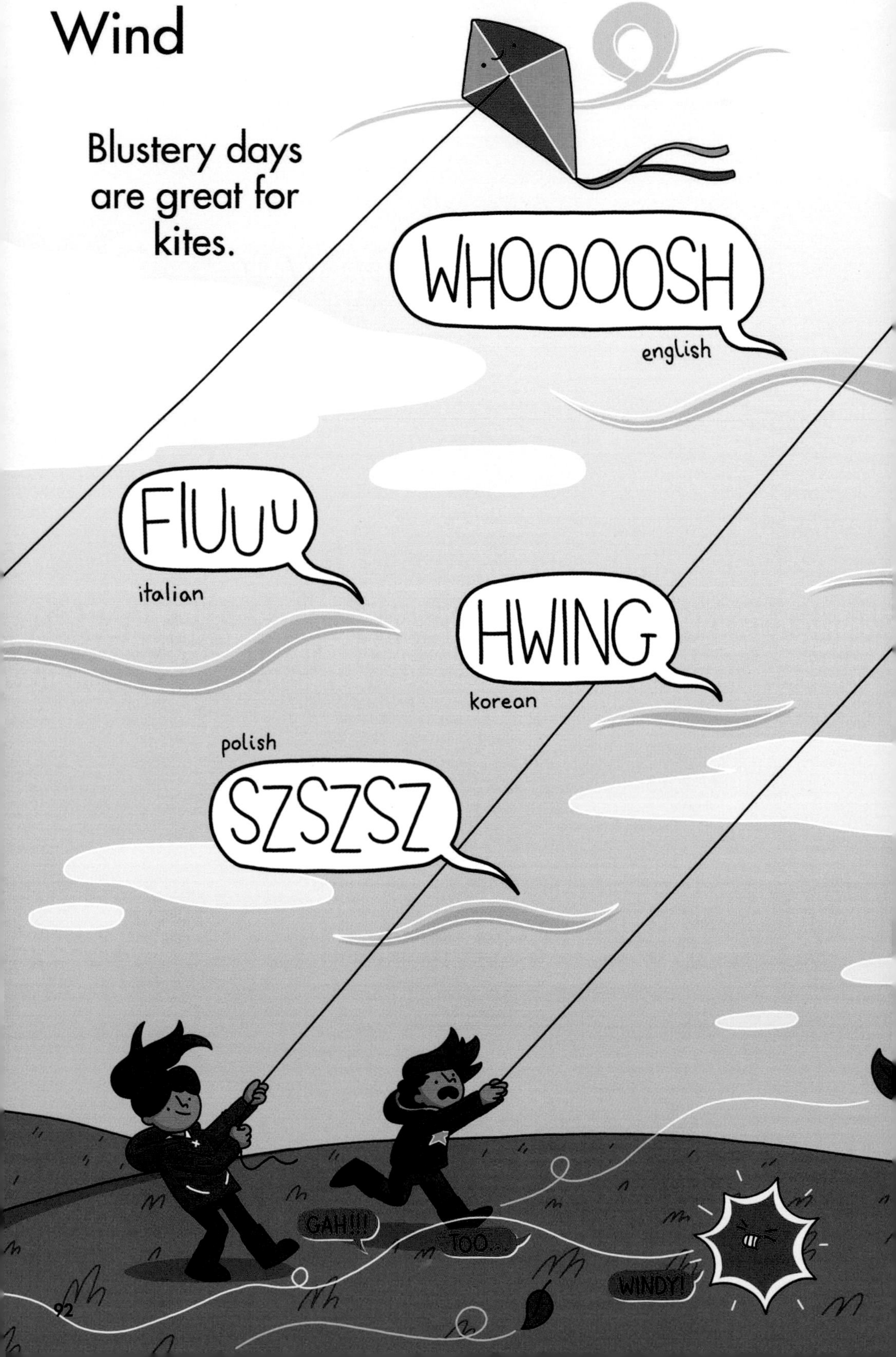
WHOOOOSH
english
FIUUu
italian
HWING
korean
polish
SZSZSZ
GAH!!!
TOO...
WINDY!

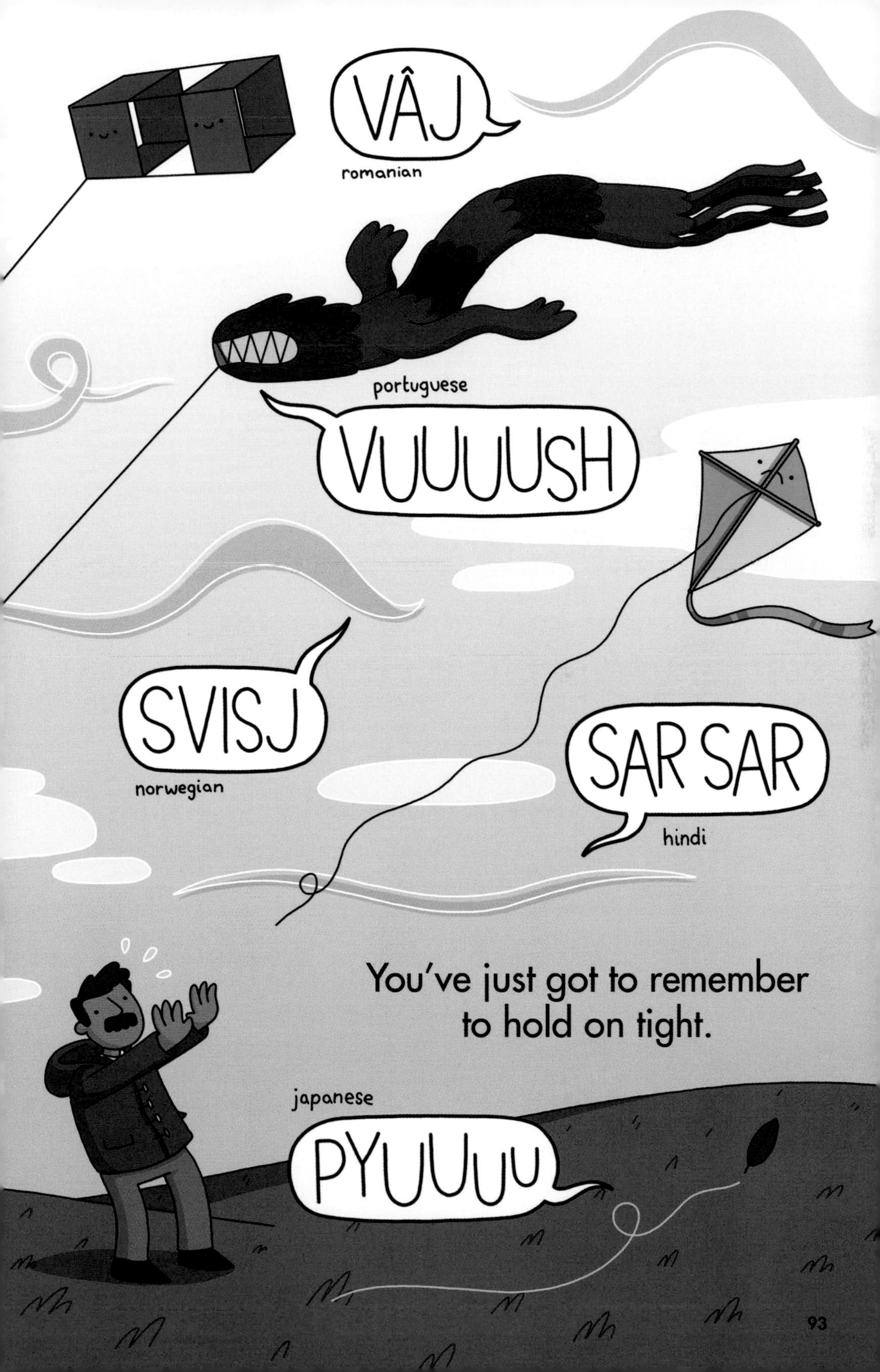
VÂJ
romanian
portuguese
VUUUUSH
SVISJ
norwegian
SAR SAR
hindi
You've just got to remember to hold on tight.
japanese
PYUUUU

Dripping

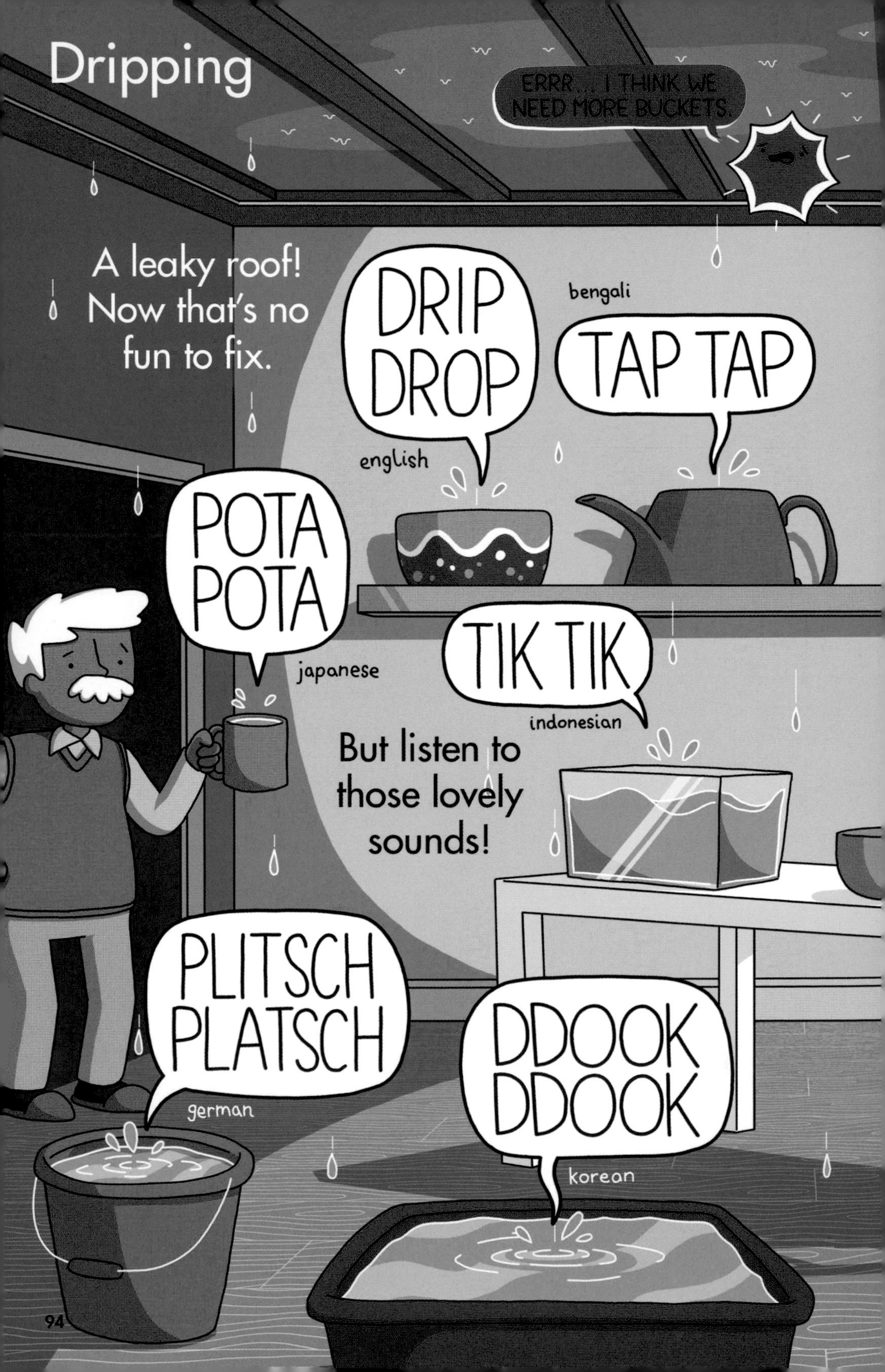
ERRR... I THINK WE NEED MORE BUCKETS.
A leaky roof! Now that's no fun to fix.
DRIP DROP
english
bengali
TAP TAP
POTA POTA
japanese
TIK TIK
indonesian
But listen to those lovely sounds!
PLITSCH PLATSCH
german
DDOOK DDOOK
korean

PLIKS PLIKS
latvian
persian
CHEK CHEK
ŞIP ŞIP
turkish
DIK DIK
chinese
KAP KAP
russian
polish
macedonian
czech
PLIM PLIM
portuguese

Splashing

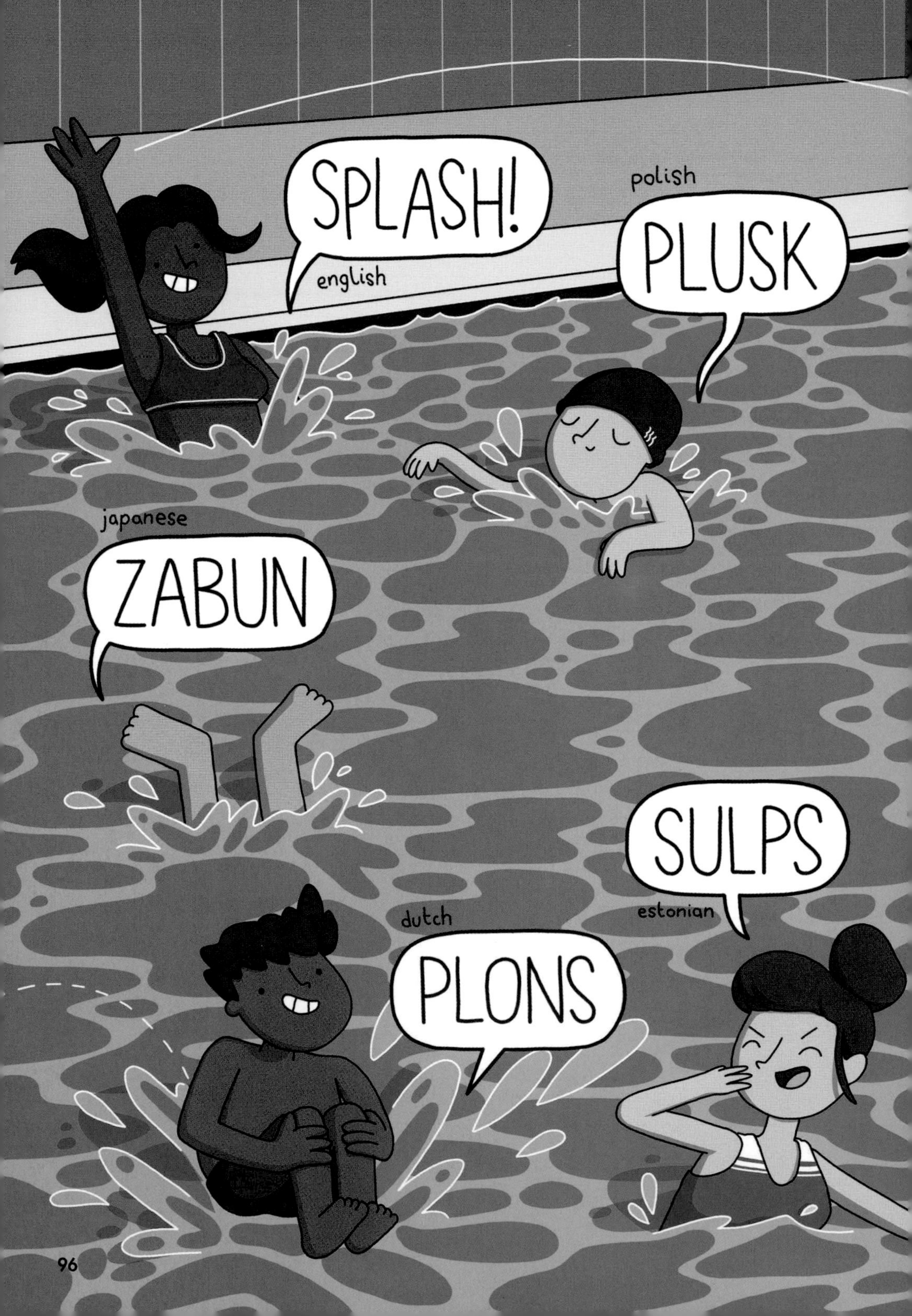
SPLASH!
english
polish
PLUSK
japanese
ZABUN
SULPS
estonian
dutch
PLONS

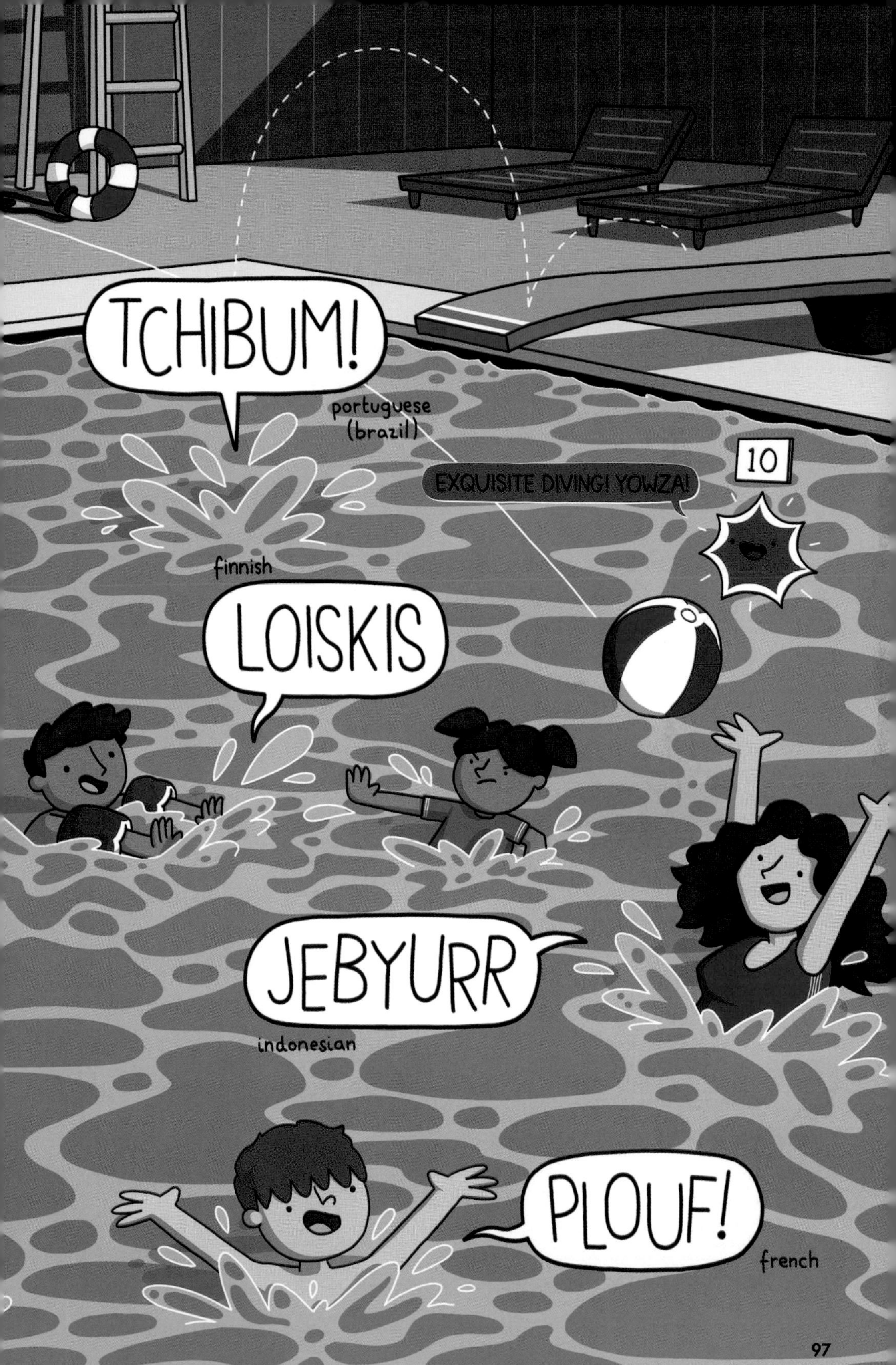
TCHIBUM!
portuguese (brazil)
10
EXQUISITE DIVING! YOWZA!
finnish
LOISKIS
JEBYURR
indonesian
PLOUF!
french

Fire

Fire may sound different around the world . . .
english
CRACKLE
arabic
TAC TAC
PACHI PACHI
japanese
danish
KNITRE
ROPOG!
hungarian

but it still toasts everyone's marshmallows!
polish
TRZASK
CHAT CHAT
hindi
MMMM... MARSHMALLOW...
PRIKS PRAKS
estonian
KNISTER
german
telugu
BAGABAGA

Ghosts

Don't be scared. These ghosts just want to say a friendly hello.

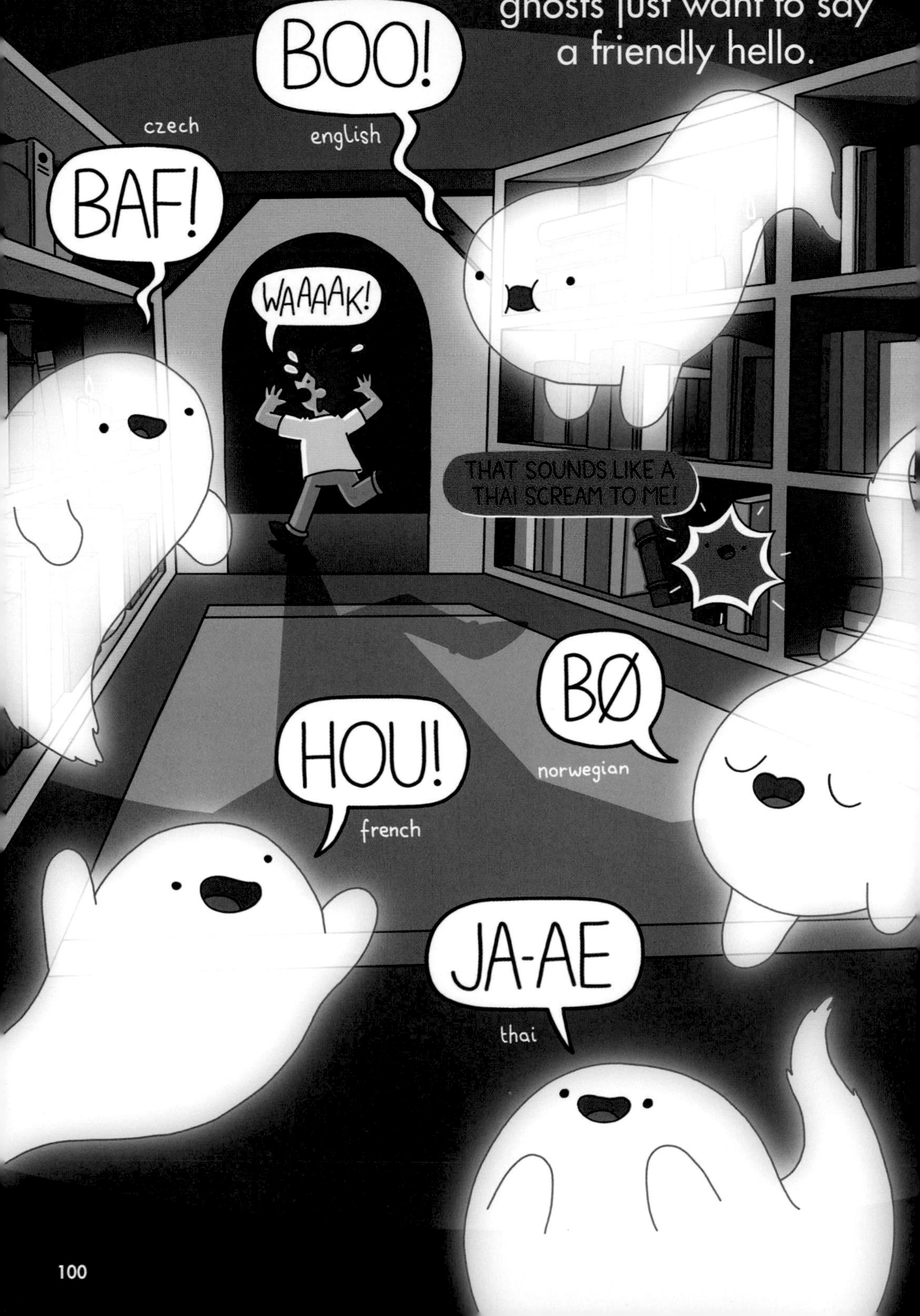
BOO!
english
czech
BAF!
WAAAAK!
THAT SOUNDS LIKE A THAI SCREAM TO ME!
BØ
norwegian
HOU!
french
JA-AE
thai

estonian
BAAAH
afrikaans
BOE
a spooky laugh
KEKEKE...
japanese
Even if some of
them might sound
a little . . . rude.
PÖÖÖÖ
finnish

NOISY MACHINES

As human progress continues, new inventions arrive all the time—and some end up a little noisier than others. From steam trains hundreds of years ago to cars today, with every noisy new invention there comes a noisy new sound.

A few languages even have onomatopoeic words for toothbrushes! The English language still hasn't gotten around to giving toothbrushes a cool sound effect. It's about time that changed!

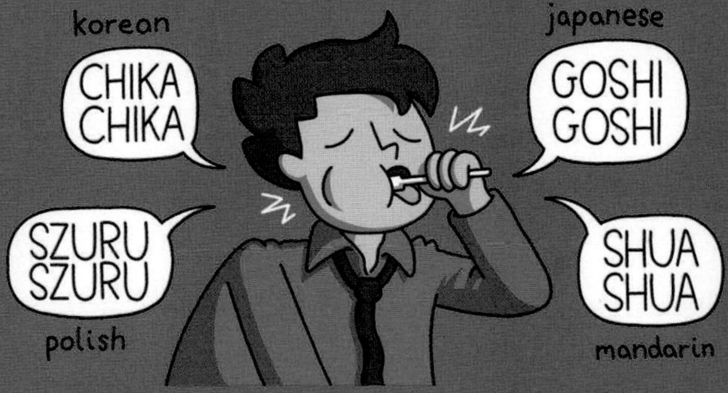
korean
CHIKA CHIKA
japanese
GOSHI GOSHI
SZURU SZURU
polish
SHUA SHUA
mandarin

What sound would you say a toothbrush makes in English?

Keep an eye on all the new inventions coming out. If you're quick off the mark maybe you can be the first to decide what it sounds like!

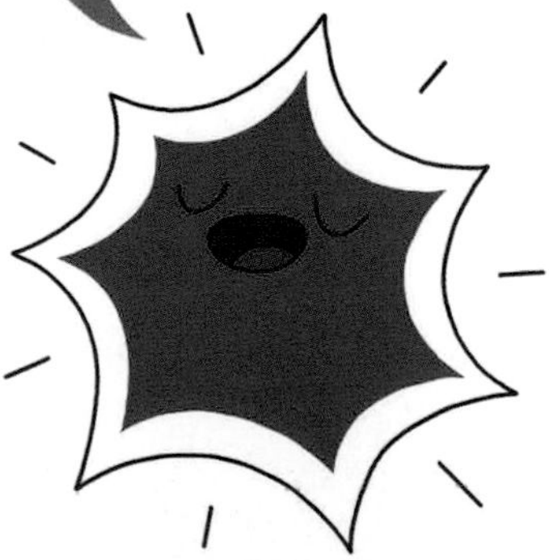

Clocks

In the Western World, clocks are all about ticking.

TICK TOCK! english

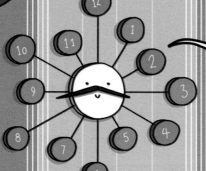

TIK TAK polish turkish dutch

TIC TAC spanish italian portuguese

DTIK DTOK thai

OH! LOOK AT THE TIME, I'D BETTER GET MOVING!

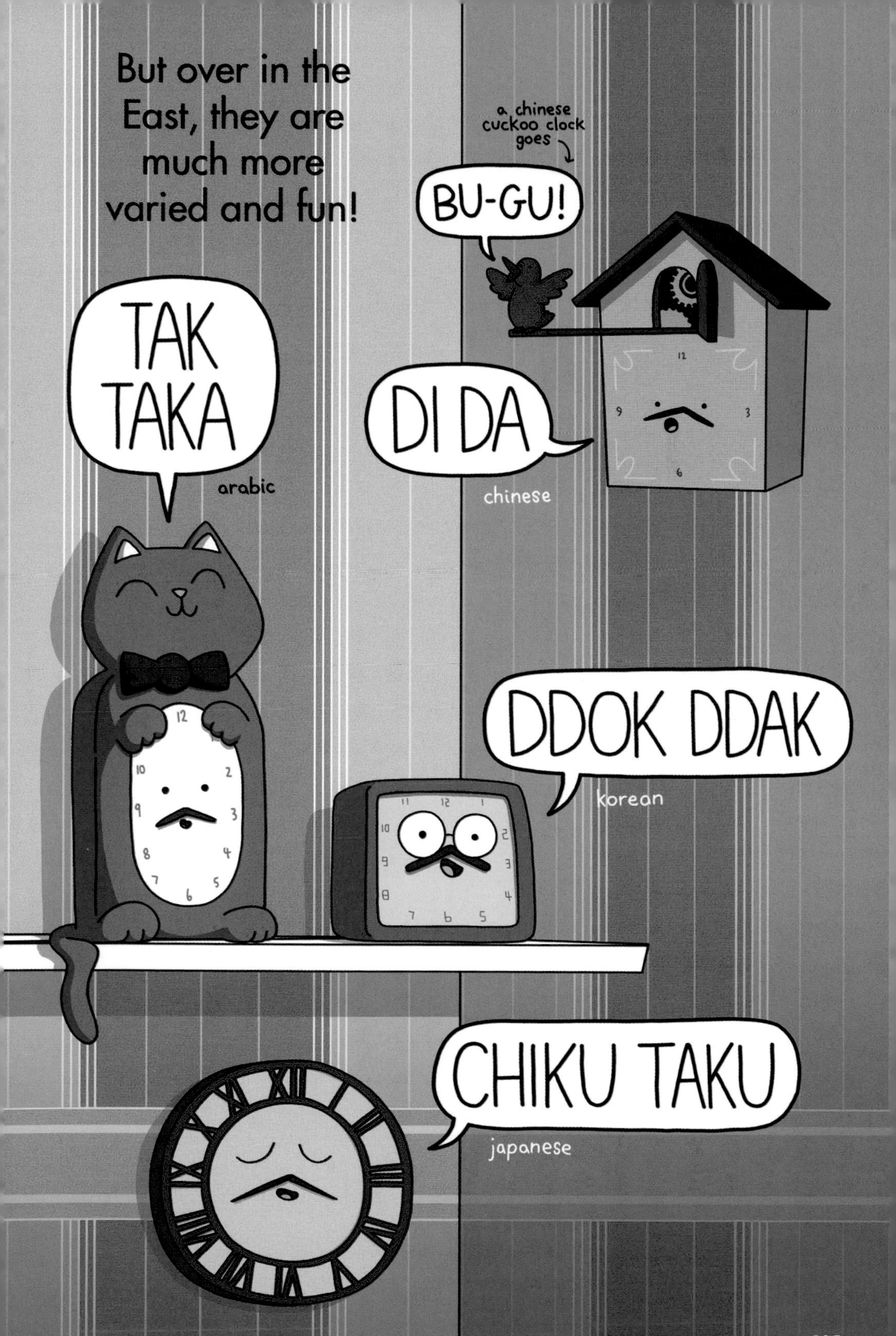
But over in the East, they are much more varied and fun!
a chinese cuckoo clock goes
BU-GU!
TAK TAKA
arabic
DI DA
chinese
DDOK DDAK
korean
CHIKU TAKU
japanese

Honking

A traffic jam is noisy wherever you go.

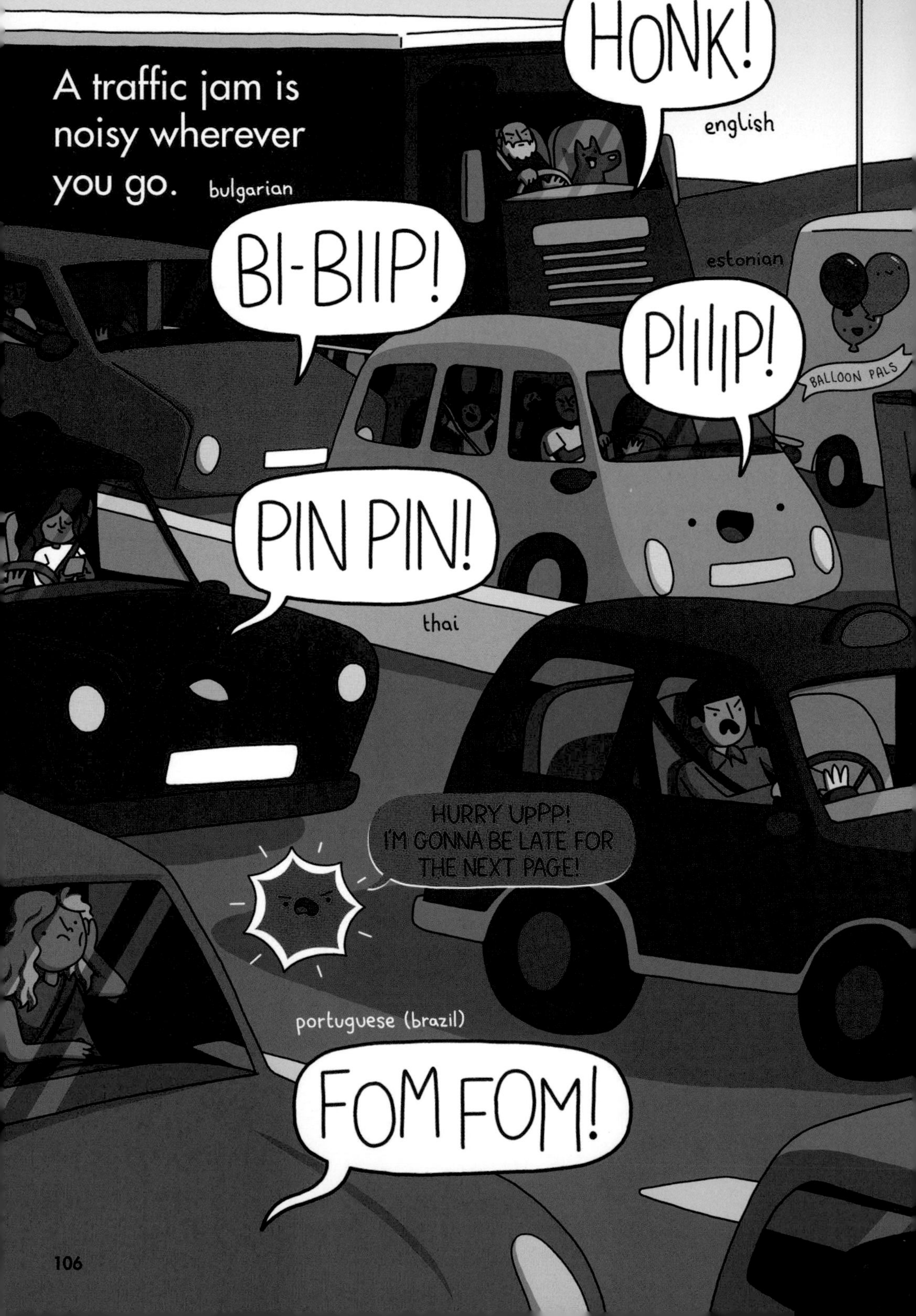

HONK!
english
bulgarian
BI-BIIP!
estonian
PIIIIP!
BALLOON PALS
PIN PIN!
thai
HURRY UPPP! I'M GONNA BE LATE FOR THE NEXT PAGE!
portuguese (brazil)
FOM FOM!

MOVE-IT
norwegian
BÆRT
finnish
TÖÖTÄTÄ
BBANG!
korean
danish
DYT DYT
vietnamese
BIMBIM!
DUDU
chinese

Driving

Off we go!
The sounds of the
open road, all
around the world.

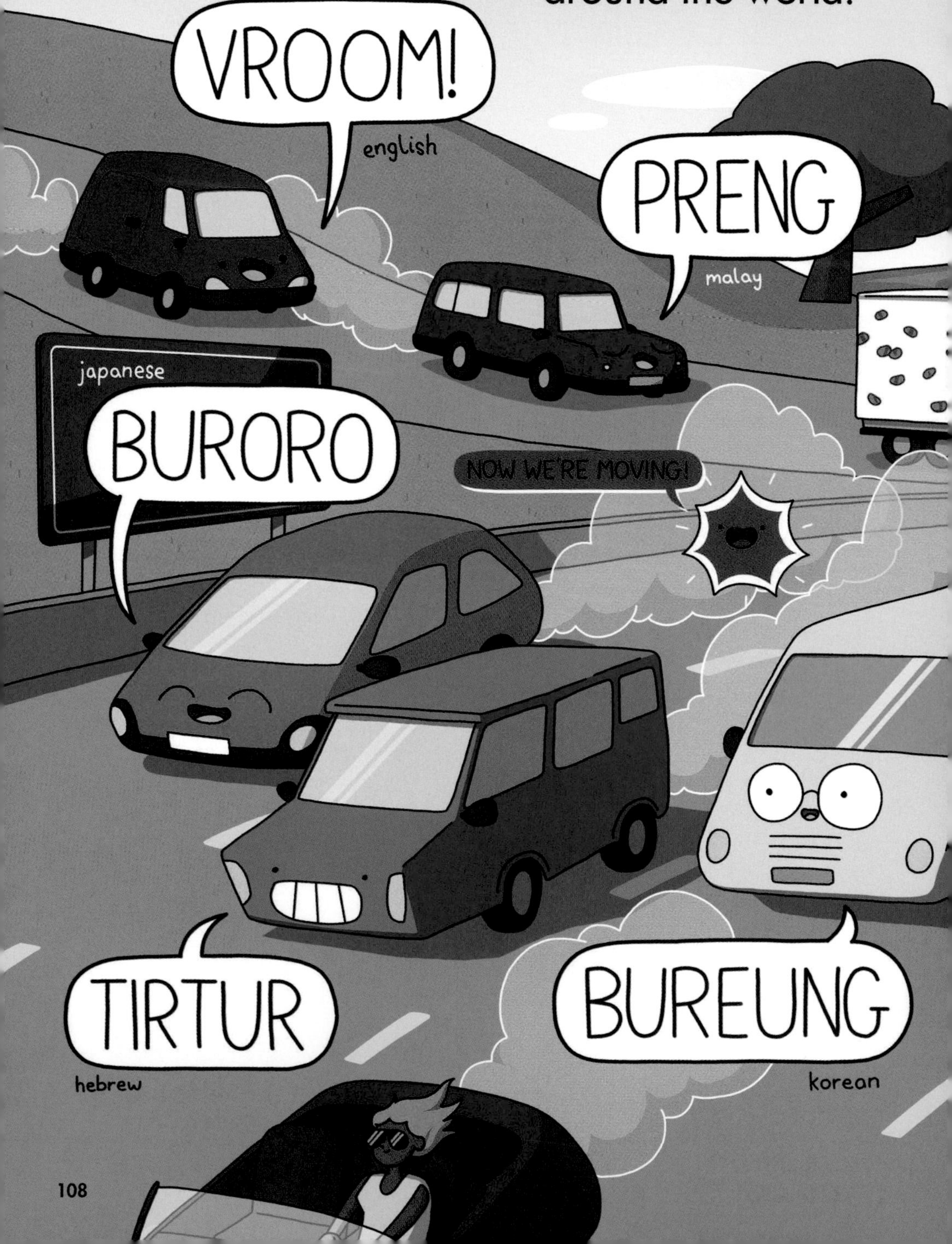
VROOM!
english
PRENG
malay
japanese
BURORO
NOW WE'RE MOVING!
TIRTUR
hebrew
BUREUNG
korean

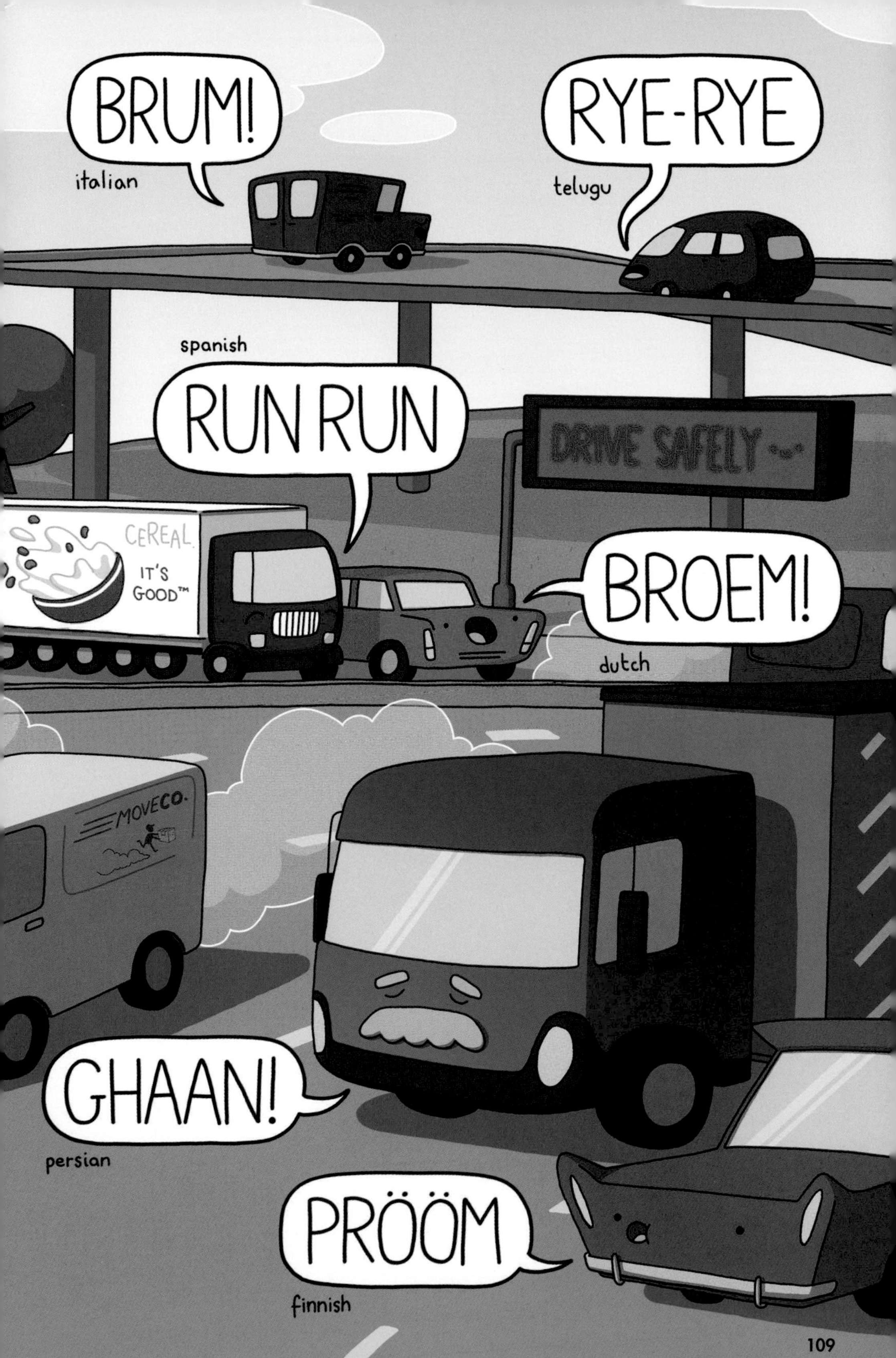
BRUM!
italian
RYE-RYE
telugu
spanish
RUN RUN
DRIVE SAFELY
CEREAL
IT'S GOOD™
BROEM!
dutch
MOVECO.
GHAAN!
persian
PRÖÖM
finnish

Trains

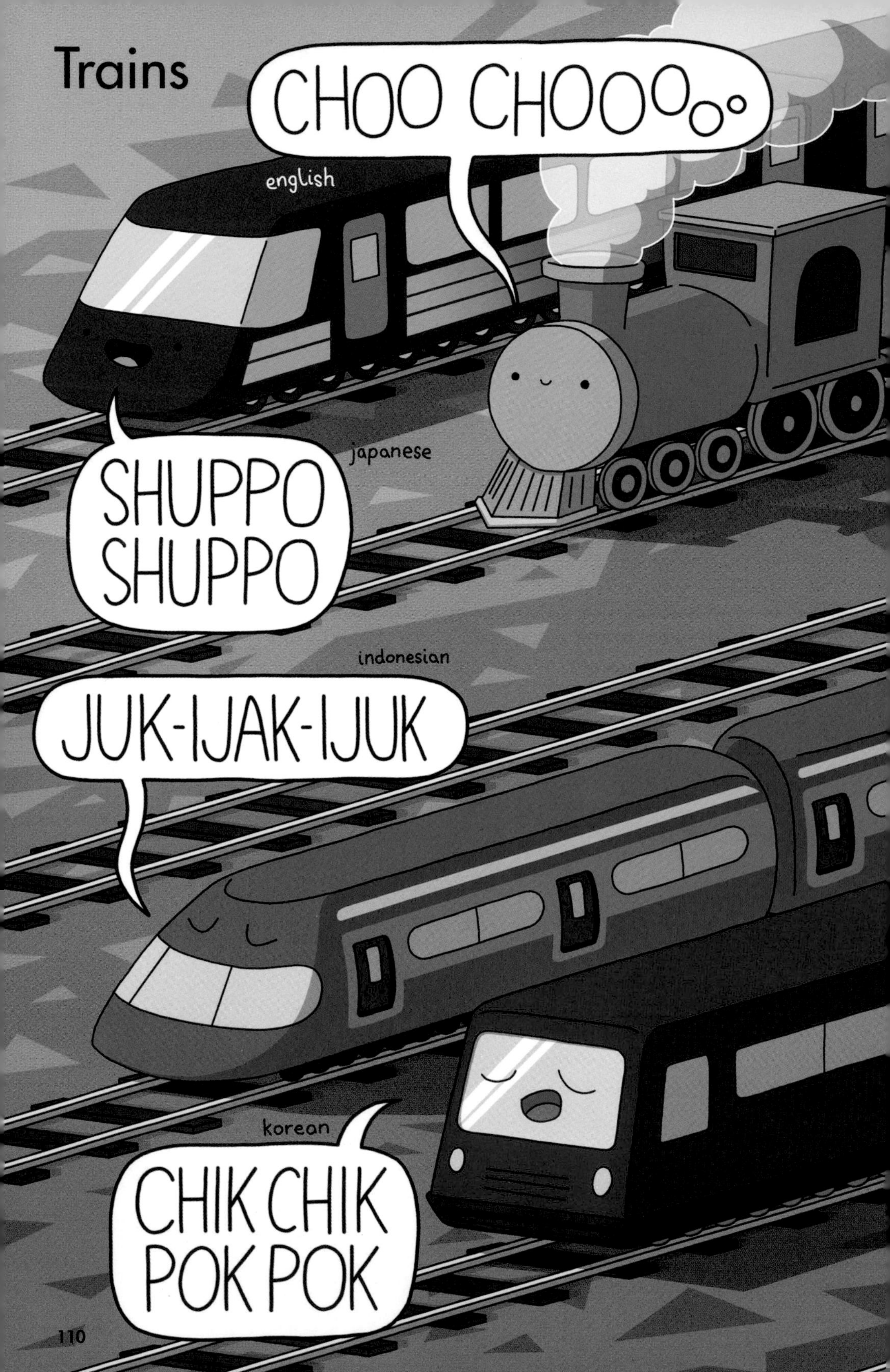

CHOO CHOOooo
english
SHUPPO SHUPPO
japanese
indonesian
JUK-IJAK-IJUK
korean
CHIK CHIK POK POK

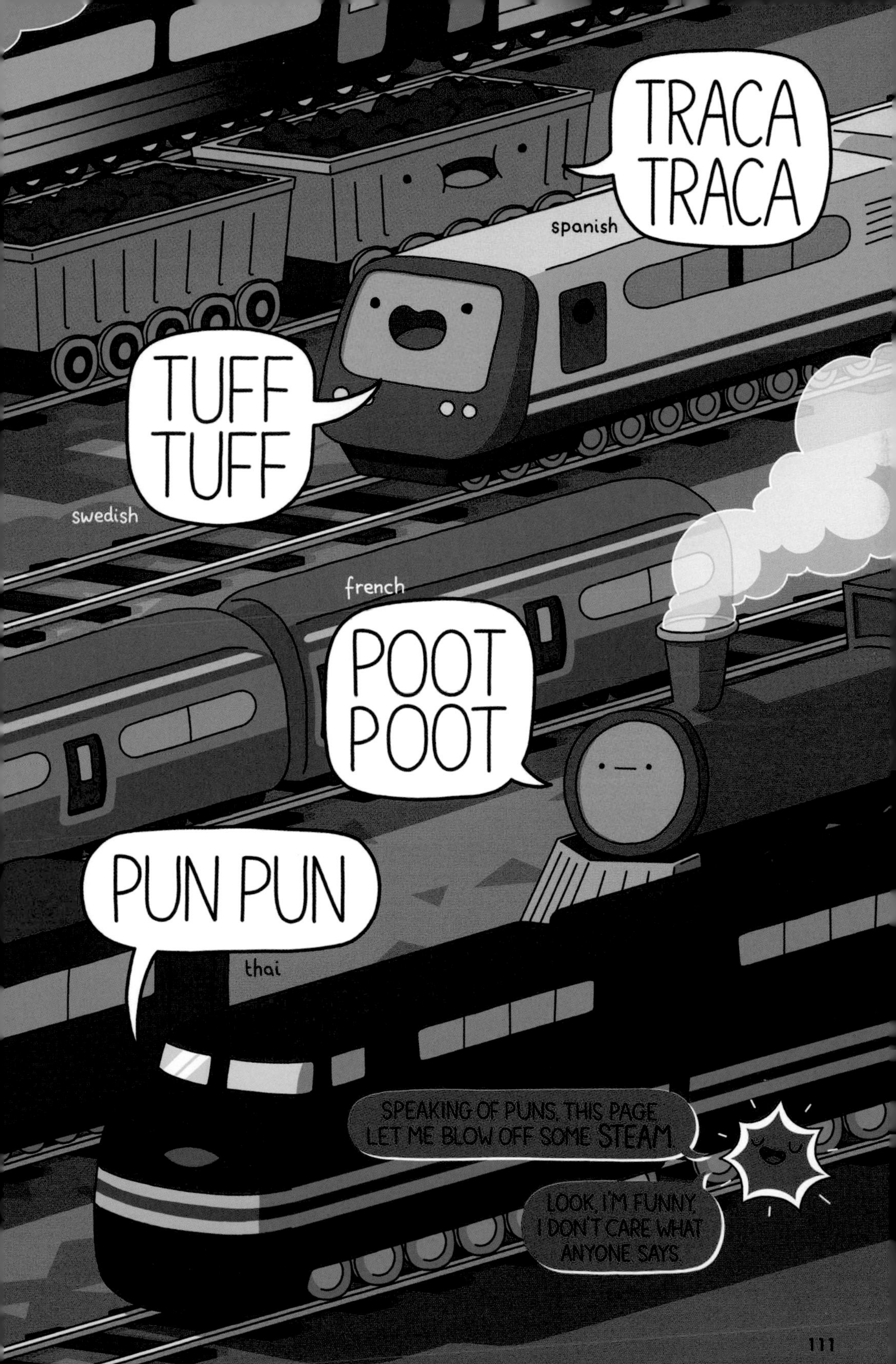
TRACA TRACA
spanish
TUFF TUFF
swedish
french
POOT POOT
PUN PUN
thai
SPEAKING OF PUNS, THIS PAGE LET ME BLOW OFF SOME STEAM.
LOOK, I'M FUNNY. I DON'T CARE WHAT ANYONE SAYS.

Sirens

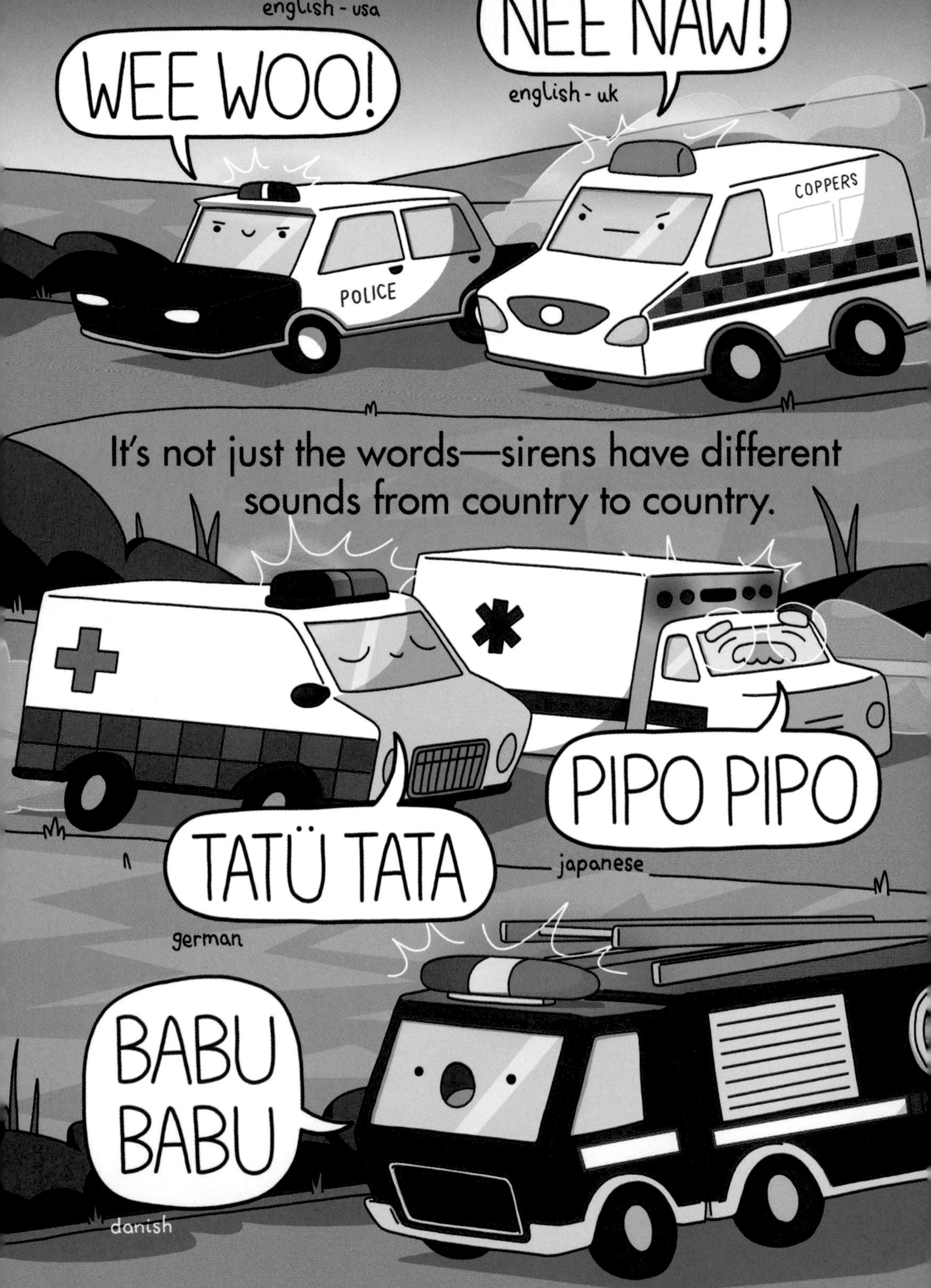
english - usa
WEE WOO!
NEE NAW!
english - uk
COPPERS
POLICE
It's not just the words—sirens have different sounds from country to country.
PIPO PIPO
TATÜ TATA
japanese
german
BABU BABU
danish

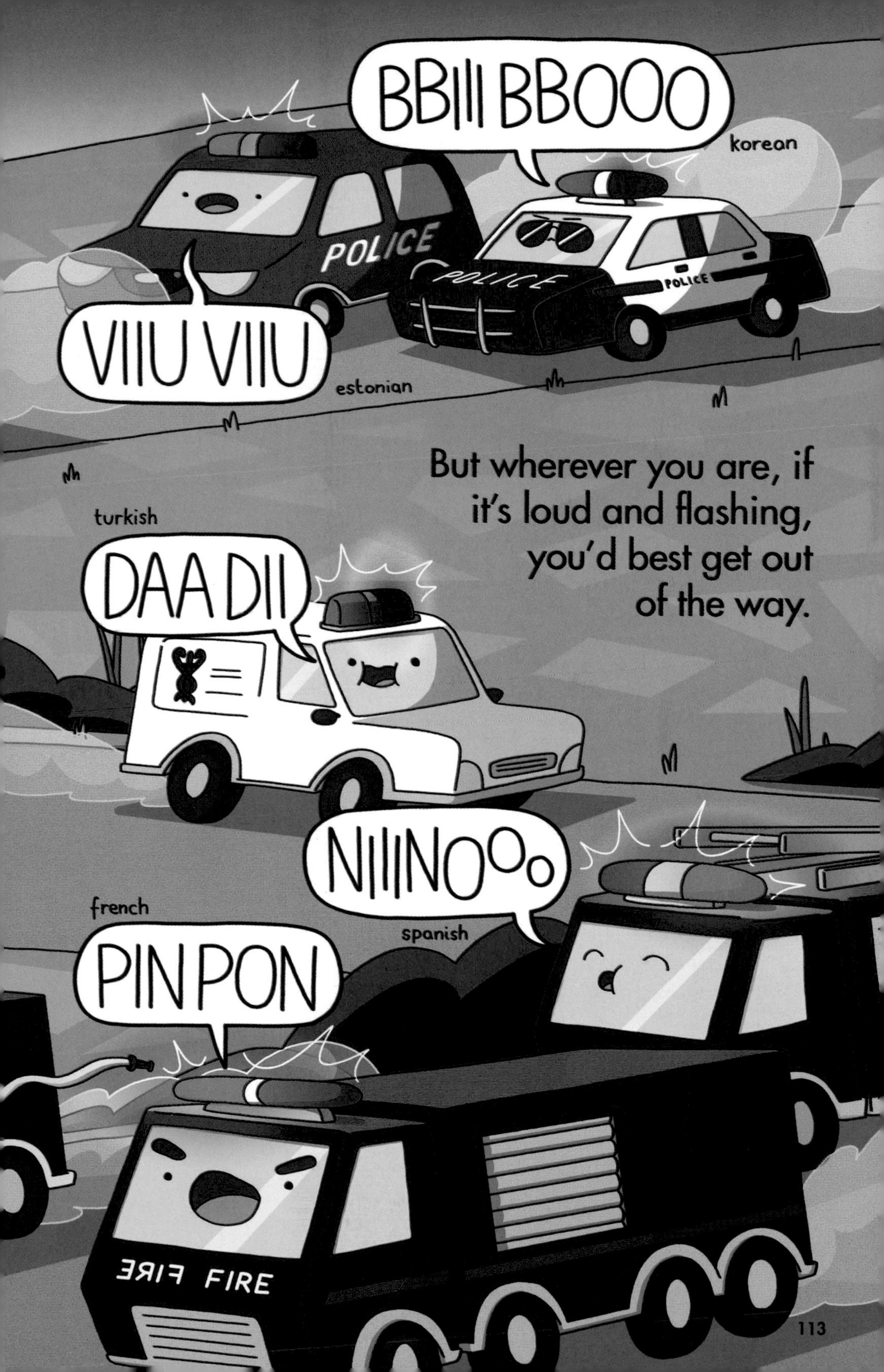
BBIIII BBOOO
korean
POLICE
POLICE
POLICE
VIIU VIIU
estonian
But wherever you are, if it's loud and flashing, you'd best get out of the way.
turkish
DAA DII
NIIINOoo
spanish
french
PIN PON
FIRE

Telephones

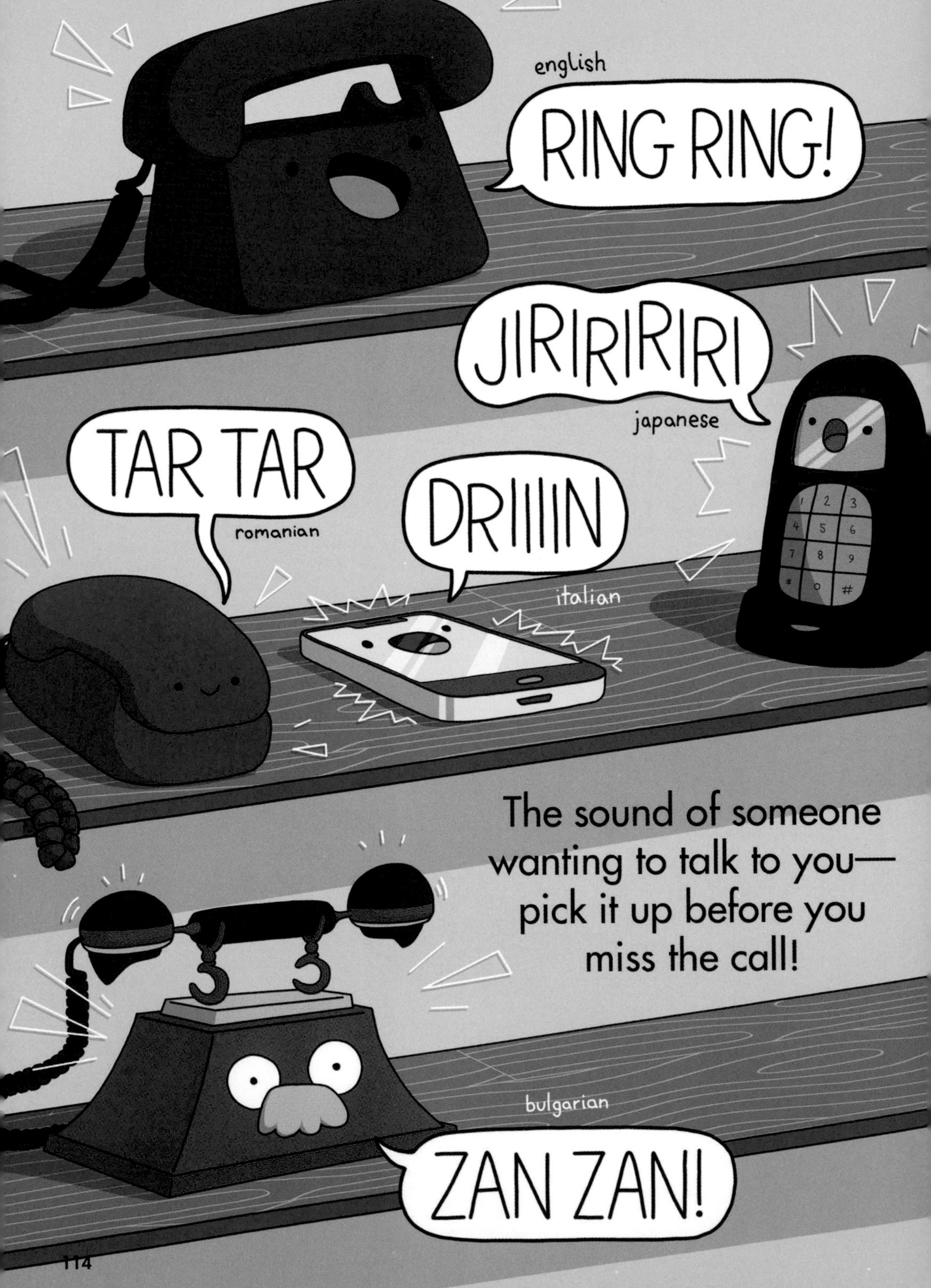
english
RING RING!
JIRIRIRIRI
japanese
TAR TAR
romanian
DRIIIIN
italian
bulgarian
ZAN ZAN!

The sound of someone wanting to talk to you—pick it up before you miss the call!

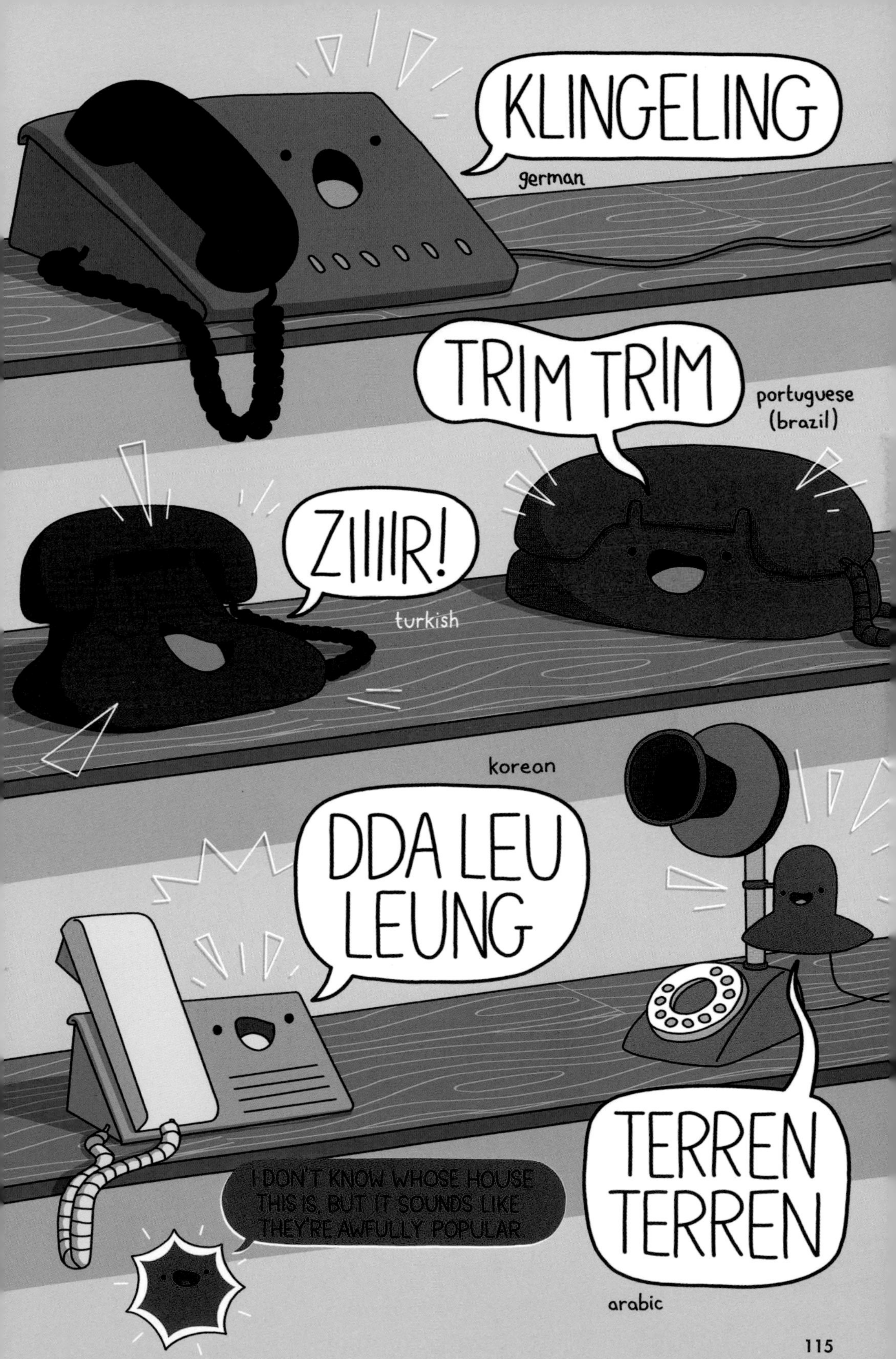
KLINGELING
german
TRIM TRIM
portuguese (brazil)
ZIIIIR!
turkish
korean
DDA LEU LEUNG
TERREN TERREN
arabic
I DON'T KNOW WHOSE HOUSE THIS IS, BUT IT SOUNDS LIKE THEY'RE AWFULLY POPULAR.

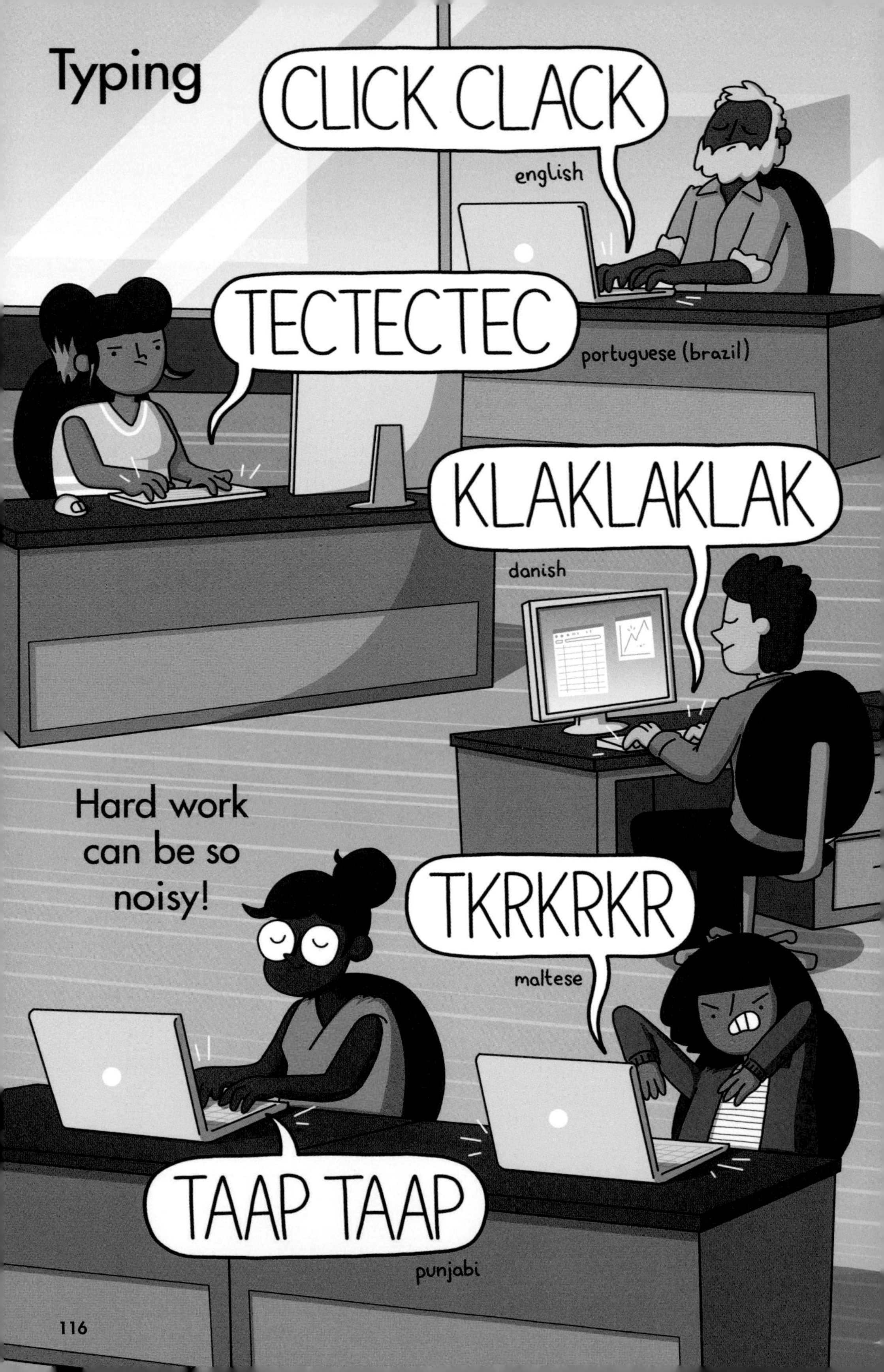
Typing
CLICK CLACK
english
TECTECTEC
portuguese (brazil)
KLAKLAKLAK
danish
Hard work can be so noisy!
TKRKRKR
maltese
TAAP TAAP
punjabi

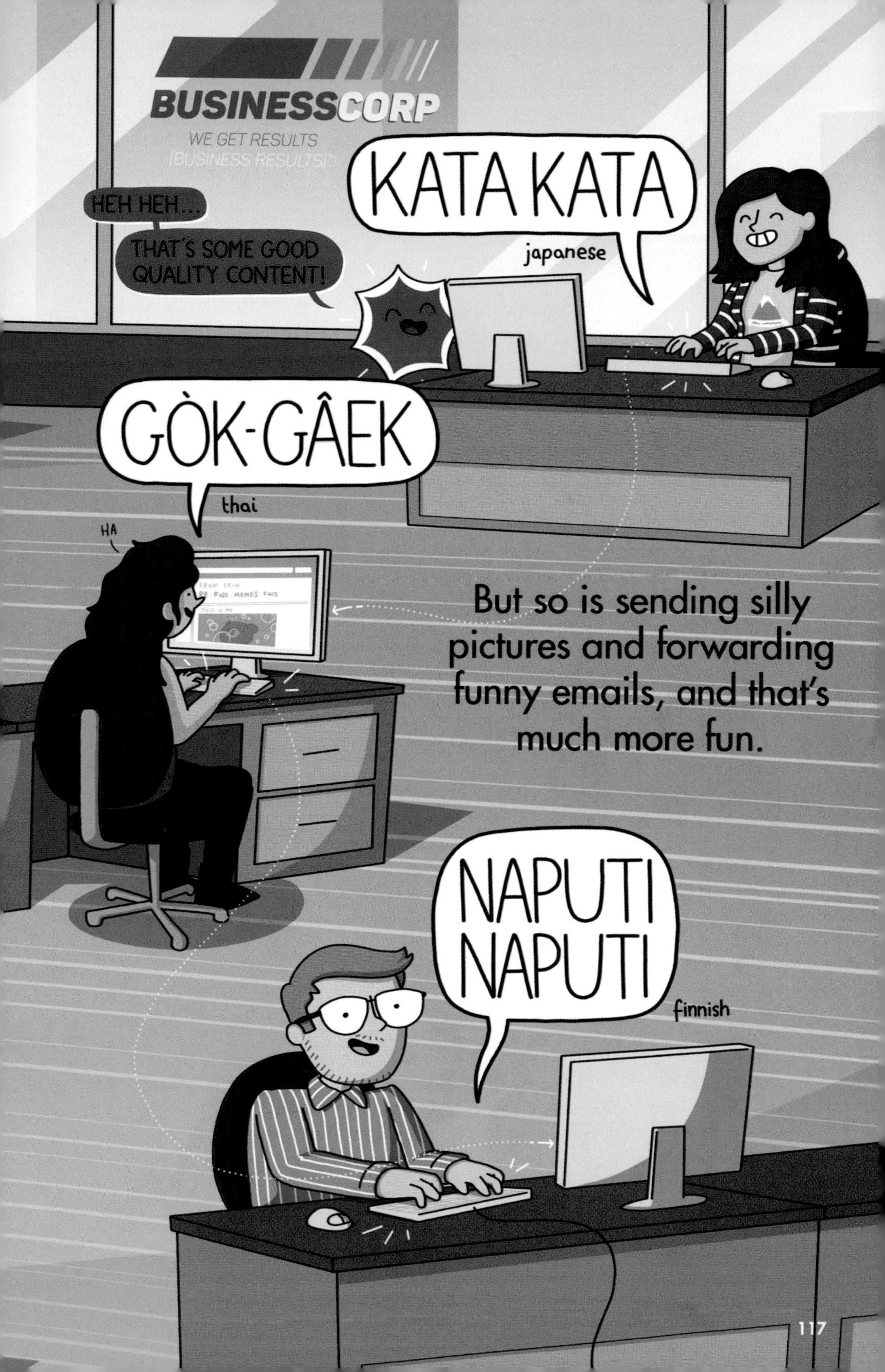
BUSINESSCORP
WE GET RESULTS
(BUSINESS RESULTS)™
HEH HEH...
THAT'S SOME GOOD QUALITY CONTENT!
KATA KATA
japanese
GÒK-GÂEK
thai
HA
But so is sending silly pictures and forwarding funny emails, and that's much more fun.
NAPUTI NAPUTI
finnish

Cameras

The sound of a captured moment.

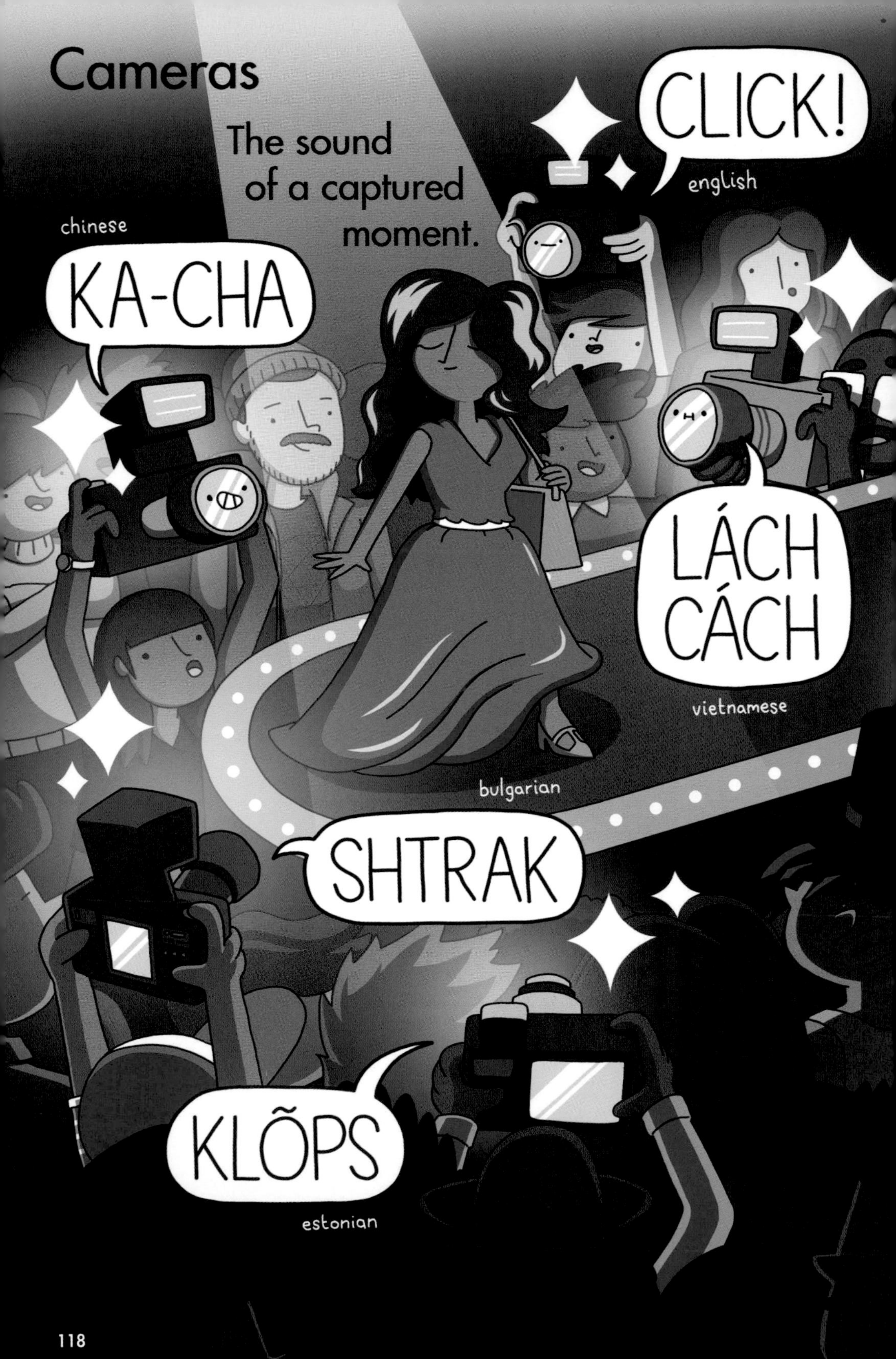
CLICK!
english
chinese
KA-CHA
LÁCH CÁCH
vietnamese
bulgarian
SHTRAK
KLÕPS
estonian

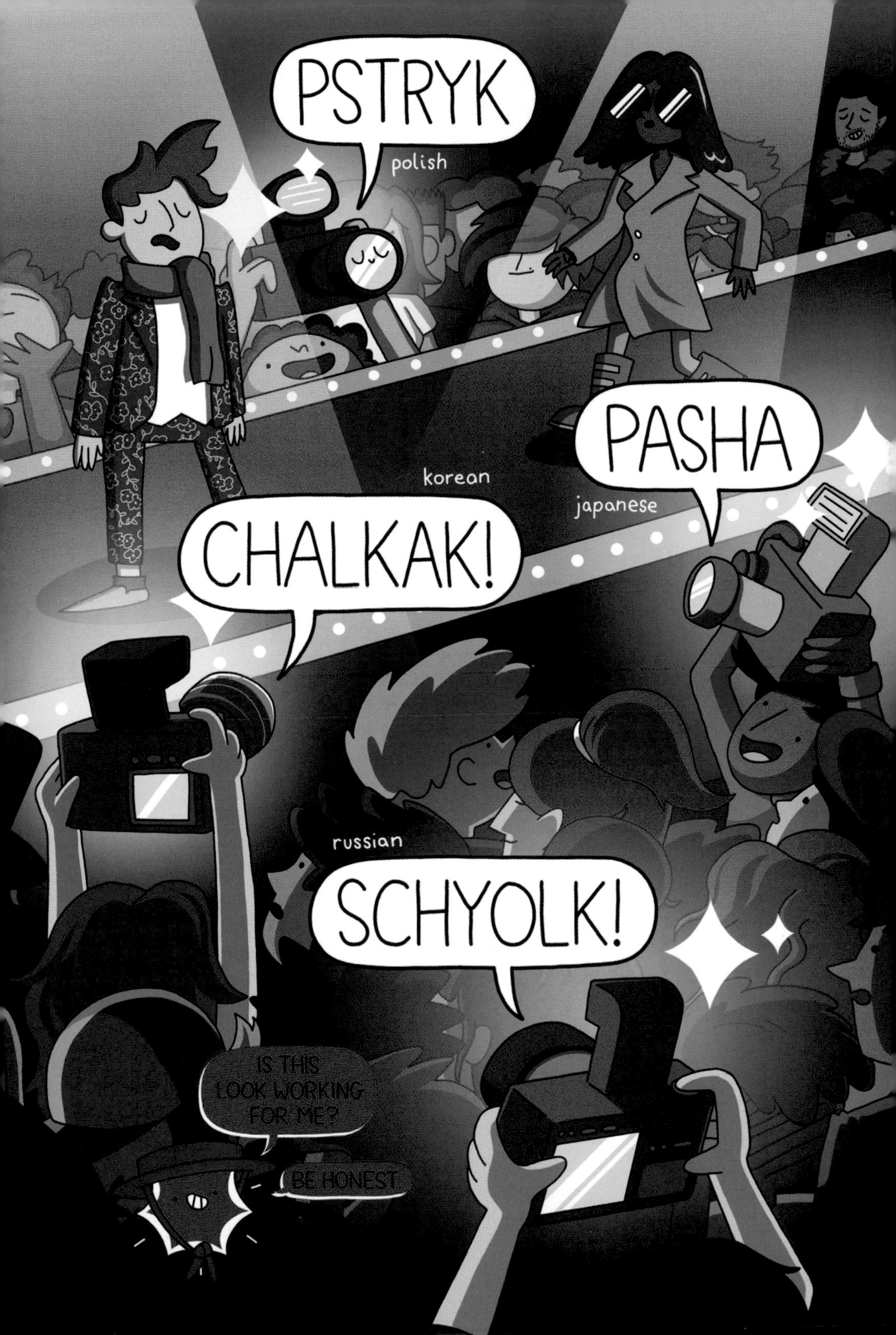
PSTRYK
polish
korean
PASHA
japanese
CHALKAK!
russian
SCHYOLK!
IS THIS LOOK WORKING FOR ME?
BE HONEST.

SOUNDS OF THE HUMAN BODY

People make a lot of strange noises. Sniffly noses, weary yawns, and big gulps—people are all so loud even when they're not talking!

It turns out there's a lot of disagreement on human noises around the world, which is understandable. I mean, try describing a burp sound without actually burping. It's not easy!

They say it's good to embrace local culture when you go on holiday, and that goes for sounds too . . .

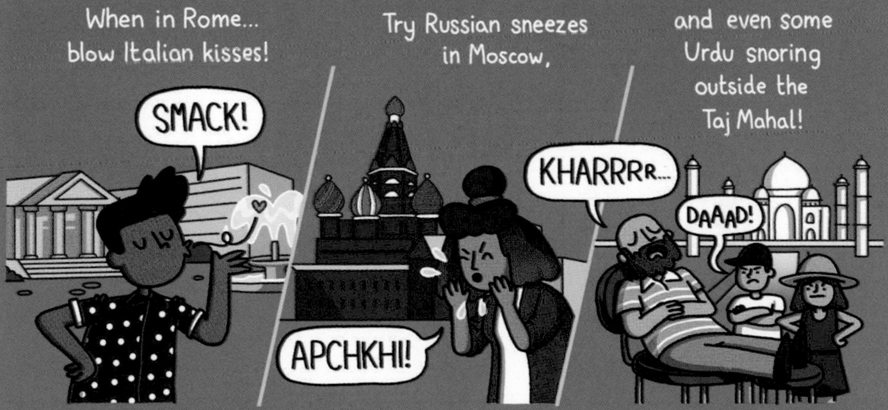
When in Rome... blow Italian kisses!
SMACK!
Try Russian sneezes in Moscow,
APCHKHI!
and even some Urdu snoring outside the Taj Mahal!
KHARRRRR...
DAAAD!

It's time to learn the sounds people are making all over the world!

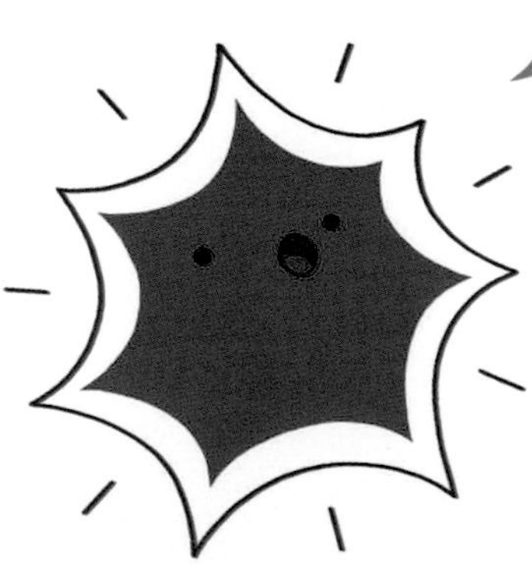

Eating

Some say it's rude to eat loudly . . .

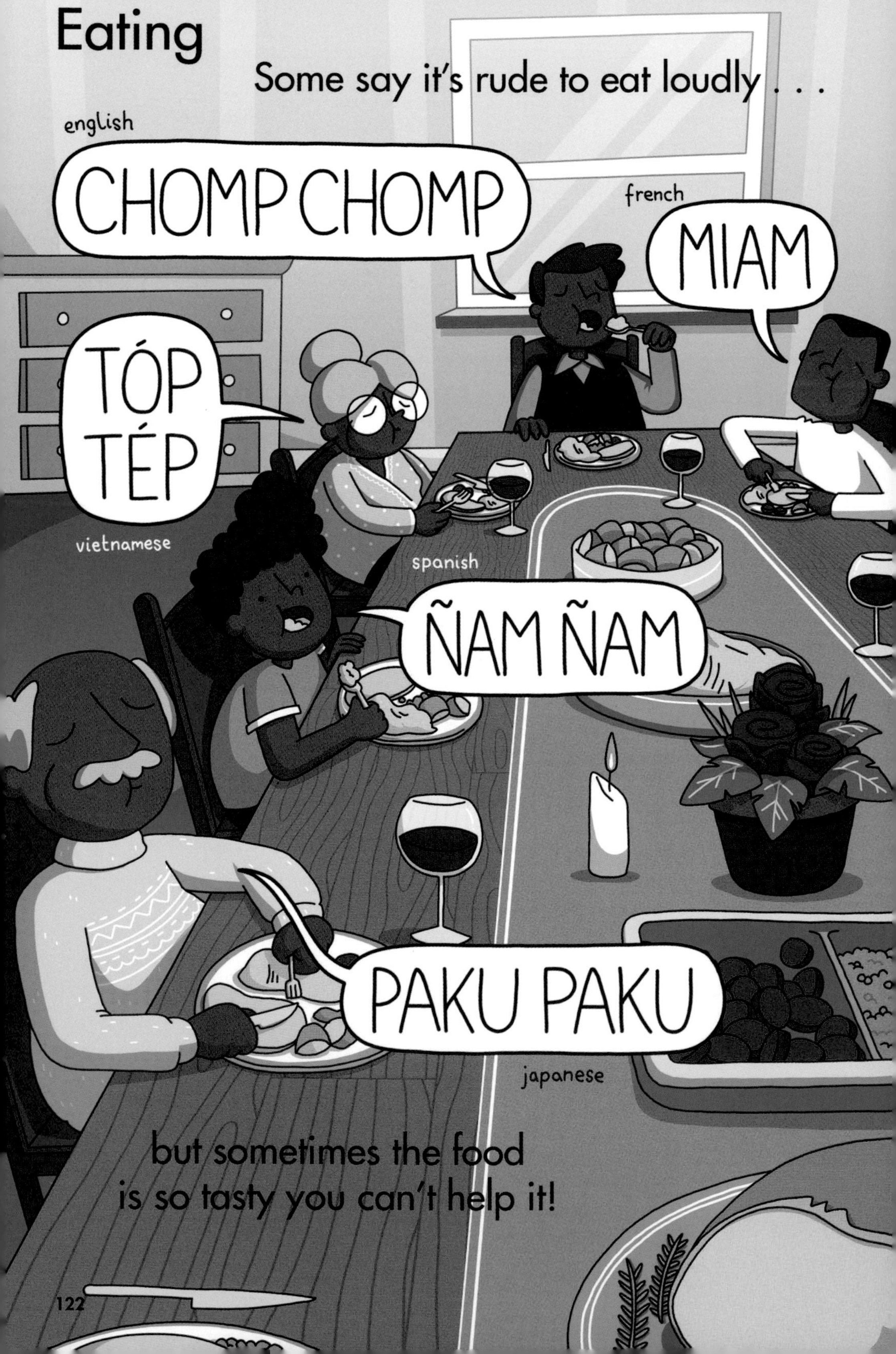
english
CHOMP CHOMP
french
MIAM
TÓP TÉP
vietnamese
spanish
ÑAM ÑAM
PAKU PAKU
japanese

but sometimes the food is so tasty you can't help it!

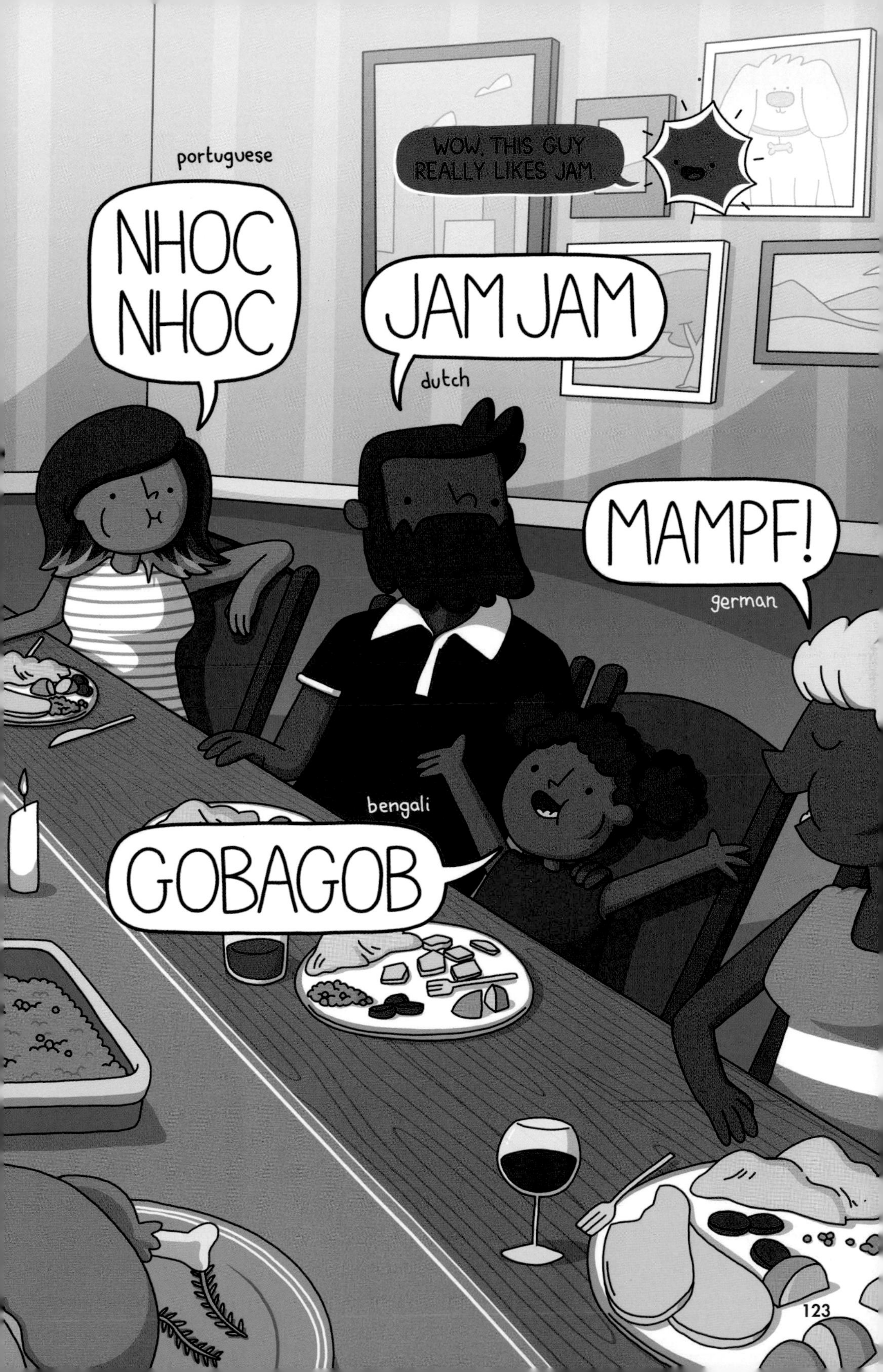
WOW, THIS GUY REALLY LIKES JAM.
portuguese
NHOC NHOC
JAM JAM
dutch
MAMPF!
german
bengali
GOBAGOB

Drinking

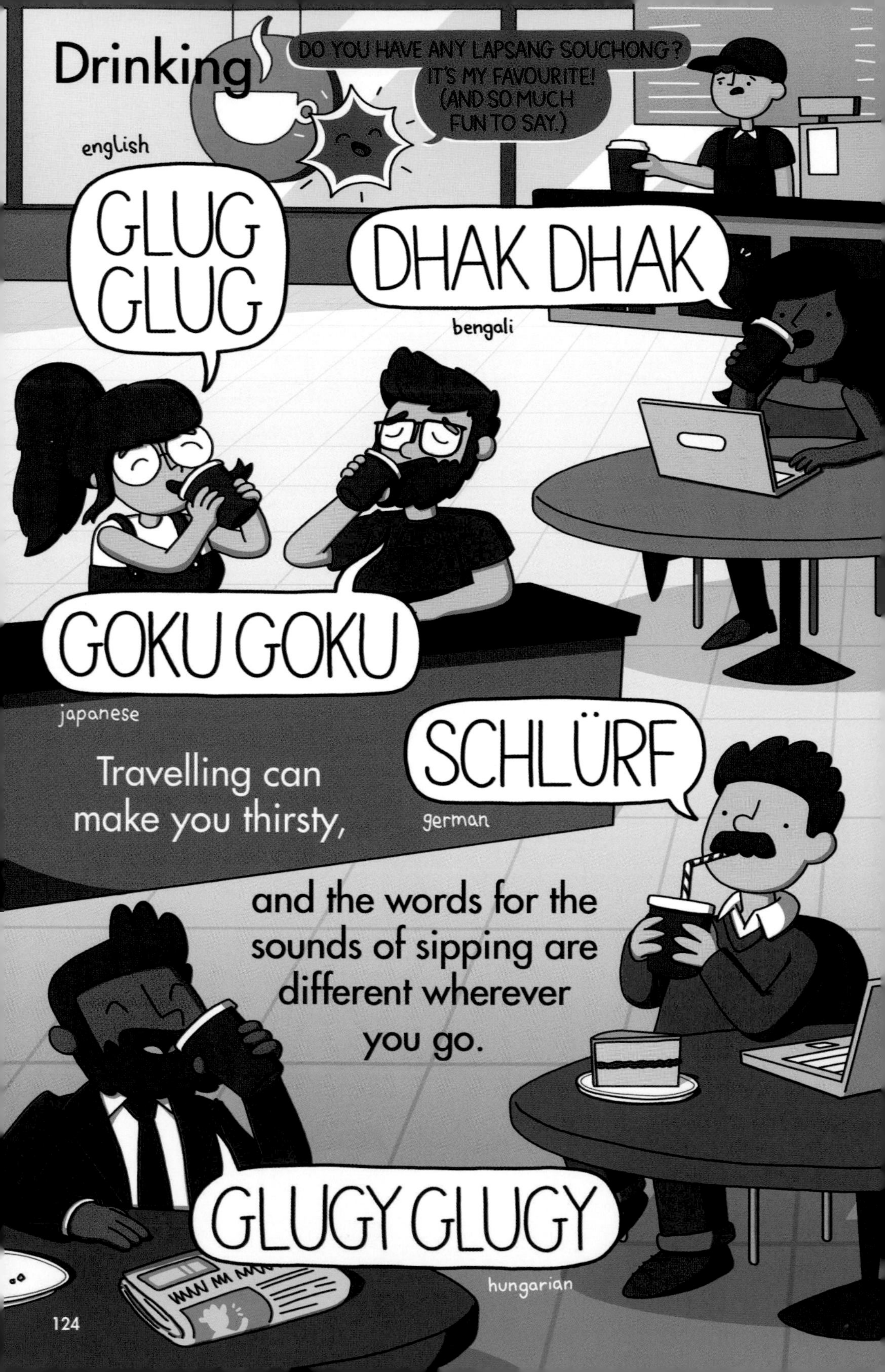
DO YOU HAVE ANY LAPSANG SOUCHONG? IT'S MY FAVOURITE! (AND SO MUCH FUN TO SAY.)
GLUG GLUG
english
DHAK DHAK
bengali
GOKU GOKU
japanese
SCHLÜRF
german
GLUGY GLUGY
hungarian

Travelling can make you thirsty,

and the words for the sounds of sipping are different wherever you go.

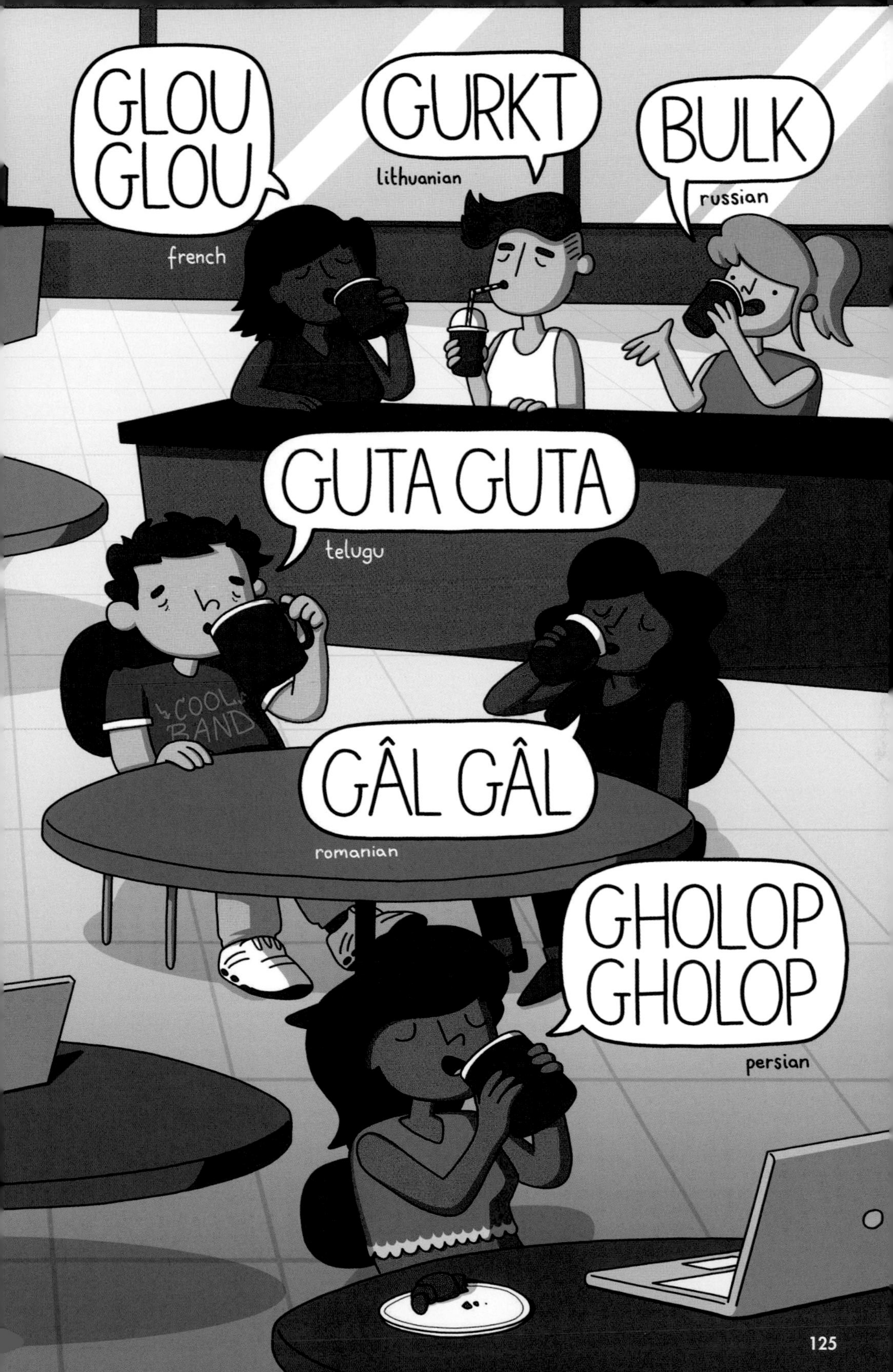
GLOU GLOU
french
GURKT
lithuanian
BULK
russian
GUTA GUTA
telugu
COOL BAND
GÂL GÂL
romanian
GHOLOP GHOLOP
persian

Kissing

On New Year's Eve, when the clock strikes midnight, the sound of smooches fills the air.

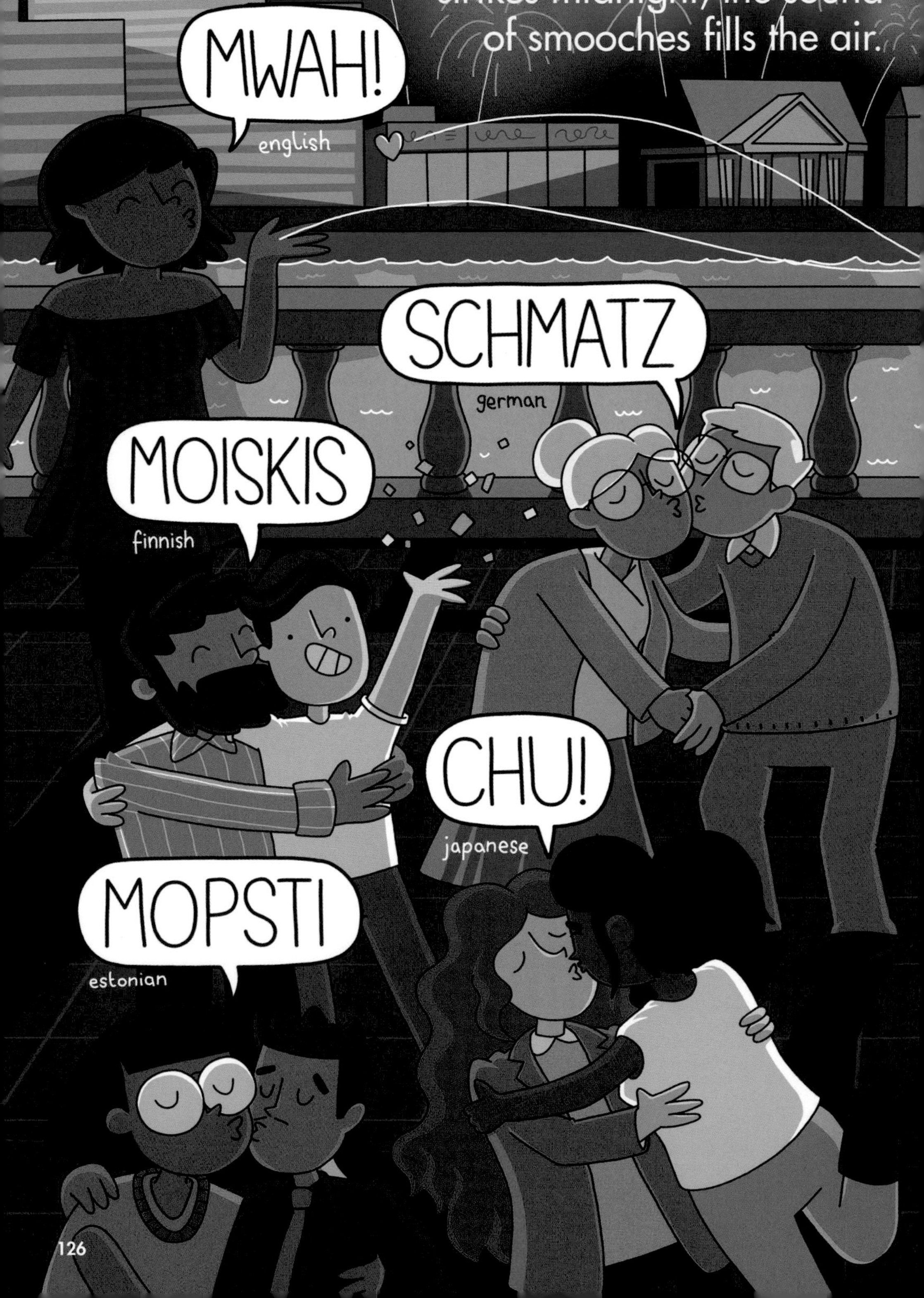
MWAH!
english
SCHMATZ
german
MOISKIS
finnish
CHU!
japanese
MOPSTI
estonian

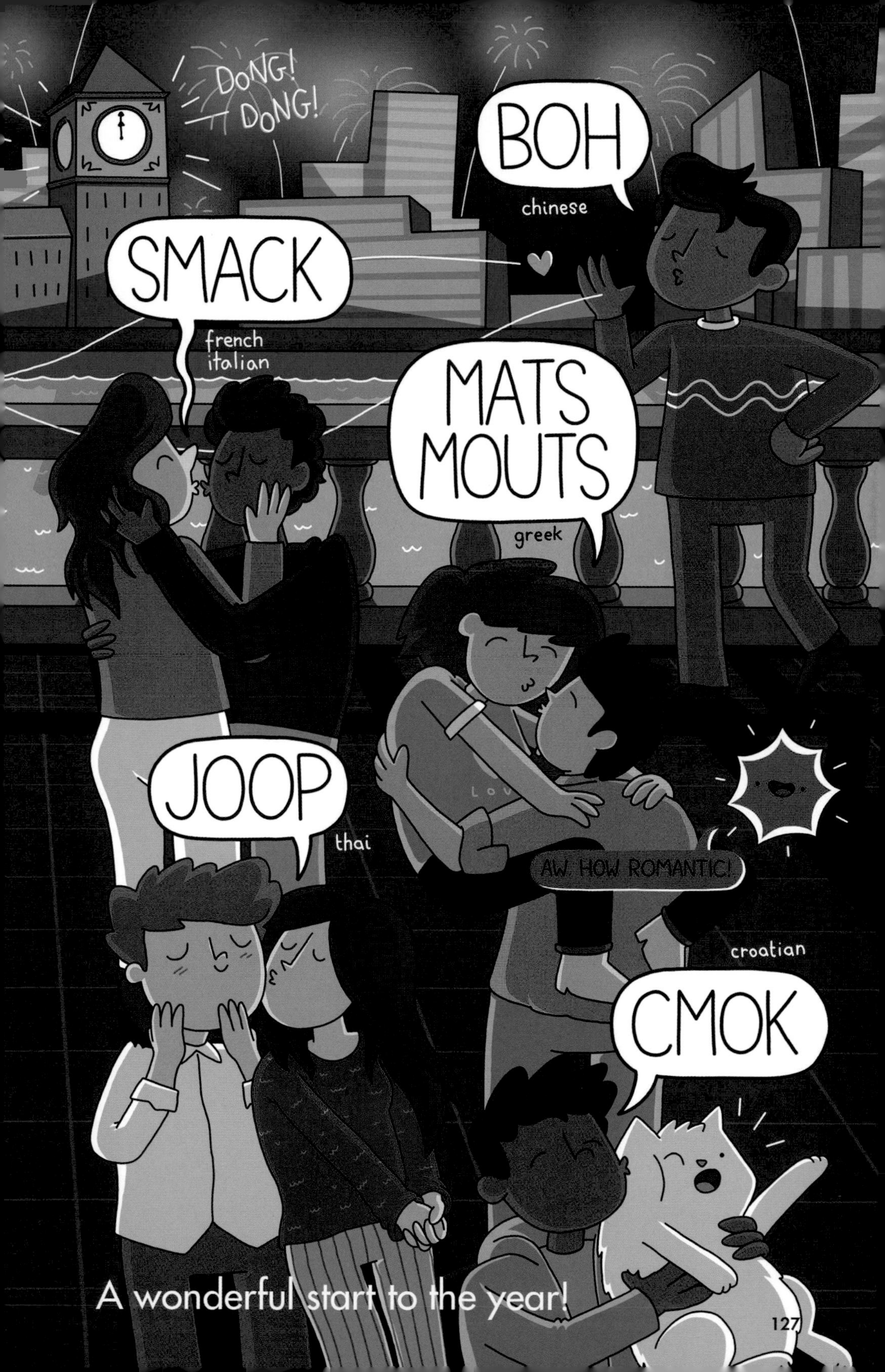
DONG!
DONG!
BOH
chinese
SMACK
french
italian
MATS MOUTS
greek
JOOP
thai
AW, HOW ROMANTIC!
croatian
CMOK
A wonderful start to the year!

Yawning

Yawning is contagious.

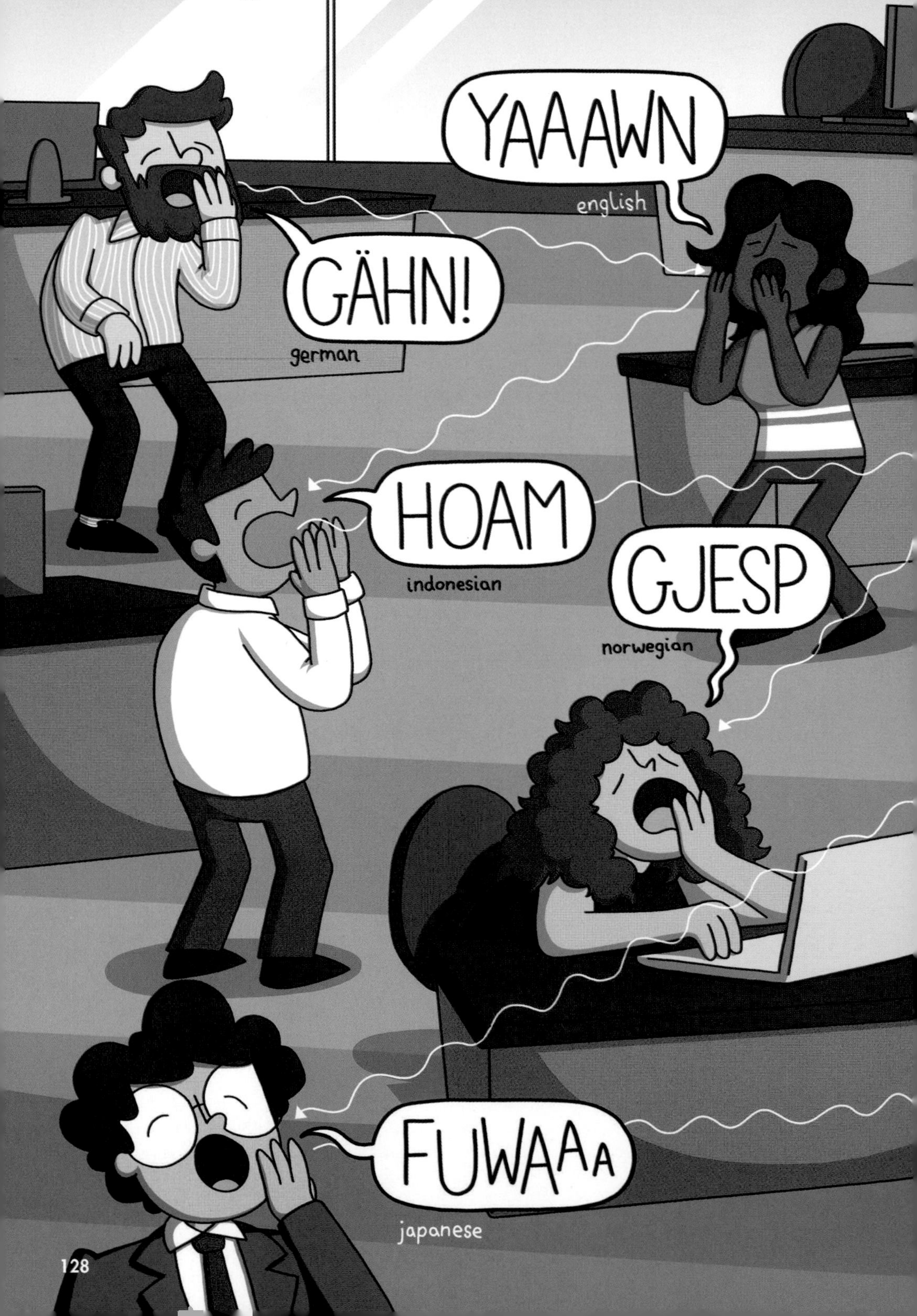
YAAAWN
english
GÄHN!
german
HOAM
indonesian
GJESP
norwegian
FUWAAA
japanese

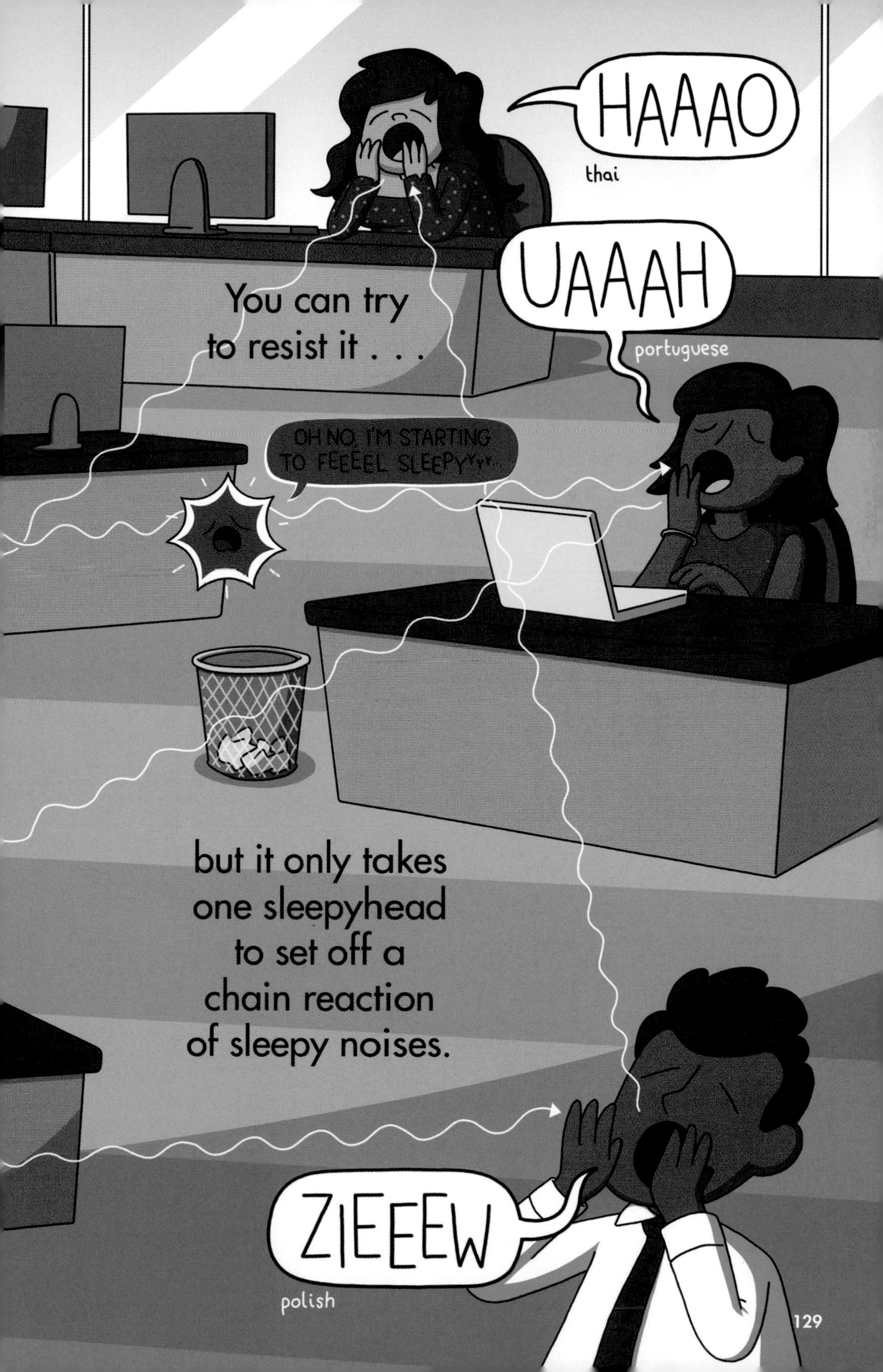
HAAAO
thai
You can try to resist it . . .
UAAAH
portuguese
OH NO, I'M STARTING TO FEEEEL SLEEPYYYY...
but it only takes one sleepyhead to set off a chain reaction of sleepy noises.
ZIEEEW
polish

Snoring

Next time you're near a noisy sleeper, listen closely.

What language are they snoring in?

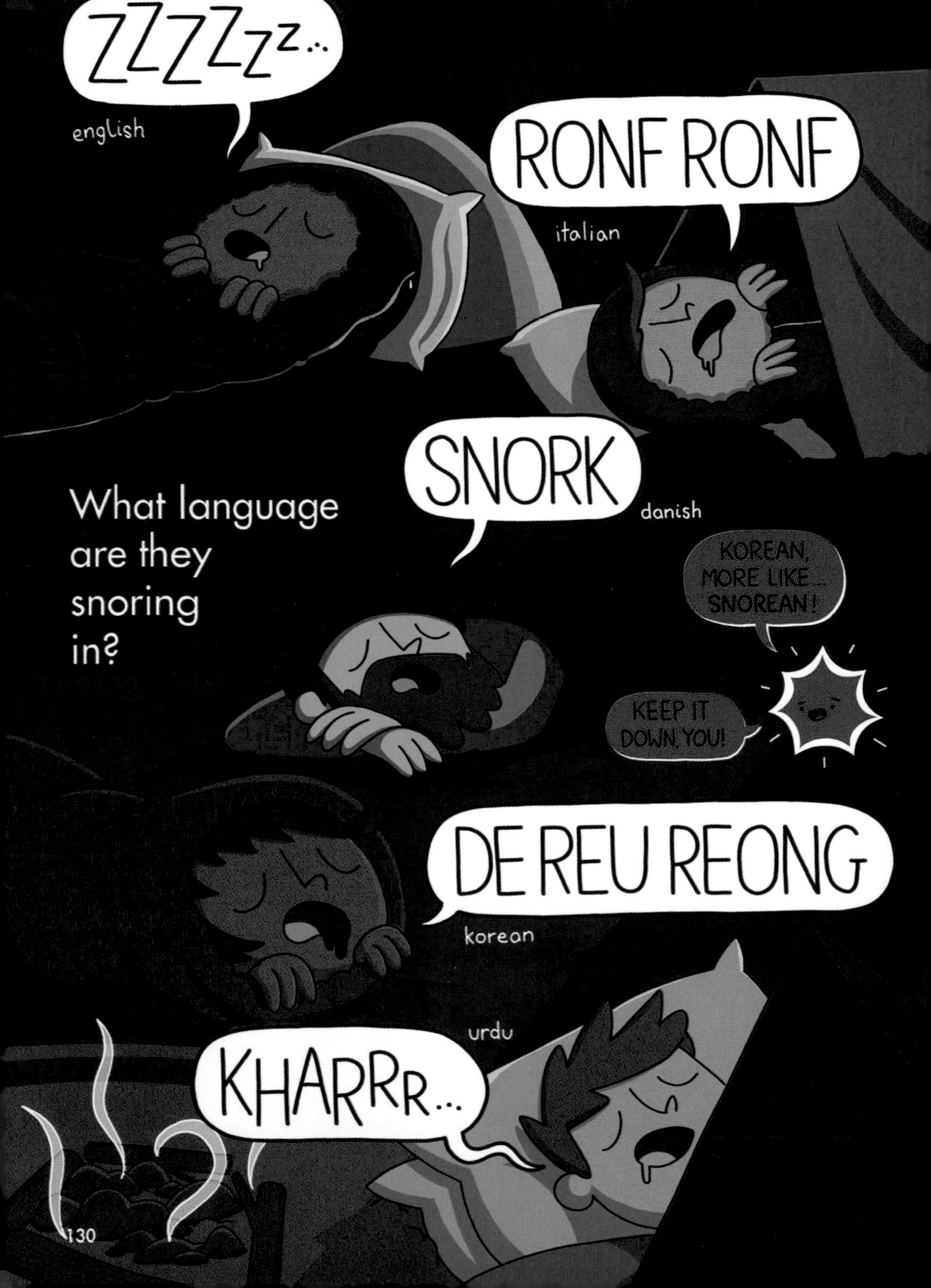

ZZZZzz...
english
RONF RONF
italian
SNORK
danish
KOREAN, MORE LIKE... SNOREAN!
KEEP IT DOWN, YOU!
DE REU REONG
korean
urdu
KHARRR...

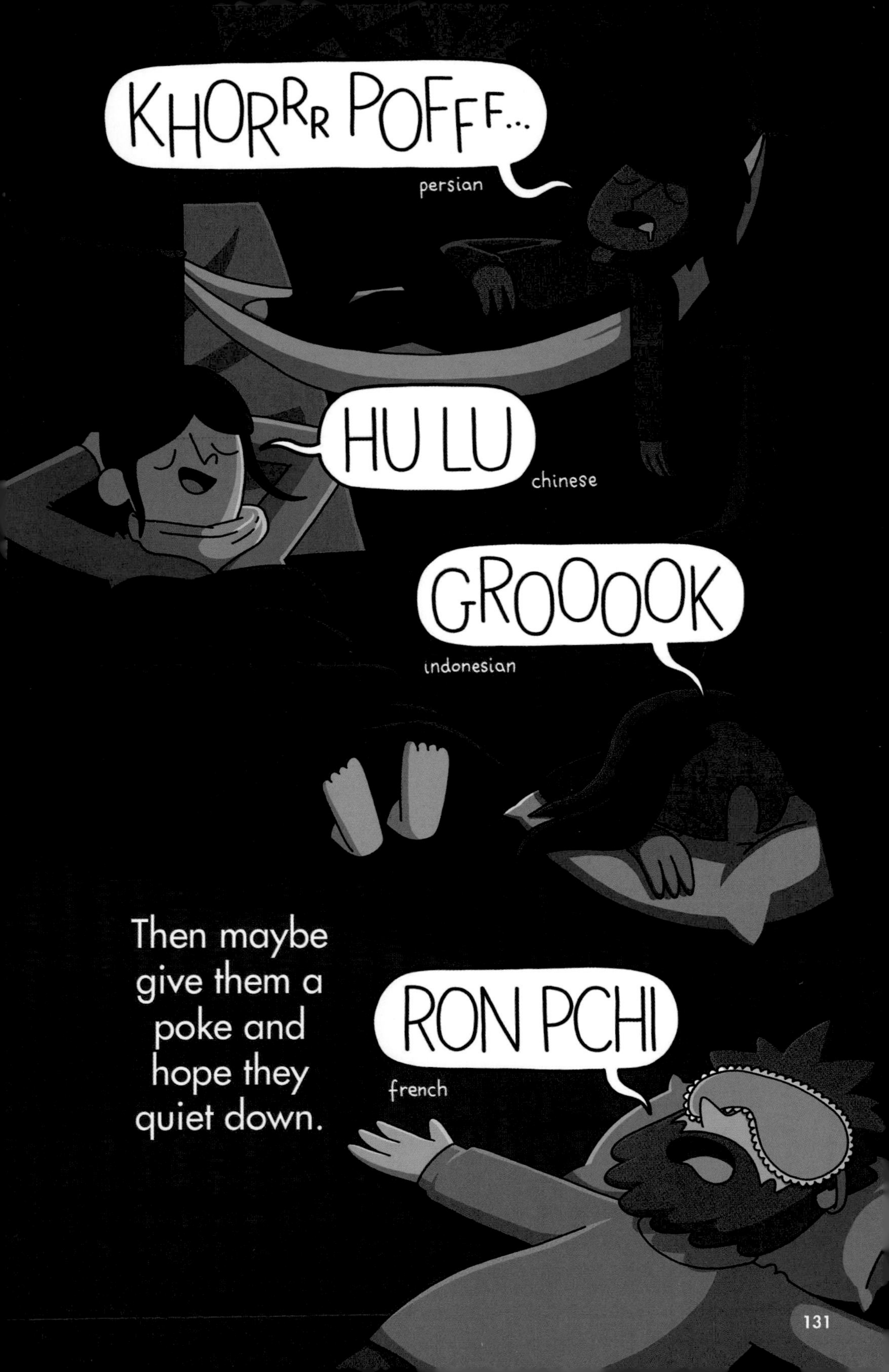
KHORRRR POFFFF...
persian
HU LU
chinese
GROOOOK
indonesian
Then maybe give them a poke and hope they quiet down.
RON PCHI
french

Sniffing

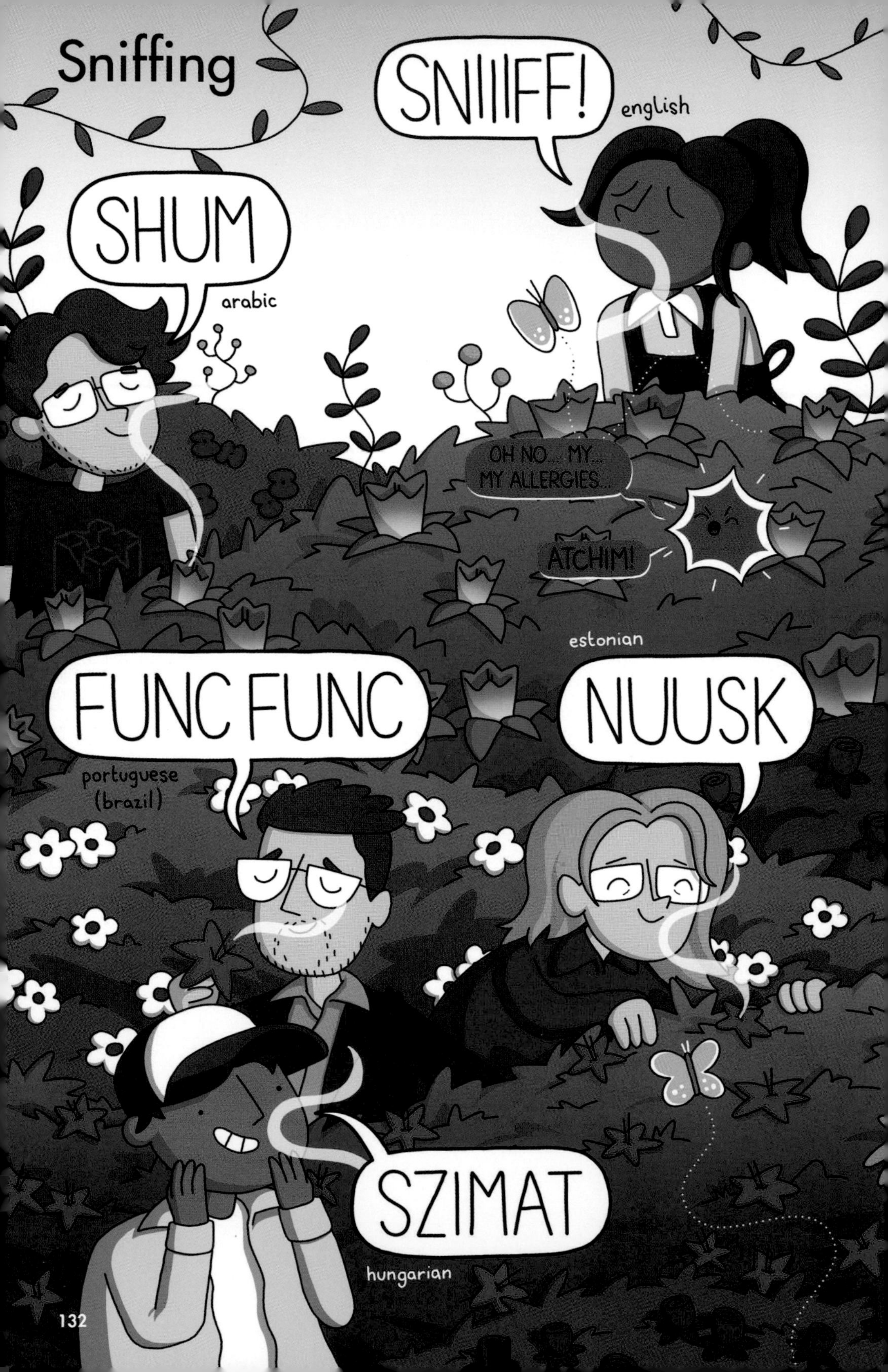

SNIIIFF!
english
SHUM
arabic
OH NO... MY... MY ALLERGIES...
ATCHIM!
estonian
FUNC FUNC
portuguese (brazil)
NUUSK
SZIMAT
hungarian

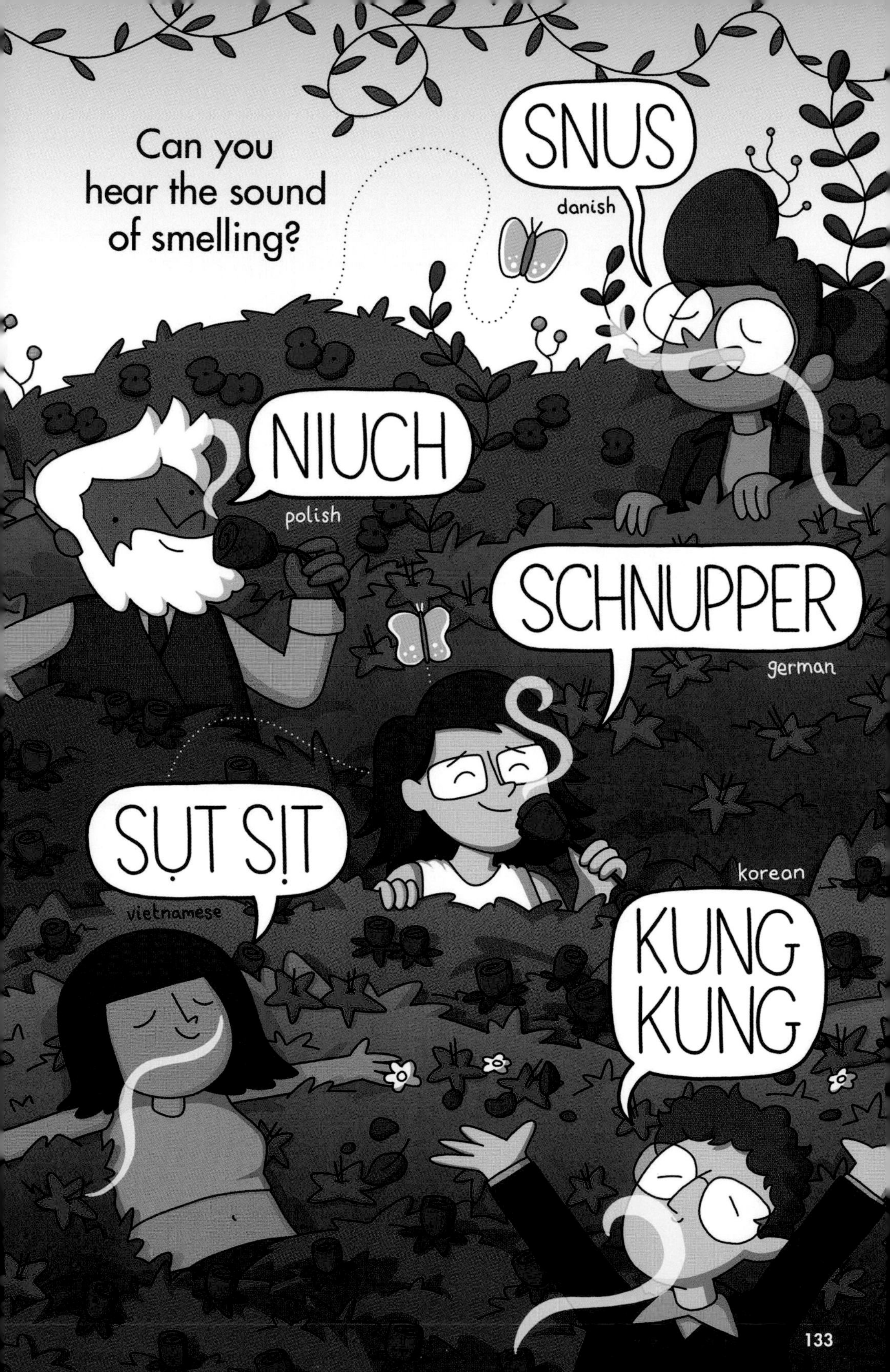
Can you hear the sound of smelling?
SNUS
danish
NIUCH
polish
SCHNUPPER
german
SỤT SỊT
vietnamese
korean
KUNG KUNG

Coughing

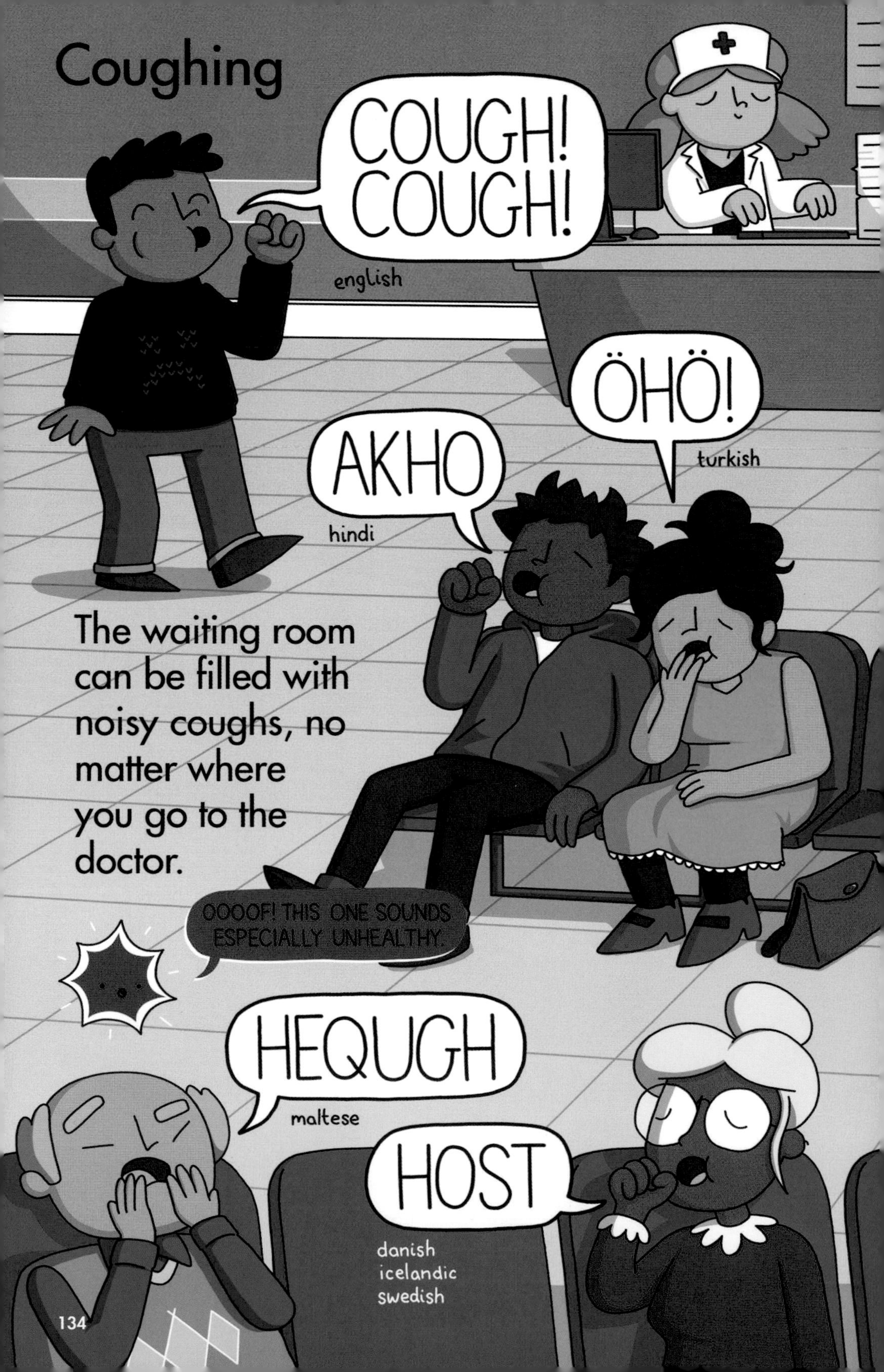
COUGH! COUGH!
english
ÖHÖ!
turkish
AKHO
hindi
OOOOF! THIS ONE SOUNDS ESPECIALLY UNHEALTHY.
HEQUGH
maltese
HOST
danish
icelandic
swedish

The waiting room can be filled with noisy coughs, no matter where you go to the doctor.

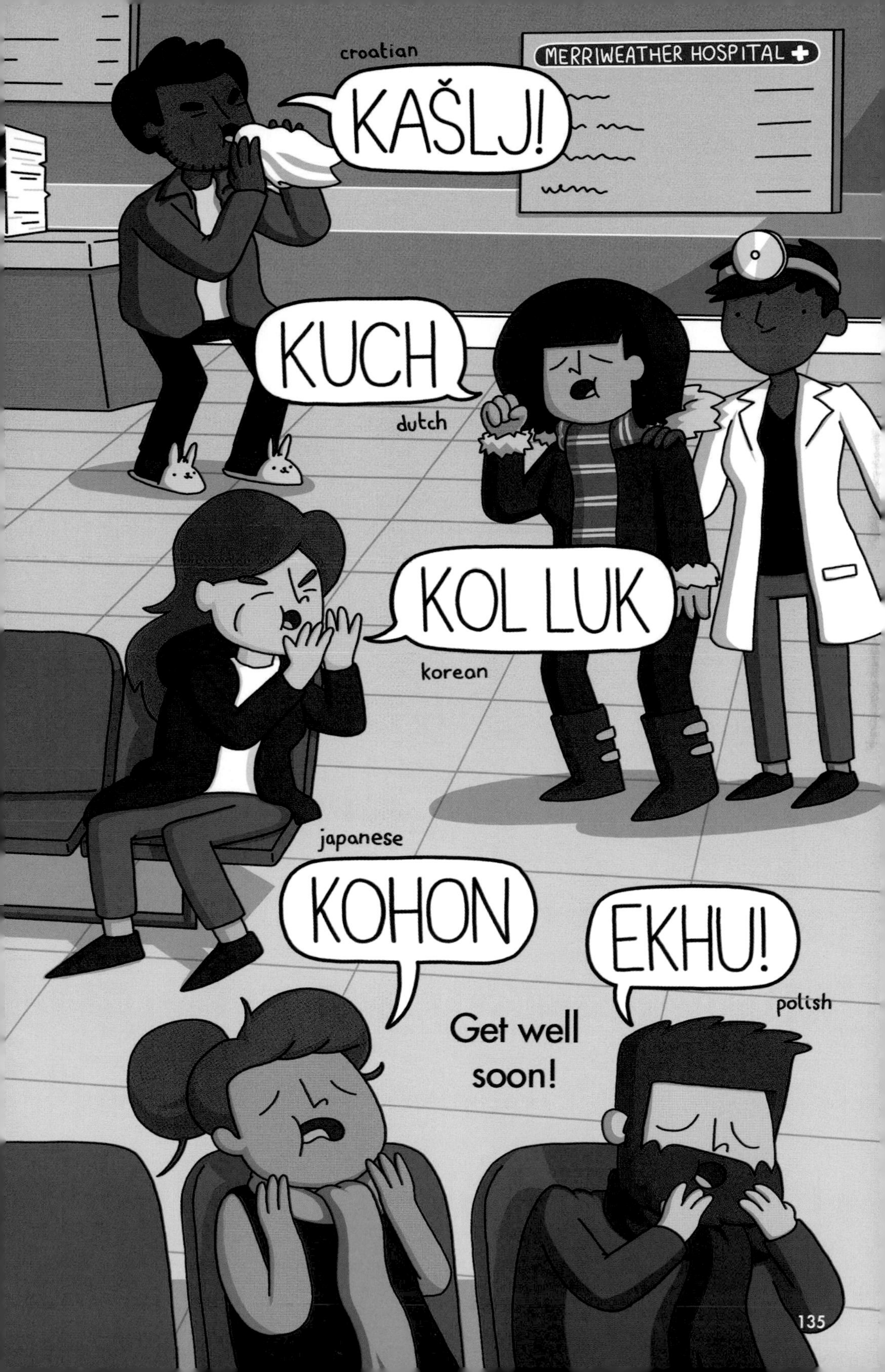
MERRIWEATHER HOSPITAL
croatian
KAŠLJ!
KUCH
dutch
KOL LUK
korean
japanese
KOHON
EKHU!
polish
Get well soon!

Sneezing

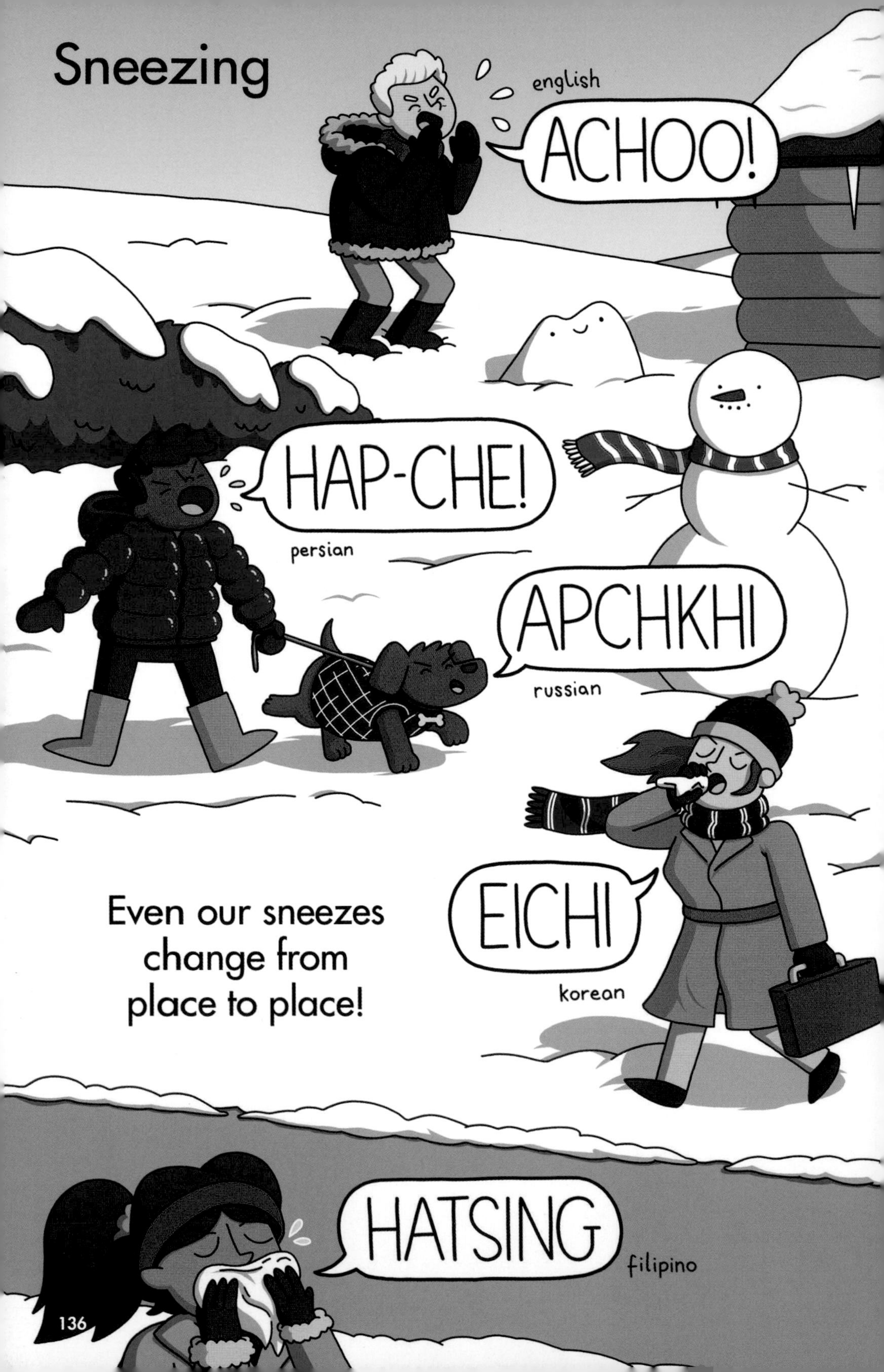
english
ACHOO!
HAP-CHE!
persian
APCHKHI
russian
Even our sneezes change from place to place!
EICHI
korean
HATSING
filipino

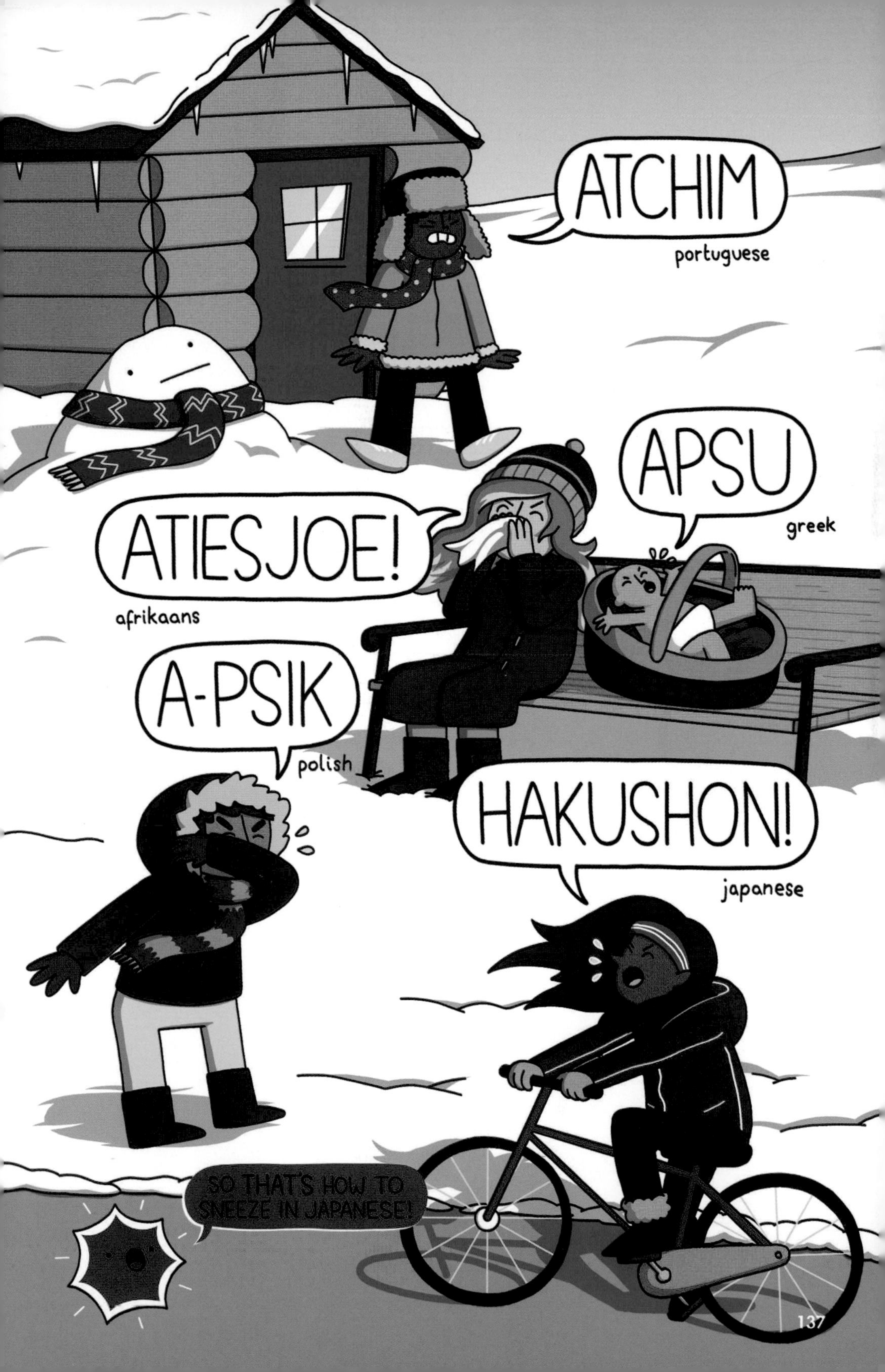
ATCHIM
portuguese
APSU
greek
ATIESJOE!
afrikaans
A-PSIK
polish
HAKUSHON!
japanese
SO THAT'S HOW TO SNEEZE IN JAPANESE!

Burping

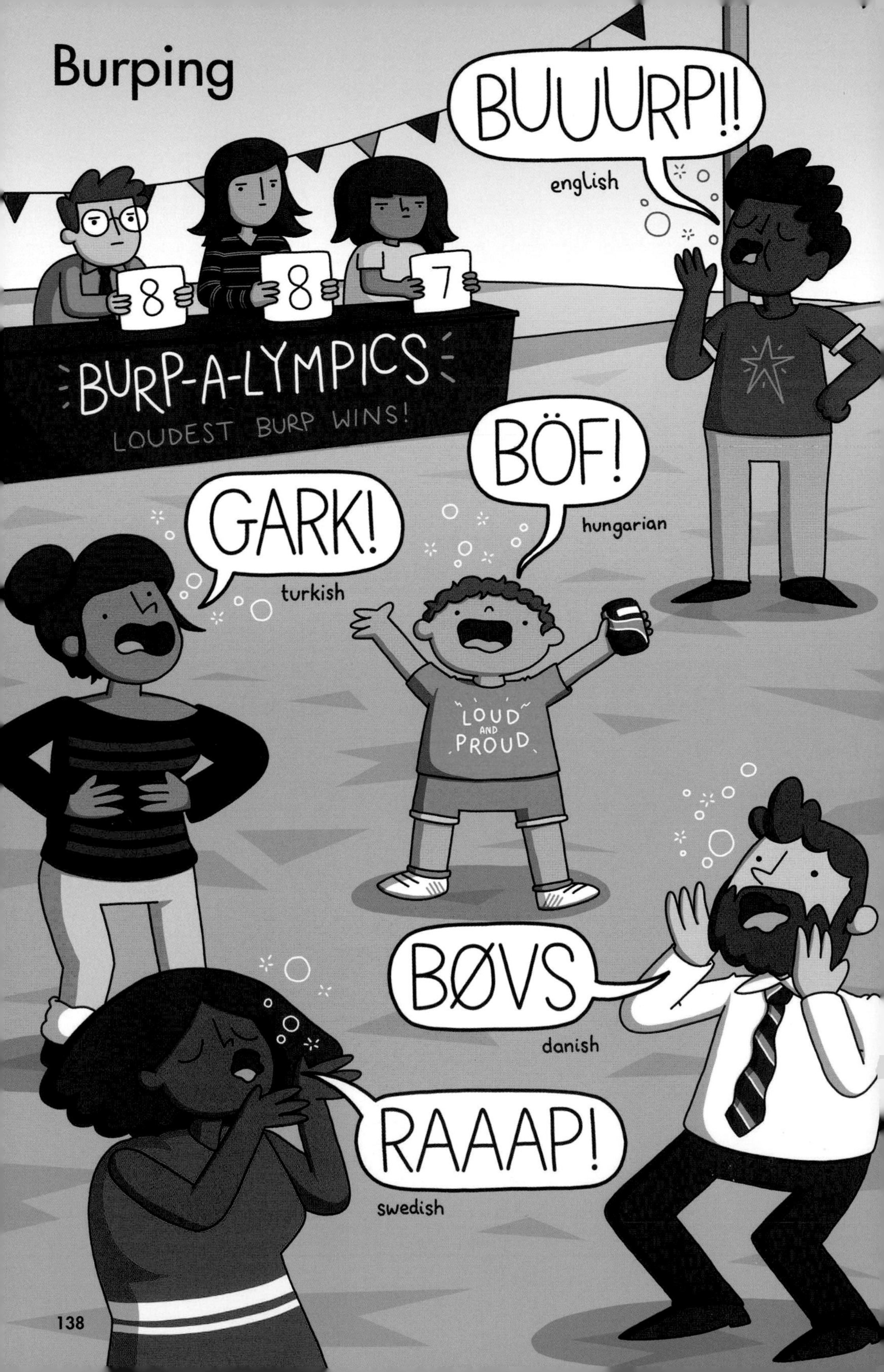
BUUURP!!
english
8
8
7
BURP-A-LYMPICS
LOUDEST BURP WINS!
BÖF!
hungarian
GARK!
turkish
LOUD AND PROUD
BØVS
danish
RAAAP!
swedish

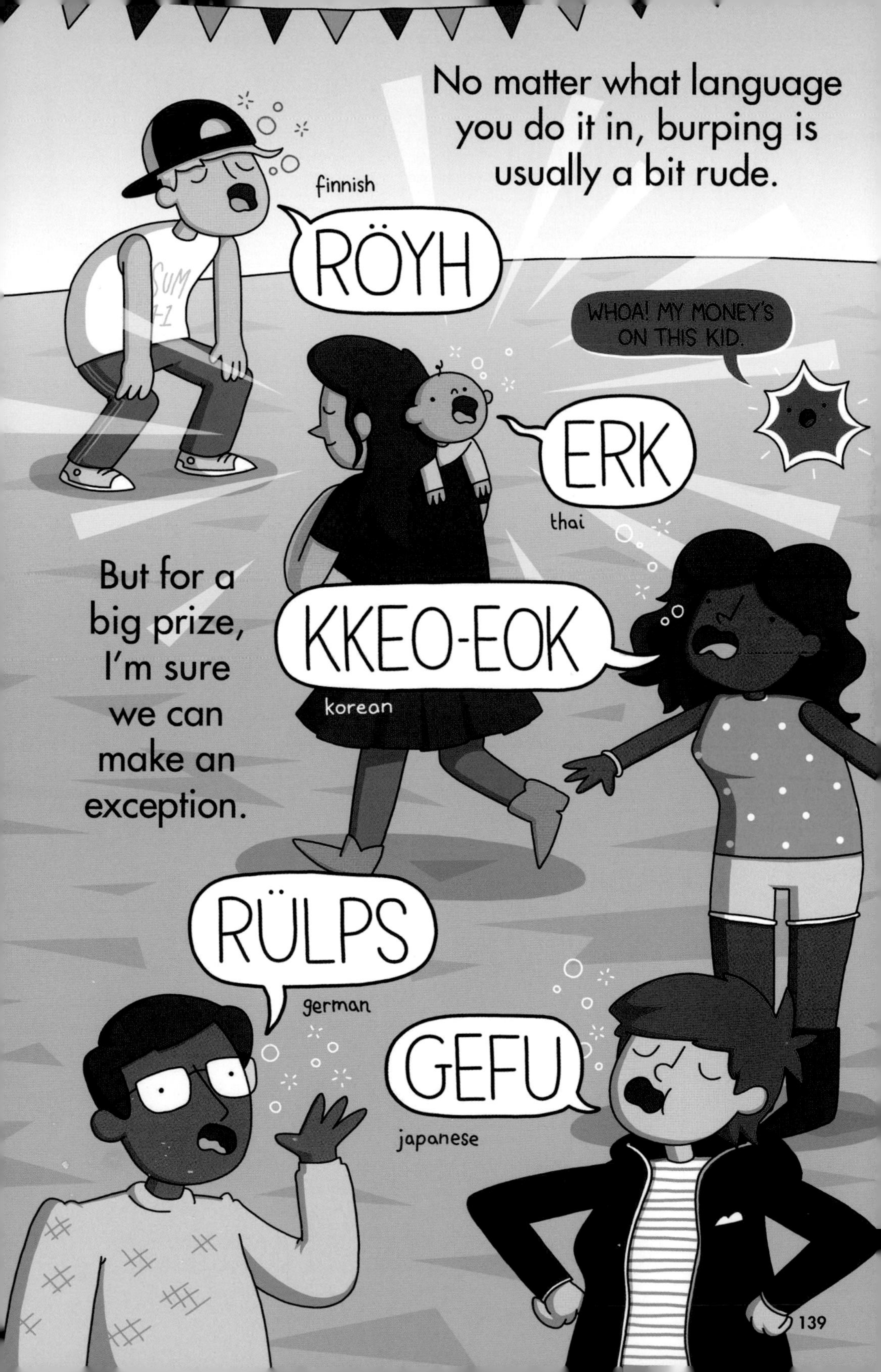
No matter what language you do it in, burping is usually a bit rude.
finnish
RÖYH
WHOA! MY MONEY'S ON THIS KID.
ERK
thai
But for a big prize, I'm sure we can make an exception.
KKEO-EOK
korean
RÜLPS
german
GEFU
japanese

Applause

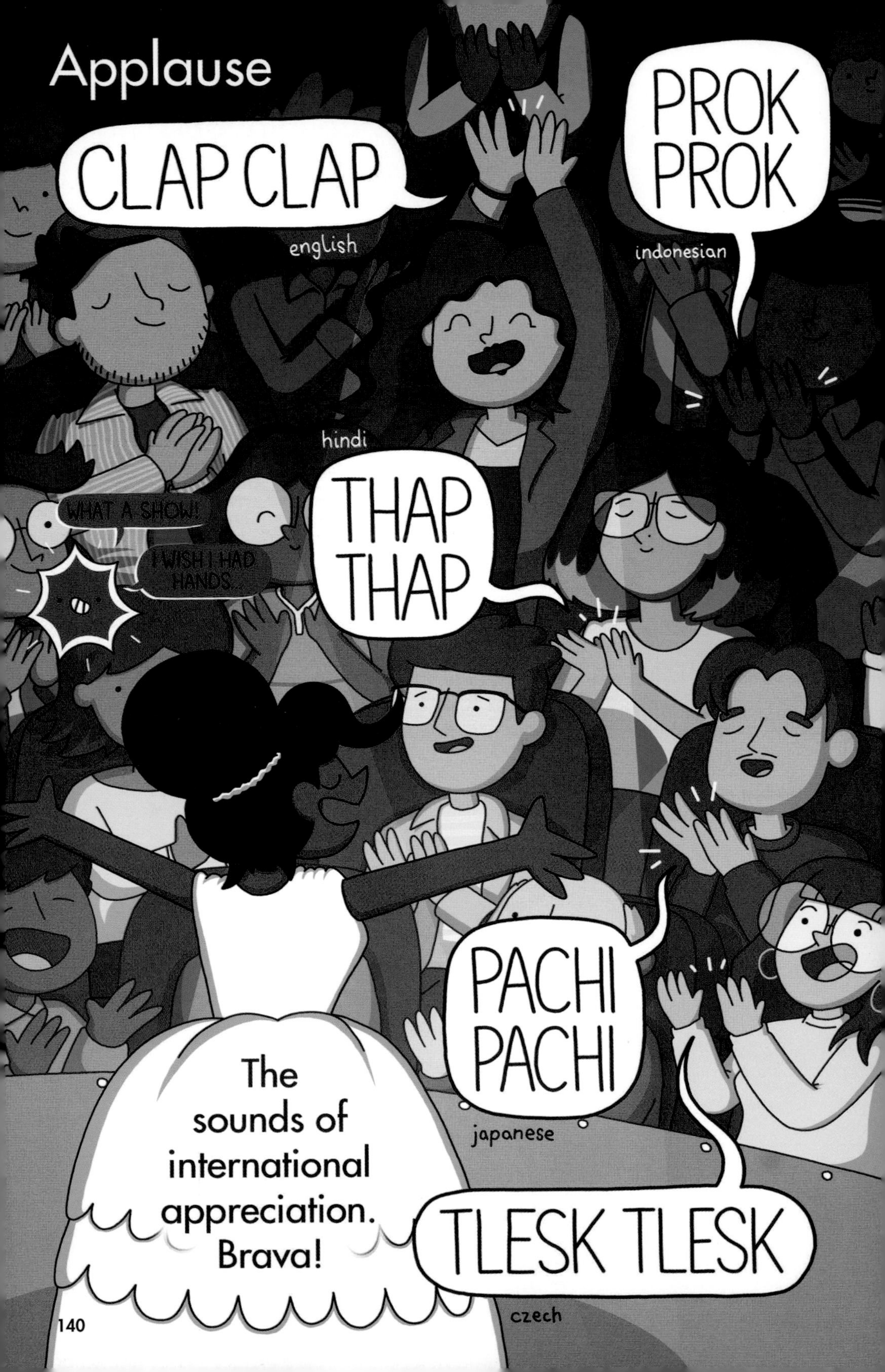
CLAP CLAP
english
PROK PROK
indonesian
hindi
THAP THAP
WHAT A SHOW!
I WISH I HAD HANDS...
PACHI PACHI
japanese
TLESK TLESK
czech

The sounds of international appreciation. Brava!

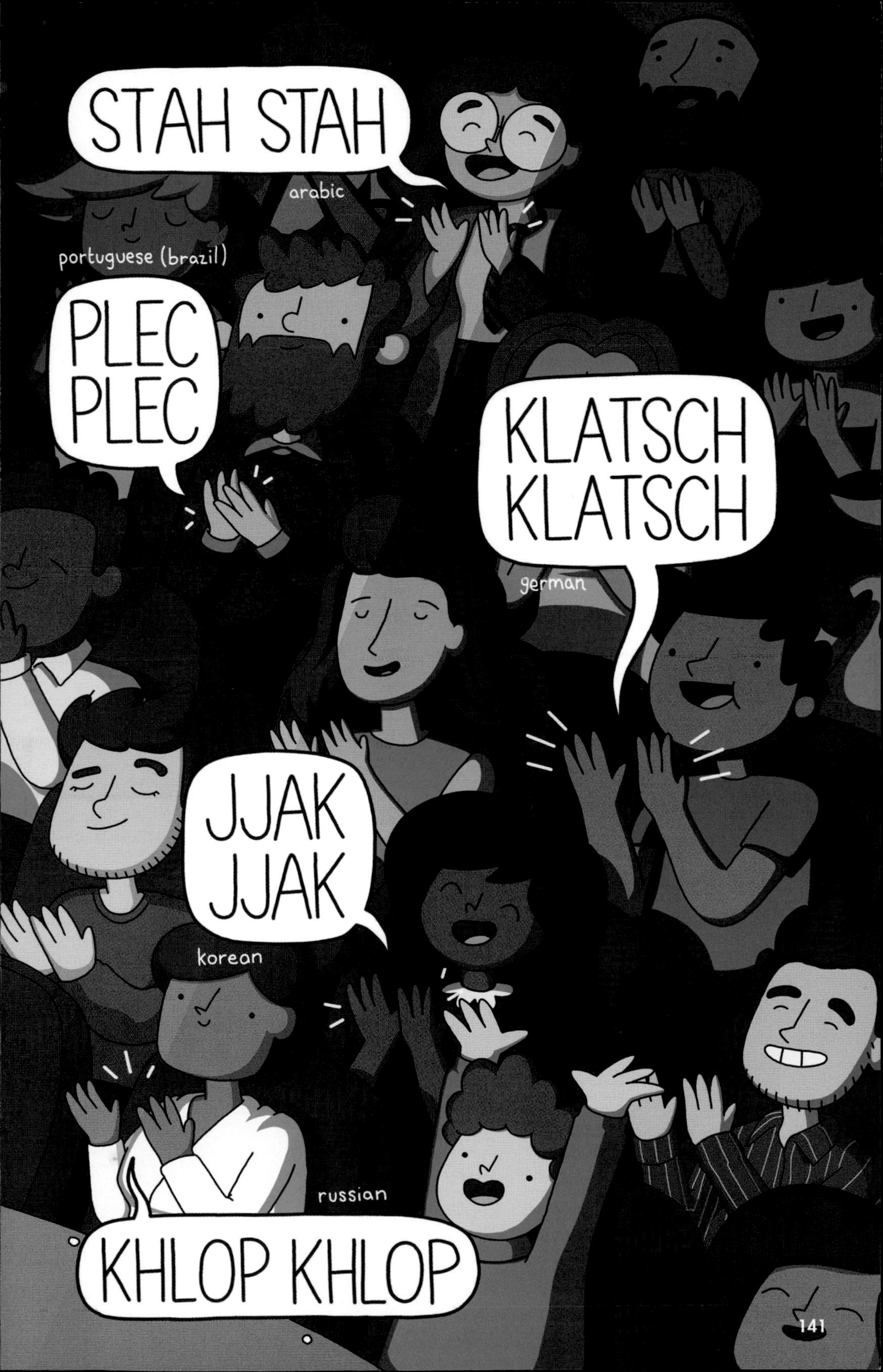
STAH STAH
arabic
portuguese (brazil)
PLEC PLEC
KLATSCH KLATSCH
german
JJAK JJAK
korean
russian
KHLOP KHLOP

Heartbeats

Hearts are so rhythmic! Let's hear how they sound on the dance floor.

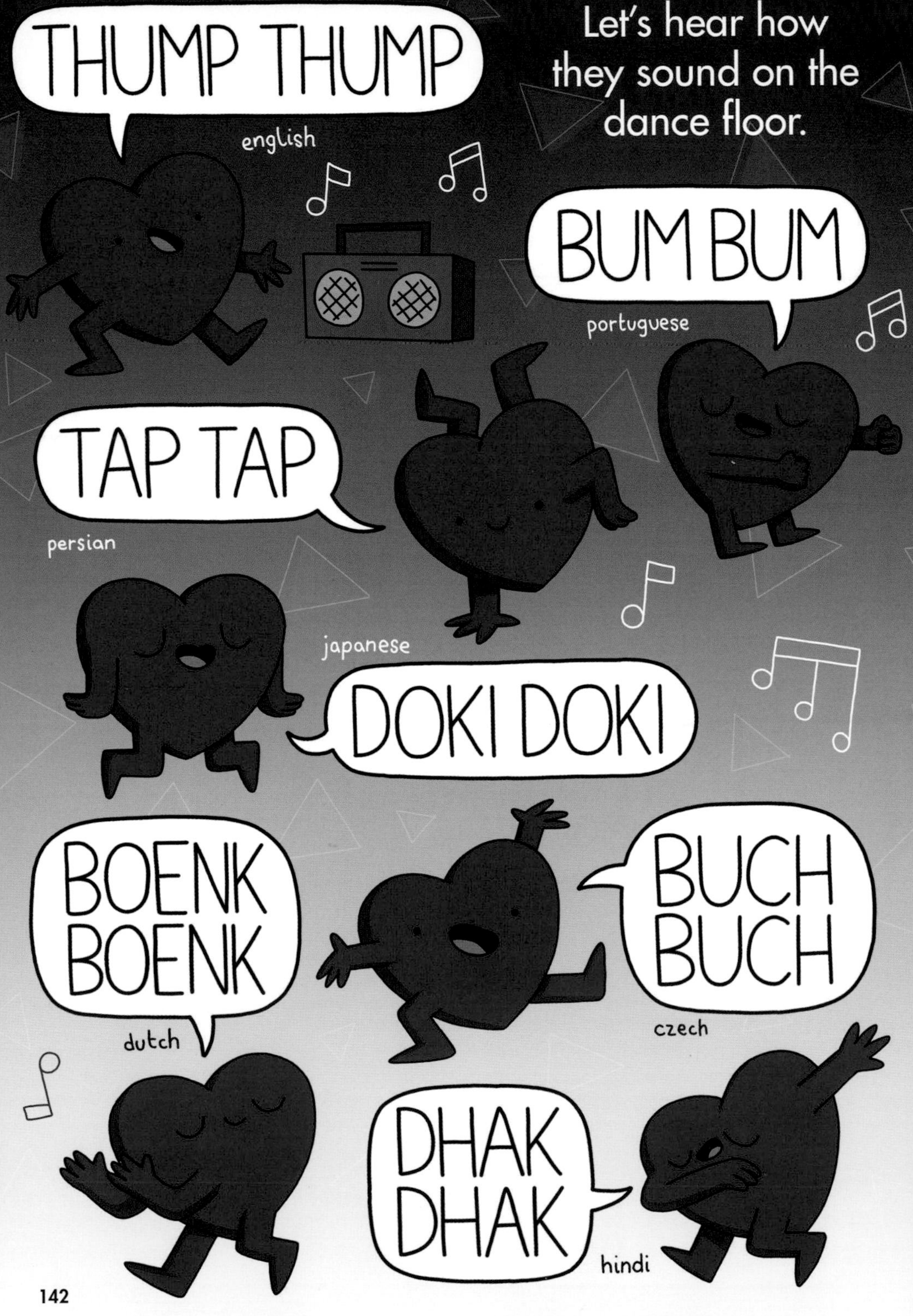
THUMP THUMP
english
BUM BUM
portuguese
TAP TAP
persian
japanese
DOKI DOKI
BOENK BOENK
dutch
BUCH BUCH
czech
DHAK DHAK
hindi

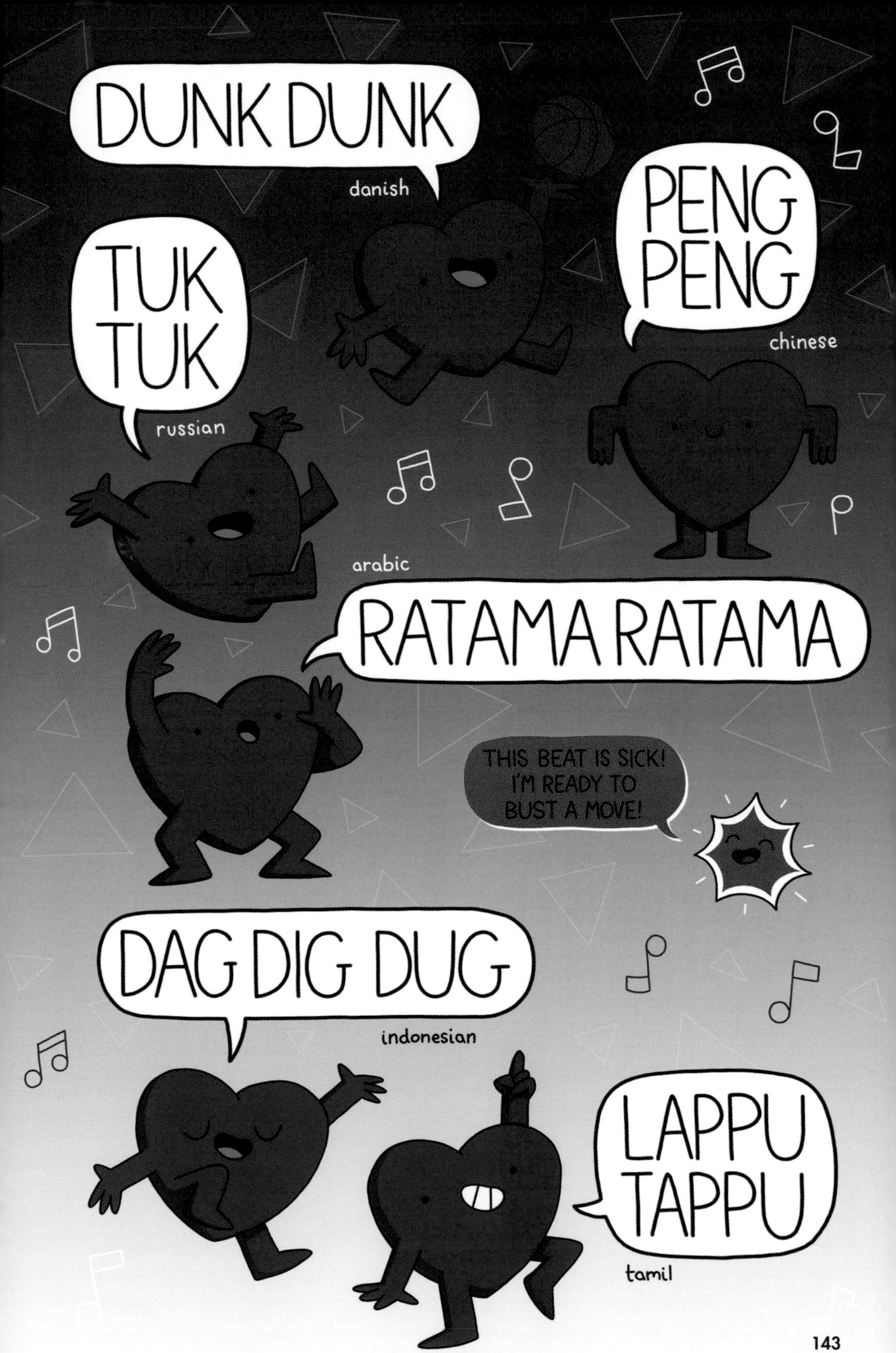
DUNK DUNK
danish
PENG PENG
chinese
TUK TUK
russian
arabic
RATAMA RATAMA
THIS BEAT IS SICK! I'M READY TO BUST A MOVE!
DAG DIG DUG
indonesian
LAPPU TAPPU
tamil

SOUNDS
OF
EMOTION

The sounds you make can reveal a lot about how you're feeling. Cries of pain, howls of laughter, and screams of joy are all part of life. It's hard to keep quiet when you're full of strong emotions.

Over in Japan (where sounds are quite specific, you might have noticed), there are noises associated with all kinds of feelings, even those you might think of as being silent. These "mimetic" words evoke a feeling or a sensation rather than a literal noise, so they're used as sound symbolism.

"WAKUWAKU"
excited
anticipation

"HARAHARA"
anxiety

"ZOTTO"
a scared
shiver

"KANKAN"
anger!

Maybe you have your own sounds for when you're feeling a certain way? Funny noises are the perfect way to express yourself, make whichever ones you like!

Cheering

Sounds are a great way to show how you feel.

There are sounds for when you're feeling happy.

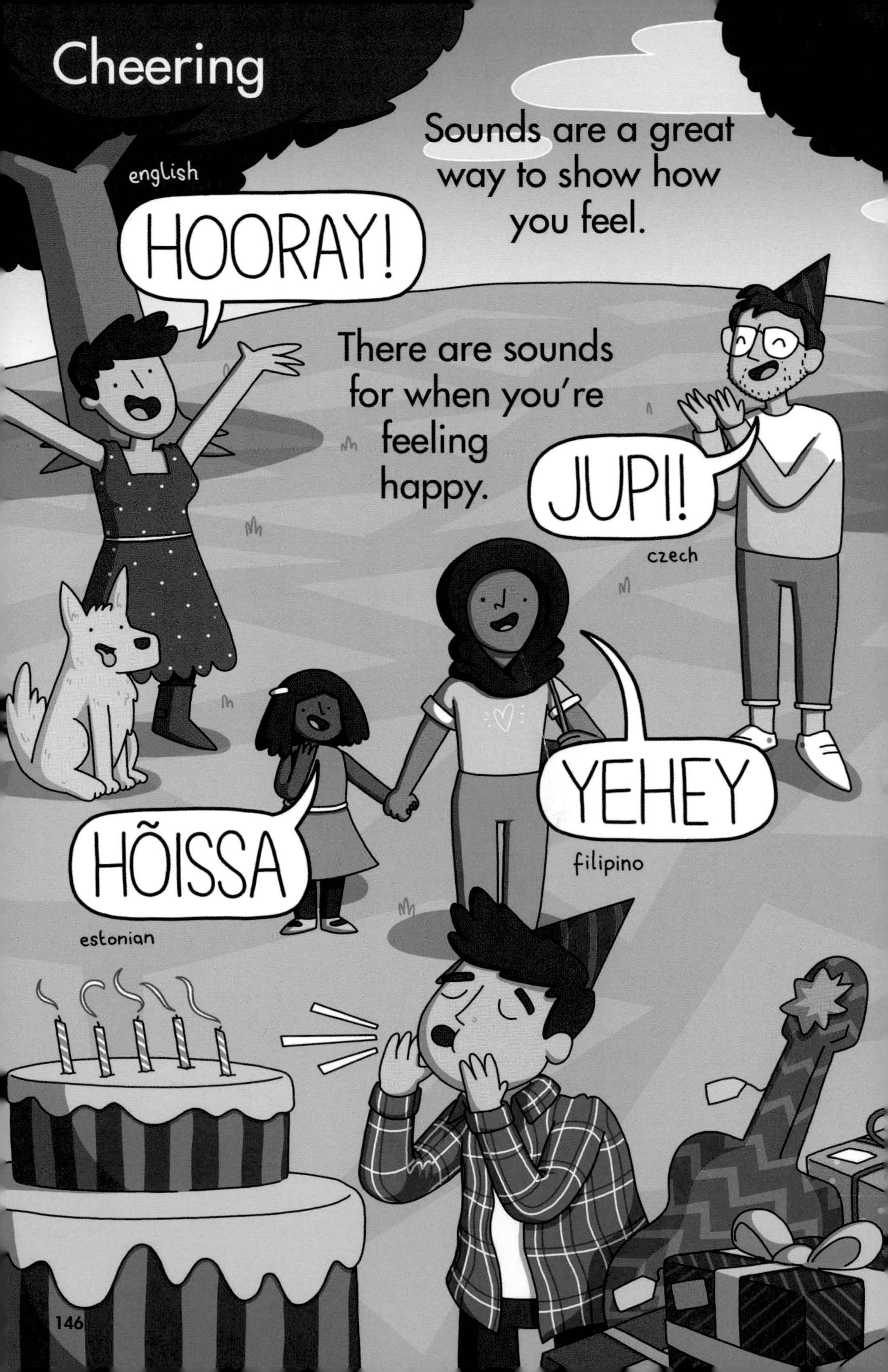
english
HOORAY!
JUPI!
czech
YEHEY
filipino
HÕISSA
estonian

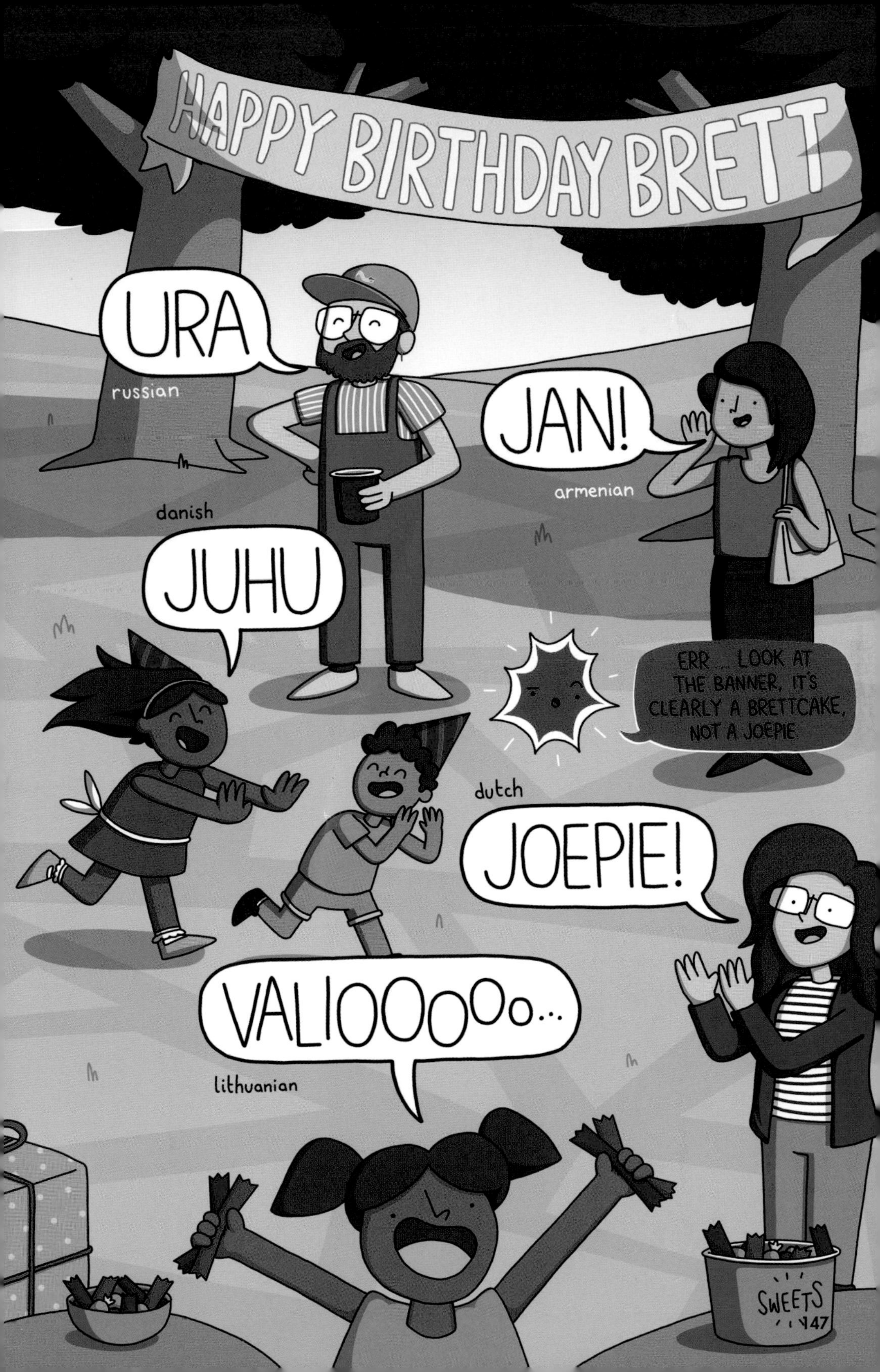
HAPPY BIRTHDAY BRETT
URA
russian
JAN!
armenian
danish
JUHU
ERR... LOOK AT THE BANNER, IT'S CLEARLY A BRETTCAKE, NOT A JOEPIE.
dutch
JOEPIE!
VALIOOOOo...
lithuanian
SWEETS
147

Crying

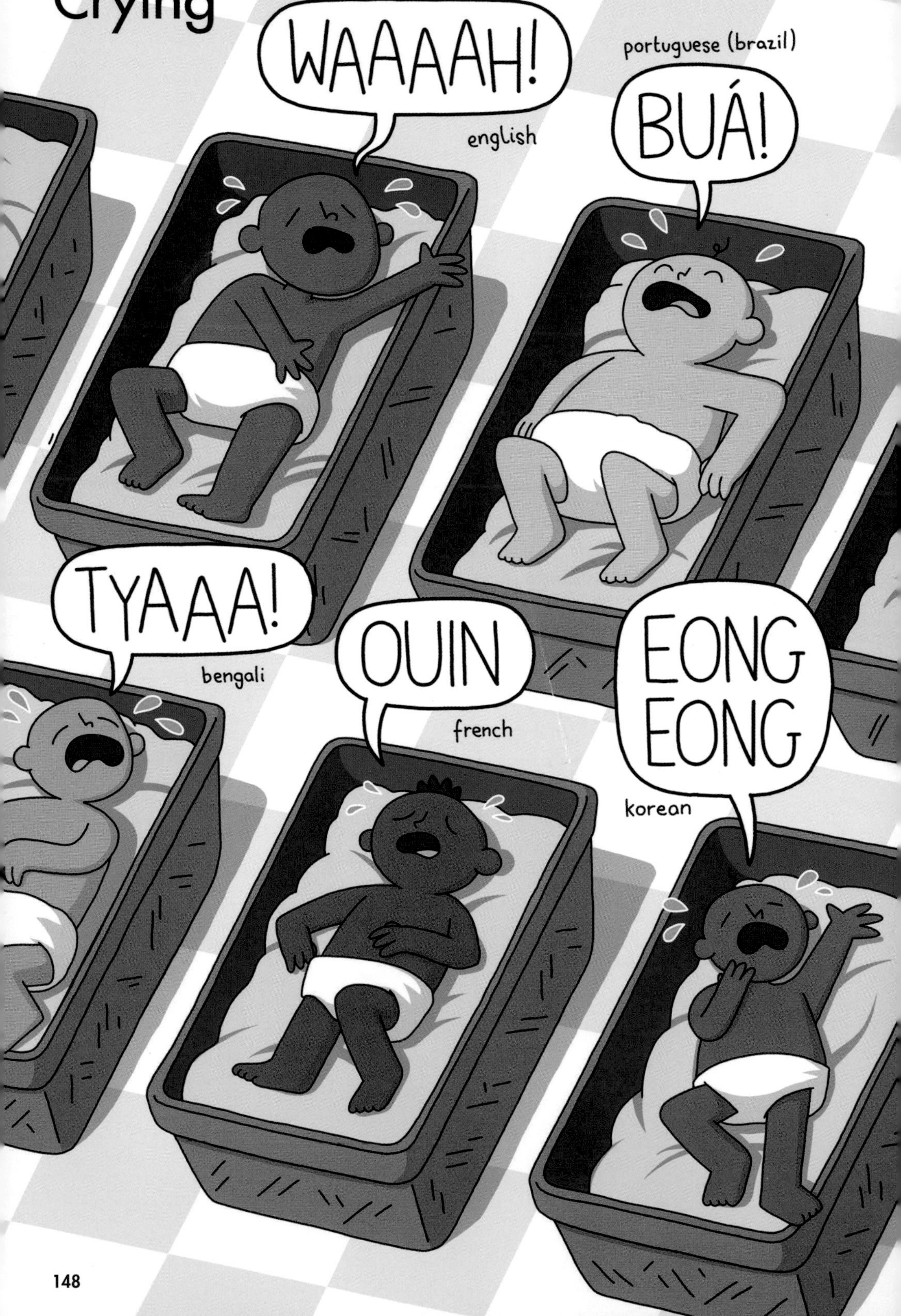
WAAAAH!
english
portuguese (brazil)
BUÁ!
TYAAA!
bengali
OUIN
french
EONG EONG
korean

There are sounds for when you're feeling sad.

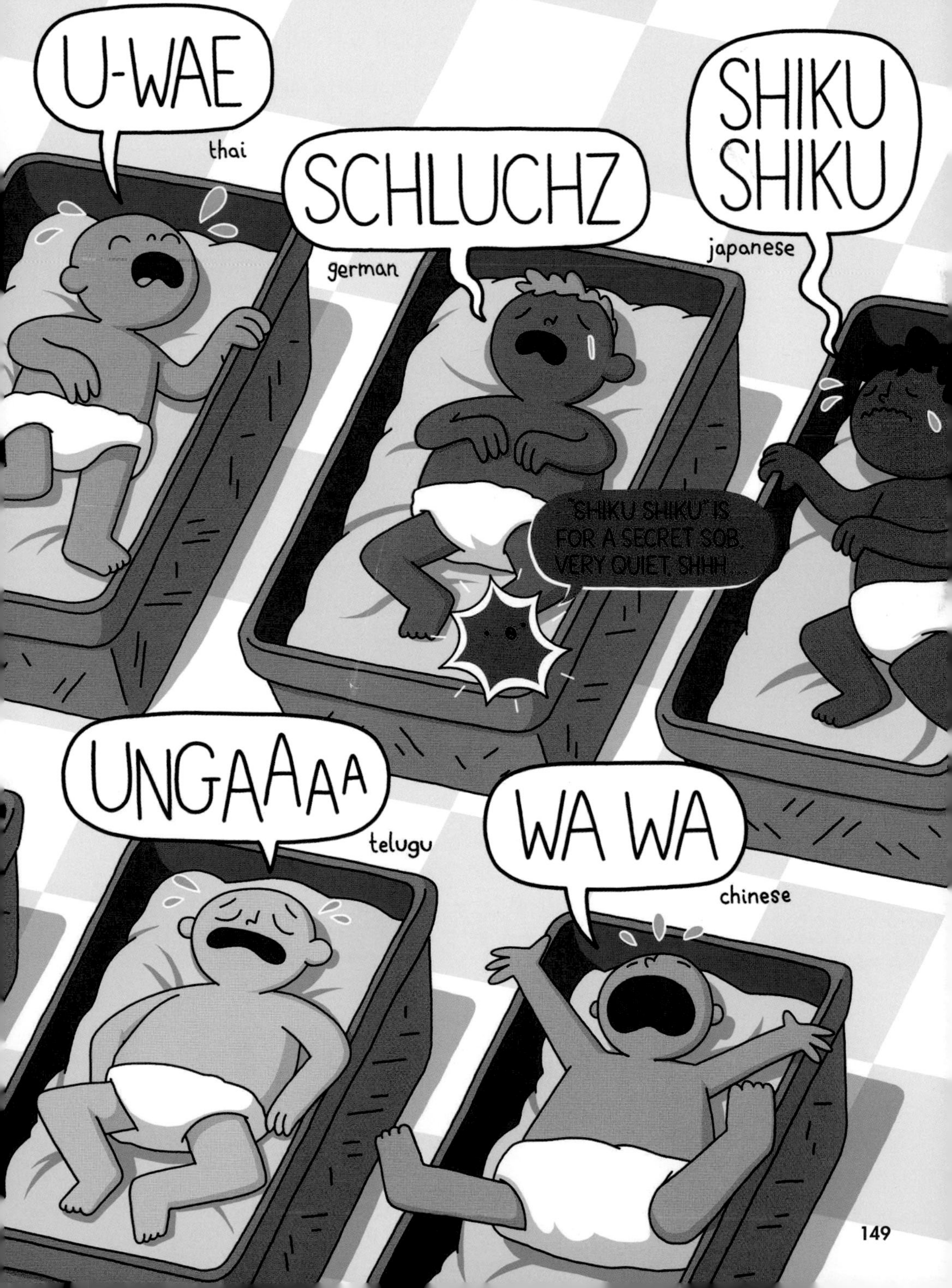
U-WAE
thai
SCHLUCHZ
german
SHIKU SHIKU
japanese
"SHIKU SHIKU" IS FOR A SECRET SOB. VERY QUIET. SHHH...
UNGAAAA
telugu
WA WA
chinese

Screaming

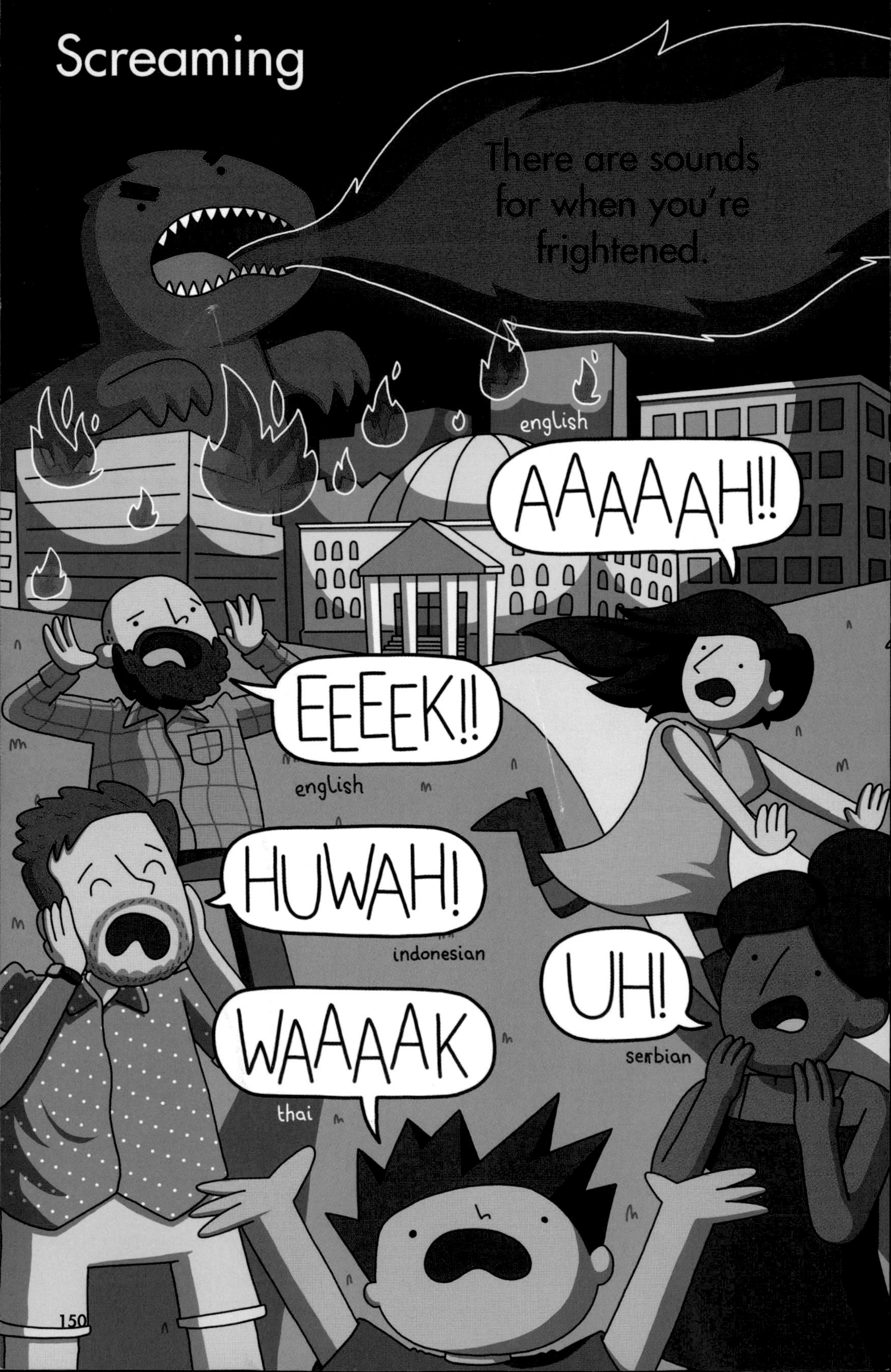
There are sounds for when you're frightened.
english
AAAAAH!!
EEEEK!!
english
HUWAH!
indonesian
UH!
serbian
WAAAAK
thai

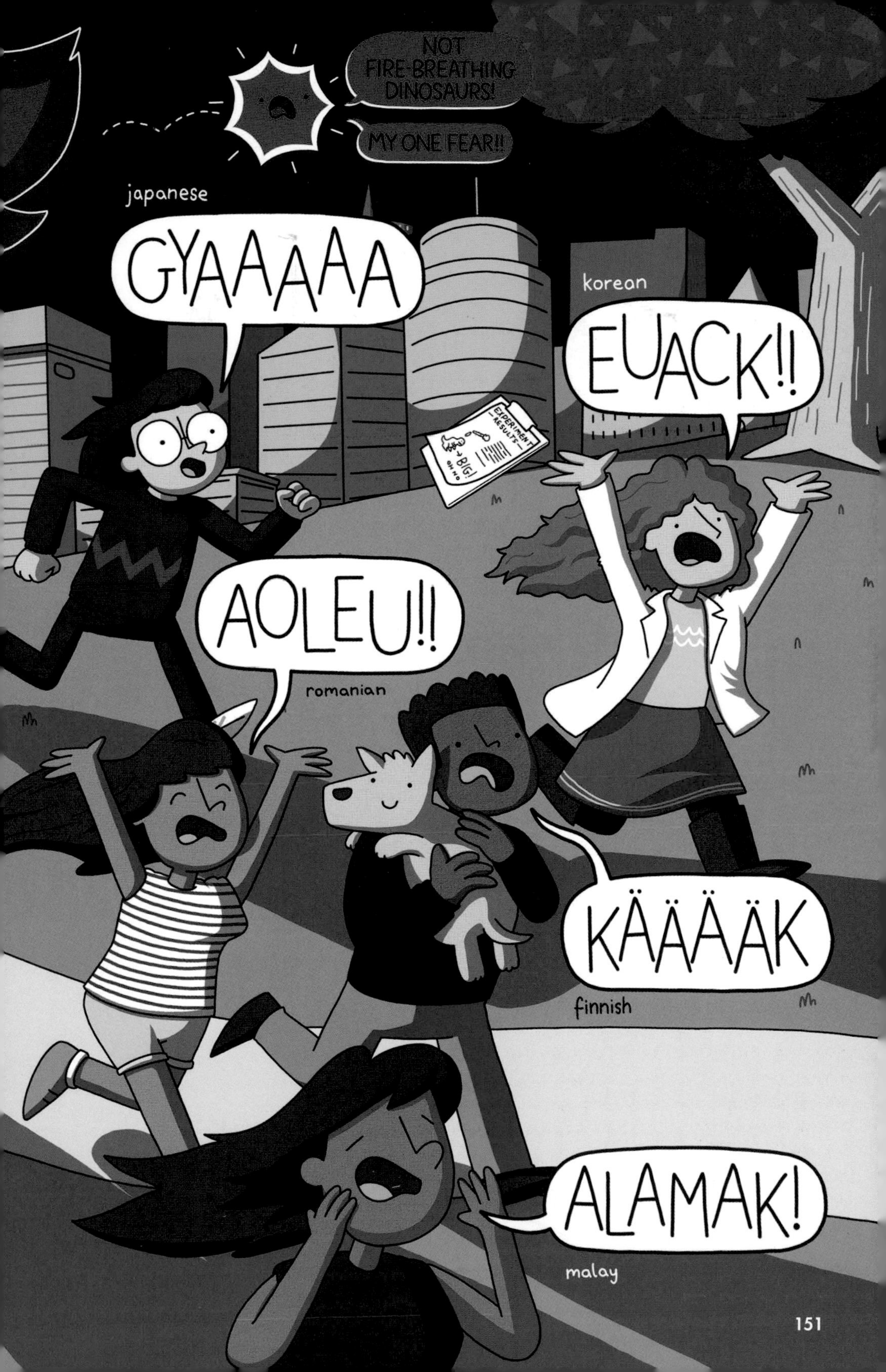
NOT FIRE-BREATHING DINOSAURS!
MY ONE FEAR!!
japanese
GYAAAAA
korean
EUACK!!
EXPERIMENT RESULTS
BIG!
OH NO
AOLEU!!
romanian
KÄÄÄÄK
finnish
ALAMAK!
malay

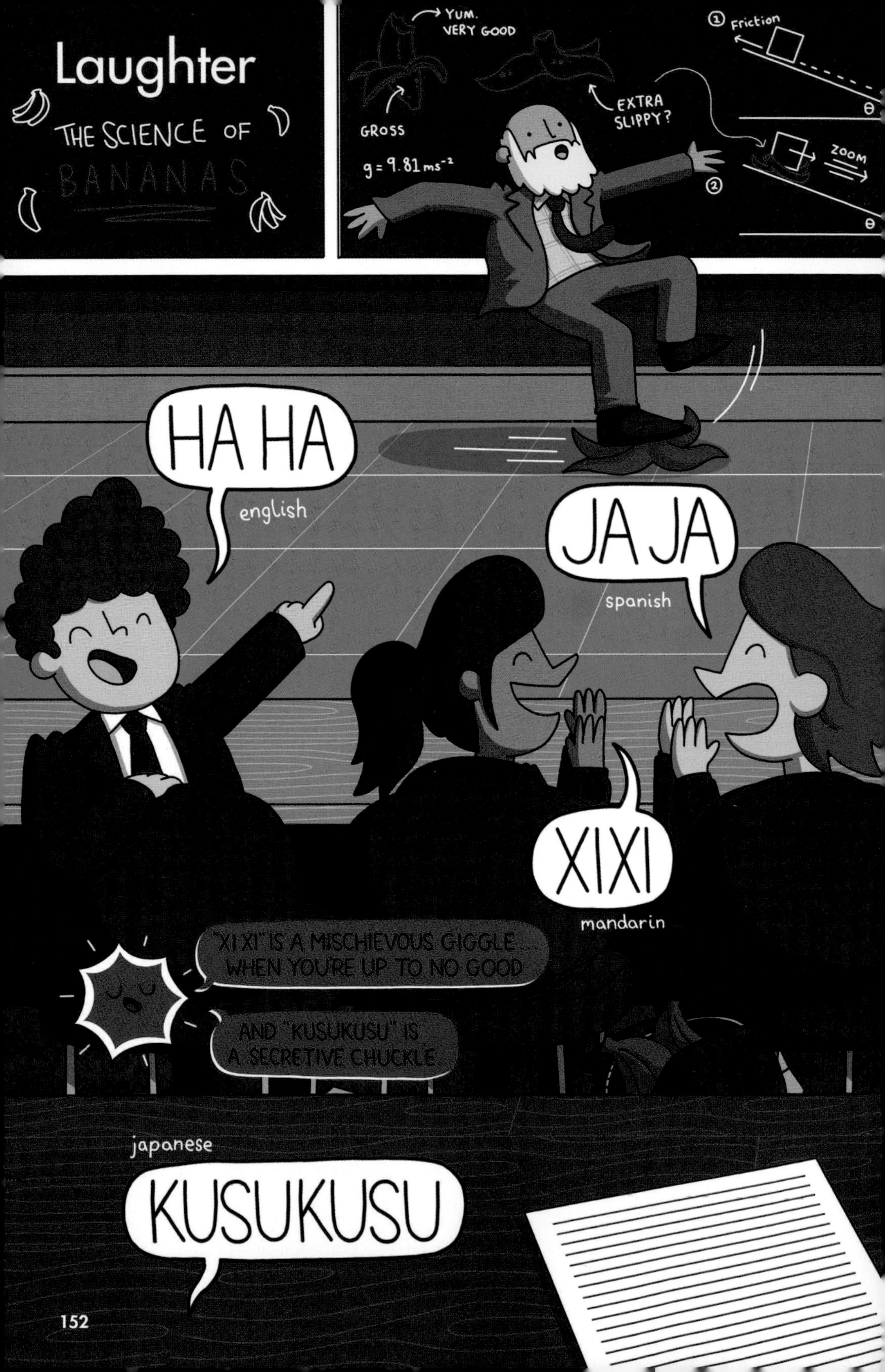
Laughter
THE SCIENCE OF
BANANAS
YUM. VERY GOOD
GROSS
EXTRA SLIPPY?
g = 9.81 ms-2
① Friction
θ
② ZOOM
θ
HA HA
english
JA JA
spanish
XIXI
mandarin
"XI XI" IS A MISCHIEVOUS GIGGLE ... WHEN YOU'RE UP TO NO GOOD
AND "KUSUKUSU" IS A SECRETIVE CHUCKLE.
japanese
KUSUKUSU

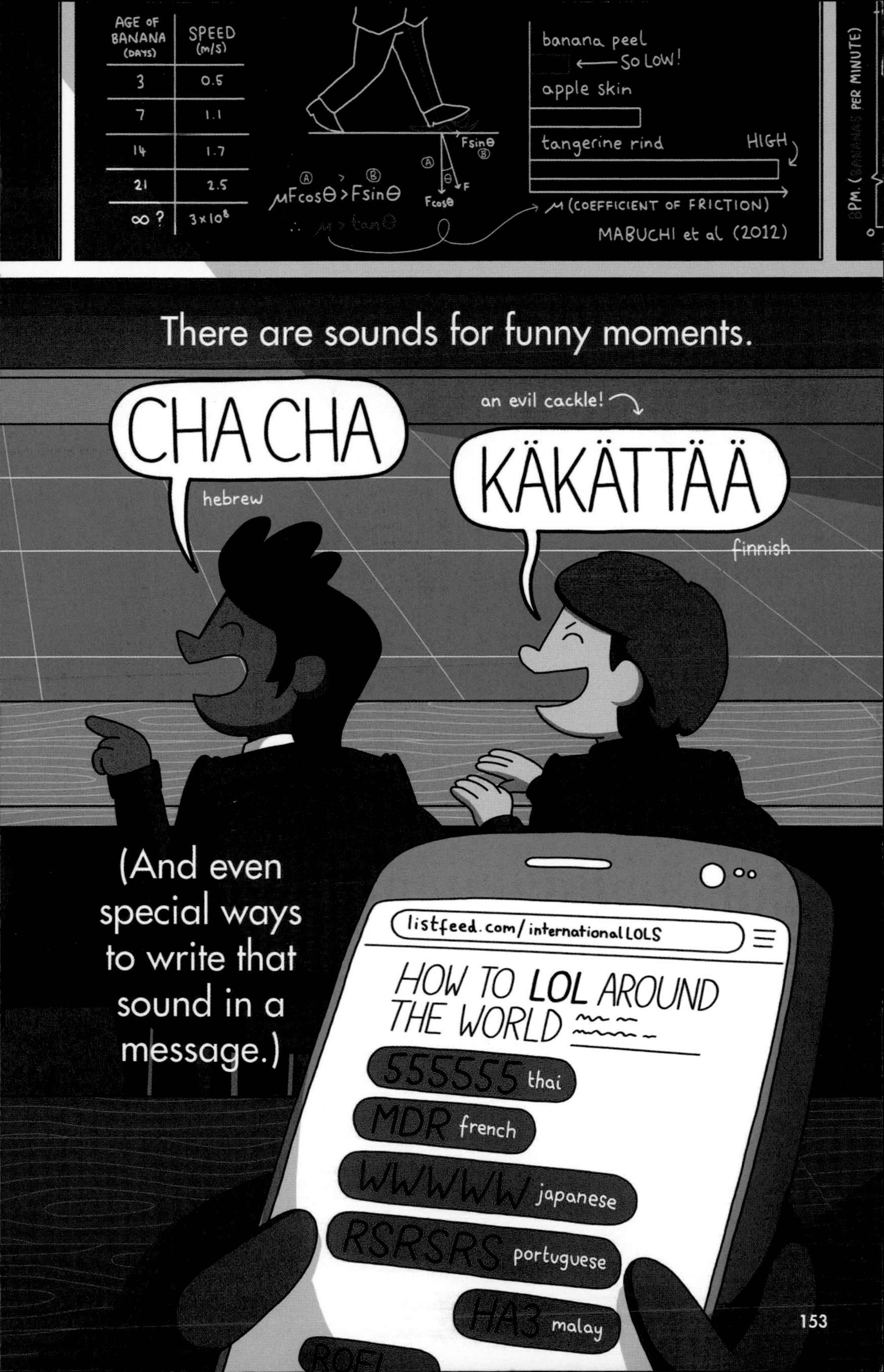

AGE OF BANANA (DAYS)
SPEED (m/s)
3 0.5
7 1.1
14 1.7
21 2.5
∞ ? 3×10⁸
μFcosθ > Fsinθ
Fsinθ
Fcosθ
F
θ
banana peel
SO LOW!
apple skin
tangerine rind
HIGH
μ (COEFFICIENT OF FRICTION)
MABUCHI et al (2012)
BPM. (BANANAS PER MINUTE)
There are sounds for funny moments.
CHA CHA
hebrew
an evil cackle!
KÄKÄTTÄÄ
finnish
(And even special ways to write that sound in a message.)
listfeed.com/internationalLOLS
HOW TO LOL AROUND THE WORLD
555555 thai
MDR french
WWWWW japanese
RSRSRS portuguese
HA3 malay

Pain

There are sounds when you get bumps and bruises.

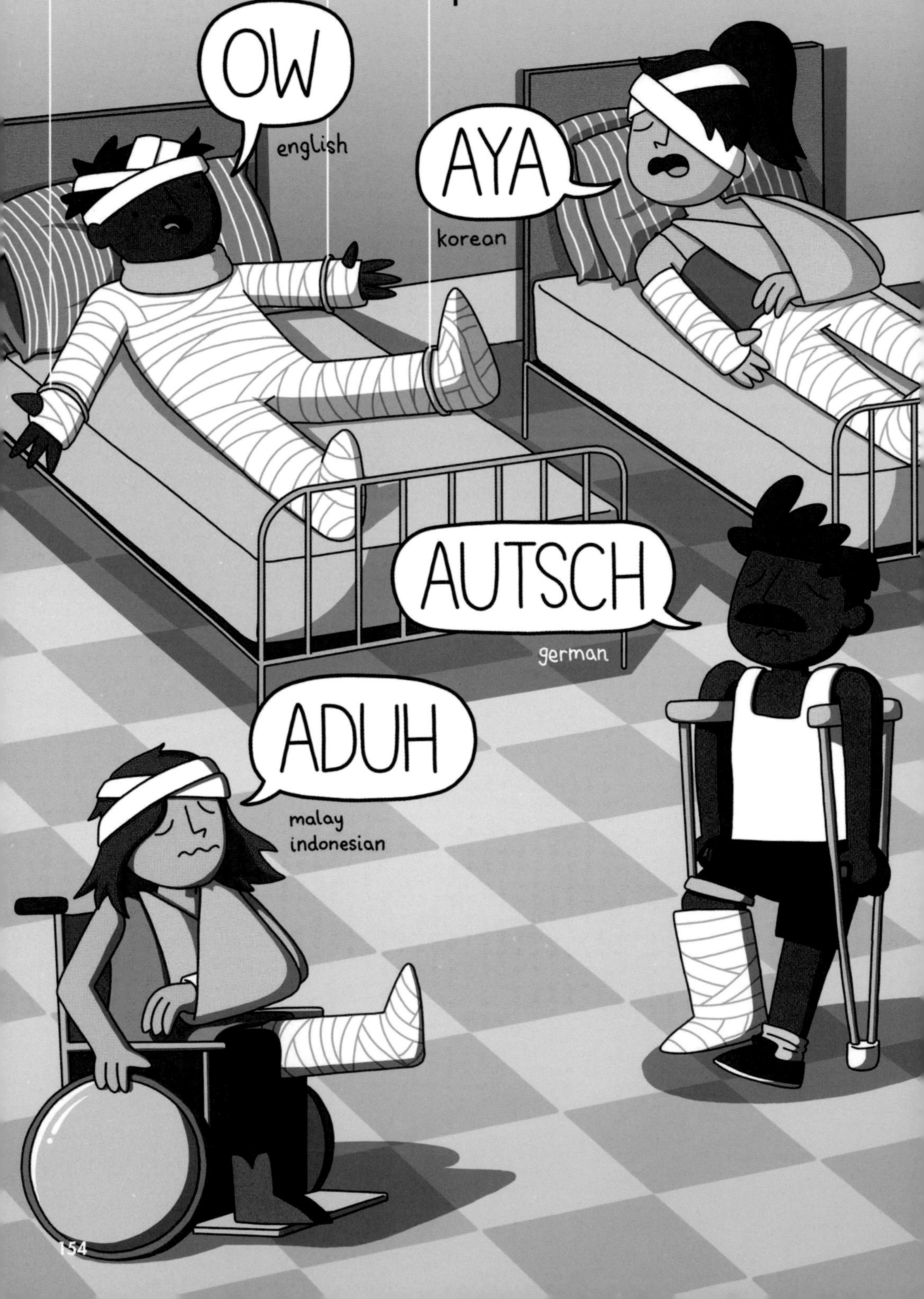
OW
english
AYA
korean
AUTSCH
german
ADUH
malay
indonesian

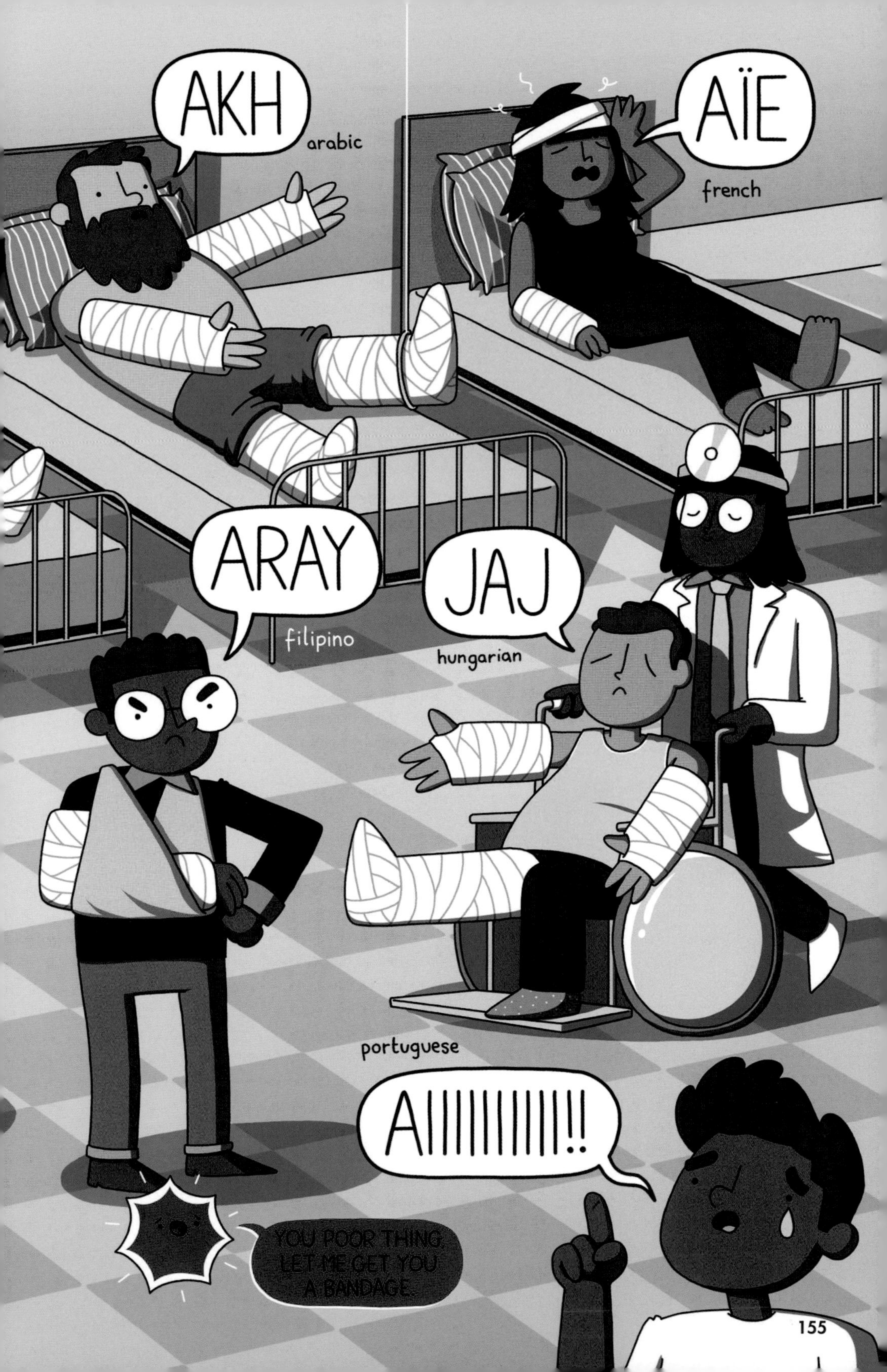
AKH
arabic
AÏE
french
ARAY
filipino
JAJ
hungarian
portuguese
AIIIIIIIIII!!
YOU POOR THING. LET ME GET YOU A BANDAGE.

Disgust

There are sounds for when something is gross.

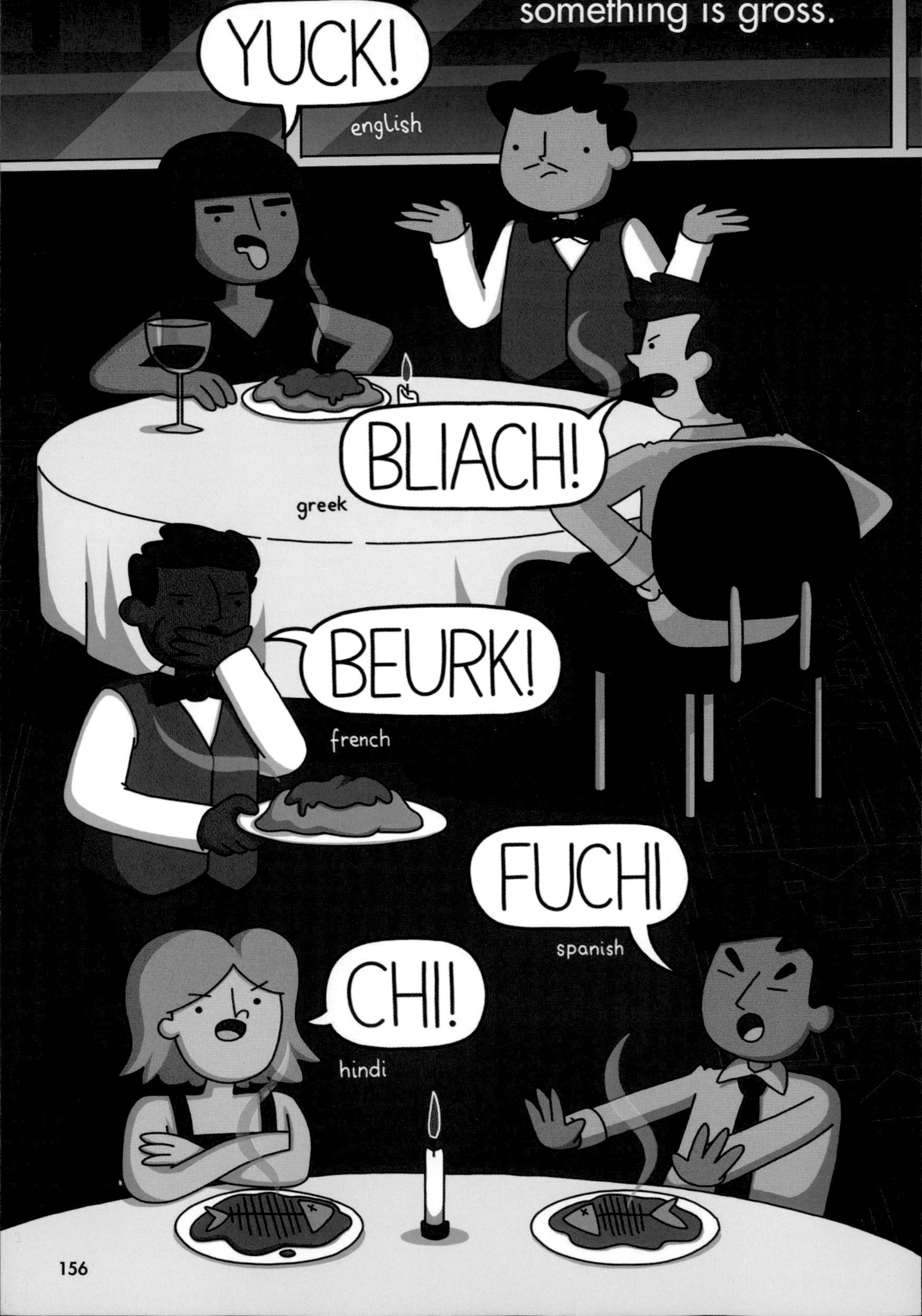
YUCK!
english
BLIACH!
greek
BEURK!
french
FUCHI
spanish
CHI!
hindi

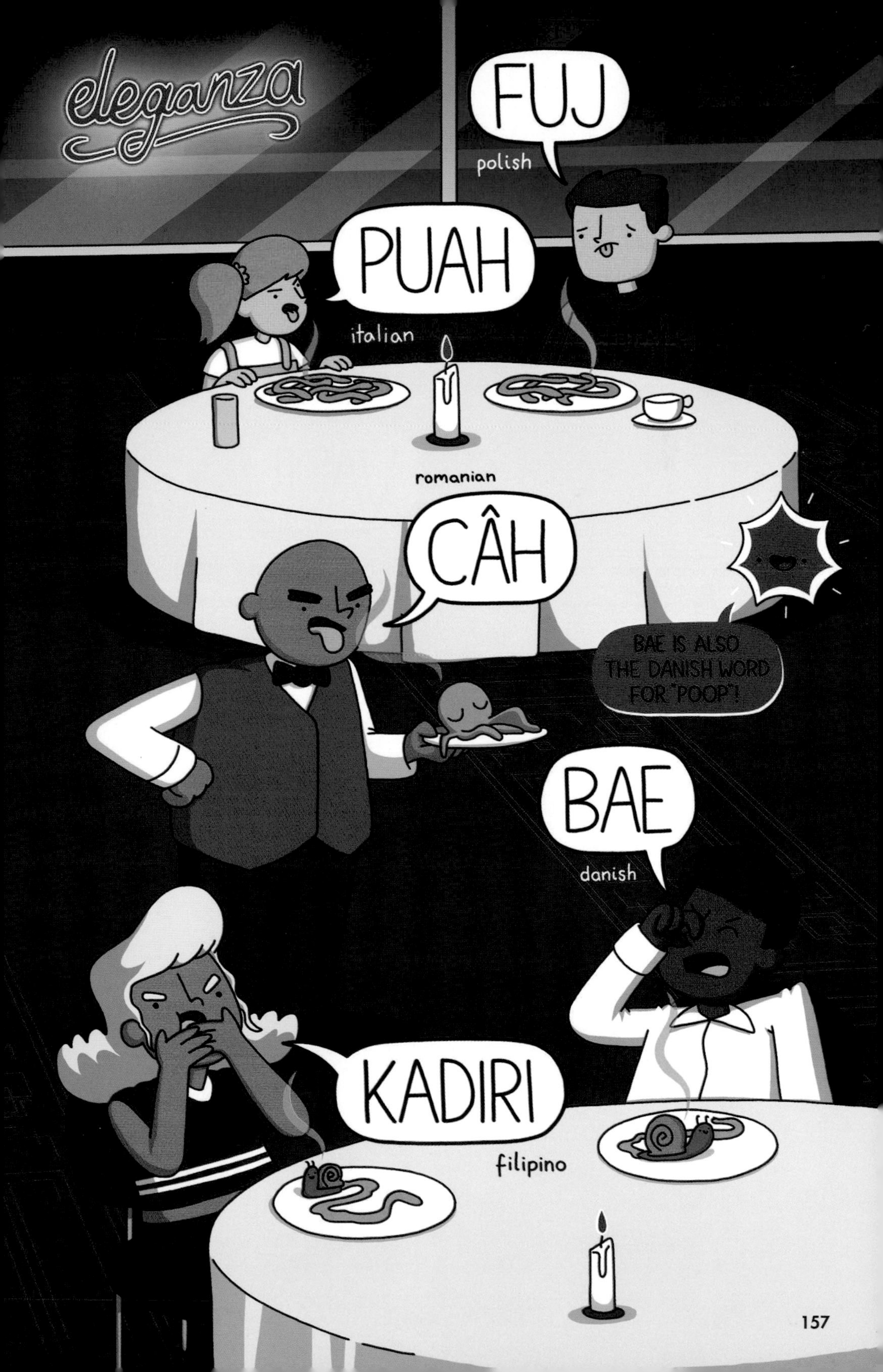
eleganza
FUJ
polish
PUAH
italian
romanian
CÂH
BAE IS ALSO THE DANISH WORD FOR "POOP"!
BAE
danish
KADIRI
filipino

Amazement

And even sounds for when you can't believe your eyes.

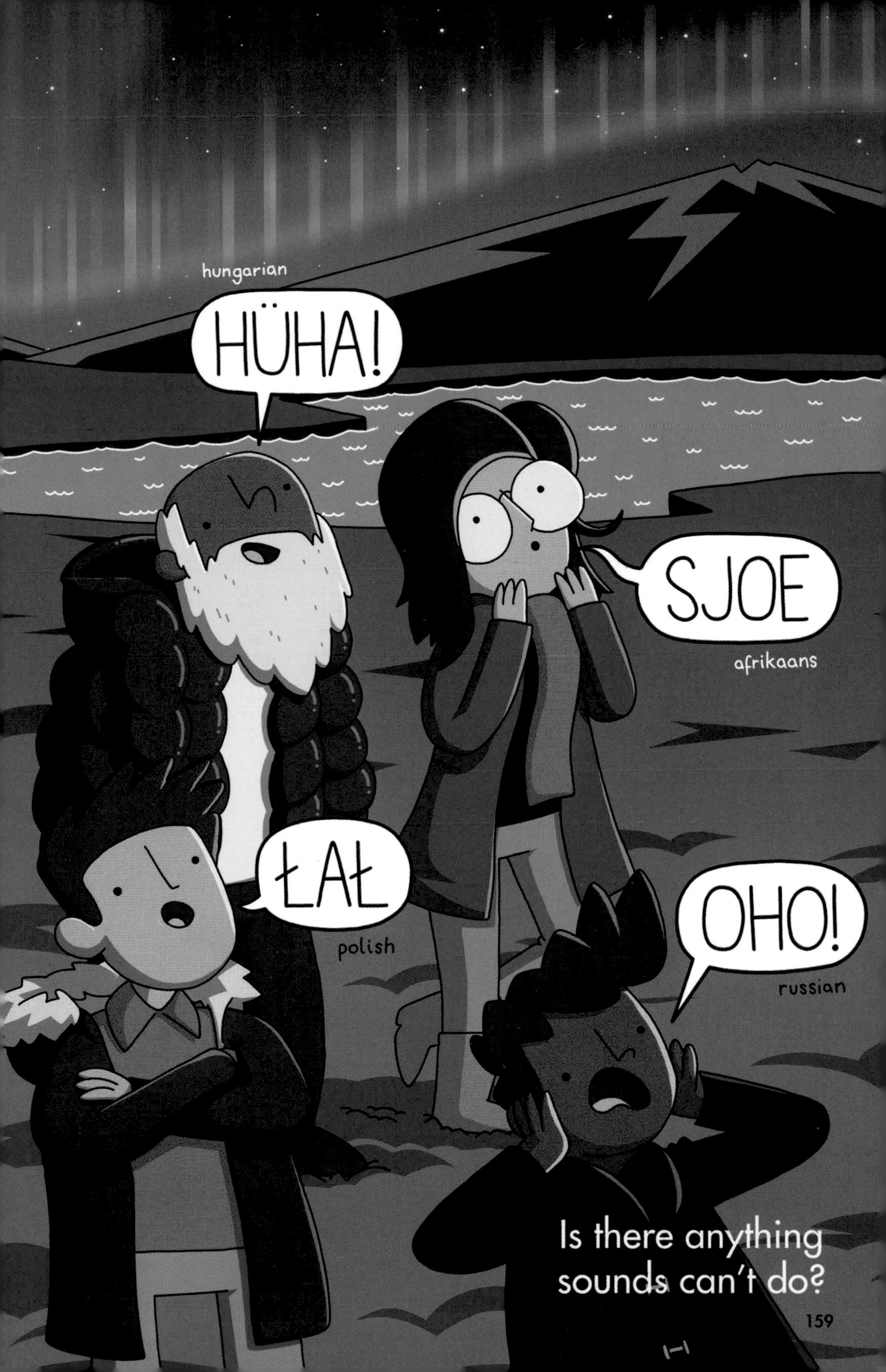
hungarian
HÜHA!
SJOE
afrikaans
ŁAŁ
polish
OHO!
russian
Is there anything sounds can't do?

All around the world there are different words for sounds: loud sounds, quiet sounds, emotional sounds, and silly sounds. And you know what?

We can't agree on anything!

Across the world, there are dozens of ways to pretend to be a dog.

But they're all equally beautiful.

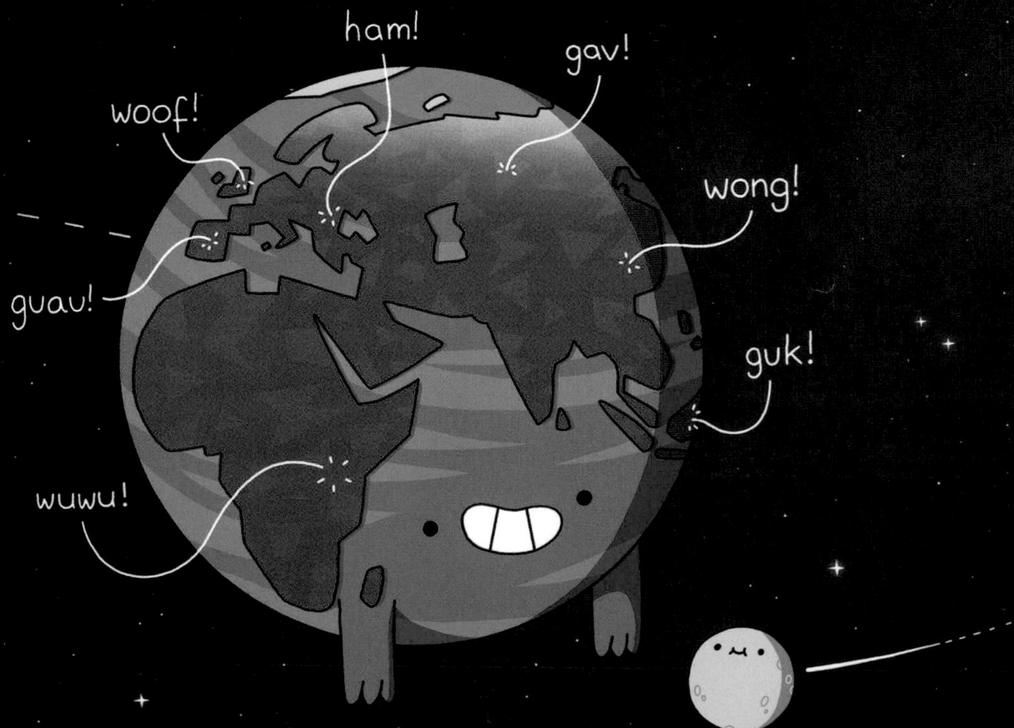
ham!
gav!
woof!
wong!
guau!
guk!
wuwu!

We live on a planet filled with diversity and countless ways to describe our surroundings. There are no right or wrong answers when it comes to sounds, just different perspectives.

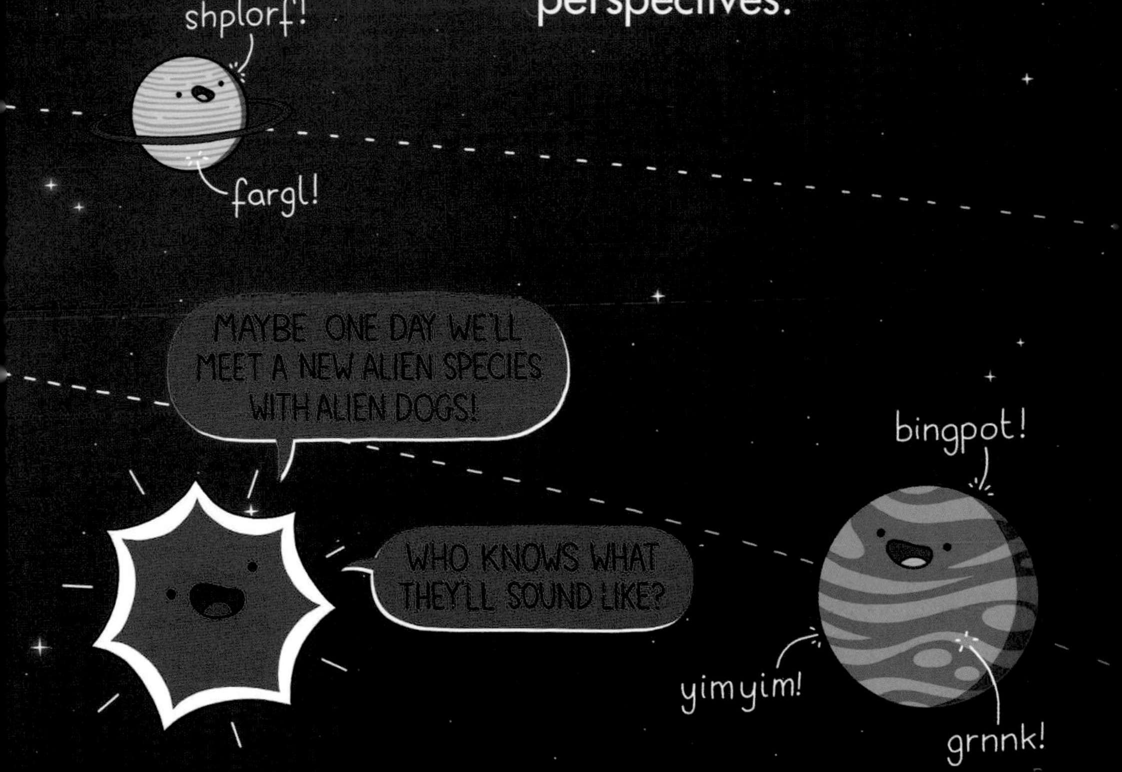
shplorf!
fargl!
MAYBE ONE DAY WE'LL MEET A NEW ALIEN SPECIES WITH ALIEN DOGS!
WHO KNOWS WHAT THEY'LL SOUND LIKE?
bingpot!
yimyim!
grnnk!

The End.

Acknowledgments

This collection would not have been possible without the contributions and suggestions so helpfully provided via social media over the past few years. Thank you to everyone who joined in.

And thanks to Marilyn, David, Eric, Iris, Joe and Dee for their incredible support.

About the Author

Dr. James Chapman is an illustrator and writer who has always been interested in language. His webcomic series, *Soundimals*, that explored the sounds animals make in different languages around the world, inspired this book. He lives in Manchester, UK.

Sounds All Around

Andrews McMeel Publishing
a division of Andrews McMeel Universal
1130 Walnut Street, Kansas City, Missouri 64106

www.andrewsmcmeel.com

19 20 21 22 23 SDB 10 9 8 7 6 5 4 3 2 1

ISBN: 978-1-5248-5076-0

Library of Congress Control Number: 2019917535

Made by:
King Yip (Dongguan) Printing & Packaging Factory Ltd.
Address and location of manufacturer:
Daning Administrative District, Humen Town
Dongguan Guangdong, China 523930
1st Printing — 1/13/20

Editor: Allison Adler
Art Director: Tiffany Meairs
Production Editor: Julie Railsback
Production Manager: Chuck Harper